Point Horror

3

The
Caroline B. Cooney
Special Edition

A Triple Dose of Terror...

Have you read these other thrilling Point Horror Special Editions?

Point Horror

3

The
Caroline B. Cooney
Special Edition

A Triple Dose of Terror...

Freeze Tag
The Stranger
Twins

■ SCHOLASTIC

Scholastic Children's Books,
Commonwealth House, 1–19 New Oxford Street,
London WC1A 1NU, UK
a division of Scholastic Ltd
London ~ New York ~ Toronto ~ Sydney ~ Auckland

First published in this edition by Scholastic Ltd, 1996

Freeze Tag
First published in the US by Scholastic Inc., 1992
First published in the UK by Scholastic Ltd, 1993
Copyright © Caroline B. Cooney, 1992

The Stranger
First published in the US by Scholastic Inc., 1993
First published in the UK by Scholastic Ltd, 1994
Copyright © Caroline B. Cooney, 1993

Twins
First published in the US by Scholastic Inc., 1994
First published in the UK by Scholastic Ltd, 1995
Copyright © Caroline B. Cooney, 1994

Printed by Clays Ltd, St Ives plc

ISBN: 0 590 54288 5

Contents

FREEZE TAG

Prologue

"Suppose," said Lannie dreamily, "that you really could freeze somebody."

The setting sun seemed to shine right through Lannie, as if she were made of colored glass and hung in a window.

Lannie's eyes, as pale as though they had been bleached in the wash, focused on Meghan.

Meghan gulped and looked away, queerly out of breath. If she kept looking into Lannie's eyes, she would come out the other side.

Into what?

What was the other side of Lannie made of?

Meghan shivered, although the evening was still warm. She felt ancient. Not old herself, but as if something in the night had quivered free from an ancient world. Free from ancient rules.

Tonight something would happen.

Meghan stared at her bare arms. A thousand tiny hairs prickled in fear. Even her skin knew.

The sun was going down like a circle of construction paper falling off the bulletin board. No longer the yellow bulb of daytime, it was a sinking orange half circle. Meghan yearned to run toward the sun and catch it before it vanished.

Meghan tried to ignore Lannie. This was not easy. Lannie

always stood as close as a sweater, trying to take your share of oxygen.

Lannie stood alone, but Meghan sat on the second step with her best friend, Tuesday, and admired the silhouette of West Trevor as he mowed the lawn.

Meghan adored the Trevor family. They were what families should be. First, the Trevors had had the wisdom to have three children, not just one like her own parents. The Trevors were always a crowd, and Meghan loved a crowd.

Second, the children had wonderful names. Mr. and Mrs. Trevor had not wanted their children to be named Elizabeth or Michael and thus get mixed up with dozens of classmates. Mixing up the Trevor offspring would never happen. There was, thought Meghan, probably no other family on earth with children named West, Tuesday, and Brown.

West Trevor. It sounded like a street, or perhaps a town in Ireland. But West Trevor was the boy on whom, in a few years, all the girls would have crushes. Meghan was slightly ahead of them. She had adored West all her life.

He was mowing around the beginner-bushes. (That's what Mrs. Trevor called them, because they were so young and newly planted they hardly even formed knobs in the grass.) Meghan admired how West so carefully overlapped each pass, making sure no blade of grass would escape untrimmed.

"Suppose," said Lannie dreamily, "that *I* could freeze somebody."

Meghan could just see Lannie opening a refrigerator, stuffing a classmate in to freeze, and walking off. Just thinking about it chilled Meghan. Even as Lannie talked, Meghan's joints seemed to harden like a pond surface turning to ice.

Meghan hated it when Lannie joined the neighborhood games.

The houses on Dark Fern Lane were new, but the families were old-fashioned. The lawns ran into each other, the kitchen doors were always open, and the children used each other's refrigerators and bathrooms.

Since the houses were so small, and everybody had a little brother or sister who was cranky, or needed a diaper change, or wanted to be carried piggyback, the older children on Dark Fern Lane stayed outside whenever they could.

Even though the Trevors' front steps were exactly like everybody else's front steps, this was where the children gathered. Mrs. Trevor was generous with after-supper Popsicles, and the Trevors had a basketball hoop on the garage where everybody learned to dunk and dribble.

West's little brother Brown hurtled out of the house, taking the four cement steps in a single bound. Brown leapt onto the back of the ride-upon mower, shouting horse commands at his big brother. He had a long leather bootlace in his hand that he swung like a lasso, telling West to jump the fence and head for the prairie.

West simply mowed on, ignoring the presence of a screaming five-year-old attached to his back.

Brown began yodeling instead. He had heard this sound on public television and now planned to be a yodeler when he grew up, instead of a policeman. Tuesday yodeled along in harmony. The Trevor family sounded like a deranged wolf pack.

For Meghan, this was yet another Trevor attraction: how close and affectionate they were. Friends, mowing partners, and fellow yodelers.

Meghan knew exactly what would happen next. Tuesday would realize that she was thirsty from all that yodeling. She would get up off the step and go into the house. Several minutes later, she would bring out a tray of pink lemonade and jelly-jar glasses. Her brothers would spot her, and come running. They'd all slurp pink lemonade and listen to the summery sound of ice cubes knocking against glass.

Tuesday would not carry the tray back. That was West's job, along with carrying back all other dishes the Trevor family dirtied. And West would never complain. He accepted dishes as easily as Meghan accepted new shoes.

Whereas in Meghan's family everybody hated dishes. It was

hard to say who hated them most — her father, her mother, or Meghan. Sometimes Meghan thought the only thing the Moores ever said to each other was, "No, it's *your* turn to do dishes."

West and Brown were framed like an old photograph: sunset and small tree, older brother and younger. They were beautiful.

"You want to spend the night, Meghan?" said Tuesday, measuring her sneaker against Meghan's. Tuesday's was larger. The Trevors were a very sturdy family.

Of course Meghan wanted to spend the night. Everybody always wanted to stay at the Trevors'. Mrs. Trevor would throw the sleeping bags down on the playroom floor and let everybody watch Disney videos all night long. She would put brownies in the oven and, just when you were ready to fall asleep, Mrs. Trevor would waltz in with hot rich chocolate treats scooped over with cold melting vanilla ice cream. Meghan sighed with pleasure.

Through the screen door, Tuesday shouted, "Meghan is staying over!" and her mother said, "That's nice, dear."

Meghan's mother would have said, "Not tonight, dear, I have to get up in the morning." Meghan could never understand what getting up in the morning had to do with going to bed at night.

Meghan smiled, in love with every member of the Trevor family.

"I'm spending the night, too, Tuesday," said Lannie. She always kept you informed of her plans.

"No," said Tuesday quickly. "Mother said I could have only one person over."

Lannie knew this for the lie that it was. Her heavy eyelids lifted like cobra hoods. For a long time she said nothing. It was cold and frightening, the way she could stay silent. No other child knew how to stay silent. They were too young.

But Lannie had never seemed young; and as the rest grew up, Lannie never seemed old either.

The fireflies came out. They sparkled in the air.

We're being mean, thought Meghan. We're treating the second step as if it were a private clubhouse.

Meghan wanted to do the right thing, the kind thing, and have Lannie sleep over, too, but Lannie was too scary. Meghan never wanted to be alone in the dark with Lannie Anveill. Lannie never made any noise when she moved. When you thought you were alone, the hair on the back of your neck would move in a tiny hot wind, and it would be Lannie, who had sneaked up close enough to breathe on your spine.

Lannie could creep behind things that hadn't even grown yet. Dark Fern Lane was a made-up name for a new little development. There was hardly even shade, let alone tall deep ferns gathering in damp thickets, behind which a child could hide. Yet Lannie crossed the street and passed through the yards as if behind screens of heavy undergrowth, unseen and unheard.

"I hate you, Meghan Moore," said Lannie.

She meant it.

Meghan had to look away from those terrible eyes, bleached like bones in a desert.

Once Tuesday and Brown announced that they were going to give Lannie sunglasses for a birthday present. They chickened out. But Lannie didn't have a birthday party after all, so it didn't matter.

Dark Fern Lane was where grown-ups bought their "first house." They said that when they entertained. "Of course, this is just our first house." Meghan kept expecting her parents to build a second house in the backyard, but they didn't mean that; they meant they lived on Dark Fern Lane until they could afford something better.

Lannie's parents had a raised ranch house the same size and shape as the rest, but there the similarities ended. Her parents were rarely home. Mr. and Mrs. Anveill did not set up the barbecue in the driveway on summer evenings. They did not have a beer and watch television football on autumn weekends. They did not make snow angels with Lannie in January. And come spring, they did not plant zinnias and zucchini.

They weren't saving up for a second house either.

They spent their money on cars.

Each of them drove a Jaguar. Mrs. Anveill's was black while Mr. Anveill's was crimson. They drove very very fast. Nobody else on Dark Fern Lane had a Jaguar. It was not a Jaguar kind of road. The rest of the families had used station wagons that drank gas the way their children drank Kool Aid.

Mrs. Anveill talked to her car, which she addressed as "Jaguar," as if it really were a black panther. She talked much more often to Jaguar than to Lannie.

Lannie was a wispy little girl. Even her hair was wispy. She was skinny as a Popsicle stick and pale as a Kleenex. Meghan felt sorry for Mr. and Mrs. Anveill, having Lannie for a daughter, but she also felt sorry for Lannie, having Mr. and Mrs. Anveill for parents.

The sun fell like a wet plate out of a dishwasher's hand. Meghan half expected to hear the crash, and see the pieces.

But instead, the light vanished.

It was dark, but parents didn't call them in yet. Shadows filled the open spaces and the yards became spooky and deep, and faces you knew like your own were blurry and uncertain.

Lannie's searchlight eyes pierced Meghan. "I hate you," she repeated. The hate grew toward Meghan like purple shadows. It had a temperature. Hate was cold. It touched Meghan on her bare arms and prickled up and down the skin.

Why me? thought Meghan. Tuesday's the one not letting her sleep over.

Again the warm glow of being wanted by a Trevor filled Meghan Moore, and then she understood Lannie's pain. Lannie loved the Trevor family as much as Meghan did. Lannie yearned to be part of that enveloping warmth and silly love and punchy fun. Lannie would never hate Tuesday. She wanted Tuesday. Lannie would hate Meghan because Meghan was the one chosen.

Lannie left the steps, silently crossing the soft grass, walking toward the lawnmower on which West and Brown still rode.

Meghan and Tuesday leaned back against each other, little

girls again, and rolled their eyes, and breathed, "Whew!" and "Close one!"

Lannie heard. She looked back, her little white skirt like a flag in the dusk. Meghan hunched down, as if Lannie might throw things. Tuesday's warmth was at Meghan's back, but Lannie's hate was on her horizon.

"Hello, West," said Lannie. This was unusual. Lannie never bothered with conventions of speech like hello or goodbye.

"Hello, Lannie," said West politely.

"Are you mowing the lawn?" said Lannie.

"No," muttered Meghan, sarcastic because she was afraid. "He's painting the Statue of Liberty."

It was impossible for Lannie to have heard all the way across the yard, but she had.

"You'll be sorry, Meghan Moore," said Lannie Anveill.

Meghan was only nine, but she was old enough to know that she had made a terrible mistake.

You'll be sorry, Meghan Moore.

I am sorry, she telegraphed to Lannie Anveill. I'm sorry, okay? But she didn't say it out loud.

"Get off of there, Brown," said Lannie sharply to the five year old. "It's my turn."

"Actually, I'm not giving turns," said West mildly. "Sorry, Lannie. But this really isn't safe and —"

"Get off, Brown," said Lannie. Her voice was flat like a table. Brown got off.

"Stop the mower, West," said Lannie, spreading her voice.

Meghan tucked herself behind the morning glory vines that had climbed to the top of the trellis and were stretching into the sky, looking for more trellis. Their little green tentacles were more alive than a plant should be, as if they were really eye stalks, like some creepy underwater jellyfish.

"Lannie," said West, "it's getting dark and —"

"Take me for a ride," said Lannie in her voice as cold as sleet, "or I will freeze Meghan."

There was a strange silence in the yard: a silence you could hear and feel in spite of the running engine.

They expected West to sigh and shrug and tell Lannie to go on home, but he did not. West obeyed Lannie, and she got on behind him as Brown had.

How could West stand to have Lannie touching him? Her long thin fingers gripping his shoulders like insect legs?

It seemed to Meghan that West and Lannie circled the lawn forever, while hours and seasons passed, and the grass remained uncut and the darkness remained incomplete.

"Stop the mower, West," said Lannie in her flat voice. "I've decided we're going to play Freeze Tag."

Brown fled. He hated Freeze Tag. Too scary. Brown usually decided to watch television instead.

"There aren't enough of us," objected West.

"Stop the mower, West," repeated Lannie. She did not change her voice at all. "I've decided we're going to play Freeze Tag."

West stopped the mower.

"I," said Lannie, "will be It."

"Surprise, surprise," muttered Tuesday, getting up and dusting her shorts.

Meghan loved Freeze Tag.

Whoever was It had to tag everybody. Once you were tagged, you froze into an ice statue, and didn't move a muscle for the remainder of the game. Eventually the whole neighborhood would be frozen in place.

You tried to impress people by freezing in the strangest position. It was best to freeze as if you were still running, with one leg in the air. It was difficult to balance while the rest screamed and ran and tried not to get tagged. But that was the challenge. Another good freeze was half-fallen on the ground, back arched, one arm frozen in a desperate wave. Good freezers didn't even blink.

At some point in the game, Meghan would get to touch West.

Or he would touch her. Meghan yearned to hold West's hand and run with him, but tag was a solo effort.

You ran alone.

You caught alone.

You froze alone.

Meghan tried to cry out, and run away, but no sound came from her throat and no movement entered her legs.

"Brown!" called Lannie.

He came instantly. Lannie's orders pulled like magnets.

"I could call my brother all my life and not get him to come," said Tuesday.

Lannie smiled at the three Trevors and the one Moore.

She still had her baby teeth, but her smile was ancient and knowing. Her eyes stretched out ahead of her fingers, which were pre-frozen, like a grocery item.

"Run!" she whispered gleefully.

They stumbled away.

The sky was purple and black, like a great bruise.

"*Run!*" Lannie shouted.

Meghan could not seem to run. She could only stagger.

Lannie laughed. "Try to get away from me," she said to Meghan. "You never will," she added.

This is not a game, thought Meghan Moore.

Her feet found themselves and ran, while her mind and heart went along for the ride. She kept looking down at those strange bare white sticks pumping frantically over the blackened grass. Those are my legs, she thought.

A queer terror settled over the flat ordinary yard. The children ran as if their lives depended on it.

Nobody screamed. Silence as complete as death invaded Dark Fern Lane.

They ran behind the house. They doubled back over the paved driveway. They tried to keep the parked lawnmower between them and Lannie.

One by one, Lannie froze them all.

She froze Brown first, and easily, because he was so little.

She froze West second, and just as easily as if West had

surrendered. As if West, although oldest and strongest, was also weakest.

Tuesday uttered the only scream of the night, as terror-struck as if her throat were being slit.

Lannie touched her, and the scream ended, and Tuesday froze with her mouth open and her face contorted.

Lannie closed in on Meghan, fingers pointed like rows of little daggers.

And yet Meghan slowed down. In some primitive way, like a mouse in the field beneath the shadow of a hawk's talons, she wanted it to be over.

Want what to be over? Meghan thought. My life?

"I won't be rude again!" cried Meghan. "I'm sorry! You can spend the night at the Trevors' instead of me."

Lannie smiled her smile of ice and snow.

Meghan's knees buckled and she went down in front of Lannie like a sacrifice. How real, how cool, how green the grass was. She wanted to embrace it, and lie safely in the arms of the earth, and never look into Lannie's endless eyes again.

Lannie stood for a moment, savoring Meghan's collapse, and then her fingers stabbed Meghan's arm.

Meghan froze.

The air was fat with waiting.

Lannie surveyed her four statues.

None of them moved.

None of them blinked.

None of them tipped.

Lannie chuckled.

She rocked back and forth in her little pink sneakers, admiring her frozen children.

Then she went home.

The soft warmth of evening enveloped Dark Fern Lane. No child shrieked, no engine whined, no dog barked. The air was sweet with the smell of new-mown grass. All was peaceful.

Mrs. Trevor came to the front door and called through the screen. "Game's up! Come on, everybody. One cookie each and then it's home for bed." Mrs. Trevor was accustomed to obedience and did not stay to be sure the children did as they were told; of course they would do as they were told.

But only the fireflies moved in the yard.

Meghan's eyes were frosty.

Her thoughts moved as slowly as glaciers.

As if through window panes tipping forward, Meghan saw Lannie leaving the yard. Lannie was happy. Meghan knew that she had never before seen Lannie Anveill in a state of happiness. Her smile shone on Meghan, as she lay crooked and stiff on the grass.

Time to go in, thought Meghan. Her expression did not change, her muscles did not sag. Her mouth was still twisted in fear, her eyes still wide with desperation.

Time to go in! thought Meghan.

But she was frozen. Time was something she no longer possessed and going in was something she would no longer do.

Lannie stepped down off the curb, contentedly glancing back at the statues of Brown and Tuesday. She headed for her house.

Mrs. Trevor came back to the screened door. "I am getting annoyed," she said, and she sounded it. "Everybody up and get going, please. I'm tired of all these grass-stained shirts. Now move it."

She returned to the interior of the house. The lights and music of the Trevors' living room seemed as distant from the dark yard as Antarctica.

Lannie stood invisibly in her own front yard.

The dark swirled around her and Lannie, too, went dark, her usual ghostly paleness pierced by night as it had been pierced by sun.

After a few minutes, she walked back across the street. Gently as a falling leaf, Lannie brushed the rigid shoulder of West Trevor.

West went limp, hitting the ground mushily, like a dumped

bag of birdseed. Then he scrabbled to his feet. He shook himself, doglike, as if his hair were wet.

Meghan wanted to call out to him, but nothing in her moved. When he walked forward, she tried to see where he was going but her eyes would not follow him. Her neck would not turn.

"Come on, Brown," said West to his brother. "Come on, Tues." His voice was trembling.

Brown and Tuesday stayed statues.

"You guys are freezing so well I can't even see you breathe," their brother said. A laugh stuck in his throat.

"They're *not* breathing," explained Lannie.

West sucked in his breath. He stood so still he seemed to have been tagged again. In a way, he was. Lannie had placed him in that tiny space after understanding, and just before panic.

Through the frost over her eyes, Meghan saw Lannie's smile, how slowly she reached forward, savoring her power, being sure that West understood. Then, making a gift to West, Lannie touched first Tuesday and next Brown.

Tuesday whimpered.

Brown moaned, "*Mommy.*"

"I froze them," said Lannie softly, as if she were writing West a love letter.

Meghan could see her own hair, sticking away from her head without regard to gravity, carved from ice.

"I can do it whenever I want," said Lannie. She seemed to be waiting for West to give her a prize.

West, Brown, and Tuesday drew together, staring at Lannie. In a queer tight voice, as if he had borrowed it from somebody, West said, "Undo Meghan."

Lannie smiled and shook her head. "I hate Meghan."

Tuesday began to cry.

West knelt beside Meghan, putting his hand on her shoulder, Meghan did not feel it, but there must have been pressure, because she tipped over stiffly. Now her eyes stared at the stems and mulch circle of one of the beginner-bushes.

I will be looking at this the rest of my life, thought Meghan Moore. This is what it's like in a coffin. You stare for all eternity at the wrinkles in the satin lining.

"Meghan?" whispered West.

But Meghan did not speak.

"Lannie," whispered West, "is she dead?"

"No. I froze her. I hate Meghan. She gets everything." Lannie chuckled. "Look at her now. No blinking. No tears. Just eyeballs."

West tried to pick Meghan up. Her elbows did not bend and her ankles did not straighten. "Lannie! Undo Meghan."

"No. It's Freeze Tag," said Lannie. "So I froze her." She turned a strangely anxious smile upon West. "Did you see me do it, West?"

They were too little to understand boy-girl things, and yet they knew Lannie was showing off for West. He was a boy she wanted, and she was a girl flirting with him, the only way she knew how.

And West, though he was only eleven, knew enough to agree. "Yes, I saw you. I was impressed, Lannie," he said carefully.

Lannie was pleased.

West wet his lips. He said even more carefully, "It would really impress me if you undid her."

"I don't feel like it," said Lannie.

Meghan stayed as inflexible as a chair, as cold as marble.

West took a deep breath. "Please, Lannie?" he said.

West, the strongest and oldest on the street, the big brother who could mow lawns, and baby-sit on Saturday nights, had to beg. Brown and Tuesday were both crying now.

"Well . . . " said Lannie.

"Promise her anything," said Tuesday urgently.

The only one who knew that West must not promise Lannie anything was the one who could not speak.

Meghan, alone and cold and still, thought: No, no, no! Don't promise, West. Better to be frozen than to be Lannie's!

The Trevors stood in a row, the three of them as close as blankets on a bed.

"You must always like me best," said Lannie.

"I will always like you best," repeated West. Lannie smiled her smile of ice and snow. She touched Meghan's cheek, and Meghan crumpled onto the grass. A normal child, with normal skin, and normal breathing.

"Don't forget your promise, West," said Lannie.

They had been whispering. When the screen door opened so sharply it smacked against the porch railings, the children were badly startled and flew apart like birds at the sound of gunshot.

"I am very angry," said Mrs. Trevor. "You will come in now. West, why is the lawnmower not in the shed? Do you think Freeze Tag comes before responsibility?"

Lannie melted away.

Meghan got up slowly, sweeping the grass cuttings off her shorts and hair.

"Don't tell," whispered Tuesday.

Nobody did tell.

Nobody would have known what to say.

Nobody quite believed it had happened.

They never did talk about it.

Not once.

Yard games went into history, like afterschool television reruns.

When Meghan grew up, and remembered the yard games, her memory seemed to be in black and white, flecked with age. Did we really play outside every night after supper? she asked herself.

Meghan could remember how it felt, as the hot summer night turned cool in the early dark.

She could remember how it looked, when fireflies sparkled in the dusk, begging to be caught in jars.

She could remember how it sounded, the giggles turning to screams and the screams turning to silence.

But they never talked.

Were their memories frozen? Or were their fears hot and still able to burn? Did they believe it had happened? Or did they think it was some neighborhood hysteria, some fabricated baby dream?

Meghan never knew if Tuesday remembered that brief death.

She never knew if West woke in the night, cold with the memory of Lannie's icy fingers.

She never knew if Brown was slow giving up his thumb-sucking because he remembered.

The only thing she knew for sure was that the neighborhood never played Freeze Tag again.

But Lannie . . .

Lannie played.

Chapter 1

For his seventeenth birthday, West Trevor was given an old Chevy truck. It was badly rusted, but this made West happy. He was taking courses at the auto body shop and would rebuild the exterior himself. The engine ran rough, but West was happy about that, too; he had had two years of small engine repair and, although this was no small engine, he ached to use what knowledge he had, and bring that Chevy truck back to strength.

Over the years, Dark Fern Lane had achieved its name. In the deep backyards near the shallow, slow-moving creek, bracken, ferns, and bittersweet had grown up in impenetrable tangles. Mrs. Trevor would not let West leave the truck in the driveway because it was so repulsive, and there was not room for it in the garage, so he drove it down the grassy hill and parked it at the bottom among the weeds and vines. From his bedroom window he could admire its blue hulk and dream of weekends when he would drive it to the vocational school shop and work on it for lovely grimy greasy hours on end.

Sometimes West just stood on the back steps of the house and stared down into the yard. "You can't even see your truck from here," Brown would point out. But West didn't care about that. He knew it was there.

West liked almost everybody. He was not discriminating. He thought most people were pretty nice. He preferred the company of boys, and next to rebuilding his Chevy, the best part of his life was managing the football team. He wasn't big enough to play, but he was crazy about the sport. Fall of his senior year in high school, therefore, was spent on playing fields or in locker rooms instead of working on his truck.

Football season would be over after Thanksgiving weekend.

West spent a lot of time thinking about what he would do next on his truck. He read and re-read his extensive collection of *Popular Mechanics, Popular Science*, and *Car and Driver*. He thought he was the happiest guy in town. He thought his life was perfect and it never occurred to West to change a molecule of his existence.

But something happened.

West Trevor fell in love.

He fell so deeply, completely, and intensely in love that even the truck hardly mattered, and football seemed remote and pointless.

What amazed West most of all was that he fell in love with a girl he had known — and hardly noticed — all his life.

Meghan Moore.

Meghan Moore, of course, had been planning this moment for years.

Girls always think ahead, and Meghan thought ahead more than most. Meghan had worshipped West since she was eight. I'm fifteen now, thought Meghan. That means I've spent half my life adoring the boy next door.

It seemed perfectly reasonable.

West had grown broad, rather than tall. Meghan was crazy about his shoulders and had spent all last year imagining herself snuggling up against that broad chest.

This year she was doing it.

Sometimes, cuddled up against West, her long thick hair arrayed across him like a veil, Meghan would feel the joy rise up in her chest and throat, and envelop her heart and mind. She would actually weep for love of West Trevor.

Furthermore, West was dizzy with love for her. West could not go down the school hall without detouring to her corner, and waving. (Making, said his brother Brown gloomily, a complete idiot of himself.) West could not have a meal unless he was sitting beside her. West could not be near a telephone without calling her. West could not sleep at night without slipping through the privet hedge that had grown tall and thick between the houses, running in the Moores' back door, and kissing her good night.

The only thing better than having a terrific boy in love with you was having the entire world witness it, and be envious, and soften at the sight.

Meghan was the happiest girl on earth.

Mr. and Mrs. Moore were not sure they liked this situation.

Meghan's interests had previously been confined to music. She was in the marching band, concert band, and jazz ensemble. She played flute and piccolo. Since she planned to be a band teacher when she grew up, she was now studying other instruments as well: trumpet, and the whole noisy range of percussion.

The entire neighborhood had been forced to follow Meghan's musical progress. There were those who hoped Meghan would attend a very distant college. Mr. and Mrs. Moore were tremendously proud of Meghan and were sure she had abilities far beyond teaching high school band. They expected her to be first flutist with the Boston Symphony Orchestra, and cut records, and be on television.

They were not thrilled that West Trevor was cutting into Meghan's practice time. With much difficulty (they had to look out the window or down at the table instead of at their daughter) they gave stern talks on sex, babies, AIDS, and life in general.

Meghan nodded reassuringly, said the things she knew they wanted to hear, and went ahead with her own plans.

Two houses away, the Trevors had other things to worry about than West's love life. Tuesday and Brown, so delightful and compatible as small children, had become extremely difficult teenagers. Mr. and Mrs. Trevor were worrying pretty much

Hi Iona.

full-time about Tuesday and Brown. They could not imagine where they had gone wrong. Tuesday and Brown's being horrible was very gratifying to the rest of Dark Fern Lane, after having had the perfect Trevor family held up in front of them all those elementary school years.

West, at seventeen, with his driver's license and his good grades and his busy life, was their success story.

Still, his mother was not sure she liked the intensity of this relationship with little Meghan Moore. "He's only seventeen," West's mother would say nervously, as if she thought West and Meghan were going to get married when she wasn't looking.

It wasn't marriage that worried West's father. He chose not to say what he had been doing with girls when he was seventeen. He thought it was just as well that the Chevy truck was not in good enough condition to drive farther than the vocational school repair bays. He tried not to laugh when he looked at his son. He had never seen a boy so thoroughly smitten.

Young love, thought West's father, smiling. There's nothing like it.

Meghan herself had everything: two parents who lived together and loved her, neighbors who included her, a boy who worshipped her, and a school in which she was popular and successful.

Meghan did not analyze these things. She did not ask why she was so lucky, nor worry about the people who were not. She was fifteen, which is not a particularly kind age. It's much better than thirteen, of course, and greatly superior to fourteen, but age sixteen is where compassion begins and the heart is moved by the plight of strangers.

Meghan was fifteen and her world was West and West was world enough.

Nobody knew what Lannie Anveill thought.

And nobody cared.

Meghan danced down the hall to West's locker. In the shelter of the ten-inch wide metal door, they kissed. Then they laughed, the self-conscious but wildly happy laugh they shared. Then they held hands and admired each other's beauty.

"I've got Mom's car for the day," said West.

They were airborne with the thought of a front seat together.

Meghan slid the strap of her bookbag over her shoulder. West slid his over his opposite shoulder. They wrapped their arms around each other's waists, and slowly made their way out of the school.

Every girl daydreams of a boy so in love he can't bear spending time away from her. There were a thousand boys in that high school and maybe ten had ever behaved like this. The girls watched West watching Meghan. They ached to be Meghan, to have West, to be adored like that. They saw how his hands and his eyes were all over her. How he was thick in the clouds of his love.

West did not see a single girl except Meghan.

Meghan, of course, saw all the girls, and knew exactly how envious they were, and got an extra jolt of pleasure from it.

Lannie Anveill fell in step with them.

Meghan could not believe it. There were certain rules of etiquette, and one was that you did not join a couple who were linked body and soul. Meghan glared at Lannie to make her go away, and Lannie glared right back. Meghan flinched. She had forgotten the power of Lannie's eyes. They went too deep.

West remembered his manners — he had fine manners; sometimes he stood behind his manners like a safety rail — and said cheerfully, "Hi, Lannie. What's up?"

Lannie stood still. She was still thin and wispy, looking little older than she had when they had played yard games. It was a little spooky, really, the way Lannie did not age. As if she would bypass all that tiresome human stuff of stages and ages. Her bleached-out eyes passed straight through Meghan and came out the other side.

Meghan, lovely in casual plaid wool pants and clinging dark sweater, felt stripped. As if Lannie did not see clothes. Only interior weaknesses.

Lannie discarded Meghan from her sight. She focused on West. Sternness left her. Hostility left her. With unusual softness, Lannie said to him, "It's time."

Meghan felt a strange tremor.

West smiled politely. "Time for what, babe?" He called girls who did not interest him "babe." He did not know how much this annoyed them.

"You remember," said Lannie.

West considered this. One of his nicest traits was being serious when being serious counted. Not every seventeen-year-old boy had figured out how to do this. "Remember what?" he asked her at last.

"Your promise," said Lannie.

Something cold shivered in Meghan's memory.

West was blank. He said, "Am I taking everybody to a movie or something? Sorry, Lannie, I'm a little off-center today." He pulled Meghan close, to demonstrate what put him off-center. "Remind me, babe."

Lannie tightened like a bow and arrow. "You must remember!" she whispered so hotly she could have lit a match with her breath.

West frowned. "Ummm. Lannie, I'm sorry, I'm not sure what we're talking about."

"Give us a hint," said Meghan. From the lofty position of Us — she had a partner, she had a boyfriend, she was a pair — she could look down on Lannie, who was alone and unloved and unpaired. It was more comfortable to be scornful than to be scared. So Meghan looked down on Lannie, and it showed.

Somewhere from the distant past she heard Lannie say, "*You'll be sorry, Meghan Moore.*" Something in Meghan Moore quivered like a rabbit as the fox's jaws close on its leg.

"You want a reminder, Meghan Moore?" said Lannie Anveill. "Fine. Tomorrow. You will be reminded."

Meghan's knees were weak. She could remember that, too. That moment when her body failed her.

Lannie turned and walked away, vanishing in the high school crowds with the same ease she used to vanish on Dark Fern Lane.

Meghan forced a giggle. When she took West's hand, hers was sweaty. I always hated it when Lannie joined the neighborhood, thought Meghan. The last thing I want her to join is *us*. She has no right.

West said, "Didn't she sound like the voice of doom?"

Meghan dropped her voice an octave. "*You will be reminded.*"

They actually laughed.

Chapter 2

It was a good morning. One of the best.

In geometry Meghan learned the new formula right away and her mind glittered with pleasure. There was nothing like mastering math to make you feel like a genius.

In history, usually so dusty and remote, the teacher read an exciting passage from an old, old journal. Meghan's skin prickled, imagining how it had been back then.

"Why is history important?" said the teacher. His voice was soft, uttering a sentence he wanted the students to carry through life. "Because . . . if you forget history, you are doomed to repeat it."

Where did I just hear that word? thought Meghan. You don't hear it very often. How dark it is. A word for death and eternal sorrow.

"*Doomed*," repeated the teacher softly.

But I have no history, Meghan thought. So I am not doomed to repeat anything.

In Spanish, Meghan was required to read a passage aloud. For the first time ever in foreign language class, her tongue knew how to sound. She felt a wild surge of triumph, and yearned to speak with somebody Spanish.

She could hardly wait for lunch, to tell West.

Sometimes school frightened Meghan. Sometimes she failed, or it failed her. Sometimes it puzzled her or left her behind.

But this was not one of those days.

She burned with excitement. She savored the feel, even the taste of the new Spanish syllables. She planned the phrases she would use to describe the new knowledge.

She danced down the hallway to where they always met, at the drinking fountain.

He was there already, smiling.

Oh, how she loved him! He was West, wide and handsome and fascinating and wonderful, and most of all, *hers*.

For years she had averted her eyes from any boy she liked. All through middle school, the more she liked a boy, the less able she was to look at him.

But she could look at West. Soak him up. Like a flower facing the sun.

He started talking first. "Guess what."

"What?" They saved things for each other; tiny tales of success to hand each other at lunch, and after school, and on the phone.

"We had a quiz in physics. Guess what I got." West was shining.

He wanted to be an engineer and design cars. He loved anything to do with motors or movement. "A hundred," guessed Meghan.

"Yes!" West hugged her with his pride. "I raised the curve," he bragged.

"Yeah, you toad," said another kid from physics. He punched West cheerfully. "I was the next highest," he confided to Meghan. "I got eighty-nine."

"Congratulations," said Meghan. West's hand on her waist was opening and closing, going nowhere and yet exploring. She loved being possessed like that — the proof of his clasp like a bracelet: this is mine, it stays here.

"You want to get in the sandwich line or the hot line?" asked West.

They checked out other people's trays. The hot plate was unrecognizable. It was brown and it had gravy, and that was all you could be sure of.

"Sandwiches," said Meghan.

"Sandwiches," agreed West.

They laughed and wanted to kiss in front of everybody, but didn't. Still, it was in their eyes and in the way they walked.

"Guess what," said Meghan.

"You got a hundred in Spanish."

"We didn't have a quiz. But listen to me talk. I'm going to knock your socks off with my accent."

"I'm ready," said West. He tugged his pant legs up so they could watch when his socks came off. Meghan giggled.

Somebody screamed.

Of course, the cafeteria was always noisy. People yelled, laughed, talked, gossiped, burped, scraped chairs, and dropped dishes. A scream was not extraordinary.

But this was a scream of terror.

It was the kind of scream that grabbed at the roots of your heart, and wrenched the air out of your lungs, and made you want your back against a wall.

Five hundred students went silent, breath caught, looking for the source of the terrible scream. Eyes sped around the room like paired animals, seeking the terror.

Meghan had a queer slicing memory, like a knife, a knife dripping with blood, and somehow it was mixed with Tuesday, and grass, and darkness, and childhood.

The last time I heard a scream like that . . . thought Meghan.

But she could not quite remember the last time she had heard a scream like that.

West sucked in his breath. Her hand was on his back and she felt his ribs and chest expand, and felt them stay expanded, as if holding onto his lungs would keep him alive. As if there were danger of not being alive.

Toppled on the floor, like a statue knocked over by a vandal, was a girl. One leg remained raised and off it, a long skirt hung like drapery.

"She fainted," said somebody.

"Give her air."

"Call an ambulance."

Teachers and cafeteria workers rushed over to help.

The girl was stiff.

"She's . . . sort of . . . frozen," said the cafeteria monitor, backing away, as if it were a virus, and would leap free of the fallen girl and attack the rest.

People touched the frozen girl with a single extended finger, and then pulled back, afraid, even wiping their hands off on their trousers.

The air swirled around Meghan Moore and West Trevor.

Old air. The air of their childhoods.

Memory.

The quiet of the night came back, and the softness of the summer, and the deepness of the horror.

Meghan remembered the morning glory by the steps, whose bright blue flowers had slid into their green envelopes, saving its glory for dawn. Meghan had always wondered what morning glories knew that people did not.

She remembered the lawnmower and the scent of the cut grass, the setting sun and the thickness of dusk.

She remembered the calm explanatory voice. *It's Freeze Tag. So I froze her.*

"Who is it, does anybody know?" said the teachers.

"Jessica," said somebody else.

The school had at least fifty girls named Jessica. Meghan did not know if this was a Jessica she knew, or a stranger Jessica.

Meghan moved slowly, dizzily, forward. The fallen girl was still and solid. Her skin did not seem tan with summer, but icy blue with winter. Her hair stuck out from her head without regard to gravity, as if carved from ice. Her shoulders did not rise and fall with the filling of lungs.

"She *is* frozen," whispered a horrified adult.

I didn't run fast enough, thought Meghan. *Lannie hated me.*

She remembered Lannie's fingers, burring into her soul. She

remembered being frozen. It didn't hurt. And I wasn't afraid, either, thought Meghan. I was just suspended. Perhaps hibernation is like that. Bears survive the winter, don't they? They just turn down the heat until spring.

But a human would not live till spring.

"It must be a seizure," said a teacher, voice trembling. He tried to move her into a sitting position, but the body did not bend. It was sickeningly stiff, as if she had died yesterday and gone into rigor mortis. "Call an ambulance!"

The girl's leg stayed high in the air, like a gymnast's photograph.

West had had to say *please*. West had had to beg.

Lannie had said, *You must always like me best*.

And West repeated like a little boy learning a little lesson, *I will always like you best*.

He never thought of Lannie again, let alone liked her best, Meghan realized. He liked cars best, and football best, and then finally he liked *me* best.

West set the lunch tray down, his face pale, upper lip fringed with sweat. "I remember," he said. His voice was vacant.

Meghan was afraid to look around. What if she met Lannie's eyes? Those terrible bleached eyes could illuminate a dark yard, like headlights of a car. Perhaps Lannie could freeze you with her eyes.

West murmured, "She's over by the windows."

Meghan forced herself to look over by the windows.

Lannie stood alone, her little wispy frame very still. As Meghan had soaked up the sunshine of West's greeting, Lannie soaked up the darkness of Jessica's freezing. Her smile was tender. Her head was tilted to the side, an artist admiring her exhibit.

West mumbled something unintelligible. He shoved both hands deep into his jeans' pockets.

He was separating himself from Meghan, and from the disaster, and even from the future.

Meghan stared at those wrists, at those pockets, and saw a

different West: a West who did not want to face this. A West who was going to stand very still and hope it all went away.

She was aware of a deep disappointment in West. His broad shoulders and his fine mind did not match his strength of soul.

It was a thought too terrible to allow. Meghan knocked it away.

Lannie slid between them, materializing as completely and silently as a chemistry experiment. Meghan's body jerked with fear. Lannie was so close, Meghan flinched. Don't touch me!

She gave Lannie another inch and Lannie smiled into the air, but did not bother to look at Meghan. She did not bother with greetings or small talk either. She never had. "We are going out now, West," she said firmly. As if West were a lottery ticket, and Lannie wanted to buy in.

West jammed his hands deeper into the pockets.

"This is your fault, anyway," Lannie said. "You should have discussed this last night, after I talked to you. I warned you this would happen."

Meghan was afraid, and fear made her stupid, and stupidity made her rude. "Lannie," she said sharply, "we had better things to talk about than you."

In the short space of time before Lannie retaliated, Meghan saw that Lannie actually experienced emotion. It had hurt Lannie's feelings that West and Meghan had not talked about her last night. Lannie looked up at West with a kind of grief and sorrow.

Lannie knew nothing of love. Yet she ached for it; all the world ached for love. Somehow Lannie could not understand why she couldn't just take West and walk off with him. Sort of like shoplifting a lipstick.

In the distance came the peculiar rise and fall of an ambulance siren, as harsh and upsetting as chalk on a blackboard.

"Lannie," said Meghan, "undo her. Jessica didn't do anything to you."

The revolving lights on top of the ambulance cast on-and-off rainbows through the slanted cafeteria windows. When a backboard was slid under Jessica, the body remained stiff and splayed.

"Get out of here, Meghan," said Lannie calmly. "West is mine now."

She's in love with him, thought Meghan. She always has been. How could I have forgotten that? We marched our love up and down Dark Fern Lane, showing off for the world. We forgot that Lannie is part of our world. "You can't do that to Jessica," said Meghan softly. "Undo her."

"It isn't a true demonstration if I undo her," said Lannie. "You would relax. You must never relax around me, Meghan. Now go away. West is mine."

"Lannie," hissed West, "what did Jessica do to deserve that?"

"She didn't do anything."

"You can't go around freezing people!" said West.

"Of course I can," said Lannie, with the annoyed air of one having to point out the obvious. "Now if this was not enough for you, I'll do another."

"No!"

"Actually," said Lannie, "I could freeze lots of people. They would close the school down. They would think they had a weird epidemic."

"I would tell them what you were doing," said West.

Lannie put her thin little arm around his big waist. She hugged him affectionately. "Would they believe it?" she said, smiling.

Across the silent frightened room a teacher said, "It must be some kind of virus. One of those new diseases. Like Legionnaire's Disease."

"Unfreeze her, Lannie!" hissed Meghan.

"No. Come on, West. We're eating together."

West actually took a step with her. Actually picked up the lunch tray on which his and Meghan's sandwiches lay.

"Let's talk about this," said Meghan quickly.

"There's nothing to talk about. West promised to like me forever, and forever is here."

Forever is here.

The words strapped Meghan down. Lannie would have West for eternity, while Meghan would go to school alone and grow up and move away.

"Actually I think I promised to like you best," said West.

"That, too," said Lannie happily.

"Undo Jessica!" shouted Meghan.

The cafeteria turned to stare in their direction.

Lannie shook her head gently, disassociating herself and West from Meghan's crazy behavior.

"You're a virus, Lannie," said Meghan.

Lannie had had enough of her. "And you're frozen, Meghan," said Lannie, reaching out.

Chapter 3

West jerked Lannie backward. Her finger missed Meghan by a molecule's width. Lannie's hand trembled, stuck out into the air, touching nothing. The finger pointed evilly on, as if it could freeze by invisible waves. But it could not. Meghan could move and breathe.

Not easily. Fear tightened her up. Her stomach was cinched in, her ribs were rigid, her ankles were stiff. Meghan managed a single half step away. It was not enough. A river between them would not have been enough.

She was going to freeze me! thought Meghan. She was tired of me and that was the answer.

After a long time, she wrenched her eyes off that shivering fingertip — was it shivering because it delivered a freeze? shivering because it was still straining forward? — and looked at West.

How large West was, how slight Lannie looked against him. She was as insubstantial as a tissue, and yet he had to struggle to hold her. West seemed both stunned and certain. Of what was he certain? Meghan did not know. She was certain of nothing now. She did not see if she could ever be certain again.

What weapon was this — this threat Lannie could carry out?

How would any of them behave normally ever again, when that finger could . . .

"I like you best, Lannie," said West. His voice was calm. It was even friendly. It did not sound like a lie. Anybody listening would have thought that West Trevor did, indeed, like Lannie best.

Meghan was no longer stiff with fear but limp with shock. Was West acting? If so, he was a brilliant actor. Or was he impressed? Memory returned to Meghan Moore. *I'm impressed, Lannie*, he had said that evening on the grass.

Power is impressive, she thought. But he has to like me best!

"We'll have lunch over by the windows, Lannie," said West in his firm adult voice. "And on our way over, Lannie," he said, giving an order, sounding like a parent, "you'll brush against Jessica. It'll count. It'll undo it. The ambulance won't have to take her. Right?"

Lannie pulled her lips together in a little girl's pout.

How strange she looked. A moment ago Lannie had been as ancient as evil, as timeless as cruelty. Now she was a little girl, lip stuck out because she had to do something she didn't feel like doing.

"I mean it, Lannie," said West. "I can't hang out with you if you're going to freeze people."

Meghan suppressed an hysterical desire to laugh.

"Okay, fine," said Lannie irritably. She snuggled herself up against West and walked so close to him she might have been standing on his shoes to walk, the way Brown used to love to do with his big brother when he was about three.

It was good that everybody in the cafeteria was so absorbed by Jessica's condition. Nobody saw the amazing combination of Lannie and West.

Actually, thought Meghan, a combination of Lannie and anyone at all would be amazing. She's always alone. Everybody's afraid of her.

Meghan's hair prickled.

Why? Why were they afraid? What experiences had other people in here had with Lannie Anveill? What had happened off Dark Fern Lane?

Meghan closed her eyes, blotting out her imagination, and in those few brief moments, West and Lannie brushed by the stretcher just as it was sliding out the cafeteria door and toward the waiting, open ambulance.

Jessica tried to sit up on the swaying stretcher, miraculously regaining consciousness and muscle.

"Oh, thank God!" cried the teachers.

Lannie smiled, accepting this description of herself.

Lannie and West really did sit together for lunch. They even talked, and faced each other, and handed each other napkins. West actually seemed to listen to Lannie, and when it was his turn, he seemed to be telling her important things, things worth focusing on.

Meghan could not seem to function. She could not figure out whether to sit alone, or find an old friend, or hide in the girls' room, or go back to class early.

My perfect day, thought Meghan Moore. My wonderful classes, my fluent Spanish, my lovely, lovely West.

Meghan hurt somewhere inside. How could West be so easy about this? How could he saunter across the cafeteria, relax with that terrible hand so close to him — touching him, even?

Was he acting?

Perhaps she froze part of me after all, thought Meghan. I'm not completely here. Part of my mind is ice. Part of my heart is snow.

Eventually lunch period ended.

Eventually Meghan found herself in gym.

She was taking tennis. The school had an indoor court. Never had it been so satisfying to whack a ball. Meghan hurled all her strength into the drills. The coach was thrilled. "Meghan, you're vicious!" said the coach happily. "I love when you play like this! This is winning!"

I will hit Lannie Anveill like this, thought Meghan Moore. I am not giving up West Trevor. And *he* is not giving *me* up, either. She's not allowed to go running around freezing people or scaring me that she might. I won't put up with it.

Meghan smashed a ball down into the opposite court. Whatever had been frozen in her melted. She was all heat. All rage.

All hatred.

Once she had thought hatred was cold. Wrong. Hate boiled in her mind and her heart. The steam of hate rose in her throat. Bubbles of hate raced through her blood.

She could actually *feel* the hate.

She could feel hate take over her body the way Lannie Anveill's evil touch had taken over Jessica's.

Meghan Moore set down her tennis racket. Meghan Moore backed away from the court, away from the shouting coach, away from the beaten opponents.

No.

I refuse.

I will not be filled with hate. I don't like people who are hateful. I like nice people. I am a nice person. I will not hate.

Meghan walked into the girls' locker room early and stood alone among the slick tiles and the stuck lockers.

She let the hate seep out of her. It did not leave quickly or easily. Hate was a lingering thing. It liked ruling the body.

She shook her hands as if shaking water off her fingers. She lifted each foot and shook it. The last little droplets of hate seemed to leave.

I won't beat Lannie with hate, thought Meghan. But I have to beat her with something. So what will it be?

" . . . because knowing your opponent will give you an edge," the coach was saying out in the gym. "You must study your opponent's technique. Then you can see the weaknesses and the flaws, and move in on them."

Know your opponent, thought Meghan Moore.

Did Lannie have weaknesses? Did she have flaws?

Meghan would have to get to know Lannie.

There was no other way.

Meghan had a study hall last period. She usually made excellent use of it. Today, as usual, the forty-four minutes were not wasted.

She did not doodle or daydream. But she did not study math or literature, either.

She reviewed her knowledge of Lannie Anveill.

Lannie never seemed to get older, or taller, or curvier. She had stayed wispy. Her hair was dry and brittle. It reminded Meghan of herbs that people who had country kitchens were always hanging from their ceilings. There was a dustiness to Lannie, as if she were very old, and had been stored somewhere. Unused.

Or unloved, thought Meghan. Nobody ever had less love.

Meghan's mother used to say that, when she insisted Meghan had to be kind to Lannie. It was blackmail kindness. You could not really feel sorry for Lannie. You were more apt to feel sorry for her parents. There was something in Lannie that precluded sympathy.

Except for the growing of trees and children, Dark Fern Lane had seen few changes when Meghan was in elementary school. Most of the families who had bought first homes there still owned those first homes.

Lannie's father was the only one on Dark Fern Lane who actually did get a second house. Lannie had been about ten.

Getting a second house, it turned out, was not necessarily good news. For Lannie's father was not going to bring his wife and daughter along to this second house. He was going to live there with his girlfriend, Nance.

Mr. Anveill promised that he would take Lannie one weekend a month. It did not sound like a lot of time to spend with your father, but it sure sounded like a lot of time to spend with Lannie. Meghan had shivered for Nance, who surely did not know what that weekend and that stepdaughter were going to be like.

And when Lannie's mother remarried, too, Meghan shivered for Jason. Jason moved into the house on Dark Fern Lane, and had to live with Lannie all the time.

One Friday, Nance and Mr. Anveill were picking Lannie up for The Weekend, and Nance happened to have a conversation with Meghan's mother, who was raking leaves across the yard and into the street. "I've been reading up on stepparenting," said Nance.

"Oh?" said Mrs. Moore.

"Experts say not to expect to get along for at least two years, let alone feel any love for the stepchild. So I don't expect a thing, and I certainly don't love Lannie, but I wish she would brush her teeth more often."

Lannie was standing there at the time. She had chosen a few pretty orange and yellow maple leaves to admire. But she did not take them inside with her. She crushed them in her hand.

And then there was the day when Jason, waxing his car (he drove a classic Corvette; the former Mrs. Anveill was not interested in men who drove dull cars) talked to Meghan's father. "I don't know how to be a parent," he confided. He seemed to feel this freed him from having to try.

That year, Lannie skipped a grade, catching up to Meghan. Lannie had never seemed especially smart, and many people were surprised that Lannie was skipped up. Meghan understood perfectly. Lannie's scheduled teacher was afraid of her. What better way to breathe easily than to bump up the source of your fear?

Beside her in study hall somebody coughed. Somebody moved his chair. Somebody dropped a book on the floor.

Meghan heard none of it. For she had remembered the dog. She had not thought of that dog in years!

Why didn't I remember? she wondered. Why didn't I add things up? What took me so long?

Jason had brought home an Irish setter. Such a beautiful dog!

Dark red, lean, and graceful.

It bounded across the narrow yard on Dark Fern Lane, whipped around the Jaguar and the Corvette parked in the drive, and rushed back to Jason to lick his hands. Jason, impossibly handsome in his sporty jacket and jaunty cap, knelt to fondle the dog.

How attractive everybody was! The fine strong stepfather!

The magnificent cars! The lovely fluid Irish setter! Meghan had been awestruck. Her own family was dowdy and dull.

Jason, laughing happily, had hugged the dog.

"He's never hugged me," said Lannie.

The dog did not yet have a name. Lannie's mother came out and she too admired the beautiful dog. "We need a name for it," said Lannie's mother with great concentration. "It must be a perfect name."

"For a perfect dog," agreed Jason.

They hugged each other, and leaned against each other, as if they and the dog were the family.

As if Lannie did not exist.

The Irish setter, loping over the green grass, passed near the two young girls. Meghan, who was not fond of dogs, shrank back.

But Lannie had put her hand out.

Meghan, in the study hall, clung to the table, sick with dizziness, as if she were about to faint. *I knew*, thought Meghan, *I knew even then*. I knew what was going to happen.

How vividly Meghan remembered Lannie's fingers. Too long for a little girl's hand. Her wrist too narrow, skin too white.

The dog tipped over, as if made of cast iron. It lay on the ground with its legs sticking out like chair legs.

"Oh, no!" cried Jason. "What's the matter? My beautiful dog!"

Lannie's mother said, "Quick! We'll take the dog to the vet."

They crooned and wept.

They rushed for help.

They showed the paralyzed dog more affection and worry than they had ever shown Lannie.

Lannie's skin was as cold and white as snow, but her eyes, her pale dead eyes, were hot and feverish with pleasure.

Meghan remembered backing away, trying to slip unseen into her house. She had accomplished it easily. Lannie had forgotten Meghan. Lannie's satisfied eyes remained for hours on the place in the grass where the dog's frozen outline was impressed.

The following spring there was another ending in Lannie's life.

People who drive Jaguars as fast as Lannie's mother either lose their driver's license or get killed. With Lannie's mother, it was first one and then the other.

Everybody on Dark Fern Lane felt obligated to go to the funeral.

Only Meghan had refused to attend.

"Darling," said Mrs. Moore, "I know funerals are upsetting, but Lannie is in school with you, and she's your across-the-street neighbor, and you owe it to Lannie to show support."

Why didn't I want to go? thought Meghan, tapping her pencil against the cover of her unopened literature book. The boy next to her stared pointedly until she flushed and stopped tapping.

Meghan tried to remember the funeral.

I didn't go, thought Meghan. I stayed home.

Why?

The answer did not come, and yet she felt it there: a piece of knowledge she had chosen to bury when she was young. When she was thirteen. A terrible age. Meghan was very grateful not to be thirteen any longer.

In any event, Lannie, at twelve, had no mother, and so of course went to live with her father and Nance. Nobody on Dark Fern Lane missed Lannie. Meghan breathed deeper and laughed longer with Lannie off the street.

Not a month later, Nance drove into Lannie's old driveway. Lannie was in the front seat with her stepmother.

The weather had turned unseasonably hot, and everybody was outdoors — because nobody on Dark Fern Lane had air conditioning — and therefore everybody saw and everybody heard what happened next.

"Lannie's father," said Nance to Jason, "has deserted us."

Jason said he was sorry to hear that, but he did not know how it involved him.

"Lannie is yours," said Nance, and she drove off faster than Jason could think of an argument.

There was Jason, in his driveway, with Lannie Anveill. "Well," said Jason. "Well, well, well."

Lannie stayed. Jason continued to lead his own life. Lannie always seemed to have clean clothes and a recent shampoo. But that was all she had.

Absolutely all.

The children on Dark Fern Lane graduated from elementary school, left middle school, and entered high school.

They no longer had neighborhood birthday parties to which Lannie must be invited. They no longer went to the same ballet classes and had to give Lannie rides. They no longer gathered for afternoon snacks at the Trevors', and had to give Lannie a plate of nachos as well.

High school was big and airy and full of strangers. Even when they had attended it for years, it was still full of strangers. Sometimes they went days without running into Lannie.

Even when they saw Lannie, they didn't think of her. They were completely absorbed by their own lives. The whole world, from the President of the United States to their mothers, was remote and bothersome.

Had any of them noticed Lannie?

Even once?

The final bell rang.

Meghan stood up, dazed.

Here's what I know about Lannie Anveill, thought Meghan Moore. Nobody loves her. Nobody ever has.

Chapter 4

And yet, for all that, when Meghan went down the usual hall at the usual time, there was West, in his usual place. And as usual, her heart leaped, her legs danced, and her lips smiled.

"West!" she said.

His smile filled his face. "Meghan."

They hugged at the locker and went arm and arm to the car.

Lannie had fallen away from their thoughts and their lives like a piece of paper dropped to the floor. How remote those hate-filled tennis-ball-smacking minutes became. How meaningless the knowledge of Lannie's loveless life. Meghan forgot again. Only teenagers can forget so completely, so often.

Meghan knew nothing except the joy and the warmth of the boy she adored. Her world was very small, and very full.

"This afternoon I'm going to work on my truck," said West happily. "It's cold out, but the sun will be shining for probably another hour and a half. I'm trying to fix the door handles."

"That's a good project," said Meghan, who thought it was the most boring thing she had ever heard of.

West beamed, and shared his door-handle restoration plans with her. It seemed that both handles had broken off on the inside. "You have to keep a window rolled down in order to get out," he explained. "And I can't be letting it rain and snow inside my truck!"

Considering that it had been raining and snowing inside that rusty old hulk for a decade now, Meghan didn't see why he felt so deeply about it. But she loved him so she said, "I could help."

She knew West didn't really like help when he worked on his truck. In fact, West didn't like company. He liked to be alone with his toolbox and his chore. But she loved him a whole extra lot today, and she wanted to sit on that dumb old front seat and watch him sweat.

"Okay," he said reluctantly.

They threaded through the escaping cars — hundreds of kids leaving school as fast as they could — and found West's mother's car. West measured his happiness by the number of days he was allowed to take the car to school. It wasn't all the time, by any means. It wasn't even half the time.

"How long before the truck is up and going?" said Meghan, meaning, How long before you and I can ride together every day?

"Long time," said West, half gloomy because there was so much to do, and half delighted because there was so much to do.

West got in his side and Meghan opened the door to hers.

Lannie was sitting in the middle of the front seat.

West froze in the act of getting behind the wheel, looking exactly like a statue in Freeze Tag — one leg in, one leg out, half his body on the seat, half still outside the car.

Meghan froze all over again. Her hand froze on the door handle and her face froze in shock, seeing Lannie ensconced in West's mother's car. Meghan's mind and heart and body raced through every emotion of the day: fear, panic, rage, and finally knowledge.

I know she isn't loved, thought Meghan, striving for understanding and decency. But I don't want her to start with West!

And Meghan especially didn't want to see Lannie so pleased with herself.

West evidently decided that good manners would carry the day. West hated not getting along with everybody. It was a character flaw, in Meghan's opinion. You couldn't always be friends with everybody. But West, like the rest of the Trevors, was endlessly polite. It gave them protection; they could stand neatly behind their courtesy.

"Hey, Lannie," said West easily. As if it were quite ordinary to bump into her in his car. As if it meant nothing now, and was not going to mean anything later. "Want a ride home? We'll drop you off."

But it did mean something, Lannie being there in Meghan's place. Meghan could not quite get in the front seat and sit next to Lannie. Not after she had remembered the dog.

West did not look at Meghan. She could not exchange thoughts by eye. What shall I do? thought Meghan, as if her life depended on it. After a moment she got in the backseat by herself.

Lannie smiled victoriously and rested a hand on West's thigh.

Meghan was outraged. That's my place! she thought. Don't you touch him! He's mine!

But she did not say anything.

None of them said anything. Meghan did not think she had ever driven down these roads and kept silent. She did not think she had ever come out of school without a thousand stories and complaints and jokes to tell.

West seemed to sit very casually in the driver's seat, rather like a van driver who'd been giving rides for a hundred years and drove with a single fingertip, a slouch, and a shrug.

They reached Dark Fern Lane without having uttered a word. And it was Lannie, taking control, who spoke first. "Drop Meghan off," said Lannie. Her voice was as cold as January.

Meghan pressed back against the upholstery. Lannie seemed to have lowered the temperature in the whole car, just by speaking. As if her breath carried frost with it.

"Aw, come on, Lannie," said West. "I had lunch with you." As if that were enough. As if Lannie Anveill would settle for that. "Meghan and I have plans." As if Lannie cared. As if Lannie were going to allow those plans to be executed.

Outside was very January. Cold and waiting, the weather

hiding behind a gray sky, waiting to blast them out of their safe houses. The ground hard as iron, expecting snow, needing snow.

In the backseat, Meghan felt queerly numb. She lifted her hands, to be sure she still had them. Drop me off, she thought. Off what? A cliff?

And suddenly she knew.

A glaze frosted her eyes, like the day she had been frozen in the yard.

A glaze of knowledge.

Lannie turned around to glare at Meghan for taking so long. Her hooded eyelids lifted and the dark irises glowed like the Northern Lights. "Get out of the car, Meghan," said Lannie, in a voice as flat as a table.

"Lannie," breathed Meghan. She was trembling so hard she did not see how she could pick up her bookbag, or find the door handle.

Lannie smiled her smile of ice and snow.

"Did you freeze your own mother?" said Meghan. "Is that why the car crashed? Because she was frozen?"

Because that's why I didn't go to the funeral, thought Meghan. I remember it now. I was sure Lannie made her mother pay for loving the dog more.

The bleached eyes swung from Meghan to West.

West's big hands tightened on the steering wheel.

"Look at me, West," whispered Lannie.

"Don't look at her," said Meghan. But Meghan couldn't look away. Nor could she move. She was afraid to lean forward and so much as rest her hand on West's shoulder. She was afraid to touch the door handle, for fear that Lannie had infected it, and it would be a carrier, as wires carry electricity.

"Is that why the car crashed?" said West. His voice, too, was flat. But his throat gave him away. It gagged.

Lannie's smile was as sharp as a splinter. "Maybe," she said. And then she laughed, and the laugh pierced Meghan's skin and hurt.

* * *

A few houses down Dark Fern Lane, the school bus stopped.

Children poured out.

Tuesday, who had a generous and romantic nature, and therefore usually let West and Meghan ride home by themselves, got off last. She separated from the little ones. Her dark blonde hair bounced against her neon pink windbreaker. She swung her yellow bookbag in a circle and jumped successfully over an ice-crusted puddle in a driveway. She was laughing. She must have had a great day, or a funny ride home, because even though she was on her own now, the laugh was still carrying her.

"Why, it's Tuesday," said Lannie sweetly. "Dear Tuesday. I've never liked her either, really. Wouldn't it be unfortunate if . . . " Lannie smiled. Then she said once more, "Get out of the car, Meghan."

Tuesday hurled her bookbag toward her own front steps — missing by a hundred yards — and headed toward her brother and her best friend. "Hi, Meggie-Megs!" shouted Tuesday.

It was a very old nickname.

Meghan hardly knew which person it meant: she felt at least a century older than the little girl who had once been called Meggie-Megs by the neighborhood.

The only sound inside the car was the sound of West trying to swallow and not managing.

For a moment Meghan was furious with West. What was the matter with him? What did he think those big wide shoulders were for? They were for taking control and throwing people like Lannie Anveill out into the street.

But muscles meant nothing.

Not against a touch like Lannie Anveill's.

West's and Meghan's eyes met. This time the message they exchanged was very clear. They were trapped. "You better get out of the car," said West, his eyes going helplessly to his little sister.

Meghan got out slowly, holding the door open, as if nothing more could happen until the door was closed: The car could not leave, Lannie could not have him, nobody could be frozen, all was well, as long as she held the door open.

"Get out," said Lannie, "or I'll freeze Tuesday."

Meghan slammed the door. She ran forward to deflect Tuesday from her path toward the car.

Lannie shifted her insubstantial weight closer to the driver. She said something. Her tongue flickered when she spoke. Snakelike.

West drove away.

"West is going somewhere with Lannie?" Tuesday said. "What is he — a mental case? Nobody goes anywhere with Lannie."

"Lannie needs to talk," said Meghan. This was an accepted teenage reason for doing anything: if people needed to talk, you needed to listen.

"Lannie?" said Tuesday skeptically. "Talk? Right. Lannie doesn't *do* talk, Meggie-Megs, you know that."

Meghan changed the subject. "You're pretty bouncy, Tues. What happened today?"

"Well!" said Tuesday, beaming. "You'll never guess!"

"Tell me," said Meghan, linking arms with her.

What would West and Lannie do on this afternoon? Where would West drive? What would Lannie want from him? Meghan tried to imagine what it would be like for West, sitting in that front seat, Lannie inches away, with her contented chuckle and her pencil-thin arms and her terrible touch.

But from the way Lannie had moved, she was no longer inches away. She was there.

The emotions ripped through her all over again: the fear, the panic, the rage . . . and even a very little bit of the understanding.

Meghan followed Tuesday into the Trevors' house. There was always a lot of food at the Trevors'. Nobody ever dieted there. There was chocolate cake and rocky road ice cream and mint candy and cheese popcorn and onion bagels and sliced strawberries. Meghan's family had things like diet Coke and celery sticks.

The kitchen was entirely white: Mrs. Trevor had redone it a few years ago and it reminded Meghan of a hospital room. It looked like the kind of room you'd hose down after the autopsy.

But the family left debris everywhere: on the counter were a bright plaid bowling ball bag, a pile of trumpet music, a stack of old homework papers, a folder of phone numbers, two pairs of sneakers, folded laundry, and breakfast dishes piled with toast crusts.

It was so real.

So ordinary.

So comforting.

Meghan knew right away that her worries were false and exaggerated.

Nobody freezes anybody, thought Meghan. I can't believe that West and I let ourselves fall for Lannie's silliness. No wonder she was laughing at us. We fell for her dumb story. Poor old Lannie needs to be the center of attention and did she accomplish it this time! I'm such a jerk.

Meghan helped herself to a handful of cheese popcorn and then a dozen chocolate chips from the bag — nobody ever got around to making cookies in this family; they just ate the chips straight — and then a glass of raspberry ginger ale and finally some of the strawberries. Tuesday meanwhile had strawberries on Cheerios with lots of milk, tossing in a few chocolate chips for variety. For quite a while there was no sound but the contented intake of really good snacks.

"They chose me to hostess the JV cheerleaders' slumber party!" said Tuesday, sighing with the joy and the honor. "It's going to be here, Meggie-Megs! Isn't that wonderful? They want to have it at my house."

It did not necessarily indicate that Tuesday had become the most popular girl on earth. Mrs. Trevor was probably just the only parent willing to have a dozen screaming ninth- and tenth-grade girls overnight. Plus Mrs. Trevor would certainly have the most food and be the most liberal about what movies they could rent.

But Tuesday didn't see it that way. Nobody ever sees popularity that way. And Lannie probably didn't see that she had blackmailed West into driving away with her; Lannie probably thought she was just getting her fair share of popularity at last.

At that moment, Mrs. Trevor came home. She was a very attractive woman. Heavy, but the kind of heavy where you would never want her to lose weight: she was perfect the way she was. All the neighborhood children called her Mom even though everybody but Lannie had a mom of their own. "Hi, Mom," said Tuesday happily.

"Hi, Mom," said Meghan.

Mrs. Trevor hugged and kissed and made sure everybody had had enough to eat. Then she made sure she had enough to eat, too. "Tell me that I did not see my son driving around with Lannie Anveill."

"You did not," said Tuesday agreeably.

"Yes, I did," said her mother. "What's going on?"

"Lannie has a crush on West," said Tuesday, "didn't you know that?"

"Of course I knew that. But West is dating Meghan."

"They're just going to talk," said Meghan.

Mrs. Trevor got out her huge coffeemaker, the one that dripped and kept for hours. Meghan was happy. She loved the smell (but hated the taste) of coffee. For a really good kitchen smell, you needed bacon, too. If Meghan told Mrs. Trevor that, Mrs. Trevor would have bacon in that skillet in a second. She would think it was a perfectly good reason to cook some: because Meghan wanted to smell it.

"I feel funny," said Tuesday suddenly.

"You do?" said her mother, all concern. "In what way, darling?"

"Frozen!" said Tuesday. She rubbed at her own skin, trying to warm herself with friction.

There is such a thing, thought Meghan, as being too understanding. Or perhaps that's not it at all. Perhaps I'm just too afraid to think about what's really happening. I'm too eager to put it on the shelf and pretend it's not there. But Lannie's come off the shelf. She's here. She's not going away.

She has West.

She could have Tuesday.

What am I going to do?

Meghan thought of saying: Mom Trevor, Lannie has evil powers, she can freeze people, she froze me once, she froze the Irish setter, and probably froze her own mother. Now she's threatening to freeze Tuesday. So since we now both want your son West, what do I do? I can't sacrifice Tuesday.

Mrs. Trevor would laugh and say, "No, really, what is going on?"

Meghan was a great fan of television real-life shows. She adored *America's Most Wanted*, and *Cops*, and *Rescue 911*, and all shows of rescue and law and order. She imagined herself calling the police. Hi, my boyfriend is driving around town with this girl who . . .

Right.

When they stopped laughing (and her call would be taped! Her voice would be forever captured on tape — so jealous of her boyfriend she called the police when somebody else sat in his car!) they'd say, "Okay, honey, get a grip on yourself."

"Do you think Lannie is capable of love?" asked Tuesday.

"No," said Mrs. Trevor. She didn't add to that.

Meghan couldn't stand it. She liked long answers. "Why not?" said Meghan.

"She never had any. I've never seen a child so thoroughly abandoned. Why, even when her mother was alive, I never saw anybody pick Lannie up, or kiss her, or hug her. She put herself to bed, nobody ever tucked her in. She ate alone, nobody ever shared a meal with her."

The coffee was made. Mrs. Trevor poured herself a big mug and added lots of sugar and milk. Meghan thought anything a Trevor did would always be sweet and warm like that.

"Poor Lannie," said Mrs. Trevor. "It's enough to freeze your heart."

Chapter 5

Tuesday and her mother discussed the slumber party. Mrs. Trevor agreed to everything.

Meghan was impressed. Her own mother would be thinking up blockades, barricades. Battening down the hatches of the house to protect the Moores against the cheerleader invasion. Her own mother would confine the girls to the yard and the basement playroom. On the night of the party, Meghan's mother would constantly roam the place, keeping an eye on things and maintaining standards.

Mrs. Trevor didn't have any to maintain, which streamlined the whole event.

Meghan wished she was a JV cheerleader and could come.

But she was not and, as the afternoon passed, she felt more and more left out of the celebration. When eventually Meghan slipped out and headed home, Tuesday and Mrs. Trevor scarcely noticed.

When Meghan was little, the front yards on Dark Fern Lane had seemed like vast stretches of green grass. When they played yard games, what great distances their little legs had had to pump! When Lannie was It, what terrifying expanses of empty space Meghan had been forced to flee over.

Now the beginner bushes were fat and sprawling. Meghan's father liked to prune and trim his bushes, and in the Moores' yard, the bushes were neat and round, like plums. But the Trevors never trimmed, and the long thin tentacles of forsythia bushes arced through the darkness. Icy fronds touched Meghan's face and twisted cords grabbed her waist.

Lannie's fingers in winter.

Meghan sobbed dry tears, tottering among the obstacles.

A raised ranch house has three doors: front door atop many steps, back kitchen door opening onto a high deck, and a door into the garage. If you go in by the garage, you must ease your body between the silent cars and the debris stacked along garage walls. There is an oily waiting stink in a garage. The darkness that has collected over the years lies in pools, sucking your feet.

In winter, the garage door was always dark.

Meghan hated the garage door. But if she went in the front, she would be exposed to Lannie's view. If Lannie was home. If Lannie was looking away from West.

And she could not go in the kitchen door, because it was latched as well as locked.

The door in the garage opened with a raspy scream.

It wasn't the door, thought Meghan. It was me.

Would Lannie have frozen Tuesday? Had Lannie frozen her own mother? It had seemed silly when she was surrounded by the warmth of Mrs. Trevor. Now, in the oily dark, it seemed so very real.

Meghan did not feel frozen this time, but suffocated. The oil that had leaked out of the cars and soaked into the cement floor came through the soles of her shoes and crawled up her veins and lay like a sheet of rubber over her lungs.

West and Lannie. Hours now. Alone together.

She got out of the garage, up the stairs, into the safer more open dark of the living parts of the house. She turned on no lights. She did not want Lannie Anveill, across the street, to see that she was home.

Although of course Lannie always knew.

And Lannie, who could materialize anywhere, anytime,

Lannie might suddenly be leaning against the wallpaper right here in this room, with her little chuckle of ice and snow.

It was a matter of will not to turn on the lights and make sure that the corners were empty. Lannie isn't here, Meghan told herself. I'm not going to be a baby and panic.

She sat in the dining room, which the Moores never used; it was just wasted space with a table and chairs. But it had a window view of West's driveway. She wanted to see him come home.

He didn't get home till supper.

He parked that car of his mother's and sat quietly for several moments behind the wheel before he opened the door and got out. What was he thinking about?

He had been alone with Lannie Anveill for three hours.

What had they done in that three hours? West . . . with his Trevor need to be courteous. Just how courteous had West been? What on earth had they talked about?

That hand on the pants leg of West's jeans. Lannie's hand. Thin and white like a peeled stick. What had that touch been like?

Had West shivered and felt sick?

Or could Lannie's hands, which froze bodies and hearts, make other changes, too?

West did not look over at Meghan's house. He did not look at his own, either. He got out of the car so slowly he looked damaged. He had to pull himself along, as if his limbs were a separate weight. He had trouble opening his front door, and trouble closing it when he was inside.

But then the door closed, and he was as lost to her as he had been driving around with Lannie.

The dining room curtains had been put up years ago and their positions rarely changed. They hung stiffly at each side of the sills, as frozen into place as if Lannie had touched them. It was utterly silent in Meghan's house. She had not turned on the television or the radio for company. Her parents were not yet home.

Meghan was so lonely she wanted to run over to the Trevors.

Not even waste time getting to the door. Leap straight through the window.

But Lannie would be watching. Lannie always watched. It was what she had done her whole life: stand in the shadows and watch.

Standing in her own shadows, watching the passing of others, Meghan thought — Life? This is not life. This is a warehouse.

Lannie had just been stored, all these years. Born and then stuck on a shelf, while others lived.

It was time to turn on the lights and go back to living herself. Meghan left the dining room, and walked through the house flipping every light switch. Then she sat by the phone.

It did not ring.

Meghan couldn't believe it. What was the matter with West? He had to know that the most important thing on earth was to call her up and tell her what was going on.

He didn't.

Meghan's parents came home. The routine in the Moore household never varied. Her mother and her father smiled at the sight of her, lightly kissed her forehead or her cheek, and asked how her day had been. How Meghan yearned for the passion at the Trevors' house — the clutter and noise and chaos and exuberance.

"I had a great day," said Meghan. The morning's academic successes might have happened ten centuries ago. "I'm really improving in Spanish. And history was very interesting."

Her parents wanted to hear her improved Spanish accent. They wanted to find out what had been so interesting in history.

But it was West's interest she wanted.

West did not call after supper.

He did not call at all.

At nine-thirty, Meghan gave up the wait and telephoned him herself.

West answered. "Hi, Meghan," he said. There was nothing in his voice.

"Are you alone?"

"No."

"Who's listening?"

"Everybody."

"What happened?"

"Tell you later."

"I have to know now. I can't sleep without knowing!"

West sighed and said nothing.

Meghan said, "I'll meet you at the truck."

They had done this a few times: crept out of their houses, walked silently over the dark backyards down the hedge lines, down the sloping grass, slick with evening frost. Then they'd sit in the front seat of the Chevy to talk. You couldn't slam the doors because it would make a noise the families might hear. Plus now that the handles didn't work from the inside, you didn't dare shut the doors anyway.

The truck interior was not romantic.

In summer, because it was in a low place where vines and tangles grew thickly, there were mosquitoes. In winter, a chill rose off the ground and could not be shaken. Meghan's feet got so cold she couldn't stand it. And this was January. Cold as Lannie's heart.

"Okay," said West finally.

"What time?"

"Same time."

"Eleven?"

"Okay."

"West, I can't tell a thing from your voice. What is going on? Is it okay? What did Lannie do?"

"It's okay," said West.

"I love you," she said to West.

There was a long silence. "Okay," he said at last.

But it was not okay.

Meghan's parents liked to be in bed by a few minutes before eleven, and at eleven, sitting up against the big padded headboard, they would watch the evening news together. In that half hour of broadcasting, Meghan could do anything and her parents would not know.

As soon as their door shut, she slipped downstairs to rummage in the closet, seeking out her heaviest coat.

On the back step, the wind bit her face and cut her skin.

She felt like an explorer on a glacier.

The backyard was long and deep.

There were no stars and no moon.

The wind yanked silently at the young trees and the hovering hedges.

The world swayed and leaned down to scrape her face.

She could not see a thing. But a flashlight would be a diamond point for Lannie to see out *her* bedroom window. Lannie must never know about the tangles, the privacy and the pleasure of the truck deep in the shadows.

How deep the yard was!

I must be taking tiny steps, thought Meghan. I feel as if I've gone so far I've crossed the town line.

The ground became mucky, and her feet quaked in the mire.

Where am I?

A hand grabbed her hair.

She tried to scream, but was too afraid. Her whole chest closed in as if a giant's hand had crushed her like newspaper for a fire.

"You walked right by," whispered West. "Come on. Truck's way back there."

Meghan's knees nearly buckled. "You scared me!" she whispered.

West led her back to the truck, where the driver's door hung open. She was amazed she had not walked smack into it and broken a bone. She climbed in first, and West got in after her, and on the wide single seat they crushed against each other.

"Tell me," said Meghan.

"About what?"

"About Lannie!"

West said nothing.

Meghan was used to the dark now, and could see his eyes. They were large and shiny. "Did you make it clear to her that you and I are going out with each other?"

West was silent for a long time. At last he said, "No."

"West! Why not?"

"Because."

Meghan hated him. Just as much as she loved him, she hated him.

West closed his shiny eyes and Meghan felt buried.

"She was serious," said West. He did not touch Meghan. He ran his hands over the torn dashboard, as gently as if he were stroking velvet. "When we talked, she slid over next to me, Meghan. She never took her eyes off me and she never blinked. I couldn't see down into her eyes. It was like riding around with a store mannequin. People shouldn't have eyes as pale as that. But she's like that all the way through. Too pale. What's human in her got washed out. Bleached away." West linked his hands together and studied them. Perhaps he had had to hold hands with Lannie. Perhaps he had scrubbed them to get the Lannie off. "She'll freeze Tuesday," said West.

"Why Tuesday?" said Meghan. "Why not me?"

West played with the broken door handles. The wind raked through the open cab door and chewed on Meghan's cheeks like rats.

Meghan thought: because West would risk me. He would call her bluff on his neighbor Meghan. But he would never call her bluff on his sister Tuesday. Tuesday matters.

West went in stages with his family. There were times he could hardly bear having a younger sister and brother. There were times he hated their dumb names and wished somebody would adopt them, or send them to boarding school. There were times when he and Tuesday and Brown bickered steadily, hitting each other, throwing things, being obnoxious.

But he loved them.

"Lannie is jealous of us," said West slowly. "We Trevors — our family works. We get along. We talk, we hug, we fight, we have supper, we share, we bicker. It works. We're a close family."

I'm jealous, too, thought Meghan. How weird that I can understand Lannie in that. Meghan thought of Lannie's cold cold eyes growing hot as tropical fever.

"Lannie is alone," said West. "She's always been alone. And she's tired of it. She's chosen me."

There was a strange timbre in West's voice, like an instrument being tuned. *She's chosen me*. Could he be proud? Could he feel singled out for an honor? That Lannie had chosen him?

"She wants an excuse, Meggie-Megs," said West softly. "She's ready to freeze somebody. I can't give her an excuse."

"Just stop her!"

"How?"

The little word sat in the cold night air and waited for an answer.

But there was none.

No parent, no police officer, no principal could prevent Lannie from touching somebody she wanted to touch. No bribe, no gift, no promise could ease Lannie's requirement. She wanted West.

"What about Friday night?" said Meghan at last.

Friday night they were going to a dance. West had never taken a girl to a dance. He'd attended plenty of them, of course. It was something to do. He didn't object to dances as an event. He'd go, and hang out with the boys, and do something dumb like hang off the basketball hoop, and bend it, and get in trouble, and have to pay for repairs.

But he wouldn't dance.

West knew all the top songs. He knew all the good groups. He owned all the best cassettes and CDs.

But he wouldn't dance.

He was a senior, and as far as Meghan was concerned, you could not have a senior year without dances.

There were to be raffles and games and prizes. There was a DJ (nobody wanted a band; they never played the songs right) and the chaperones were somebody else's parents. That was key. A good dance never had your own parents there. There was even a dress code this time: dresses for girls and a shirt tucked in with a tie for boys. Meghan could hardly wait.

"You have to understand," said West Trevor.

He meant he was not taking Meghan to the dance. Meghan could have overturned the truck on top of him. "Lannie won't freeze Tuesday!" shouted Meghan. "She knows you won't go out with her if she freezes your own sister!"

West swallowed. Meghan could hear the swallow. Thick and difficult. "She said she would."

If Meghan cried, West would not comfort her. He was frozen in his own worries: he had to protect his little sister. That was first with him.

I want to be first! thought Meghan.

She slid away from him, and jerked open the handle on the passenger door. The handle being broken, of course it didn't work. She tried to roll down the window so she could open the door from the outside. That handle didn't work either. She fumbled and muttered instead of storming away. There was nothing worse than a slamming exit — and no door to go out of. Eventually she had to look back at West.

He was laughing.

"You bum," said Meghan. She absolutely hated being laughed at.

West's grief and confusion evaporated. His long crosswise grin split his face. His head tipped back with the laugh he was choking on. He had never been more handsome. "Don't be mad," he said. His hands unzipped her heavy jacket. "So I have to take Lannie to some old dance." His hands tugged at Meghan's thick sweater. "Big deal," said West. He leaned forward, hands and lips exploring. "I'll wear Lannie down somehow," he promised, "and get rid of her. It'll be us again, okay?"

The cold and the wind were forgotten. The torn seat and the

broken handles meant nothing. The heat of their bodies left them breathless and desperate.

Yes, yes, it was okay! What was Lannie Anveill, against the strength of true love?

Meghan's adoration for West was so great it seemed impossible they could survive the pressure; they would explode with loving each other. Her arms encircled his broad chest in the tightest, most satisfying embrace.

More, thought Meghan Moore, more, more, more, more, I will never have enough of you, West. More. More.

A thin white hand ran through West's hair and resettled it gently behind his ear.

The hand was not Meghan's.

A long narrow fingernail traced West's profile and stopped lightly on his lip.

The finger was not Meghan's.

A wrist as bony as a corpse inserted itself gracefully, slowly, between West's face and Meghan's. Fingers like falling snow brushed lightly on Meghan's cheeks.

"He's mine," whispered Lannie Anveill in Meghan's ear.

Meghan heard, but saw only mistily.

She felt, but through many layers.

Neither West nor Meghan moved away from each other. But there was no more heat between them. Their excitement had been iced over. They might have been anesthetized, waiting for some terrible surgery.

The only thing that moved was Lannie's hand, stroking here, touching there.

Lannie covered her victims like a snowdrift with her hatred for one, and her love for the other.

The game of Freeze Tag had gone on.

Lannie was still It.

Chapter 6

Winter wind prowled over Dark Fern Lane.

Snow crept behind shutters and blanketed steps.

Cars left in driveways were rounded white monuments, casting fat meaningless shadows where streetlights touched them.

In the yellow halos beneath the streetlights, snow seemed not to fall, but to hang, separate flakes caught in time. Listening.

Listening to what?

Dark Fern Lane was full of listeners.

Tuesday Trevor was so wide awake it felt like a disease.

Her eyes strained to climb out of their sockets.

Her lungs tried to turn themselves inside out.

Her blood circulated in marathons.

What is the matter with me? thought Tuesday. Her heart revved, and raced, and took corners on two wheels.

After a long time, Tuesday got out of bed. Silently she walked down the narrow hall to the boys' room. The door was cracked, in order that West could slip back in without making noise. Without making noise, Tuesday opened her brothers' door all the way.

West was not back.

Tuesday crossed the dark bedroom without bumping into anything. Since the windows looked out only onto yards and woods, her brothers never pulled the shades down. She looked out their window. Snow was falling. West's footprints in the old snow were covered now. She knew he was in the Chevy but nobody else would. If search parties went out, they would not think of the truck. How long had he been out there? Her heart revved again, fueled by worry.

"Do you think they're all right?" whispered Brown.

Tuesday jumped a foot. She'd been sure he was asleep. She shrugged.

She said, trying to sound knowledgeable, "I guess they're having fun."

"It's awfully cold out to have that much fun," said Brown.

Tuesday and Brown felt weird thinking about their own brother with their own best friend Meghan.

"Gag me with a spoon," said Brown, who hoped that when he was a high school senior he would not disgrace himself like that.

Tuesday had to deep breathe twice in order to say her next sentence out loud. "Lannie's there, too."

Brown sat up. "You saw her light go on?"

"I saw her cross the street."

Brown was full of admiration. Nobody ever saw Lannie cross the street. She just vanished and then reappeared.

"She loves West," said Tuesday.

"She always has. Talk about making me gag. I think we'd have to give West over to terrorists for a hostage if he ever loved Lannie back."

"Lannie's the terrorist," said Tuesday. I am terrorized, thought Tuesday. "Let's go down to the yard and check on them," she said.

"Yeah, but . . . what if . . . West and Meghan . . . you know . . . like . . . ick," said Brown.

What did Lannie have to do with it? Why was Lannie out there in the snow at one in the morning?

"Something happened in school," said Tuesday. How odd her voice sounded. Like somebody else's. She tried to catch her voice and bring it home. "This girl. In the cafeteria. At first everybody thought it was an unexplained paralysis. A girl named Jodie. But then somebody said it was Jennifer, and she had fallen down and broken her spine. And then somebody else was sure it was Jacqueline and she had a fever and some virus attacked her brain and turned her stiff as a board."

"Get to the point," said Brown.

"It was some girl, okay? And Lannie froze her. The way she did that time when we were little and Freeze Tag was real."

"It was never real," said Brown.

"Then why are you pulling the covers back up? It's because you remember that night, Brown."

"Do not."

"Do so." Tuesday looked back out onto the snow. The wind caught and threw it, as if the wind were having a snowball fight with its friends. The backyard tilted downhill, and vanished into the dark. A cliff to the unknown.

Tuesday stared at her little brother. He stared back.

"Okay," said Brown. "Let's go look. But it's going to be tough living with West if it turns out we're just interrupting the good parts."

The door of the truck cab was open.

Lannie was swinging on it, pushing herself back and forth with one small foot. She was smiling as she looked inside.

She knew Tuesday and Brown had joined her but she did not look at them. She was too pleased by the inside of the Chevy.

Brown took Tuesday's hand. She was glad to grip it. They did not let themselves touch Lannie. They peered into the truck.

Two statues. As cold and white as marble.

Carved in a half embrace; lips not quite touching; eyes not quite closed.

Lannie chuckled. "Hello, Tuesday," said Lannie. "Hello, Brown."

The snow ceased to fall. The wind ceased to blow. The world

was smooth and pure and white. It lay soft and glittering and glowing on all sides.

"Are they dead?" whispered Brown.

"Just frozen." The chuckle was full of rage.

I have to reason with her, thought Tuesday. I remember that night in the grass. The last time we ever played Freeze Tag. West reasoned with her. He told her he was impressed. "I'm impressed, Lannie," said Tuesday. "They look very real."

Lannie favored Tuesday with a look of disgust. "They are real. They are your brother and your neighbor." She made "neighbor" sound like "roadkill."

"They'll die if they're left out here," said Tuesday.

"If they wanted to stay inside, they should have," said Lannie. "He promised to like me best." Her voice was slight, and yet filling, like a very sweet dessert. "He broke his promise."

Tuesday wet her lips. Mistake. The winter wind penetrated every wrinkle, chapping them. "Let's give West a second chance," said Tuesday. She had to look away from her frozen brother. "He'll keep his promise now." She wondered if West could hear her, deep inside his ice. Could he hear, would he listen, would he obey? It was his life.

"They didn't believe I could do it."

Tuesday suffocated in the sweetness of Lannie's tiny voice. "I believed you," said Tuesday quickly. She smiled, trying to look like an ally, a friend, a person whose brother was worth rescuing.

Brown was not willing to cater to Lannie. "You're a pain, Lannie," he said angrily. "You don't have any right to scare people."

"But people," said Lannie, smiling, "are right to be scared." Her hair was thin and did not lie down flat, but stuck out of her head in dry pale clumps.

"Undo them right this minute," said Brown. "Or I'll go and get my mother and father."

Lannie laughed out loud. "It won't be the first time in history two dumb teenagers froze to death while necking in a stupid place at a stupid time."

"Or call 911," said Brown. "They'll save them."

"No," said Lannie gently. "They can't."

Even Lannie's words could freeze. Tuesday's leaping lungs and throbbing heart went into slow motion, and her skipping mind fell down. No. Rescue teams cannot save them. Our mother and father cannot save them. That terrible little phrase "froze to death" hung in front of all Tuesday's thoughts like an icicle hanging off a porch.

At first Tuesday was going to say, *Brown and I will do anything you want, anything at all, if only you'll undo West and Meghan.* But she thought better of it. What promise would Lannie extract? What kind of terrible corner would Brown and Tuesday be in then?

So she said, "You love him, Lannie. He's better alive. Much more fun."

"He broke his promise."

"But he's learned his lesson now. He's in there now, listening. He's ready, Lannie."

Lannie appeared to consider it. Her eyes shifted from hot to cold like faucets in the shower. "I love doing this," she told Tuesday at last. Her voice was curiously rich.

Rich with what?

Desire, thought Tuesday. Not for West, and yet it was desire. An unstoppable desire to cause hurt.

The texture of the snow changed.

It became very soft, like an old cozy blanket.

The moon shone through the thin moving clouds, and the snow sparkled in the darkness of night.

The temperature dropped like a falling stone.

She has to undo them! thought Tuesday. What can I offer her? What do I have? My brother! My best friend!

Tuesday scraped through her mind, hunting for anything, the barest scrap, to offer Lannie Anveill.

Lannie swung on the truck door again, making a wide smooth pocket in the snowdrifts. She might have been a six-year-old at a birthday party. Any minute she might lie down in the snow and make an angel.

Lannie. An angel.

Tuesday did not let herself fall into hysteria. She said brightly, "I know, Lannie! You can come to the JV cheerleader slumber party!" Her voice was stacked with false enthusiasm. "At our house! And we'll have a great time."

Lannie stopped swinging. She looked briefly at Tuesday, and briefly into the truck.

"But not Meghan," added Tuesday quickly. "She won't get to come. Only you."

Lannie tilted her head.

"All you have to do is unfreeze them," coaxed Tuesday. She made her voice rich, too. Desire for Lannie's company. Desire to be a friend to Lannie. "And you'll have a boyfriend, a dance, and a party, Lannie. All coming up soon. Won't it be fun?"

Brown was staring at his sister as if they had never met before.

"Well," said Lannie finally.

"Great!" cried Tuesday. "You're going to undo them! You're coming to my party!"

"I'll undo West," said Lannie. "Meghan stays."

Chapter 7

"Only," said West, "if you bring Meghan back, too."

His voice swirled in the dark. It did not seem like a voice at all, but like a wind, a separate wind. A dervish, perhaps.

Meghan lay frozen, stiff against the seats and the dashboard and the broken handles. Snow falling through the open door of the truck rested on her face. She could not feel its touch but she knew its weight. It was drifting around the hollows of her cheeks and eyes. Soon she would not be visible, she would be one with the rest of the blanketed world.

A statue forgotten until spring.

"No," said Lannie. Her voice was no longer rich with hurtful desire. It was a statement voice, a voice for making lists and issuing decrees.

No.

It was a forever "No." A "No" which would not change, which could not be bought, or compromised, or threatened. It was a real "No."

She was not going to undo Meghan Moore.

I am frozen, thought Meghan.

It was queer the way her thoughts could continue, and yet on some level they, too, were frozen. She did not feel great emotion: there was no terrible grief that her young life had stopped short. There was no terrifying worry about whatever was to come — a new life, a death, or simply the still snowy continuance of this condition. There was simply observation and attention.

It's like being a tree, Meghan thought. I'm here. I have my branches. I have my roots. But my sap no longer runs. I weep not. I laugh not. I simply wait. And if the seasons change, I live again, and if the seasons do not, I die.

She was surprised to feel no fear. She had been so fearful of Lannie before. Perhaps fear, too, froze. Or perhaps there had never been anything to be afraid of.

West shook his head. "Then it's off, Lannie."

What's off? thought Meghan. What did I miss, being a tree?

She could see very little now. The snow lay right on her open eyes. There was only a yellow hole in the black of the night. It was the nightlight shining out of Tuesday's bedroom window.

Nightlight, thought Meghan. What a pretty thought. The real night, this night, this night I am going to have forever — it has no lights.

She would be in the dark very soon.

The dark always. The dark completely. The dark forever.

"I don't want Meghan back," explained Lannie. "I like her frozen. She's fun to freeze. She knows it's coming, you see. It's much more fun when they see it coming, and they know what's going to happen." Lannie chuckled. "I like it when they get scared and you can see it in their eyes."

Yes, thought Meghan. I was scared enough for her. I screamed loud enough to bring armies, but armies didn't come. The snow soaked up my scream. The snow and West's embrace. I screamed into his chest. I don't know if he screamed or not. We stopped moving so fast.

"Now my mother," continued Lannie, "she didn't know." This was clearly a loss to Lannie. She had wanted her mother to know. Meghan found that she could be even colder, that her heart could still shiver, with the horror of Lannie Anveill.

"And that girl in the cafeteria," said Lannie sorrowfully, "of course she didn't know what was coming either."

The glaze on Meghan's eyes was greater. The snow lay on them and didn't melt. Meghan didn't blink. The yellow nightlight from Tuesday's room up on the slope grew dim and vanished completely.

"But Meghan," Lannie went on contentedly, "she knew. She watched my finger move closer."

Lannie's voice thickened with pleasure. Tuesday whimpered. Meghan wondered how long she would be able to hear. Were her ears going to freeze now, too?

"And closer!" breathed Lannie hotly. "My finger moved only an inch and it moved slowly. Like the blade of a guillotine coming down on her throat. And Meghan knew what would happen and she was afraid."

Meghan could see nothing at all now, would never see anything again, but she knew that Lannie smiled. She knew the exact shape and texture of that smile. She knew it was the closest Lannie Anveill could come to happiness.

West's voice shook. Meghan loved him for that. She wished that West could know he was still loved. West said, "I will like you best, Lannie." His voice shook even harder. "But not if you leave Meghan out here in the snow."

Lannie sniffed. This noise did not fit the dark and the falling snow and the fear. For Lannie, fear and falling were perfectly normal, and so she sniffed, annoyed, calling West Trevor's bluff.

"And that's that," said West.

Lannie did not undo Meghan. It had been a forever "No." West had simply not understood. Meghan had. She lay quietly under her blanket of snow.

"Come on, Brown," said West. "Come on, Tuesday. School tomorrow. We have to get some sleep."

Meghan heard the snow crunch under their departing feet as West shepherded his younger brother and sister up the hill toward the house.

She heard no voices.

Neither Tuesday nor Brown argued with their brother.

They left her.

They walked on into the warmth and the safety and light.

Now the missing emotions came: they slid like a glacier falling off an alp. Meghan fell a great terrible distance into greater fear than she had ever believed existed. She was alone. Only Lannie Anveill stood beside her. She was cold. There was no warmth anywhere. She was lost. There was no rescue in this world.

Meghan's body lacked the capacity to reflect her agonies. She wept, but without tears. She shuddered, but without shaking. She screamed, but without sound.

Her only friends — the only ones who knew — who cared — Tuesday and Brown and West — *they had left her*.

Something besides her flesh froze.

She had fallen, truly fallen, heart and mind and soul and body, into Lannie's clutches.

Lannie had clutched her once, with only one finger, and would never have to clutch her again. Nature would do the rest.

Meghan's soul wept for the ending of her life, for the grief her parents would feel, for all those years she would never have, all those joys and hopes and frustrations she would never taste.

Lannie stomped her little foot in the snow. It made a pathetic little noise in the greatness of the night. "I thought he was bluffing," she said angrily. "I didn't think he'd actually leave you here in the snow, Meghan."

She knows I can hear her, thought Meghan. How does she know that?

She has frozen and tortured others before me.

She will freeze and torture more in the future.

Lannie kicked the snow around, like a little kid sulking in her room.

She doesn't really have much power, thought Meghan. Power is hers just one fingertip at a time, so to speak. West walked away, and he's gone, and she lost her game.

And I — I lost, too.

"Oh, all right," said Lannie. Disagreeably, as if she had been asked to share a small piece of cake. "All right!" she yelled up the hill at West. "Are you listening? I said, all right!"

All right, what? thought Meghan. She was very, very cold. She was not going to have many more thoughts. Or many more minutes. So it didn't really matter.

Lannie poked her in the side. It was a jab, actually, again like a little kid sulking — pinching the other kids because she wasn't getting enough attention.

Meghan's hand was moving. Brushing the snow off her eyes. She was shaking her hair. Struggling to get up. Bumping the narrow confines of the dumb, awful, cold, stupid truck.

Memory sifted away, leaving her with only bits and pieces of what had happened.

What am I doing here? she thought.

January? Meghan looked at her watch. She had to scrape off a crust of ice with her nail. One in the morning? And I'm out playing stupid games in a rusty truck in a snowstorm?

Meghan was so cold she really was frozen. She was unable to gather herself up. She floundered, but did not manage to accomplish anything.

"Fine, stay there," said Lannie.

Oh, yes. Lannie. Lannie who liked to see them shiver before she froze them. Lannie who liked her victims to know.

Meghan remembered.

And then West's arms were around her. He was sliding her out the door, lifting her in his arms like a baby, warming her with his embrace.

Oh, West! West! You did come back for me! Her lips were very cold, but his were very warm, and when they met she melted a little, and smiled a little, and was safe a little.

You lose, Lannie, thought Meghan.

From the lovely protection of West's arms, from the sweet cradle of his holding her, she looked clearly at Lannie. It was the first time since she had been frozen that she could really see.

Perhaps it was not a good thing to see reality clearly. Reality was frightening. For Lannie Anveill stood very still. And very jealous.

And very close.

And her hand — that hand Meghan had watched descending so slowly — that hand was lifted like a weapon.

Not pointing at Meghan.

Not pointing at West.

But at Tuesday.

Tuesday stood very still, as if she'd met a deadly snake on a forest path. Been trapped by a mad dog. Threatened by a mad bomber.

Perhaps she was.

Perhaps Lannie was all three of those.

Lannie's eyes, bleached of humanity, focused dead and glassy on West. "Well?" she said.

West set Meghan down in the snow. He stepped away from her. "I'm sorry," he said to Lannie.

She did not accept the apology. Her hand remained extended, only half an inch now from Tuesday's bare cheek. And Tuesday knew what was coming. And Tuesday flinched. And Lannie chuckled.

"It was just habit," said West.

Lannie regarded him stonily. "You were going to carry her home."

What made me think that love could conquer evil? thought Meghan. What stupidity persuaded me that because West and I love each other, everything will be all right?

A cracked smile pasted itself on West's face. He was splintered and broken. But this was his baby sister. This was his family.

"You know what I'd like, Lannie?" he said. His smile was in a hundred pieces. But he flirted anyway.

"What?" said Lannie, testing him.

"I'd like to carry *you* home." His smile solidified and became real. He took a step toward Lannie. She lowered her hand. He took another step toward Lannie. She smiled at him. Meghan wanted to gag, but West smiled even more widely.

He picked Lannie up easily. She appeared to weigh nothing.

As if she were not a person at all, thought Meghan, but a husk of one. Stuffed with hay instead of flesh and bone. Perhaps that dry straw hair is her stuffing coming out.

West did not glance at his sister, his brother, or his girlfriend. He carried Lannie diagonally up the sloping backyard, heading toward her house. They both laughed now. What joke could they possibly be sharing?

West waded through a drift that reached his thighs. Lannie dragged her hand through it, leaving trails of long thin fingers.

"Are you okay, Meghan?" whispered Tuesday.

Oh, sure, thought Meghan. Fine. I go through this sort of thing all the time and it never leaves a mark.

And then she thought, If I can laugh at it, maybe I am okay. But will West be okay? What has he just promised? What have we just gotten ourselves into?

Brown, being younger, was on another subject entirely. "Nobody else woke up," marveled Brown, staring at the houses on Dark Fern Lane.

But the parents had never woken up to Lannie. They went on feeling sorry for her, because she had never been loved.

There was a reason for that, thought Meghan Moore. Lannie is not loveable. She is only hateable.

West was a silhouette in the dark, climbing and crunching the snow. Lannie in his arms was a pair of boots sticking out on one side, and wispy hair and dangling scarf on the other.

What is her power? thought Meghan. Did she always have it? Who gave it to her? What evil force was her real parent?

It gave Meghan some peace to know that Mrs. Anveill, whatever she might have deserved, had at least not known what was coming. It was good that Lannie's mother had driven that Jaguar so fast she did not know she was to be frozen forever.

What was this game of Freeze Tag?
Was it truly *forever?*
Did Lannie have West *forever?*
Could Lannie hold the neighborhood hostage *forever?*

Chapter 8

In the days that followed, Meghan found out how cold it is to be without best friends.

How frozen you are when you are frozen out of love.

West never looked at her. Not once. Perhaps he did not dare. Perhaps Lannie had given an order and he knew the consequences were too terrible. But oh! how Meghan would have liked a phone call. A note. A single sad look across a room. Just so they could say: *yes, it happened; it hurts; we're afraid; we're apart.*

But West did not try to communicate with Meghan. Over and over she told herself: he's protecting me, he knows what Lannie will do if he so much as raises an eyebrow in my direction. But Meghan was not sure. Girls in love are never sure.

Bad as that was, not having a best girlfriend was even worse. For you could always count on your next-door-neighbor girlfriend. You could say anything and everything to each other, and you always did.

Tuesday never looked at Meghan either. She had that party after all: the JV cheerleader slumber party. And Meghan was not part of the preparation, and not part of the afterglow. Meghan was alone.

Tuesday's protecting me, too, Meghan told herself. It's my face Lannie's hand touched: the hand that holds freezing in its palm.

But Meghan Moore did not feel protected. She felt terribly, terribly alone. Abandoned and deserted. Without a friend in the world.

After school, when West had the use of his mother's car, it was Lannie who got in the front seat with him and drove away. It was Lannie who met him at his locker. Sat with him during his lunch. Telephoned him in the evening.

But it was Meghan who was supposed to make explanations to the world. Nobody wanted to walk up to West and say, "What are you doing, are you insane, have you lost your mind?" and nobody would have dreamed of walking up to Lannie.

West's best friend, Richard, who found girls a little unnerving at the best of times and preferred them to stay on their side of the room, actually sought Meghan out. "So what's going on? *Lannie?* Is West crazy?"

Meghan did not know what to say. What explanation was she supposed to give? The real one was too absurd. Nobody would believe it. They would say Meghan was the crazy one. So she said nothing and her eyes filled with tears because she did not know how to gather allies and mount an army against Lannie Anveill.

Richard said, "He was supposed to be restoring his Chevy this winter. I was going to work on it with him. It was bad enough that right after football he started *dating* all the time." This meant Meghan. Richard employed the word "dating" as if West had started selling military secrets to the enemy and should be shot. "But now — Lannie!" said Richard. "She has to be the creepiest person I've ever known in my life."

"I agree," said Meghan glumly.

"But after you?" said Richard, trying to get a grip on this girl thing.

Meghan said nothing.

Richard said, "Well. West and I were supposed to go to the big car graveyard down in Bridgeport, and find parts for his truck. We were going to look for handles so he can repair his, and open the doors from the inside. And Lannie said that didn't interest her, and West said he'd see her tomorrow then, and Lannie said, 'No, you'll see me today,' and West said, 'Fine.' Do you believe that? He didn't even argue with her? He's going to stay with her instead of going to the car graveyard with me?" Richard was scandalized. "At least when he dated you," said Richard, "he also would do normal things."

Meghan managed a real smile.

"What is there to smile about?" said Richard.

But it was impossible to explain.

Then there was Valerie. Valerie was a lovely girl, a junior, the year between Meghan and West. Valerie, too, had always had a crush on West. She was pretty relaxed about it, and teased herself, and asked Meghan for dating details so she could pretend it was herself dating West. Valerie took one look at Lannie on West's arm and said to Meghan, "What is going on here? I mean, I thought at least if he dumped you, he'd take me! But no — he's going out with that pale-faced shrimpette from the zoo."

"Don't let her hear you say that," said Meghan. She looked around fearfully. A girl who would send her mother to a frozen death in a Jaguar would certainly do the same to a Valerie about whom she did not care at all.

"Everybody says that!" cried Valerie. "She is *so* strange."

Meghan nodded.

"What does West see in her?" demanded Valerie. "He took her to Pizza Hut, Meghan! I mean, he was willing to be seen in public with that girl."

Eating off the same pizza wedge. It was enough to make you want to cram it in their faces, thought Meghan.

And then there was Su-Ann. Su-Ann, not Meghan's favorite classmate by any means, said with a snide smile, "Second half of West's senior year, Meghan, and it looks like you're out of the picture. No senior prom for you, huh, babe?"

Meghan said nothing.

"Back to riding the schoolbus like a peasant, huh, babe?" said Su-Ann. "No more rides from the cute boyfriend, huh, babe?"

"Don't call me babe," said Meghan. "Don't call me anything. Get away from me."

"Sure," said Su-Ann easily. "Like the rest of the crowd."

Su-Ann left Meghan alone.

Everybody, it seemed, was leaving Meghan alone. She was so lonely she could have wept all day every day. She wanted to talk to West, and ask what it felt like to be near Lannie like that, and what they were going to do about it. She wanted to talk to Tuesday, and ask what West was like to live with now, and what Mr. and Mrs. Trevor said, and what would happen next?

She wanted to be on a team.

She wanted to fight back.

But how did you fight a Lannie?

If West, who could wrestle and tackle, could not fight, how could Meghan? What was the weapon?

Was there a weapon?

"Hello, darling," said her mother. The kiss they always shared rested gently on Meghan's cheek. "How was your day?"

Meghan could not help it. Her eyes filled with tears.

"Sweetie!" said her mother. "Tell Mommy. What's wrong?"

Mommy. As if she had called her mother Mommy since second grade. "It's West," said Meghan.

"I know. Breaking up is so awful. Has he hurt you? Do you want me to kill him?"

Meghan managed a giggle. "I don't want him killed. I just —"

Just what? Meghan did not even know. Whenever she saw Lannie, she remembered, and she believed, and the frozen horror of the girl sapped Meghan's strength and turned her knees to jelly. But when she was not around Lannie, it was all impossible, and she was embarrassed, and felt stupid and hopeless.

They went down the hall together to the bedroom so her mother could take off her shoes. This was always first priority at the end of a workday. Mrs. Moore kicked off the high heels, wiggled her bare toes in the carpeting and said, "Aaaahhhhhhhhh."

"Why don't you get a job where you can wear sneakers, Mom?"

"I hate sneakers. I love high heels. I love shoes. I love being dressed up. I even love work. It just involves a certain sacrifice, that's all." Her mother kissed her again. "Now tell me everything." They flopped back on the king-sized bed, shoulders and heads hitting the fluffy rank of pillows at the same instant. Staring up at the ceiling, they snuggled their sides together.

Meghan suddenly remembered a thousand snuggles like this.

A thousand days after daycare in which she and her mother had bed-flopped to share heartaches and triumphs.

On cold days they pulled a comforter up over themselves and on hot days they turned the fan straight into their faces, so their hair blew up onto the headboard.

Meghan suddenly remembered the purse her mother used to have when Meghan was little. Oh, it was practically a suitcase. Mrs. Moore practically needed wheels to move it. How many days had her mother reached down into the capacious bottom of that handbag, and made all kinds of excited noises and raised her eyebrows and twitched her lips and said, "*What* do I have in *here?*" while the little Meghan waited, full of anticipation. And each day, a tiny treat: a single chocolate kiss, a package of bright colored paper clips, the monogrammed paper napkin from a restaurant or a giveaway vial of perfume from the department store.

How thrilled Meghan had always been.

When you were little, it only took a little.

But I never wanted to be here, thought Meghan. I always wanted to be over at the Trevors'. What was the matter with me? Home was wonderful. Why was I so sure theirs was more wonderful?

"Mom? Did it ever bother you that I spent so much time at the Trevors'?"

"Oh, yes. It bothered your father more, though. I knew you needed the company. You're very sociable. You like noise and people. There aren't enough of us here, and your father and I are too quiet for you. It used to hurt Daddy's feelings terribly that the instant we finished dinner you'd bolt out the door and go to the Trevors', where things were fun."

"Did it hurt your feelings?"

"In a way. I always wished the neighborhood kids would come here for a change. Sometimes I'd stock up on Popsicles or candy popcorn or jelly doughnuts and hope I'd be the one who got the kids, but I never was."

Meghan had always thought her mother disliked the mess of visitors. She turned on the bed to stare at her mother. They never did this. They seemed to talk most easily staring upward at the ceiling and not at each other. How pretty her own mother was. What a nice profile she had.

Why did I want Mrs. Trevor all this time? thought Meghan, and she was suffused with guilt. She buried herself against her mother's warm hug and they lay softly on the bed without speaking.

After a long time the lump in Meghan's throat went away.

She had told her mother nothing. She had said nothing about the horror of Lannie, and the taking of West, and the freezing of her own flesh. And yet, she was so comforted! Her mother was so solid. So there. So safe.

So *mine*, thought Meghan.

She knew with a stab of understanding that she had been able to spend such huge amounts of time at other people's houses because she had known absolutely that her parents would love her anyway. She had been safe doing anything at all. Safe in love.

And Lannie . . .

What had Lannie been?

Unsafe.

Without love. Without even a molecule of love.

Unsafe.

If you are not brought up in the safety of love, thought Meghan Moore, you yourself become unsafe. It is unsafe to be near Lannie. She is as dangerous as a collapsing bridge or a caving-in cliff. All because of love.

"Ohmygosh!" said Meghan, remembering things out of no-where, the way your mind does sometimes, all on its own. "Mom, don't you have a meeting tonight? We haven't even thought about supper! You're late! You haven't even changed yet! Ohmygosh!"

Her mother said, "It's only a meeting. You and I needed a hug. We haven't had a good long hug in ages."

Meghan's eyes filled with tears. Her mother had been there, waiting for this hug, and Meghan hadn't been home.

"It'll be okay in the end, darling," said her mother softly, lips moving against Meghan's hair as she squeezed her daughter. "I'm so sorry you're having trouble with West. I know you've always adored him. I know how it must hurt. But you'll tough it out. You're my strong girl. You'll do the right thing. You'll make it."

Chapter 9

Meghan *was* strong. But to be strong alone — it was hard.

She wanted to be strong together!

After two weeks of being discarded like something you can't even recycle in the garbage, Meghan went over to the Trevors' after school just the way she always had. She had the courage to do this only because she knew that West had his mother's car that day, and she had seen him drive away after school with Lannie, and the car was not back. So only Tuesday would be there, and possibly Brown, if he didn't have sports.

Meghan didn't knock. She had never knocked at the Trevors', just walked in. "Hi, Tues," she said nervously.

Tuesday leaped up from the television. She raced across the room and flung her arms around Meghan. "I'm so glad you're here!"

There. That was the welcome and those were the words. Some of the leftover frozenness in Meghan's lonely heart eased.

"It's been so weird," said Tuesday. "West doesn't talk to anybody. Not me, not Brown, not Mom, not Dad. I guess he uses up all his speech and energy with Lannie and he comes home this drained-out old thing. Sits over his homework without seeing the page, without lifting the pencil. Mom and Dad are beside themselves. You won't believe this, but they think he's lovesick."

"Over Lannie?"

Tuesday nodded. "Over Lannie. Brown and I tried to inch into an explanation that the sick one is Lannie, and the trapped one is West, and the one in danger is you. But you know parents. Even mine. They just got annoyed and stomped around when we reached the Freeze Tag part. West didn't like it either. He wouldn't even back us up. He just looked at his hands and said he didn't know what we were talking about."

Looked at his hands, thought Meghan. Why his own hands? Did Lannie pass it on? Can he do it, too, now? She swallowed, trying to gag down this horrible image. "I didn't even try with my parents," she said. She checked the window. There were no cars approaching. All they needed was for West and Lannie to drive up while she was on the premises.

"West had to take her to the library," said Tuesday.

"She studies?"

"She says so," Tuesday shrugged. "She's attached herself to him like a starfish to a rock."

"How can he stand it?" Meghan could not bear it that West was managing. Was there something redeemable in Lannie that West had managed to find? If anybody was going to find good things in an evil person, it would be a Trevor. They were big on silver linings.

Mr. Trevor came in. He got out of work at about the same time the kids got out of school, so he was usually home in the afternoons. "Hey there, Meggie-Megs!" he said, much too heartily. "Say! We haven't seen much of you lately. How've you been, kid?"

"Fine," said Meghan, because what other answer could you give a grown-up?

"Sorry you and West sort of split up," muttered Mr. Trevor.

Meghan said nothing.

"They didn't sort of split up," said Tuesday. "Lannie forced herself on West."

Mr. Trevor did not look as if he believed that. Clearly, he believed it took two to tango; if West was dating Lannie, it was because West wanted to date Lannie.

"Lannie stinks," said Tuesday, laying it on the line.

"I'm sorry," said her father, addressing both girls, "that this turn of events has happened, but life is like that when you're young. You fall in love lots of times with lots of different people. So let's not say anything unpleasant about West's girlfriend."

Tuesday threw her arms in the air. "Let's," she said. "Let's say lots and lots of unpleasant stuff about West's girlfriend. And then let's *do* something unpleasant to West's girlfriend."

Mr. Trevor frowned and left the room.

But Tuesday and Meghan grinned at each other. The grin of conspirators. Allies. Teams. They even winked.

"I'm staying at the Trevors' for supper, Mom," said Meghan into the telephone. "And I'll be studying with Tuesday. I'll be home around ten, okay?"

"That's pretty late for a school night," said her mother. "How about nine?"

Nine. Meghan wasn't sure it was going to be manageable before nine. "Fine," she said to her mother. "I'll be home by nine."

The thought of crossing the open space between the houses after dark was so scary Meghan almost quit right then. She would have Lannie's eyes following her, Lannie's knowledge, Lannie's plans.

"You can crawl across the grass the way they do in desert warfare," suggested Tuesday, giggling. "Belly flat, head down, bullets whizzing through your hair."

For Tuesday it had become fun. An adventure.

But then, Tues wasn't the one who had been frozen in the truck. Tuesday hadn't felt snow piling up on her open eyes. Tuesday hadn't felt the cold passing into her heart, taking her into another world.

Tuesday's pretty bed jutted out into the room, leaving a space between the hanging bedspread and the wall. From the doorway you could not see down into that space. Meghan unrolled the sleeping bag in which she had spent so many nights and lay down, hidden. The afternoon grew dark. Tuesday and her brothers and parents had dinner. They made a lot of noise. None of it was West. Five people for dinner and four talked.

But he would talk tonight.

Mr. and Mrs. Trevor would watch their favorite TV programs and the children would be sent to their desks to do homework.

Well, they would do homework. But it wouldn't be a school assignment.

Meghan stayed beneath the level of the windowsill, just in case Lannie was lurking outside, peeking, staring, thought-policing.

It was eight-fifteen before Tuesday led West into her silent unlit bedroom.

"Sit on the floor," Tuesday said to him, and burst into a spatter of giggles.

"Tues, I'm tired," he said. "I can't play games anymore. Isn't it enough I have to play this endless game with Lannie?"

Meghan crept out from behind the bed.

West stared at her. She held a finger to her lips.

He sagged in a funny way, as if he were being rescued. "Oh, Meghan!" he said, and he said nothing more, but it was enough. He sat down next to her, and Tuesday sat with them, which Meghan regretted, but then, tonight's plan did not call for a kiss. It called for strategy.

"What's going on in here?" hissed Brown.

"Crawl in," whispered Tuesday.

Brown checked out the participants. "War council!" he said delightedly, and dropped down, and crawled. He would make an excellent desert warfare soldier, he had that belly technique down perfectly.

The four of them lay on their stomachs, propping their heads up with their cupped hands.

"What," said Tuesday, "are we going to do?"

"You're asking me?" said West. "You think I've come up with something?"

"Where does Lannie get this power?" said Tuesday. "Maybe we can cut off her source."

West shook his head. "I asked her how she calls it up. I was half thinking *I* could freeze *her*. If I knew how. She said she'd stage a demonstration for me. She said she'd freeze that gym coach I don't like."

"Wonderful," said Brown.

"Exactly. I start yelling 'No, no, no, no, no!' and Lannie says to me, 'Don't worry, West, it's easy, all I have to do is touch him, you won't be involved. I'd do that for you,' she says. Like I'd be happy afterward."

"But Lannie must touch you all the time," said Tuesday. "And you don't freeze."

"She does touch me all the time. But I don't touch her. It's not so bad if I just sit there and let her do what she wants."

It sounded pretty bad to Meghan. But still, Meghan began to enjoy herself. This was nice, this meeting of the best friends, plotting in the dark, hidden by the furniture, safe from the bleached eyes.

"I give Lannie hundreds of excuses for why I can't see her every waking minute," West said. "I use sports, chorus, home-work, term papers, weather, baby-sitting, Tuesday, Brown, Mom, Dad, Grandma."

"Grandma?" said Tuesday.

"I said when you're eighty years old and you're stuck in a nursing home five hundred miles away, you want to hear from your oldest grandson. I've written a lot of letters."

Meghan giggled. West's face split into the old familiar grin. Oh, she loved him so much! Okay, they were going to whip this thing. Together they were going to knock Lannie out of commission.

"You should have been here at breakfast this morning," Tuesday told Meghan. "It was so funny. Mom says to West, 'You can have the car, dear.' And West says, 'No thanks Mom,' because the last thing he wants is to be alone with Lannie yet again. And Mom goes — 'There's no such thing as a seventeen-year-old boy who doesn't want the car. Are you sick? Are you taking drugs?' So after we make our way through the no-I'm-not-on-drugs conversation, Mom wants to know the truth about why West doesn't want the car. And the best my stupid old brother can come up with is — it's tough finding a parking space."

"Oh, yeah, Mom believed that," said Brown. Tuesday and Brown burst into gales of laughter. West flushed. Meghan rested her hand on his. It was their only touch. The only touch in so long! He lowered his gaze and seemed to draw comfort from her hand. No doubt it was very different from the one that had been touching him these last weeks.

Tuesday became very businesslike. She did not want this evening to deteriorate into some sort of icky romantic thing. "I think," said Tuesday, "that you've given it enough of a shot, West. Now in the morning, you march up to Lannie and you tell Lannie it's been fun, but it's time for you to move on."

West looked at his sister incredulously. "After what she did to Meghan?"

"It's worth a try," said Tuesday.

West shook his head. "She'll hurt somebody."

"We'll keep our distance."

"She'll run after you."

"Don't be a wimp," said Tuesday sharply. "You have to let Lannie know the score. Otherwise, this could go on forever."

Tuesday made it sound so simple. Meghan tried to believe her. That West could just say, *Hey, Lan, been fun, see ya around, back to normal now, don't hurt anybody, 'kay?*

"Okay," said West, nodding, trying to give himself courage. "You're right. It can't go on forever."

Meghan ate a huge breakfast, having skipped dinner the night before. Her mother was delighted. Mothers always loved seeing you eat breakfast. Even though Meghan had fixed it herself, her mother seemed to feel she could take credit for it.

But she was not so eager to go outside.

For this was the morning. West was to tell Lannie to skip off and leave him alone. Leave them all alone.

To whom was Lannie the most dangerous?

Would she turn on West, for breaking his promise? Would she turn on Meghan, for being the one West still wanted? Would she turn on Tuesday, for being the sister who started things?

This won't work! thought Meghan. He mustn't do it! Lannie isn't going to say, oh, well, it was worth a try, have a nice life without me, West! Lannie's going to attack!

Meghan rushed to the telephone and stabbed at the familiar buttons, to call West, tell him no, no, no, no, no!

She didn't get past the second number.

West, Tuesday, and Brown were already outside. West had his mother's car keys in his hand; was unlocking the doors. Tuesday was getting in front — Lannie's place. Brown was playing Indian and hollering and whooping and generally attracting attention.

Meghan set the phone down gently. She got into her coat. She pulled on her mittens. She tightened her scarf. Perhaps Lannie's touch could not go through clothing. Perhaps wool or goosedown could save Meghan.

Right, she thought. There is no getting away from Lannie.

Meghan came out her front door.

Lannie came out hers.

The Trevor children looked up Dark Fern Lane, and saw them both.

West, Tuesday, Brown, Lannie, and Meghan all knew. This was a test. The game had reached another level. They looked at each other and, even from her front door, Meghan could feel the heat and the cold, the hatred and the love, the fear and the need.

No one else did.

Two houses up, the rest of the Dark Fern Lane children waited for the buses. There were two kindergartners at that stop, two first-graders, no second-graders, one third-grader. Then there was quite an age skip up to Brown. Lannie intended for Brown to be on that bus, not riding in the car with West and herself.

The little children played in the snow.

They pushed each other down and then got up and admired the dents their bottoms had put in the snow. They swung their lunches and bookbags in circles and let go, so the bright colored containers spun out like trajectiles and hit the others lightly. They laughed six-year-old laughs and made six-year-old jokes.

The third-grader showed off, doing a cartwheel. The littler ones had no idea how to accomplish such a marvelous move, but they tried. They flung their legs up an inch or two and giggled proudly.

Lannie Anveill walked through them. Stringing her fingers along as if she were hanging laundry on a line.

Perhaps she was.

They froze.

The two kindergartners, the two first-graders, the one third-grader. They hung in their positions like statues.

"No," whispered Tuesday, who had started this. "No, please."

Lannie stopped midway between her statues and the Trevors. Directly in front of Meghan's. Meghan might as well have been frozen. She could not move. Could not think.

"Hi, West," said Lannie across the frozen yards.

He did not speak. Perhaps he was as terrified as Meghan.

"Your heart is not in this, West," said Lannie.

He did not move either. Had she frozen him without even touching?

"I want your heart, West," said Lannie.

There was a thick dense silence.

Lannie's smile was tiny and yet tall: her mouth opened up and down, instead of sideways, in a terrifying leer.

The five little children remained frozen in the snow. Perhaps their mothers were not looking out the window. Perhaps their mothers thought it was part of a game.

It was.

But not a game anybody should ever play.

Freeze Tag.

No, please, thought Meghan. Not the little children. Not just because I want to be the one at Pizza Hut with West. Set them free. Let them go.

"Lannie," said West. His head sank down, so that he was looking at his own chest, the front of his own winter jacket. He seemed to lose some of the vertebrae in his backbone, and grow shorter and less strong. His voice scratched. He walked toward Lannie like an old man weighted with stones.

"You have my heart," said West.

Chapter 10

"You know," said Meghan's father, "I haven't seen Jason lately."

Meghan and her mother were going through the movie listings. Once a month the Moore family had Movie Saturday. Driving to the huge, twelve movie theater that had opened a few years ago, they saw one movie at four o'clock, came out dizzy and pleased, went to have hamburgers, french fries, and shakes, and came back for a movie at seven. During the first movie they had candy and during the second movie they had popcorn.

Meghan loved Movie Day. When she watched a movie, she fell into it. It was completely real and completely absorbing. Even a bad movie was good when you saw it on a big screen. Whereas bad movies when you rented them to watch at home were just plain bad movies.

This month was a toughie: They wanted to see everything. "It's better than the months when we don't want to see anything," her mother pointed out.

"I mean, I usually at least see Jason coming and going," said Meghan's father.

Meghan had not been thinking about Lannie for several weeks now. Ever since West had had to go on his knees to beg her to unfreeze the little children at the bus stop, she had decided just not to think about it again. There was nothing she could do.

Nothing anybody could do. And as long as Lannie had West, the world was safe.

You have my heart, Lannie, West had said.

Meghan didn't think about that either. It had sounded so true. You could almost see his heart, that day, red and bleeding and beating. As if he carried it over to her and set it down so she could have it.

Lannie had danced back among the children, as light as an elf on top of the snow. Flying past the little ones, she seemed hardly even to touch them. She skimmed along like a swallow in the sky.

But the children fell over in the snow, real again. There was a moment when they were all close to tears. All close to calling, *Mommy! Mommy come and get me! Mommy, something's wrong!*

But the yellow schoolbus had turned the corner, and the children lined up to get on, bickering over who deserved to get on first. Shouting about who would sit with whom. And if they crowded closer to each other for warmth, and if a short, cold memory lay like ice on the backs of their necks, they did not say so out loud.

Nobody had ever said so out loud.

If I'm not thinking about Lannie, thought Meghan, I'm certainly not thinking about Jason.

Meghan tapped on the newspaper column with her bright blue soft-tipped pen. Meghan liked to write in many colors. She liked to underline in vivid yellow. She liked to make lists in black. She liked to address envelopes in red. She liked to take notes in blue. She had written very few letters in her life, but when she considered writing one, she considered writing it in blue, too.

Mrs. Moore said, "This movie is supposed to be a really truly weepy huggy romance. I am in the mood. I want love and loss. I want finders keepers. I want rings and music."

Meghan's vow to herself never to think about it again evaporated, as it did, in fact, nearly every day. Sometimes hundreds of times a day.

I want West, thought Meghan. He is all of those. I am going

to a movie with my mother and father to watch an actress pretend to be in love with an actor. A month ago, I was the lover. I was loved.

And now . . .

What was happening now?

"It kind of bothers me," said Meghan's father. He circled the kitchen, wanting his women to listen. Say something. Finish up his thoughts and his sentences for him.

Not me, thought Meghan.

At last Meghan's mother responded to him. "You could go over and check," she pointed out.

But Mr. Moore and Lannie's stepfather were not actually friends. They waved over the pavement. They occasionally met in the driveway when each was polishing his car. Once or twice they had each had a beer in hand on a hot summer day and had stood talking.

Jason never seemed to have a part in the life of Dark Fern Lane. He drove out or he drove in, but he did not drive among.

In fact, now that Meghan thought about it, what did Jason do?

Mr. Moore left the kitchen, and the long white counter over which his wife and daughter had spread the newspaper. He crossed into the living room, spread back the curtains that lay gauzily over the picture window, tucked the fern fronds out of the way, and looked diagonally across the street at Jason's house.

"There's Lannie," said Mr. Moore. "Meggie-Megs, go find out from Lannie."

Leave the safety of her house?

Walk right up to Lannie Anveill? Who froze children like used clothes for a garage sale?

Get close to Lannie? Who when she was done freezing or unfreezing would set her hand back down? As if it were not attached, but was a purse or a book she was carrying around.

Say to her: *Lannie . . . we haven't seen Jason lately.*

"What do you think could have happened to him?" said her mother lightly.

Meghan could think of one thing, anyway. But her mother was not talking to Meghan. Meghan's fingers tightened. The blue dot beneath her pen spread an amoeba of ink over the movie listings.

"He's probably just out of town," said Mr. Moore.

But Jason's job had never seemed to involve overnight travel. Besides there was Lannie. Would he leave a fourteen-year-old?

Of course, it was Lannie.

It was not as if they were talking about a normal fourteen-year-old.

And yet . . .

"Go ask Lannie, Meghan," said her mother.

Meghan did not move.

"I know you're still upset about West going out with her," said her father, as if this were pretty small of Meghan; an event so minor her father could hardly believe his daughter even *noticed* when her boyfriend dropped her. "But I want you to ask."

Meghan was against part of growing up.

There suddenly were times when she was supposed to do the hard parts, when up till now they had always fallen into her parents' laps. "You ask her," she said.

Her father sighed a little, shrugged slightly, went to his office, and shut the door.

"It certainly isn't very much for your father to ask of you," said her mother sharply. "I think it's rather unpleasant of you to refuse him such a simple request. He's worried about his neighbor and you can't even be bothered to set his mind at rest."

At rest? Since when did Lannie's answers set anybody's mind at rest?

Meghan trudged heavily down the half stairs that divided their raised ranch house in the middle. Most of the families on Dark Fern Lane had replaced the thick hairy carpet that originally covered their stairs. When she was little, Meghan had loved that old orangey-brown carpet, with its loops as thick as an old-fashioned mop. Every house had either orangey-brown or else avocado green. It made even the houses of strangers seem familiar, because you remembered the carpeting so well. The year Meghan was in sixth grade, suddenly no grown-up on Dark Fern Lane could stand the sight of shag. Carpet vans were parked on Dark Fern Lane all the time. Now everybody had sophisticated nubbly champagne wool.

The orange shag had been cozier. Shabby, but comforting.

There was something cold and businesslike about the knots of pale wool.

Plus you had to remember to wipe your feet on the doormat before you came inside, a step everybody had omitted back when they had shag carpeting.

Meghan could not waste much more time worrying over carpet. She went out the front door.

Her father was correct. Lannie was there.

Standing thin and small in her driveway.

Perhaps she was waiting for West to pick her up.

Perhaps West had just dropped her off and she was still thinking about it, staring down at his house, watching him go inside.

Meghan walked slowly across the yard. The last snow had melted and the temperature had dropped even lower. The ground was hard as pavement, and the frozen grass crunched like breakfast cereal under her shoes.

It was difficult to imagine herself and the Trevor children young enough and carefree enough to play yard games here. It seemed decades ago, a topic for history class.

It was me, thought Meghan. There was a time when I did not know what Lannie could do.

She had put on her jacket but not mittens or hat, and the wind chewed on her exposed skin, mocking her for thinking she could come outside and live.

Meghan gathered her courage and looked straight across the street. Straight at Lannie. Firmly, without flinching, because this was not a personal thing, this was a parental order. In the game of Freeze Tag, it didn't count.

Lannie had no eyes.

Only sockets.

Meghan stopped dead, gagging, unable to walk closer.

Lannie smiled. The smile rested humanlike under the empty sockets. The smile was full of those baby teeth, small as birdseed. Meghan had a horrible feeling that birds had already been there: feeding on the face, taking the eyes, preparing to peck at the teeth.

Then Lannie was right up next to her, so wispy and unsubstantial that Meghan felt as heavy as a truck. Who had moved? How did Lannie do this — empty herself from one spot and fill another, without Meghan ever seeing her accomplish it?

The sockets were not empty after all.

The same old eyes, bleached out and cruel, stared up at Meghan.

Lannie smirked.

It was the smirk that brought Meghan back. Such a middle-high kind of look. An *I've got what you want* taunt. Meghan's chin lifted. She would not be intimidated. "Hello, Lannie," said Meghan.

Lannie of course said nothing. Just waited.

"My father is worried," said Meghan.

Lannie of course said nothing. Just waited.

"About Jason," said Meghan.

Lannie smiled.

"He hasn't seen Jason lately," said Meghan. Talking to Lannie was like being in a track meet. She was winded from four short sentences.

"Well," said Lannie, linking her arm in Meghan's as if they were friends. "You haven't seen Jason lately either, have you?"

Lannie's arm turned to metal. It might have been a shackle on Meghan's wrist.

"It's time you saw Jason," said Lannie softly. "Come on over to my house, Meggie-Megs." Lannie had never used the nickname. It sounded somehow evil, as if Lannie had got a hold of some essential depth in Meghan and could control it.

"I just have to tell my father where he is," said Meghan, trying to resist. But Lannie did not let go. Meghan was going with Lannie Anveill whether she wanted to or not. They walked in lockstep.

I do not want to go into that house, thought Meghan Moore. I do not want to be alone with Lannie!

Lannie, who always knew what you were thinking, knew what she was thinking. "You won't be alone with me," said Lannie. Her voice dripped ugliness. Her tiny body shuddered with taunting. "Jason is there."

Lannie escorted Meghan in her front door.

It was identical to every other front door on Dark Fern Lane. It opened onto a rectangle of fake slate tiles. Four steps led down to the family room and the garage. Nine steps led up to where the kitchen opened straight onto the stairs. The living room was at the left, with only a metal railing to keep you from falling off the couch and into the stairwell. Jason had not replaced his shag carpeting. Layers of avocado green fluff, flattened in the center from years of footsteps, climbed both ways.

Lannie did not take Meghan up to the living room or kitchen.

They went down the four stairs to the fake cork floor that covered all family rooms.

Or had. Meghan's mother and father had continued the new nubbly champagne wool all the way down and across. They had replaced the plain metal railing at the living room rim with a delicate white wooden bookcase, half solid and half see through, so books were firmly placed and special possessions were beautifully displayed.

I'm thinking so hard about my own house, thought Meghan. I'm so afraid to think about Lannie's.

They did not go into Lannie's family room either.

It occurred to Meghan that she had never been in Lannie's family room. The same rather dark half-basement room with the high windows that let in so little light — the room where most people watched TV and sorted laundry and kept the video games and the board games and the outgrown Fisher-Price toys and the piles of paperbacks and magazines.

Did Lannie have any of those?

Had any family ever gathered in that family room?

When Lannie's relatives wanted to be happy, they drove away. They got in their cars.

Perhaps it was a room for solitary confinement, instead of family.

Meghan shivered.

Lannie smiled.

They turned right, into the tiny claustrophobic hall with a laundry closet on one side, a half bath on the other, and the garage door at the end. The garage door was flimsy; hollow wood that clunked lightly when closed. Most of these doors had broken and been replaced over the years. Lannie's had not.

Lannie opened it.

The two-car garage under the bedrooms was completely dark.

Lannie flipped the electric switch and the room was flooded with light from two overhanging fluorescent tubes.

Jason sat in his Corvette.

He had a smile on his face.

One hand on the wheel.

One hand on the gearshift.

The motor was not running. But Jason was driving. The garage had been completely dark. But Jason was driving. The garage was very very cold. But Jason was driving.

Lannie's arm dropped from Meghan's.

Meghan walked slowly toward the Corvette. Jason did not look up at her. Jason did not stop smiling. Jason did not stop driving the silent motionless car.

Between the Corvette and the leaf rakes hanging against the side of the garage, Meghan stood trapped. Lannie's bright glittering eyes pierced her like stabbing icicles. Meghan backed up, pressing herself against the cold wooden studs of the garage. "You froze him."

Lannie nodded.

"But — but he's — your only family."

"No. He was just Jason."

"He didn't deserve to — umm — I mean . . ." Meghan's voice trailed off. She was having difficulty thinking. "When did you do it?" she said. "Can you undo it?"

Lannie shook her head. "It's been quite a while. I'm surprised nobody missed him before this, actually."

Meghan had been in there, in that frozen state, where Jason was now. She well remembered the feeling. She knew every sensation Jason had had — or not had — as the cold took him over.

But she, Meghan, had returned.

How long had Jason sat behind that wheel? How long had he sat there, knowing that the glaze over his eyes was to be permanent? That the cold in his bones would be forever?

"Does West know?" whispered Meghan.

"Oh, yes." Laughter etched new lines on Lannie's parchment skin. "I made him sit next to Jason for a while," she said, smiling. "West behaves very well now."

Meghan, clutching her stomach, retreated around the Corvette.

"Don't throw up," said Lannie. "I'd only make you clean it yourself, Meghan. Jason is fine this way. It's not that much of a change from his usual personality, you know."

Lannie came closer and closer. Meghan had nowhere to go. The lawnmower blocked her exit. She had no strength in her bones anyway.

Once again Lannie's hand closed on Meghan's arm. But nothing happened. Meghan did not freeze. She did not become an ice statue. Blood still ran in her veins and thoughts still poked through her mind like electric shocks.

Oddly practical thoughts. Groceries and electric bills. How was Lannie going to keep going all winter? All year? All future years?

"I'll be fine," said Lannie. "If anybody gives me a hard time, you know what will happen to them."

Meghan knew.

"I'd prefer you didn't tell your father," said Lannie.

Meghan felt thick and hopeless.

"Because," said Lannie Anveill softly, "you know what I will do if anybody gives me a hard time, Meghan Moore."

Chapter 11

The front seat of the old truck was warm and toasty. All the short February day, sun had gleamed on yesterday's snow. The truck cab was momentarily a greenhouse in which orchids could thrive.

Meghan sat far over on her side, and West sat far over on his.

The distance between them could be measured in inches or in hearts. They did not want to touch each other. They had not discussed this. Perhaps they thought that Lannie would know. That she could read the history of this afternoon in West's eyes.

Or perhaps whatever had once been between Meghan Moore and West Trevor had grown too cold for the sun to soften.

Meghan tugged each finger of her glove forward and bent the tips down, and then tugged each finger back till it fit again. She thought deeply about the pattern knit into the gray wool. She studied the long crack in the windshield.

"There must be something!" said West. His voice was low. Lannie was a hundred miles away and yet West thought she could overhear.

I must think so, too, Meghan realized. I am afraid of what will happen tonight when she comes over here. Some afterglow of me will be lingering on West, and for Lannie it will be as vivid a message as searchlights in the dark, and she will lust to hurt one of us. That terrible desire will be back in her speech and her heart. If she has a heart.

"Some reversal!" said West urgently. "Something we can turn against her."

Oh, how I want this to end! thought Meghan. But what can be turned against a girl who possesses Lannie's power?

Yet even Lannie had to follow certain rules. Her history class had gone to the state capitol for the day and would not be back until late. Meghan constantly checked her watch and the lowering sky. What was late? How did the school define that? What if Lannie were to return when Meghan and West were sitting together?

What would she do?

Meghan was irked with herself. Meghan knew perfectly well what Lannie would do.

"Some technique," said West. And then, with a sort of ferocity in his voice, like a pit bull fastening its jaws, he spat out, "Something to *destroy* her."

Meghan swerved in the little cozy space to look at him. He was not handsome, spitting his words. He was ugly and mean. He did not see Meghan. He did not see the truck or the snow or the sky. He saw only his neighbor. Lannie Anveill. Being destroyed.

A terrible word. Armies destroy cities. People who don't want them any longer destroy dogs.

I don't want to destroy a person, thought Meghan. Even Lannie. Even with her history. I do not wish to destroy. "Can't we just cure her?" said Meghan.

"Is there a cure for evil?" demanded West.

Meghan did not know. She was new to evil.

"You're the one Lannie was going to leave frozen! She laughed when she was going to let you die in the snow! You're the one she hates most, because you have everything!" said West.

To Meghan's horrified ears, West sounded as full of hate as Lannie. As though West, too, hated Meghan, and hated the world, and all good families. His mouth looked awful. Twisted and biting down. West, her sweet good West. Meghan looked away.

"You should be first in line to wipe her out!" cried West.

But I'm not, thought Meghan. I never want to be in that line at all. I want to be in line to save people. Not the line to destroy them.

She tried to explain this to West, but he could not listen. He huffed out an angry hot lungful of air, full of swearing and cursing. In the small space between the cracked windshield and the torn seats, his words expanded. She was breathing pain and ugliness instead of oxygen.

"You think you can teach Lannie to be sweet and forgiving?" demanded West. His anger was as frightening as Lannie's.

Meghan flinched.

"We've set an example all our lives. Both our families are kind and generous. Lannie hasn't picked up any of it, believe me. A girl who would freeze her own mother? Freeze the dog? Freeze my sister? Freeze you? Freeze Jason and keep him there like a trophy?"

I never quite believed it, thought Meghan. I was there for all of that. I was one victim, and I saw the rest. Yet even now, in the afternoon sun, I cannot quite believe it.

West changed characters as swiftly and completely as if he'd been changing clothes. He set down anger and put on contemplation. Drumming his fingers on the dashboard, West frowned in an intellectual sort of way. As if he were a professor deciding how to explain a new concept.

He was handsome again, and yet Meghan was suddenly afraid of him, too. *Too?* she thought. Am I bracketing West with Lannie? What am I afraid of?

Now she was afraid of the truck, too. The handle that did not work. The doors she could not open. The bulk of West's body that blocked the only exit. Meghan laced her ten fingers together and ordered herself to be rational.

"No," said West meditatively. "I think Lannie has to be ended."

How little emotion lay in his voice. *Lannie must be ended.*

Meghan fixed her eyes on the swirling sunlight outside the

truck. The sun spoke of truth and beauty and goodness. Perhaps it was locked out. Perhaps all she needed to do was open a door.

That day Lannie froze the children.

Girls have perfect conversational recall. Boys can hardly even remember the topic. If she were to quote West to himself, West would draw a blank. I said that? he would say. No, I didn't, Meghan.

Your heart is not in this, West, Lannie had said. *I want your heart.* And West had said, *You have my heart.*

She does have his heart, thought Meghan. Horror like some grotesque virus exploded her innocence.

Lannie has his heart. That's why I don't want to touch him. She has a grip on his heart. We're alone in this truck, and yet her fingers are curled around his heart.

Even West's voice was like Lannie's. The same flatness to it, because love and heart had been ironed out of it.

No doubt Lannie had whispered that to herself when she decided she had had enough of Mrs. Anveill. *My mother must be ended.*

"West," whispered Meghan. "Did you hear yourself? Have you thought about what you're saying? *Lannie must be ended.* That's evil. It means killing Lannie."

West hardly looked at her. Now a sort of hot thick eagerness poured out of him, like a poisoned drink. "Exactly," he said.

He shared her desires, too. Her aching, throbbing desire to inflict pain.

Oh, Lannie, Lannie! thought Meghan. Give me back his heart! His fine good heart! You've taken it!

She wanted to cleanse West of Lannie. They did that in olden days. They purged people of evil. Ancient priests and ancient rituals reached down into the heart and soul and tore out the evil and left the person exhausted but clean.

West is unclean, thought Meghan. His heart is Lannie's.

"Last night," West announced casually, "I considered driving into the bridge abutment."

The bridge had been rebuilt. Huge concrete pylons and immense concrete walls.

"Lannie won't use a seatbelt," West told her. He looked happy. "I seriously thought of simply driving into the cement at seventy-five miles an hour."

"West! You'd be killed."

He nodded without regret. "Yes. We'd both be killed."

She could not bear it that West had come to this. "No, West. We will not do that. We will not think of doing that. We are not going to *end* anybody. We are not going to end Lannie and we are not going to end you."

"Then where will *this* end, Meghan?" said West. He spoke reasonably, as if discussing homework or radio stations. "Where will Lannie take us? Are we going to grow up and reach our twenties and thirties and middle age and old age, with Lannie still there threatening us? Lannie still freezing people who annoy her? Lannie still ruining all our lives?"

Meghan could not sit in the ruined truck any longer. It was too symbolic. West was the rusted-out body. "Let's go up to the house," she said. Now it was her own voice that had become toneless. All the music had passed out of her. There would be no melodies and no harmonies now. Only the flat, ironed, heartless-ness of Lannie . . . and West.

West got out of the truck. Meghan slid over the seat and hit the ground with both feet. She felt better standing on the ground. A little more connected to whatever goodness was left in the world. She headed up the hill while West fussed with the truck, checking the windows and slamming the door. As if the truck mattered. As if anything mattered when a fine young man could discuss without the slightest worry the "ending" of another human being.

"I just don't see what problem you have with this, Meggie-Megs," said West, genuinely puzzled. "I mean, think of Jason in that garage! How can you possibly mind Lannie being ended when you know what she does for fun?"

"That's Lannie!" cried Meghan. "Lannie's sick and twisted. But we're not! We can't do it just because she does!"

"Now, Meggie-Megs," said West.

She could not bear it that he was abusing her baby nickname like this. Meggie-Megs had been a curly-haired toddler to whom afterschool snacks and bear hugs were the whole world. Meggie-Megs had been a name for innocence and laughter, not the "ending" of another human being.

West was still discussing Lannie's "end" as they went into the house.

His brother and sister were watching a video. Tuesday was partial to James Bond and, as Meghan entered the family room, James Bond was also facing down Evil. He would win, of course. In the movies, Good triumphed over Evil. And so cleverly. Driving the best cars and using the finest of electronic devices.

Meghan did not feel clever. She felt utterly and completely depressed, and utterly and completely unable to stop the expansion of Lannie.

"See," said West, flopping down on the big raggedy armchair, "I was also thinking that I would teach Lannie to drive. And what I could do is, send her off by herself after I've rigged whatever car I use to teach her. There'd be a nice symmetry to that besides. She killed her mother in a car. It's only fitting that she should die in a car. Don't you think so?"

Tuesday and Brown looked up from the video.

Meghan could not bear it. "West, *murder* can *not* be next on our list."

"It isn't murder," said West, slightly surprised. "It's ending Lannie."

The family room divided into two temperature zones. There was the warm and friendly side on which Tuesday and Brown sat. There was the cold and vicious side where West sat.

Meghan stood in the middle of the room, the sleet of West's plans hitting her on one side; the stunned sweetness of Tuesday and Brown warming her on the other side.

"West?" said Brown.

West did not even look at his little brother. He was caught up in a daydream, a dream in which he would do all the things to Lannie which creatures do to each other in Saturday morning cartoons: They flatten each other, they push each other off cliffs, they drop dynamite down on each other's chimneys.

Meghan knew then that she really was an ex-girlfriend.

There was no going back.

This was not West: the Trevor she loved best. This was a stranger who would slice off another life as easily as slicing a wedge off a melon.

"And then . . . " said West eagerly.

Tuesday began to cry but West did not see her. A smile was curving on West's face. Meghan could see Lannie in it, as if Lannie had taken up residence inside West.

"Or another way . . . " said West excitedly.

Brown stared at his fingernails, the way boys did, making fists and turning them up. Girls spread their fingers like fans and held them away.

Meghan went home.

She could not bear another burden.

She lay awake for a long long time. Once or twice she got out of bed and went to a window from which she could stare at Lannie's house, and think of the people who lived there: the one who breathed and the one who did not. Once or twice she got out of bed and went to a window from which she could stare at the Trevors' house, and think of the people who lived there: the friends she still understood and the friend she had lost.

And once more she got out of bed, and very, very quietly opened a door at the other end of the hall, and looked in on two sleeping parents. Truly, thought Meghan Moore, I am loved. I have seen now what it is to be unloved and I know why Lannie is jealous.

I do have everything.

* * *

In school the next day, Meghan asked Lannie to sit with her.

"What is it you want from me?" said Lannie, when they were alone together.

"I just want to talk."

Lannie shook her head. "Nobody feels that way with me. You want something from me. Say what it is." Her eyes, like faucets, ran both hot and cold. Meghan could neither look at Lannie nor look away. She could not go on being courteous and full of fibs. "I want to talk about West," she whispered. Her lips did not move easily. How did Lannie do her freezing? She had even frozen Meghan's courage, and Meghan had had so much of it when she left home this morning!

"Oh?" said Lannie.

"I'm worried about him," said Meghan.

"Oh?"

"You've made him so cold!" Meghan burst out.

Lannie smiled. "His heart is colder," she agreed.

Meghan felt herself bowing forward, the weight of her worries folding her up. Her shoulders sagged, her muscles went limp, her arms drooped.

Coldhearted.

One of those phrases people toss about easily, without consideration, without knowing what it truly means. Meghan knew. She had two coldhearted people to go by.

And what is a cold heart?

A heart without love. Without compassion.

A heart that does not worry about others. A heart that does not care if somebody else pays a price just for being near it.

Heart and soul. They are so close! So intertwined. What kind of soul could a coldhearted person have?

Perhaps, thought Meghan Moore, *no soul at all*.

Perhaps the cold heart has frozen the soul out.

"Did you touch him to do it?" she whispered.

"I didn't have to touch him. I just had to be there. Showing him my way." Lannie smiled her smile of ice and snow. "He's a good follower, West."

Meghan was crying now. Her tears were hail on her own cheeks: blisteringly cold tears that peppered her skin instead of running down her cheeks.

What would melt the heart of Lannie Anveill? What could possibly release the heart of West Trevor? "You froze him," said Meghan through the hail of her tears.

"Yes," said Lannie, chuckling. "He's mine."

Chapter 12

Sunshine is a blessing.

Morning is a blessing.

Agony is less and fear is diminished in the sparkle and the gold of an early sun.

Meghan was slightly restored. She dressed in a corner of her bedroom where a shaft of sunlight made a warm square on the floor. If only I could pick that up, she thought, and carry it with me. Stand in it all day long.

But she did not raise the shade to let more sun in, for Lannie's house also lay to the east.

There is a way out of this, she told herself. Then she said it out loud for additional strength. "There is a way out of this!" she called. If a cold heart has frozen West's soul, I will just have to warm him up.

She smiled to herself. "Perhaps West could be defrosted," she said to the sunshine square. It was a word for refrigerators or plastic bags of vegetables. "I am probably the only girl in America," she said ruefully, "who has to defrost her boyfriend."

Well, it made Meghan laugh, anyway. Now how to get West to laugh so warmly? How to defrost his heart, and locate his soul, and peel him away from Lannie's influence, and save the world from Lannie?

In the sunshine, she believed that it could be done.

In the sunshine, she believed that she was the one who could do it.

And luckily, the sun stayed out all day. No clouds passed in front of it, no snowstorms blew in from Canada. Her classes in the morning were on the east side of the building and in the afternoon on the west. She never did lose that square of sunlight. And so after school, she went for help. She chose her history teacher, whom she adored and who seemed to have so many answers! The woman knew dates and wars and prime ministers and ancient enmities. She knew rivers and treaties and battles and kings.

Meghan launched right into it. "Suppose," said Meghan Moore, "that a person's soul froze. How would you teach him to love again?"

Her teacher smiled. "My dear, mankind has been trying to teach love to the frozen for thousands of years. That's half of every religion and every philosophy."

Meghan did not want to waste time reading every religion and every philosophy. "Who's right?" she said briskly.

"My dear, mankind has gone to war trying to decide who's right. They've lynched their neighbors, disowned their children, and built a million sacred edifices."

Meghan did not really want details at a time like this. "I understand, but in your opinion, who is right?"

"Everybody."

Meghan looked at her teacher with some irritation. "You wouldn't accept that answer on a quiz," she pointed out. "You'd say, 'Be more specific.'"

"Life is not a quiz," said the history teacher.

"Are you taking me seriously?" demanded Meghan. "I really need to know the answer to this question. *Who is right?*"

"And I said everybody. Love is right. In any language, in any history, in any religion, if you love your neighbor, if your heart is generous, if you show mercy and act justly, then you are right."

Love my neighbor.

Well, I have two neighbors here, thought Meghan Moore. Lannie and West.

Does this mean I have to love Lannie? That means I have to love Evil. Because Lannie is evil. She's a poison seeping from an abandoned tank into the water supply, and no one notices until all the children on the street have cancer. How can I love that?

I've always loved West. I've loved him all my life, and especially this year, and what do I have to show for it?

A cold heart in somebody else's hands.

Show mercy and act justly.

Show mercy to whom? Lannie's future victims? Lannie? Myself?

And what is justice? To do what West wants? End Lannie Anveill?

She had come for answers, and the history teacher seemed to think that they had been given to her. The history teacher smiled happily as she packed her briefcase with papers to correct that night.

To Meghan it did not feel like an answer. It felt like more questions.

She left the school. The sun still shone. The square of gold was still at her feet. But she knew nothing.

Least of all what to do next.

Chapter 13

The sun set and the snow began. Clouds as thick as continents rolled in, bleak and bruised. From out of those dark pain-ridden whirls came snow so white it stretched credulity. Nothing could be that white. That pure. That perfect.

Winter deepened in one brief afternoon.

Dark Fern Lane had never seen so much snow. It drifted thigh deep. Tires on the road surface made a whole new sound: scrunching and crunching in treads.

It was a Friday. The rules of school nights were suspended.

But not one child frolicked in the snow. Not one family had turned on a porch light or a garage light, and come out to roll a snowman in the dark. Not one snowball had been formed, not one snowfort built, not one angel made. No one had plucked the icicles from the porch overhang and pretended to be a unicorn. No one had gathered a plateful of the best and whitest snow, and poured hot maple syrup on it to make instant candy.

For another generation, yard games were over.

Those children who had been frozen like laundry — they remembered.

They had been aware, inside their motionless bodies and their unblinking eyes. They had known. They had felt Lannie's fingertips.

They were staying inside.

They would always stay inside.

Only Meghan went out into the snow, and only then because she had seen West in his mother's car stop for Lannie and drive away with her. Drive carefully, she had thought after the vanishing car. Don't do anything bad. Come home safe!

She waded through wonderful drifts, snow as deep as company on Thanksgiving.

"Meggie-Megs!" said Tuesday delightedly. "Come on in! It's freezing out there! You are so brave! Brown and I are hibernating till spring."

Meghan joined Brown and Tuesday in the family room. "Are your parents home?"

"Nope. They've taken up square dancing. Isn't that hysterical? You should see them. Dad's wearing cowboy shirts and a bowler and Mom's wearing a red calico skirt with ruffles."

Meghan wished she had seen them. It sounded so cute. She smiled, thinking of Mr. and Mrs. Trevor.

"It's good that they're gone," said Tuesday briskly. "We have things to decide."

Brown nodded. He sat up on the edge of the couch. Whatever they were going to decide could not be done slouching. "First," said Brown, "how much does West actually like her?"

Here we go again, thought Meghan. There's no getting away from Lannie Anveill.

"When West kisses Lannie, it looks real," said Brown. "Is he an actor? Or does he love her?"

"He started as an actor," said Tuesday, "but I think it became real. That's a danger with playing games so hard and so well. You forget it's a game. It gets into your bloodstream." Tuesday stood up. "Microwave popcorn anybody? Cheese or plain buttered?"

"Plain buttered," said Brown. "It's not only a game, but Lannie has beaten him at it. He's getting to be as sick and twisted as she is."

Tuesday brought out the popcorn. Their six hands went into

the bowl together. They sat close to share. Food helps a person think.

"I have to believe," said Meghan, munching, "that good is stronger than evil. That somehow this will work out all right."

"It won't," said Tuesday.

"I saw Jason," said Brown. He crammed more popcorn into his mouth.

"Well, there's no helping him now," said Tuesday. "And probably no helping West either. We have to look out for ourselves."

The popcorn stuck in Meghan's throat.

"So the question here is," said Brown, rubbing a popcorn against the side of the bowl to slick up extra butter and salt, "how do we end Lannie?"

The cold seeped into Meghan's heart again. Yet another sweet Trevor suggesting that Lannie should be "ended."

"Could she freeze herself?" asked Tuesday. "Could we play Freeze Tag and somehow she freezes herself?"

Brown shook his head. "If that could happen, she'd have frozen herself when she brushed her hair or put on lipstick."

"I'm thirsty," said Tuesday. "Meggie–Megs, you want Coke, Dr. Pepper, cider, hot chocolate, raspberry ginger ale, or milk?"

This was too big a decision to be executed from the family room. The three of them went into the kitchen to inspect the actual containers. Once she had seen the bottles, Meghan knew she needed water first, to wash down the salt and butter, and then she could concentrate on the hot chocolate. "Do you have marshmallows?" she said.

"It comes with them. See?"

Meghan saw. She would ask her mother to get that kind. "I could offer myself," said Meghan. "I could say: Here. Freeze me. I am yours. Do not hurt other people who are not involved."

"Lannie'd just freeze you and leave you," said Brown, "and go on to her next victim. You wouldn't accomplish anything by that except to join Jennifer or Jacqueline or whoever she is on the hospital ward."

"I thought Lannie unfroze her."

"That was a while ago. There's been another one."

"What did Jennifer or Jacqueline do to Lannie?"

"Wasn't friendly, I guess."

"I know," said Tuesday. "We could lock her away."

"You own a jail, maybe?" said Brown. He shrugged and gave up. He found the remote and turned on the television. This was Brown's only answer to all difficulties.

Homework too hard? Watch TV.

Family too annoying? Watch TV.

Lannie too scary? Watch TV.

It had very little to do with the history teacher's answer to all difficulties. Mercy and justice.

Tuesday and Meghan watched helplessly. It's difficult to have a television on and not get sucked in. How remote, how impossible the family on the TV screen seemed. How could they laugh so hard and so often?

We used to laugh like that, thought Meghan. Back before we knew all about Lannie Anveill.

Beneath her feet she felt the rising and slamming of the automatic garage door, rarely used. She heard the growl of a car engine and its abrupt cessation. She heard a door slam. West is here, she thought.

She heard a second door slam.

"Lannie's with him," said Tuesday.

Brown turned up the television volume. It might have been a weapon or camouflage. He was wrapped in a canned laugh track, safe even from Lannie Anveill.

Feet hit the stairs, and up through the raised ranch came West and Lannie.

Meghan's grandmother had had an awful saying of which she was very fond: Speak of the devil, and he appears.

They had spoken of Lannie, and she had appeared.

No one said hello.

Brown did not look up from the television. Tuesday did not

look up from the popcorn. West did not look up from his shoes. Meghan practiced locking her fingers together.

Lannie chuckled.

It was such an inappropriate sound that Meghan did look up. She caught Lannie unaware. Lannie was nervous.

Because we don't like her! thought Meghan, astonished to see this flicker of humanness. Lannie wants to be popular like anybody else. We're afraid of her and we don't want her around and it makes her nervous!

Lannie and West dropped onto the couch opposite Meghan and Tuesday. It's good they have two sofas, thought Meghan. It would be tricky to have to sit next to each other.

"Turn that down," said Lannie.

Brown did not pretend he couldn't hear her. He notched the volume down, and he didn't play around, taking it slowly and being infuriating. He didn't want to see that finger of hers moving toward him.

The people on television giggled and sparred and chatted but you could not quite hear them; they might suddenly have become ghosts whose presence was only fractional.

Lannie smiled.

West looked away.

"Popcorn?" said Tuesday brightly.

"We ate," said West.

So they sat, waiting for Lannie to leave, waiting for the torture to be over. But this was Lannie, of course, who enjoyed torture, and so she was not going to leave.

"Oh!" said Brown suddenly.

They all looked at him.

He sparkled, the way you do when you've just had a brilliant idea. "Lannie!" said Brown.

She raised her eyebrows.

"I know what! Why don't you and I go out?" he said. "I'd be a great date. And that way, Meghan could still be with West."

Meghan was so touched she wanted to weep. Brown was offering himself in exchange.

Lannie hooted with laughter. "You?" she said. "You're a little boy! You're eleven years old! Get a life! You're so pathetic, Brown."

"You're the one who's pathetic! You know perfectly well, nobody would ever date you because he wanted to!" shouted Brown. "You have to threaten them with freezing to get them to sit in the same room with you. You have to keep Jason in the car to scare everybody to death just in order to get a ride to school!"

"West promised to like me best," said Lannie defensively, "and he does. So there."

"He does not!" screamed Tuesday. "He hates you! He loves Meghan!"

I cannot bear it, thought Meghan. I cannot go on like this. I will have to give up. I will have to have another life, with other friends.

Meghan looked at the three Trevors as if for the last time. She thought of school and all the people she knew there — thought of scrounging among them like a bag lady, hoping to find a discarded friend for herself. She thought: I'm a sophomore and I have nobody. I have to start all over.

"Do you really love Meghan?" Lannie asked West in a deathly cold voice. She held her hands away from her sides, like a police officer whose holster and stick make him walk funny. But Lannie didn't need a holster nor a stick. Just a fingertip.

"Of course not," said West. He put his arms around Lannie. She vanished in his embrace, as small as a kindergartner. Then he kissed her hair.

"How romantic," said Brown. "Must be like kissing a bale of hay."

West did not respond to this. Nor did he even glance at Meghan, whose hair he had once loved to touch. Is he protecting me? wondered Meghan. Or has he forgotten me? I can't tell. I don't know.

"Go home and get warmer clothes, Lannie," said West. "We'll go ice skating. It's Friday. The rink's open till midnight."

Lannie said shyly, flirtatiously, "I'm not very good."

West smiled. "I'll hold you up."

Meghan's heart broke.

Did anybody ever want to hear anything else? *I'll hold you up.* It's what we all want, thought Meghan. Somebody to catch us when we're afraid of falling.

Oh how I want him back! I want West Trevor! We held *each other* up. We were a pair. A perfect pair.

Meghan was weary. I'm going home, she thought. There's no point in coming back here. I have to stay away and start over. By myself.

Silently and seemingly without motion, Lannie eased herself out of the Trevor house. Lannie's vanishing always gave Meghan the shivers.

From across the room West said, "Never touch me again, Meghan."

She thought she would fall over. He didn't have to say that! He could leave it alone, without stabbing her with those words!

"Lannie knows we're meeting," West said tonelessly. "She gave me her power. If I touch anybody other than Lannie, they'll freeze."

West left to get the car out again, get Lannie again, go hopelessly on with his half-life again.

Brown watched his brother leave.

Tuesday watched her brother leave.

But Meghan could not bear to look at the West she would never again have, and so she watched Tuesday.

A strange flicker crossed her best friend's face.

An expression both calculating and cruel. Meghan had to look away, and when she looked back, the expression was gone, and

Meghan convinced herself she had never seen it. Tuesday — sweet Tuesday of summer nights and pink lemonade — would not look like that.

It was the face of a cold heart.

A frozen soul.

Chapter 14

Snow fell for days.

They had never experienced such weather. The sky would not change, would not back off, would not turn clear and blue. Endlessly, the sky dumped snow down upon them. School was canceled because the snowplows could not keep up with the amazing amounts of snow. After a while there was no place for the plows to push the snow, and the roads became narrower, flanked by mountain ranges of previously shoveled snow.

Brown didn't mind. He was the kind of person who could watch a million hours of television and then watch a million more. He just sat there with the TV on, staring. Tuesday had a "kitchen attack" and suddenly made real sugar cookies which she cut out in hearts and decorated with red glaze or chocolate chips.

Tuesday called Meghan to see if she had any other cookie cutters because Tuesday had a lot more cookie dough and no more shapes.

Meghan's mother had once been given a collection of cookie cutters. They were still in the original box, lying on the original white tissue.

So much for finding new friends, thought Meghan. She put on her layers of protection against the winter and stormed her way to the Trevors' with her collection. She and Tuesday rolled out dough on the kitchen counter and argued whether — in February — they could properly use the Christmas tree or the Santa.

There was a knock at the front door.

Tuesday went to get it. Meghan took the opportunity to snitch a long thin slice of raw dough. Meghan loved raw cookie dough.

"Hi," said Lannie at the door. Like a normal person. A regular greeting and everything.

Meghan pressed herself into the corner of the kitchen, where she would be invisible if Lannie came up the stairs.

"Hi, Lannie," said Tuesday.

"Is West here?"

"Not yet. He went out to get a part for his truck. He's going to work on it today."

West hasn't looked at his truck in ages, thought Meghan. Strange how a person's only sister sees so little. You would think Tuesday would know that West is so caught between Lannie and real life that rusted trucks and stalled engines have slipped his mind. But no, she thinks he's still down there every day, working on the Chevy.

"Why don't you wait for West in the truck?" said Tuesday.

It's awfully cold out, thought Meghan. I'm not sure that Lannie should be . . . what am I doing?

Meghan shook off her thoughts.

I'm trying to protect Lannie's health? I don't mind if Lannie catches cold. I hope Lannie gets such a bad cold she's home for a year!

"West will be back in a while and you know the first thing he'll do is run down there to look at his truck," said Tuesday.

From her corner Meghan looked out the kitchen window. There was only one, and it was a small dark square above the sink. Mrs. Trevor was trying to grow little plants on that window, but they didn't get enough sun, and all she had were thin bottles of water and sad little cuttings of fading greens. There had been no sunset because the sun had never been visible. The dark sky had simply grown darker, and now, in the hour before supper, the darkness had a fullness to it, as if it had finally consumed everything in its path and was ready for a nap.

Tuesday went on and on about the truck.

After a while, Brown woke from his television coma and joined Tuesday in the little entry between the stairs. "Here," he said, "I'll put on the backyard light for you." He hit the switch that turned on the light at the bottom of the deck stairs which led up to the kitchen door. Now the snow sparkled.

Barely, way down the sloping yard, Meghan could see the mounded tops of a row of cedars that had grown up near the truck. You could not quite see down as low as the truck. The white spires of the cedars marked the spot.

How peacefully the snow lay. Snow covers all ugliness, thought Meghan.

Tuesday coaxed Lannie around the house. Tuesday even went with her partway, although Tuesday had neither coat nor boots on. "He'll be there soon," Tuesday said twice.

Lannie waded down the sloping yard, past the snow covered vines and hedges and underbrush. Meghan turned off the kitchen lights so that Lannie would not see her, illuminated next to the cookie dough. She could hardly see Lannie. In fact, Lannie's shadow was clearer than the real Lannie.

Lannie's little body, forcing itself against the high drifts and packed snow, dipped down and disappeared from sight.

Meghan pulled the shade over the kitchen window before she turned the light back on.

"Now let's set the table," said Tuesday briskly. "Mom's exhausted from her new job. I've promised to do dinner twice a week. She cut a seafood recipe out of *Family Circle*. Doesn't this look yummy? You chop the onions and sauté them, and I'll start the biscuits."

"What does sauté mean?" said Meghan uneasily. She was not familiar with kitchens. Her own family had take-out, or fixed meals that involved heating rather than recipes, like steak and baked potatoes.

In the end, Tuesday even had to demonstrate the purpose of the chopping board. Had to show Meghan how to dice the onion without also dicing her fingertips. How to scrape the onions into the skillet without dumping half of them in the crack between the stove and the counter. "This is work," said Meghan. "I'm exhausted from a single onion."

She and Tuesday giggled.

"Now you've got to prepare the scallops," said Tuesday. She took a wrapped package out of the meat compartment of the refrigerator and ripped it open.

"Those horrible mushy white things? We're going to eat those?" Meghan was horrified.

"Yes. We're going to love them. Now here's what you do."

And then she had to do things with garlic as well, and parsley had to be torn, and then she was given a tiny little broom, or paintbrush, with which to slather melted butter on the tops of the almost-baked biscuits. When they came out of the oven again, minutes later, they were crusty and golden and smelled of heaven.

There was quite a rush as everybody else got home, and the table had to be set, and her parents had to be telephoned for permission for Meghan to eat at the Trevors' again, and Meghan had to work through her guilt for once again not being home with her own family.

The real treat was sitting next to West again.

His smile was normal, his laugh was genuine.

Mr. Trevor had had a great day at work and regaled them with stories. "This is the best dinner I've had in years!" he kept saying. "Meghan, you did the garlic and onion?"

"I taught her how, Dad," said Tuesday.

He shook his head proudly. "What a pair!"

"I'll have seconds," said West.

Meghan was beaming.

"Excellent dinner," pronounced Mrs. Trevor. Then she giggled in that special Trevor way. "Of course, I'd like any meal that somebody else fixed, so my standards are pretty low."

"You guys would not believe," said Tuesday, "what I had to teach old Meggie-Megs here. Good grief. She doesn't know an onion from a potato."

"What's for dessert?" said Mr. Trevor, holding a fork in one hand and a spoon in the other, ready for any eating style.

"Drop that silver," said Meghan.

"Cookies," said Tuesday, bringing out a tray lined with a Christmas napkin she'd dug up from somewhere.

"Santa Clauses!" shouted Mr. Trevor. He bit off a Santa head and declared it the tastiest cookie he'd had in his life.

Meghan had never dreamed that the mere cooking of food could bring so many compliments. She would have to tell her parents. Perhaps the Moores would try cooking, too, one day.

West cleared the table, scraped the dishes, loaded the dishwasher, ran hot soapy water for the pots. Dishes had always been his job. And he had never complained. His mother put on the coffee. Mr. and Mrs. Trevor always liked to sit around the table sipping that awful stuff after a big meal.

"So," said Mrs. Trevor, smiling broadly at her son, and then equally broadly at Meghan, "you two are back together again? Lannie's out of the picture?"

I forgot Lannie! She's still waiting for him down in the truck! Meghan swerved to look at Tuesday, so Tuesday would give West the message. Certainly Meghan didn't want to deliver it. She was as full of happiness as the night was full of dark. She didn't even want to utter the name, because it would break her happy spell like an icicle hitting the pavement.

Both Tuesday's eyelids went down slowly, in a sort of double wink. How like Lannie she suddenly looked. Hooded, evil eyes. Eyes that had seen terrible things. Eyes that had seen through to the other side.

"Lannie's out of the picture," agreed Tuesday. She, too, smiled broadly. She met West's eyes and now his smile came out. Meghan could not move. Out of the corner of her eyes she checked Brown. No smile had ever been wider.

Meghan did not need to be out in the snow to be cold. Her hands, her heart, her thoughts: They chilled as if her friends had refrigerated her.

"All we need now," said Mr. Trevor, "is ice cream. A really good dinner isn't done till you've had your ice cream. Meghan, dish it out!"

Meghan got up from the table. She circled the big flat dining room table, and crossed the kitchen to the refrigerator.

The inside of the freezer was rimmed with frost crystals. Ice cubes tumbled out of the ice maker and fell into a clear plastic box. They looked like stones for a pyramid. Her fingers grazed the metal edge of the freezer and for a scary moment they stuck to the cold. She peeled herself away and got the ice cream container out.

So cold in there. How chilly the boxes of vegetables and desserts must be. Meghan shut the door, leaving the cold boxes to their dark frozen lives. They had to lie there until somebody wanted them. They had no exit without human hands. There were no handles on the insides of refrigerator doors.

Handles.

There are no handles on the inside of the truck doors, either, thought Meghan Moore. Lannie cannot get out of the truck.

Nobody knows she's there.

The snow is coming down. The truck is getting colder and colder. Lannie can scream and kick and bite. But she will never get out. There are no handles on the inside.

By morning . . .

By morning, Lannie Anveill will be frozen.

Like Jason, she will sit behind the wheel. She may sit all winter. Because Mr. and Mrs. Trevor never go down there.

And nobody else knows she's there.

"I boiled water," said Mrs. Trevor cheerily. "People who don't want coffee with their ice cream may have tea, herb tea, spiced cider, or instant hot chocolate."

West smiled. He would have coffee, please. Cream and sugar.

Tuesday smiled. She would have herb tea, please. With honey.

Brown smiled. He would have hot chocolate, please.

They were not smiling for coffee, tea, or chocolate.

They were smiling because they knew where Lannie was.

Those were not even smiles across their faces.

They were gashes.

Tuesday knew.

West knew.

And Brown, grinning down into his ice cream — Brown knew.

"Meghan?" said Mrs. Trevor.

"Spiced cider," said Meghan. It's not my responsibility, she thought. Tuesday sent her down there. Tuesday's the one letting it happen.

Only three people would know where Lannie Anveill was. How she got there. What happened to her.

No.

Actually, four people.

Three Trevors . . . *and one Moore.*

Meghan Moore.

Meghan's cider spilled on the table.

She set the mug down. Then set her trembling hand on her lap.

No, West. We will not do that. We will not even think of doing that.

Then where will this end, Meghan? Where will Lannie take us? Are we going to grow up and reach our twenties and thirties and middle age and old age, with Lannie still there threatening us, ruining our lives?

You won, Lannie. You froze him.

Yes. He's mine.

Evil can infect. Evil can spread. Evil has such great and terrible power that it infiltrates even the best of human beings.

I, thought Meghan Moore, am the one who became evil.

I am the one sitting here with a mug of spiced cider, waiting for the cold and terrible hours of night to pass, so that Lannie Anveill turns to ice and snow.

My heart.

My heart is frozen.

Meghan Moore got up from the table. She walked to the back door. It was difficult. Her feet dragged and she bumped into the jamb. The doorknob did not fit her hand and the wind when she opened the door assaulted her.

She heard voices behind her, but they were Trevor voices. The voices of people to whom things came easily. The voices of people who expected things to work out their way. Meghan did not know if she still loved the Trevors.

The one I have to love most, she thought, is me.

If I don't love myself, I cannot go on.

The cold was no longer an enemy. Instead it woke her and embraced her with its demands.

This is what it means, thought Meghan Moore, to choose the lesser of two evils. Lannie is evil, but it would be more evil to stand aside and silently let her die.

Meghan had never gone through snow so deep, through darkness so thick. She found the truck by feel. She opened the door of the cab and Lannie fell into her arms.

Meghan helped Lannie walk.

"Come in my house where it's warm," said Meghan.

Lannie said nothing.

Perhaps she was too cold to speak.

Or perhaps . . . she had waited all her life to come in where it was warm.

Chapter 1

It was cold in the music room. Somebody had cracked the windows to freshen the stale school air. But Nicoletta had not expected her entire life to be chilled by the drafts of January.

"Nickie," said the music teacher, smiling a bright, false smile. Nicoletta hated nicknames but she smiled back anyway. "I called you in separately because this may be a blow. I want you to learn the news here, and not in the hallway in front of the others."

Nicoletta could not imagine what Ms. Quincy was talking about. Yesterday, tryouts for Madrigal Singers had been completed. Ms. Quincy required the members to audition every September and January, even though there was no question as to which sixteen would be chosen. Nicoletta, of course, as she had been for two years, would be one of the four sopranos.

So her first thought was that somebody was hurt, and Ms. Quincy was breaking it to her. In a childlike gesture of which she was unaware, Nicoletta's hand caught the left side of her hair and wound it around her throat. The thick, shining gold turned into a comforting rope.

"The new girl," said Ms. Quincy. "Anne-Louise." Ms. Quincy looked at the chalkboard on which a music staff had been drawn. "She's wonderful," said Ms. Quincy. "I'm putting her in Madrigals. You have a good voice, and you're a solid singer,

Nickie. Certainly a joy to have in any group. But . . . Anne-Louise has had voice lessons for years."

Nicoletta came close to strangling herself with the rope of her own yellow hair. Madrigals? The chorus into which she had poured her life? The chorus that toured the state, whose concerts were standing room only? The sixteen who were best friends? Who partied and car-pooled and studied together as well as sang?

"I'm sorry," said Ms. Quincy. She looked sorry, too. She looked, to use an old and stupid phrase, as if this hurt her more than it hurt Nicoletta. "Since each part is limited to four singers, I cannot have both of you. Anne-Louise will take your place."

The wind of January crept through the one-inch window opening and iced her life. How could she could go on with high school if she were dropped from Madrigals? She had no activity but singing. Her only friends were in Madrigals.

I'll be alone, thought Nicoletta.

A flotilla of lonely places appeared in her mind: cafeteria, bus, hallway, student center.

Her body humiliated her. She became a prickly mass of perspiration: Sweaty hands, lumpy throat, tearful eyes. "Doesn't it count," she said desperately, trying to marshall intelligent arguments, "that I have never missed a rehearsal? I've never been late? I've been in charge of refreshments? I'm the one who finds ushers for the concerts and the one who checks the spelling in the programs?"

"And we'd love to have you keep doing that," said Ms. Quincy. Her smile opened again like a zipper separating her face halves.

For two years Nicoletta had idolized Ms. Quincy. Now an ugly puff of hatred filled her heart instead. "I'm not good enough to sing with you," she cried out, "but you'd love to have me do the secretarial work? I'm sure Anne-Louise has had lessons in that, too. Thanks for nothing, Ms. Quincy!"

Nicoletta ran out of the music room before she broke down into sobbing and had the ultimate humiliation of being comforted by the very woman who was kicking her out. There had been no witnesses yet, but in a few minutes everybody she cared about would know. She, Nicoletta, was not good enough anymore. The standards had been raised.

Nicoletta was just another ordinary soprano.

Nicoletta was out.

There was a narrow turn of hall between the music rooms and the lobby. Nicoletta stood in the dark silence of that space, trying to control her emotions. She could hear familiar laughter — Madrigal friends coming to read the list of the chosen. She thought suddenly of her costume: the lovely crimson gown with the tight waist and the white lace high at the throat, the tiny crown that sat in her yellow hair. People said that the medieval look suited her, that she was beautiful in red. And beautiful she always felt, spun gold, with an angel's voice.

Ms. Quincy followed her into the safety zone of the dark little hall. "Go down to Guidance, now, Nickie," she said in a teachery voice. "Sign up for something else in the Madrigal time slot."

I'll sign up for Bomb-Making, thought Nicoletta. Or Arson.

She did not look at Ms. Quincy again. She walked in the opposite direction from the known voices, taking the long way around the school to Guidance. In this immense high school, with its student body of over two thousand, she was among strangers. You had to find your place in such a vast school, and her place had been Madrigals. With whom would she stand now? With whom would she laugh and eat and gossip?

Of course in the Guidance office they pretended to be busy and Nicoletta had to sit forty minutes until they could fit her in. The chair was orange plastic, hideous and cold, the same color as the repulsive orange kitchen counters in Nicoletta's repulsive new house.

Her parents had gotten in too deep financially. Last autumn, amid tears and recrimination, the Storms family had had to sell the wonderful huge house on Fairest Hill. Oh, how Nicoletta had loved that house! Immense rooms, expanses of windows, layers of decks, acres of closets! She and her mother had poured themselves into decorating it, occupying every shopping hour with the joys of wallpaper, curtains, and accessories.

Now they were in a tiny ranch with ugly, crowded rooms, and Nicoletta was sharing a bedroom with her eleven-year-old sister, Jamie.

In their old house, Jamie had had her own bedroom and bath; Jamie had had three closets just for herself; Jamie had had her own television and *two* extra beds, so she could have sleepovers every weekend.

The ranch house had only two bedrooms, so now Jamie slept exactly six feet from Nicoletta. The seventy-two most annoying inches in the world. Nicoletta had actually liked her sister when they lived in the big house. Now the girls could do nothing except bicker, bait, and fight.

Fairest Hill.

Nicoletta always thought the name came from the fairy tale of Snow White: *Mirror, mirror, on the wall, who is the fairest of them all?*

And in those pretty woods, on top of that gentle sloping hill in that lovely house, she, Nicoletta, had been the fairest of them all.

Now she could not even sing soprano.

It was difficult to know who made her maddest — her parents, for poor planning; the economy, for making it worse; Ms. Quincy, for being rotten, mean, and cruel; or Anne-Louise, for moving here.

Within a few minutes, however, it was the guidance counselor making her maddest. "Let's see," said Mr. Parsons. "The available half-year classes, Nicoletta, are Art Appreciation, Study Skills, Current Events, and Oceanography." He skimmed through her academic files. "I certainly recommend Study Skills," he said severely.

She hated him. I'm not taking Current Events, she thought, because I sit through television news every night from five to seven as it is. I'm not taking Oceanography because deep water is the scariest thing on earth. I'm not taking Study Skills just because he thinks I should. Which leaves Art Appreciation. Art for the nonartistic. Art for the pathetic and left-behind.

"I'm signing you up for Study Skills," said Mr. Parsons.

"No. Art Appreciation."

"If you insist," said Mr. Parsons.

She insisted.

That night, as a break in the fighting with Jamie, Nicoletta received three phone calls from other Madrigal singers.

Rachel, her sidekick, the other first soprano next to whom she had stood for two lovely years was crying. "This is so awful!" she sobbed. "Doesn't Ms. Quincy understand friendship? Or loyalty? Or anything?"

Cathy, an alto so low she sometimes sang tenor, was furious. "I'm in favor of boycotting Madrigals," said Cathy. "That will teach Ms. Quincy a thing or two."

Christo, the lowest bass, and handsomest boy, also phoned.

Everybody, at one time or another, had had a crush on Christopher Hannon. Christopher had grown earlier than most boys: At fifteen he had looked twenty, and now at seventeen he looked twenty-five. He was broad-shouldered and tall and could have grown a beard to his chest had he wanted to. Nicoletta was always surprised that she and Christo were the exact same age.

"Nickie," said Christo, "this is terrible. We've all argued with Ms. Quincy. She's sick, that's what I say. Demented."

Nicoletta felt marginally better. At least her friends had stood by her and perhaps would get Ms. Quincy to change her mind and dump this horrible Anne-Louise.

"I have to take Art Appreciation instead," she said glumly.

Christo moaned. "Duds," he told her.

"I know."

"Be brave. We'll rescue you. This Anne-Louise cannot possibly sing like you, Nickie."

She entered the Art Appreciation room the following day feeling quite removed from the pathetic specimens supposed to be her classmates. Christo, Cathy, Rachel, and her other friends would turn this nightmare around. In a day or so she'd be back rehearsing like always, with a cowed and apologetic Ms. Quincy.

Without interest, Nicoletta took her new text and its companion workbook and sat where she was told, in the center of the room.

A quick survey of the other students told her she had laid eyes on none of these kids before. It was not a large class, perhaps twenty, half boys, which surprised her a little. Did they really want to appreciate art, or were they, too, refusing to take Study Skills?

The teacher, a Mr. Marisson, of whom she had never even heard let alone met, showed slides. Nicoletta prepared to go to sleep, which was her usual response to slides.

But as the room went dark, and the kids around her became shadows of themselves, her eye was caught not by the van Gogh or the Monet painting on the screen but by the profile of the boy in front of her, one row to her left.

He had the most mobile face she had ever seen. Even in the dusk of the quiet classroom, she could see him shift his jaw, lower and lift his eyes, tighten and relax his lips. Several times he lifted a hand to touch his cheek, and he touched it in a most peculiar fashion — as if he were exploring it. As if it belonged to somebody else, or as if he had not known, until this very second, that he even had a cheek.

She was so fascinated she could hardly wait for the slide show to end.

"Well, that's the end of today's lecture," said Mr. Marisson, flipping the lights back on.

The boy remained strangely dark. It was as if he cast his own shadow in his own space. His eyelashes seemed to shade his cheeks, and his cheeks seemed full of hollows. His hair was thick and fell onto his face, sheltering him from stares.

Nicoletta, who had never had an art-type thought in her life, wanted to paint him.

How weird! she thought. Maybe Mr. Marisson put him in the class just to inspire us. Perhaps this is how van Gogh and Monet got started, emotionally moved by a stranger's beautiful profile.

Never had the word *stranger* seemed so apt. There was something genuinely strange about the boy. Essentially different. But what was it?

Nicoletta could not see straight into his eyes. He kept them lowered. Not as if he were shy but as if he had other things to look at than his surroundings.

Class ended.

People stood.

Nicoletta watched the boy. He did not look her way nor anybody else's. He did not seem aware of anyone. He left the room with a lightness of step that did not fit his body: His body was more like Christo's, yet his walk might have been a dancer's.

Nicoletta rarely initiated friendships. She tended to let friendship come to her, and it always had: through classmates or seatmates, through group lessons or neighbors. But she wanted to look into this boy's eyes, and unless she spoke to him she would not have the privilege.

Privilege? she thought. What a strange word to use! What do I mean by that? "Hi," she said to his departing back. "I'm Nicoletta."

The boy did not register her voice. He did not turn. He might have been deaf. Perhaps he was deaf. Perhaps that was his mystery; his closure from the rest. Perhaps he really was hidden away inside his silent mind.

She stopped walking but he did not.

In a few moments he vanished from sight, blending with crowds and corridors.

After school, Nicoletta saw Christo, Cathy, Rachel, and several of the others. She ran up to them. They would have spoken to Ms. Quincy again. She could hardly wait for their report.

"Hey, Nickie," said Christo. He rubbed her shoulders and kissed her hair. Affection came easily to Christo. He distributed it to all the girls and they in turn were never without a smile or a kiss for him. But that was all there was. Christo never offered more, and never took more.

Nor did he say a word about the first Madrigal rehearsal in which Anne-Louise, and not Nicoletta, sang soprano.

"So?" said Nicoletta teasingly, keeping her voice light. She was mostly talking to Rachel, her sidekick. Her fellow sufferer in soprano jokes. (Question: A hundred dollars is lying on the ground. Who takes it — the dumb soprano or the smart soprano? Answer: The dumb soprano, of course. There's no such thing as a smart soprano.)

Rachel looked uncomfortable.

Cathy looked embarrassed.

Even Christo, who was never nervous, looked nervous.

Finally Rachel made a confused gesture with her hands, like birds fluttering. Awkwardly, she mumbled, "Anne-Louise is really terrific, Nicoletta. She has the best voice of any of us. She is — well — she's —" Rachel seemed unable to think of what else Anne-Louise might be.

"She's Olympic material," said Christo.

Rachel managed giggles. "There's no soprano division in the Olympics, Christo."

But it was very clear. Anne-Louise was miles better than Nicoletta. Nicoletta was not going to get back in. She was not going to be a Madrigal again. Her friends had put no arguments before Ms. Quincy.

"But come with us to Keyboard, Nickie," said Rachel quickly. "There's so much to talk about. You have to tell us about Art Appreciation. I mean, is it wall-to-wall duds, or what?"

Keyboard was the city's only ice-cream parlor with a piano. Perhaps the world's only ice-cream parlor with a piano. For years and years, before Nicoletta was even born, the high school Madrigals had hung out there, singing whenever they felt like it. They sang current hits and ancient tunes, they sang Christmas carols and kindergarten rounds, they sang rock or country or sixteenth-century love songs. In between, they had sundaes, milk shakes, or Cokes, and stuck quarters in the old-fashioned jukebox with its glittering lights and dated music.

Okay, thought Nicoletta, trying to breathe, trying to accept the slap in the face of Anne-Louise's superiority. We're still friends, I can still —

Anne-Louise joined the group.

She was an ordinary-looking girl, with dull brown hair and small brown eyes. But the other singers did not look at her as if *they* saw anything ordinary. They were full of admiration.

She'll wear my crimson gown, thought Nicoletta. She'll put my sparkling crown in her plain hair. She'll sing my part.

Christo rubbed Anne-Louise's shoulders and kissed her hair exactly as he had Nicoletta's. Anne-Louise bit her lip with embarrassment and pleasure, and said, "Are you sure you want me along?"

"Of course we do!" the rest chorused. "You're a Madrigal now."

And I'm not, thought Nicoletta.

Rachel and Cathy protested, but Nicoletta did not go to Keyboard with them. She claimed she had to help her mother at home. They knew it was a lie, but it certainly made things easier for everybody. With visible gratitude, the new arrangement of Madrigals left in their new lineup.

Nicoletta headed for the school bus, which she rarely took. Christo had a van and usually ferried Madrigals wherever he went. But she did not get on the bus after all.

Walking purposefully down the road, knowing his destination, was the dark and silent boy from Art Appreciation.

The high school was not located for walking home. It had been built a decade ago in a rural area, so that it could be wrapped in playing fields of the most impressive kind. No student lived within walking distance. Yellow buses awaiting their loads snaked around two roads, slowly filling with kids from every corner of the city.

Yet the boy walked.

And Nicoletta, because she was lost, followed him.

Chapter 2

The first two blocks of following the boy meant nothing; anybody could reasonably walk down the wide cement.

But then the boy turned, and strode down a side street, stepping on every frozen puddle and cracking its ice. DEAD END said the sign at the top of the street. Nicoletta had never even noticed the street. The boy surely knew everybody on his street, and he would also know that she did not live there, had no business walking there. That she had no destination at the DEAD END.

At no other moment in her life would she have continued. Nicoletta was conventional. She was comfortable with social rules and did not break them, nor care to be around people who did.

But all the rules of her life had been broken that day. She had lost her circle, her pleasure. She had been found lacking, and not only that, she had been replaced by someone better.

The sick humiliation in her heart was so painful that she found herself distanced from the world. The rules were hard to remember and not meaningful when she did remember them. She was facing a terrible empty time in which the group she loved forgot her. If she filled the time by going home, she'd have a crabby sister, a small house, and a nervous mother. She'd have television reruns played too loud, a fattening snack she didn't need, and homework she couldn't face.

So Nicoletta crossed the road, and followed the boy down the little lane.

She had his attention now. An odd, keep-your-back-turned attention. He didn't look around at her. At one point he paused, and stood very still. She matched him. He walked on; she walked on. He walked faster for a while; she did, too. Then he slowed down. So did Nicoletta.

Her head and mind felt light and airy. She felt as if she might faint, or else fly away.

She was mesmerized by the task of making her feet land exactly when his did. He had long strides. She could not possibly cover as much ground. She was carrying her books, hugging them in her arms, and they grew heavy. She hardly noticed. Her head was swimming and there was nothing in the universe but the rhythm of their walking.

The houses ended.

The road narrowed.

The trees that had neatly stayed inside hedges and yards now arched over the street. Latticed, bare branches fenced off the sky. In summer this would be a green tunnel. In winter it was grim and mean.

The asphalt ended. The road became dirt ruts.

Nicoletta would have said there were no dirt roads in the entire state, let alone this city. Where could the boy be going?

Trees grew as closely as fence posts. Prickly vines wrapped the edge of the woods as viciously as concertina wire. Stone walls threaded through the naked woods, the lost farms of early America. For a moment, she felt their souls: the once-breathing farmers, the vanished field hands, the dead wives, and buried children.

At the end of the dirt lane, an immense boulder loomed like a huge altar from some old-world circle of stones.

Nicoletta had the strangest sensation that the stone greeted the boy. That the stone, not the boy, changed expression. They knew each other.

Nicoletta kept coming.

Some boys would have readied for combat. They would have slipped into the athletic stance used for obstructing or catching. This boy was simply there.

Very, very slowly he turned to see whose feet had been matching his, what person had trespassed on his road. Dark motionless eyes, falling heavy hair, smooth quiet features. Not a word. Not a gesture.

People often asked Nicoletta if her shining gold hair was really hers. They often asked her if her vivid green eyes were really hers. The general assumption was that extremely blonde hair and very green eyes must be the result of dye and contact lenses. She hated being asked if parts of her body were really hers.

And yet she wanted to ask this boy — *Is that really you?* There was something so different about him. As if he wore a mask to be pulled off.

There were about twenty paces between them. Neither he nor she attempted to narrow the distance.

"Hi," she said at last. She struggled for a smile, but fear gave her a twitch instead.

He did not ask her what she was doing, nor where she was going.

"I followed you," she said finally.

He nodded.

A flush of shame rose up on her face. She was a fool. She was utterly pathetic. "It was just something to do," she offered him.

Still his face did not move.

She struggled to find explanations for her ridiculous behavior. "I had a bad day. I lost all my friends. So — you were walking — and I walked, too — and here we are."

His face did not change.

"Where's your house?" she said desperately.

At last he spoke. But he did not tell her where his house was. He said softly, "You can't have lost *all* your friends." His voice was like butter: soft and golden. She loved his voice.

"No," she agreed. "Probably not. It just feels like it. It turns out I'm not as important as I thought."

He said, "I'll walk you back to the road while you tell me about it."

She told him about it.

He simply nodded. His expression never changed. It was neither friendly nor hostile, neither sorry for her nor annoyed with her. He was just there. She wondered what his mouth would look like smiling. What his mouth would feel like kissing.

Nicoletta talked.

He listened.

She poured out her feelings as if he were her psychiatric counselor and she was paying by the hour. She had to face this boy tomorrow, and every day for the rest of the school year! And yet here she was describing the workings of her heart and soul, as if he were a friend, as if he could be trusted.

It was horrifically cold. She had not worn clothing for a hike in the outdoors. She shifted her books, trying to wrap her cold hands inside one another.

The boy took off his long scarf, which was plain, thin black wool, with no fringe and no pattern. He wrapped it gently around her freezing ears, brought the ends down and tucked them around her icy fingers. The wool was warm with his heat. She wanted to have the scarf forever.

She had to know more about him. She wanted to see him with his family, standing in his yard. She wanted to see him in his car and in his kitchen. She wanted to see him wearing jeans and wearing bathing trunks.

"Will you be able to get home from here?" he asked instead. They were standing next to the bright yellow DEAD END sign. A few hundred yards ahead, traffic spun its endless circuit.

She could not let their time together end. In fact, standing with him, they did not seem to be in normal time; they were in some other time; a wide, spacious ancient time. "Were you just going for a hike or do you live down there?" Nicoletta said.

He regarded her steadily. "It's a shortcut," he said finally.

He's very, very rich, thought Nicoletta. He lives on an

immense estate by the ocean. Acres of farm and forest between us and his circular drive. Perhaps his mother is a famous movie star and they live under another name. She said, "I'm Nicoletta Storms."

"Nicoletta," he repeated. How softly he sounded each consonant. How romantic and European it sounded on his lips. Antique and lyrical. Not the way her classmates said it, getting the long name over with. Or switching without permission to Nickie.

"What's your name?" she said.

For a while she thought he would not tell her; that even giving out his name to a classmate was too much personal expression for him. Then he said, "Jethro."

"Jethro?" she repeated. "What an odd name! Are you named for an ancestor?"

He actually smiled. She was lifted up on that smile like a swallow on a gust of summer wind. His smile was beautiful; it was wonderful; it was buried treasure, and she, Nicoletta, had uncovered it.

Their city was one of the oldest on the East Coast. She had never previously met a native, but there had to be some. Perhaps Jethro was a descendant of the *Mayflower*. That was the kind of name they gave boys back then. Jethro, Truth, Ephraim.

"Ancestors," he agreed. The smile slowly closed, leaving behind only a sweet friendliness.

"How did you like Art Appreciation?" she said. She did not want to stop talking. "Do you know a lot about art or were the slides new to you?"

"Everything is new to me," the boy answered, and gave away the first tiny clue. Slightly, he emphasized *everything*. As if not just art were new — but everything. The world.

"Let's have lunch together tomorrow," she said.

He stared at her, eyes and mouth flaring in astonishment. And blushed. "Lunch," repeated Jethro, as if unfamiliar with it.

"Meet me in the cafeteria?" said Nicoletta. She wanted to kiss him. Rachel would have. Rachel would have stood on her tiptoes, leaned forward, and kissed long and slow, even the first time. Rachel felt kissing was the world's best hallway activity. Teachers were always telling Rachel to chill out.

Instead the boy touched her face with his fingertips.

And Nicoletta, indeed, chilled.

It was not the hand of a human.

Chapter 3

"Of course he's a human," said her sister Jamie. Jamie was absolutely disgusted with the end of the story. "Nick, you blew it. I cannot believe you turned around and ran!" Jamie was always convinced that she would handle any situation whatsoever a hundred times better than her older sister. Here was yet more proof.

Nicoletta hated defending herself to a child of eleven. But it happened constantly. There was no decision Nicoletta made, including, of course, being born, which met with her sister's approval. "I was scared."

Jamie flung up her hands in exasperation. "If you had enough guts to follow him into the dark and dank and dreary woods . . . "

"They weren't dark or dank or dreary. The sun was shining. There was still snow on the ground in the forest. It was more silver than dark."

"My *point*," said Jamie, with the immense disgust of younger sisters who were going to get things *right* when *they* started dating, "is that he started talking to you! Flirting with you. You even invited him to meet you for lunch. Running away from him was stupid, stupid, stupid, stupid, stupid."

Their father said, "Jamie. Please. You are entitled to your opinion, but saying it once is enough."

The worst thing about this minihouse was the way they had to function in each other's laps. There was no privacy. All conversations and confrontations became family property. Nicoletta thought of their lovely house on Fairest Hill, and how she should have had an entire suite in which to be alone and consider her — well, Jamie was right — her stupidity.

"Besides," said their mother, "of course the boy's hands were cold. You'd been in the woods for hours and he didn't have any gloves on and it's January." Mother sniffed. She did not like fantasy, and when the girls were quite small, and liked to make things up, their mother put a stop to it in a hurry. "Not human," repeated Mrs. Storms irritably. "Really, Nicoletta."

Nicoletta had told them about Jethro because it was easier than telling them about Madrigals. She could not bring herself to say that part out loud. *I'm not in it anymore. You won't go to concerts anymore. You won't have to iron my beautiful medieval gown ever again. Somebody else — somebody named Anne-Louise — gets to dress up and sing like an angel and hear the applause from now on.*

"Speaking as the only man in this family, . . . " said Nicoletta's father. He looked long and carefully at his hands, as if reading the backs instead of the palms. "I want to say that if some girl followed me home, walked after me for miles through the woods, and told me she had a crush on me, and then I walked her all the way back to the main road, I would certainly have been hoping for a kiss. And if instead of throwing her arms around me, the girl *fled* . . . well, Nickie, I would feel I'd done something incredibly stupid or had turned out to be repulsive close up. I'd want to change schools in the morning. I'd never want to have to face that girl again."

Wonderful, thought Nicoletta, wanting to weep. Now I'll never see him again.

She struggled with tears. In the other house, she could have wept alone. In this one, she had witnesses. The small-minded part of her tried to hold her parents responsible, and hate them instead of herself, for being a complete dummy and running from Jethro.

She remembered the cold touch of his hands. I don't care what

Mother says, thought Nicoletta. Jethro's hands were not normal. He scared me. There really was something strange about him. Something terribly wrong, something not quite of this world. I felt it through his skin. I can still feel it. Even though I have washed my hands, I can still feel it.

"So," said her father, his voice changing texture, becoming rich and teasing, "what'll we do tonight, Nickie? Want me to play my fiddle?"

Jamie got right into it. Nothing brought her more satisfaction than annoying her big sister. "Or we could slice up a turnip," Jamie agreed. "That would be fun."

Right up until high school, Nicoletta had loved the *Little House* books. How unfair that she had to live now where the family could go to McDonald's if they got hungry, check out a video if they got bored, and turn the thermostat up if they got chilled. A younger Nicoletta had prayed every night to fall through a time warp and arrive on the banks of Plum Creek with Mary and Laura. She wanted a covered wagon and a sod house and, of course, she wanted to meet Almanzo and marry him. In middle school, Nicoletta had decided to learn everything Laura had to learn; quilting, pie making, knitting, stomping on hay. Nicoletta's mother, who hated needlework and bought frozen pies, could not stand it. "You live in the twentieth century and that's that. Ma Ingalls," Nicoletta's mother said, "would have been thrilled to live like you. Warm in winter, snow never coming through the cracks, fresh fruit out of season."

When she was Jamie's age, Nicoletta had made her fatal error. "Daddy never gets out his fiddle and sings songs for me when it's snowing outside," she'd said.

Her father laughed for years. He was always making fiddle jokes.

The second fatal error came shortly after, when Nicoletta tried eating raw sliced turnip because the Ingalls considered it a snack. Nicoletta's mother had never in her life even bought a turnip because, she said, "Even the word gives me indigestion."

Only last Christmas, Nicoletta's stocking had included a raw turnip and a paring knife. "Instead of potato chips," said the card. "Love from Santa on the Prairie." It was Jamie's handwriting.

Nicoletta's *Little House* obsession ended with Madrigals: The singing, the companionship of a wonderful set of boys and girls from tenth to twelfth grade, the challenge of memorizing the difficult music filled Nicoletta the way her pioneer fantasies once had.

She thought of her life as divided by these two: the *Little House* daydream years and the Madrigal reality years.

And now Madrigals were over.

She was not a Madrigal singer. She was just another soprano, good enough only for the ordinary non-audition chorus.

Unwillingly, Nicoletta looked at the photograph of herself on the mantel. Every few years these photos were replaced, when the old one began to seem dated and ridiculous. Nicoletta's portrait had been taken only last fall, and she stood slim and beautiful in her long satin skirt, crimson fabric cascading from her narrow waist, white lace like sea froth around her slender throat. Her yellow hair had just been permed, and twisted like ribbons down to her shoulders. In her hair glittered a thread of jewels. She seemed like a princess from another age, another continent, dressed as a Nicoletta should be dressed.

Now she hated the portrait. People would come to the house — Rachel, Cathy, Christo — and there it would sit, pretending nothing had changed.

I don't want this life! thought Nicoletta, her throat filling with a detestable lump. Who needs high school? It hurts too much. I don't measure up. I'm not musical and I'm a jerk who runs away from boys and makes them wish they attended school in another town. I don't care what my mother says. Laura Ingalls had it good. Blizzards, starvation, three-hundred-mile hikes, scary badgers, and flooding creeks.

She thought of Jethro. His profile. His odd, silent darkness. His quiet listening while she poured out her pain.

"I got kicked out of Madrigals," Nicoletta said abruptly. "Ms. Quincy tried everybody out again, and a new girl named Anne-Louise is better than I am, so I'm out and she's in and I don't want to talk about it."

Chapter 4

She did not dream of Madrigals.

She dreamed of Jethro.

When she awoke much earlier than usual it was quickly and cleanly, with none of the usual muddleheaded confusion of morning. She arose swiftly and dressed without worry.

That in itself amazed Nicoletta. Choosing clothing normally took her half an hour the night before, and then in the morning half an hour to decide that last night's choice would not do, and yet another half hour to find clothing that would fit the day after all. It was amazing how an outfit that had been absolutely the right choice for last Thursday was never the right choice for the following Thursday.

She did not brush her hair; Nicoletta's permed curls were too tight for a brush to manage. She ran her fingers through it, fluffing and smoothing at the same time. She put on a simple black turtleneck, a plain silver necklace, and narrow dangling silver earrings. She wore a skirt she rarely touched: It had two layers, a tight black sheath covered by a swirl of filmy black gauze. The skirt was dressy, but the plain turtleneck brought it down to school level.

She did not look romantic. She looked as if she were in mourning. For Madrigals? Or for the boy she would not meet for lunch after all?

Jethro.

Her school bus did not pass the strange little country lane she had never before noticed. When she got off the bus, she looked for him, but she had never seen him wandering around the school before, and she did not see him now. In the halls, her eyes scanned the taller people, searching for him, both aching and scared that she would actually spot him.

First-period history, she covered a page in her notebook with the name Jethro. It looked historical. Where did it come from? It sounded Biblical. Who was Jethro and what had he done? She wrote it in script, in plain print, in decorated print, in open block letters. She wrote it backhand and she wrote it billboard style, enclosed in frames.

Second-period English, the other person in her life with an O name sat beside her. Christo. "Hi, Nick," he said cheerfully.

She had always admired Christopher's endless cheer. It seemed an admirable way to face life: ever up, ever smiling, ever optimistic and happy.

Now it seemed shallow. Annoying.

Am I comparing him to Jethro or am I angry with him for still being in Madrigals, for making peace in a single day with the fact that I have been replaced? "Hi, Christo," she said. He had not even noticed how she skipped a beat before answering him.

The teacher had visited England last year and, sad to say, taken along his camera and several million rolls of film. Today he had yet more slides of where famous English authors had lived and gone to college and gardened. It was the gardening that most amazed Nicoletta. Who could possibly care what flowers bloomed in the gardens that no longer belonged to the famous — and now dead — authors? In fact, who could possibly have cared back when the famous authors were alive?

Nicoletta sat quietly while the teacher bustled — fixing his slides, flipping switches, lowering screens, focusing.

Christo murmured in her ear. "Nicoletta?"

His use of her whole name startled her. She turned to look at him, but his face was so close to her they touched cheeks instead.

"There's a dance Friday," whispered Christo. "I know it's late to be asking, but would you go with me?"

Nicoletta was stunned. Christo? Who showed affection to everybody equally? Christo, who never appeared to notice whether he was patting the shoulder of Nicoletta or Rachel or Cathy, or — now — Anne-Louise? Christo, for whom girls seemed to be just one generic collection of the opposite sex?

Christo. Who was certainly the best-looking and most-yearned-for boy in school.

She absolutely knew for a fact that Christo had never had a date.

One of the things Madrigals spared you was dating. You had your crowd; you had your portable group. You had people with whom to laugh and share pizza. Rarely did any of them pair up, either within or without the group.

On the big white screen at the front of the class, appeared a dazzling slide from inside a cathedral. Great gray stones held up a gleaming and terrifying stained glass window. The glass people were in primary colors: scarlet arms, blue gowns, golden heads. If Jethro were hers, she, too, would be as vivid as that: Together they would blind the eye.

If I go to a dance with Christo, how can Jethro ask me out? Nicoletta thought. *I want to be with Jethro.*

Christo's hand covered hers. She dropped her eyes, and then her whole head, staring down at his hand. His hand was afraid. She could feel uncertainty in the way he touched her. Christo, who touched everybody without ever thinking of it, or knowing he was doing it, was fearful of touch.

The slide changed and a gargoyle appeared on the screen. Carved stone. An unknowable man-creature stared out from oak leaves that were both his hair and his beard, which grew into him and, at the same time, grew out of him. *It's Jethro*, thought Nicoletta.

"That sounds wonderful," she murmured, mostly to Christo's hand. "I'd love to go. What dance is it?"

"Fund-raiser," said Christo. "It'll be at Top o' the Town."

A famous restaurant where in years past her father had taken her mother for special occasions, like Valentine's Day or their anniversary. Nicoletta had never been there. It was not a place that people wasted on children.

I'm not a child, thought Nicoletta. I'm a young woman, and Christo knows it. Christo wants me. He doesn't want any of the others. Not Rachel or Cathy. And not this Anne-Louise. But me.

She looked nervously at Christo in the half-dark of the class-room. He was truly nervous. His easy smile puckered in and out. He had needed the dark to do this; he had chosen a place where they could not possibly continue the conversation or else people would hear, and because lights would come on in a moment, and the teacher would begin his lecture.

She was amazed at the discovery that Christo was afraid of anything at all, let alone her.

But when she looked at him, she still saw Jethro.

Who is Jethro? thought Nicoletta, that he has consumed me. Who am I, that I am letting it happen? Mother is right; daydreaming and fantasy are silly and only lead to silly choices. I'll stop right now.

Then came chemistry.

Then came French.

Then came lunch.

And Jethro was there.

He had come. He was waiting. He did mean to meet her.

She saw him from far across the room. Her whole body shivered, and she did not understand him the way she had to her surprise understood Christo. She could not imagine who that person Jethro was. He was as hidden to her as the gargoyle in its mask and crown of oak leaves.

She could not smile. There was something frightening about

this boy who also did not smile, but who stared at her in his dark and closed way. She walked toward him, and he moved toward her, exactly as they had in the lane, surrounded by thorns and vines and boulders that spoke.

They were only a table's distance apart when Christo caught Nicoletta's arm.

Nicoletta could not have been more astonished if an army had stopped her. She had thought her coming together with Jethro was inevitable, was destined, was a part of the history of the world before it had even happened. And yet Christo, who touched anything and whose touch meant nothing, had stopped it from happening.

"I'm over here, Nickie," Christo said eagerly. "You didn't see me."

She looked up at Christo.

She looked back at Jethro.

Jethro had already turned. There was no face at all, let alone the smile she wanted. There was only a back. A man's broad back, unbent, uncaring. Departing.

Jethro! her heart cried after him.

But this time she did not follow him. She sat with Christo, and within moments everybody that Christo and Nicoletta knew had learned that Christo had arranged his first date ever. With Nicoletta.

The attention was better even than Madrigals. Better even than solos or applause.

And she didn't want it.

She wanted Jethro.

Chapter 5

After lunch, Jethro did not come to Art Appreciation.

Nicoletta stared, stunned, at his vacant seat.

"Is Jethro absent?" asked the teacher.

"He was here at lunch," said Nicoletta. Her lips were numb.

"He's cutting," said Mr. Marisson disapprovingly. He pressed down hard with his pencil in the attendance book.

He cut class because I cut him, thought Nicoletta. Oh Jethro! I was going to explain it to you — I was going to —

But what was there to explain? She had behaved terribly. She had arranged to meet Jethro in the cafeteria. He had done so and then what had she done? Walked off with another boy.

His empty seat mesmerized her as much as the occupied seat had.

His name filled her head and her heart, as if it really were her heartbeat: *Jeth-ro. Jeth-ro.*

Like a nursery rhyme her head screamed Jeth-ro, Jeth-ro. And of course, after school up came Chris-to, Chris-to, smiling and eager and offering her a ride home.

It was by car that romance was established. When a boy gave you rides, or you gave him rides, it meant either you lived next door and had no choice, or you were seeing each other. If you didn't want the school to make that interpretation, you had to fill your car with extras. Christo had always filled his van with extras.

But now he stood alone. He must have told them already that they had to find another way home. For the usual van crowd was not there and the much-complimented Anne-Louise was not in evidence.

But Nicoletta could not go home with Christo.

She had to find Jethro. She had to go back down that lane, follow that shortcut he took to his house, and locate him.

How many lies it took to make Christo go on without her! How awful each one of them was. Because, of course, he had to believe her lies, or else know that she was dumping him. Know that she did not want to be alone with him and go for a ride with him.

When you're in love, the possibility that the object of your love has better things to do is the worst of all scenes.

So Christo just smiled uncertainly and said at last, "I'll call you tonight."

"Great," said Nicoletta, smiling, as if it were great.

They did not touch. For Christo it was the not-touching of a crush; physical desire so intense it pulled him back instead of rushing him on. For Nicoletta, it was a heart that lay elsewhere.

But Christo did not know.

Love rarely does.

Nicoletta waited inside the lobby until she saw Christo's van disappear.

And then she gathered her books and her belongings and ran out the school doors, up the road, across the street, and down the quiet lane.

There was no Jethro ahead of her. Of course not. He had left at noon, abandoning his lunch and his classes. Because of her.

She ran, and was quickly out of breath.

Today there was no sun. The last of the snow had vanished into the brown earth. The words Jamie had used were now, horribly, the right ones. These woods were dank and dark.

At the end of the lane she saw the boulder, big and scarred and motionless. Of course it's motionless, she said to herself, it's a rock. They're always motionless.

And yet the huge stone sat there as if it had just returned from some dreadful errand.

The stone waited for her.

It's a rock, she said to herself. Put there by a glacier. That's all it is.

She might have come to the end of the world instead of the end of a little dirt road. The sky lay like an unfriendly blanket over a woods that was silent as tombs.

She clung to her books as if to a shield. As if spears might come from behind that great gray stone and pierce her body. It took all her courage to edge around the boulder.

On the other side of the rock was a footpath of remarkable straightness. In a part of the world that was all ups and downs, crevices and hills, rocky cliffs and hidden dells, here was an utterly flat stretch of land and a trail from a geometry test: The quickest way between two points is a straight line.

What are the two points? thought Nicoletta. Is his house at the other end?

Jethro, she thought. I'm coming. Where are you? What will I say to you when I find you? Why am I looking?

She walked down the trail.

When she looked back over her shoulder, the boulder was watching her.

She whimpered, and picked up speed, running again, trying to turn a corner, so the stone could not see her. But there were no corners and no matter how far she ran, the stone was still there.

The silence was complete.

She could hear nothing of the twentieth century. No motors, no turnpikes. No doors slamming, no engines revving, no planes soaring.

The only sounds were her own sounds, trespassing in this dark and ugly place.

Abruptly the trail descended. She heaved a sigh of relief as mounded earth blocked her from the terrible boulder. She wondered where she would come out, and if perhaps she could return to her own home from another direction. She did not want to go back on that path.

The trees ended, and the vines ceased crawling.

The ground was clear now, and the path became a narrow trail on top of a man-made earthen embankment. Suddenly there were lakes on each side of her, deep, black, soundless lakes with a thin, crackled layer of ice. She could go neither left nor right. Not once had there been a choice, a turning place, a fork in the road. Now she could not even blunder off into the meadow or the forest, because the trail was the only place to put a foot.

The trail ended.

She could not believe it.

It had stopped. Stopped dead. It simply did not go on.

In front of her was a rock face, a hundred feet high. Behind her lay the narrow path and the twin lakes.

She was being watched. She could feel eyes everywhere, assessing her, wondering what she would do next. They were not friendly eyes.

She wanted to scream Jethro's name, but even drawing a breath seemed like a hostile act in this isolated corner. What would a shout do? What horrible creatures would appear if she screamed?

She put a hand out so she could rest against the rock face, and her hand went right through the rock.

She yanked her hand back to the safety of her schoolbook clasp. Tears of terror wet her cheeks. Mommy, she thought. Daddy. Jamie. I want to go home. I don't want to be here.

It was a cave.

It was so black, so narrowly cut into the cliff, that at first she had not seen it. It was nothing natural. It had been chipped by some ancient tool. The opening was a perfect rectangle. She did not even have to duck her head walking in.

The wonder was that she did walk in.

Even as she was doing it, she was astonished at herself. She — a girl who hated the dark, or being alone in the dark, or even thinking of the dark — was voluntarily entering an unknown cave.

Was she so terrorized that terror had become an anesthetic, flattening her thoughts? Or was she finally getting a grip on her ridiculous, fabricated fears and handling them like an adult?

She stepped into the cave.

She had expected absolute black darkness, especially with her own body blocking whatever weak sunlight might penetrate at this angle, but the cave walls themselves seemed to emanate light. They were smooth and polished like marble. She slid a bare hand over them and the texture was rich and satisfying. The cave was not damp or batlike. It seemed more like an entrance to a magnificent home, where she would find beautiful tapestries and perhaps a unicorn.

She followed a shaft of light. Even when the cave turned and the opening to the world behind her disappeared. Even when the cave went down and she had to touch the wall for support.

Part of her knew better.

Part of her was screaming, *Stop this! Get out! Go home! Think!*

But more of her was drawn on, as all humans are drawn to danger: the wild and impossible excitement of the unknown and the unthinkable.

She did not know how far she went into the cave. She did not know how many minutes she spent moving in, deeper in, farther from the only opening she knew.

She paused for breath, and in that moment the cave changed personality. Gone was the elegant marble. In a fraction of a second, the walls had turned to dripping horrors.

Holes and gaping openings loomed like death traps.

Whistling sounds and flying creatures filled her ears and her hair.

She whirled to run out, but the cave went dark.

Completely, entirely dark.

Her scream filled the cave, echoing off the many walls, pouring out the holes like some burning torch.

"Jethro!" she screamed. "Jethro!"

She touched a wall and it was wet with slime. She fell to her knees, scraping them on something, and then . . . the something moved beneath her.

She was not falling. The earth was lifting, arranging itself against her, attaching itself to her. She actually tried to fall. Anything to free herself from the surface of the underworld that clung to her, sucking like the legs of starfish.

"Jethro!" she screamed again.

Tentacles of slime and dripping stone wrapped themselves around her body.

I will die here. Nobody will know. Who could ever find me here? Nobody has been in this cave in a hundred years. This is some leftover mine from olden days. Abandoned. Forgotten.

And Jethro — he could live anywhere. What on earth had made her think that the walk through the woods necessarily led to Jethro's house? What on earth had made her think that she would find Jethro by following a path that led only to a cave?

Nothing on earth, she thought. Something in hell. This is an opening to some other, terrible world.

The creatures of that other world were surfacing, and surrounding her, dragging her down with them.

"Jethro!" she screamed again, knowing that there were no creatures, there was only a mine shaft; she must stay calm, she must find her own way out. She must stop fantasizing. She must be capable.

She tried to remember the calming techniques that Ms. Quincy used before Madrigal concerts. Breathe deeply over four counts. Shake your fingertips. Roll your head gently in circles.

It turned out that you had to be pretty calm to start with in order to attempt calming techniques. Screams continued to pour from her mouth, as if somebody else occupied her.

I'm the only one here, Nicoletta told herself. I must stop screaming. This is how people die in the wilderness. They panic. I must not panic. I am the only one here and —

She was wrong.

She was not the only one there.

The cave filled with movement and smell and she was picked up, actually held in the air, by whatever else was in the cave with her.

A creature from that other, lower, darker, world.

Its skin rasped against hers like saw grass. Its stink was unbreathable. Its hair was dead leaves, crisping against each other and breaking off in her face. Warts of sand covered it, and the sand actually came off on her, as if the creature were half made out of the cave itself.

She could not see any of the thing, only feel and smell it.

It was holding her, as if in an embrace.

Would it consume her? Did it have a mouth and jaws?

Would it carry her down to wherever it lay?

Would it line its nest with her, or feed her to its young?

She was no longer screaming. Its terrible stench took too much from her lungs; she could not find the breath to scream, only to gag.

And then it carried her up — not down.

Out — not in.

And spoke.

English.

Human English.

"Never come back," it said, its voice as deep and dark as the cave itself.

She actually laughed, hysteria crawling out of her as the screams had moments before. "I won't," she said. I'm having a conversation with a monster, she thought.

"It isn't safe," it said.

"I could tell."

The walls became smooth and they glowed. The beautiful patterns of the shiny entrance surrounded them.

She looked at what held her and screamed again in horror. She had never had such a nightmare, never been caught in such a hideously vivid dream. The features of the thing were humanoid, but the flesh dripped, like cave walls.

Old sayings came true: There was literally light at the end of the tunnel.

Real light. Sunlight. Daylight!

She flung herself free of the thing's terrible embrace. Falling, slipping, running all at the same instant, Nicoletta got out of the cave.

Never had a gray sky been so lovely, so free, so perfect.

Never had dark lakes and bleak woods been so appealing, so friendly.

She held up her hands to the real world, incredibly grateful to be back. The sight of her bare hands reminded her she no longer held her schoolbooks.

The thing stood slightly behind the mouth of the cave, so that its shadow but not itself was visible. The books sat neatly in a pile by the opening. Had Nicoletta set them down like that?

"Don't come back," the thing said again, with a sadness so terrible that Nicoletta dissolved from fear into pity. Nicoletta knew what loneliness was, and she heard it in that awful voice.

It lives down there, she thought. It's caught forever in that terrible dark.

How ridiculously petty to be fretting for a larger house and a separate room. She could be sentenced to *this*, whatever this was! She would never have gotten out without this creature's help. She would have died down there.

She felt a strange bond between them, the bond of rescuer and rescued. Her need to run and scream had ended with the sunlight. "Are you alone?" she asked.

"No," it said sadly. "Alone would be better."

What terrible company it must have, to think alone was better.

"Don't come back," it whispered. "Not ever. Don't even think about it. Not ever. *Promise*. Promise me that you will never even think about coming back here."

Chapter 6

A strange and difficult promise. *Don't even think about it.*

A promise not to go back would be easy to keep. Neither wild horses nor nuclear bombs could have made Nicoletta go back.

But not even *think* about it?

Not wonder who or what it was? What sort of life it led?

Not wonder about its name, or gender, or species?

It had saved her life. Who could forget such an event?

A strange evening followed that weird and inexplicable afternoon.

She walked through a house which only that morning she had hated. But how wonderful it was! For it had walls and warmth, lamps and pillows. It had love and parents and food and music.

Her sister did not infuriate her. Jamie actually seemed beautiful and even worthy. She was alive and giggling and pesky, which was how little sisters are meant to be. What did Jamie have to do with caves and monsters?

Nicoletta had always told her family everything. Other girls who said they could not communicate with their families confused Nicoletta. What could they mean? Nicoletta simply arrived home from school and started talking. So did Jamie. So did Mother and Dad. Not communicate?

For the first time in her life, she did not communicate.

She did not tell them about the quiet lane, the staring stone, the straight path, the descending cave. As for the creature who brought her up from the depths, by the time she had reached home, she could no longer believe in him herself. He could have been nothing but an hallucination. She had not known her imagination was so active; in fact, Nicoletta thought of herself as having little or no imagination.

Such a thing could not have happened, and therefore it had not happened.

And so she remained silent, and shared none of it, and it swelled in her mind, filling her with confusion and disbelief.

Several times she drew a deep breath to begin the story somewhere. Each time she looked away and said nothing. She did not want a lecture on safety. Safety alone could consume weeks of scolding. Just the idea of Nicoletta walking alone into an unknown woods would outrage her parents. But when she told them she walked straight into an abandoned mine shaft — well, please.

But what kind of mine could it have been? Who had mined it? Who had smoothed those lovely walls, and what mineral caused the elegant glow?

A monster lives in it, she imagined herself saying to her father. The monster has cave skin: sand skin: rock skin. It has calcified leaves for hair and crumbling stones for fingers.

It occurred to Nicoletta that her family might just laugh.

She did not want anybody laughing at the creature. It had saved her. It had carried her out.

And yet — she wanted to talk about it. She was a talker and a sharer by nature.

And more than anything, she wanted to go back.

On that very first evening, sitting quietly at the dining table — while Jamie did geography homework and Nicoletta pretended to do algebra — while her mother balanced the checkbook and her father finished the newspaper — Nicoletta thought — *I want to go back.*

Jethro was familiar with the path. Surely he had followed it to its end at least once. Jethro would not have flinched from entering that shining cavern. He would have walked in as she had.

That's why Jethro didn't want me to follow him any farther, she thought. He's met the monster, too! The monster asked Jethro never to tell either!

In school tomorrow she would ask him about it. She would see if his eyes flickered when she said "cave." It would not be breaking a promise if you talked with a person who already knew.

When the phone rang and it was Christo, Nicoletta could hardly remember who that was. She could barely remember Madrigals, her group of friends and her great loss. Christo wanted to know what color dress she would wear. Nicoletta actually said, "Wear to what?"

Christo laughed uneasily. "The dance Friday, Nicoletta."

She detested rudeness in people. She was ashamed of herself for not having her thoughts where they belonged. Quickly she said, "I was kidding. I'm sorry. It was dumb. I have this lovely pale pink dress. Are you getting me flowers? I adore flowers."

Nobody had ever given her flowers. Why was she implying that she had had the honor often?

Christo said his mother was recommending white. Roses or carnations.

Nicoletta said she would love white roses.

But before her eyes was the blackness of caves.

And inside her mind was a slipperiness. She had a secret now, she who had never had a secret. The secret wanted to be in the front of her mind, consuming her thoughts. She had to push it to the rear, and behave like a normal human being, and flirt with Christo and miss Madrigals and study algebra.

"Let's have lunch again tomorrow," Christo said.

She hesitated. What about Jethro? Well, she would talk to Jethro in Art Appreciation. Or follow him again.

"Yes," she said. "Lunch was fun today." She couldn't even remember lunch today.

* * *

And lunch the next day blurred as well.

She had difficulty paying attention to Christo. Everything she did was a fake. She was sufficiently aware to know that, and be appalled at herself. She knew that Christo half-knew.

She knew he was thinking that perhaps this was what girls were like: that easy friendship evaporated, to be replaced by hot and cold flirtation. And she knew that while he was hurt by her distance, he was also fascinated by it. He had never experienced that with a girl; all the girls adored him. Christo was thinking more about Nicoletta than he had ever thought about a girl.

And am I flattered? thought Nicoletta. Am I falling in love with him? Am I even thinking about my first formal dance and my first bouquet?

No.

I am thinking about a boy in art whose last name I do not even know. I am thinking about a cave in which I thought I might die and a monster in whom I no longer believe because there is no such thing as a monster.

Lunch ended and she rushed to Art Appreciation, barely taking time to wave good-bye to Christo.

"He would have kissed you," whispered Rachel as the girls rushed up the stairwell together. "He wanted to kiss you in front of everybody, I can tell. I know these things."

Two days ago, Nicoletta had thought that the loss of her girlfriends in Madrigals would kill her. Now she just wanted Rachel to vanish so that she could concentrate on Jethro.

And because passing period was only three minutes, Rachel had no choice but to vanish, and Nicoletta entered Art Appreciation.

Jethro was present.

She was filled with exuberance. It was like turning into a hot-air balloon. Flames of delight lifted her heart and soul.

"Jethro," she said.

His body stiffened in his seat but he did not turn.

She knelt beside his chair and looked up into his face.

He remained frozen. How perfect he was. Like a statue —

sculpture from some Dark Age. She wanted to stroke his face and hair, as if he were artwork himself, and she could study the curves and surfaces.

He relented and looked down at her.

"I'm sorry about lunch," she said, keeping her voice so soft that nobody could share their words. "But I have to talk to you. Something happened yesterday, Jethro. I have to tell you about it."

She stared into his eyes, looking for a clue to his thoughts.

Jethro wet his lips, as if she were frightening him.

"After school?" she said. "Let's walk down the lane together."

He was shocked.

She might have suggested that they bomb a building.

"Just a walk," she whispered. "Just a talk. Please."

He shivered very slightly.

She could not imagine what his thoughts were. His eyes gave her no more clues than a sculpture would give and he used no words.

The teacher cleared his throat. "Uh — Nicoletta? Excuse me?"

She got to her feet, and in the moment before she slid into her seat she stroked the back of Jethro's hand.

He spent the entire class period looking at his hand.

As if nobody had ever touched him before.

Chapter 7

They stood where they had stood before, beside the stone. With Jethro beside her, she was not afraid of the stone. It still seemed alive, as if left over from another world, it held a spirit. A woodland power. But it no longer threatened her.

"And you promised?" said Jethro.

How measured his speech was. How carefully he pondered each word before he actually put it in his mouth and used it. Nicoletta realized that everybody else she knew used speech cheaply: It meant little. To Jethro, every syllable was precious. He squandered nothing.

"I didn't actually make any promises," said Nicoletta. How she wanted to touch him again. But he was more like the stone than like a boy. He was entirely within himself, and only the few spare syllables of speech escaped his control. "I left," explained Nicoletta. "I was afraid."

Jethro nodded. "I can understand that you were afraid." His eyes looked down into an emotional cave of their own.

"I want to go back," said Nicoletta. She felt light and bright, as if she were the flame of a candle.

He was shaken. "Caves are dangerous, Nicoletta." He had never used her name before. She took his hand as if it were her possession, as if they had both agreed that she might have his hand, and again he stared at the way her fingers wrapped around his. He seemed caught in emotion so deep that there were no words for it. Perhaps even a person used to speech, like Nicoletta, could not have explained his emotion.

"Please don't go back," said Jethro. His voice was meant only for her. It was not a whisper, and yet it did not carry; it was intended to travel only as far as her ears and then stop. He sounded as if he had had a lifetime of practice at preventing his speech from being heard. It was the opposite of what anybody else did with speech. "It's dangerous, Nicoletta."

"Then you do know!" she said. "You *have* been in there, Jethro. You know what I'm talking about."

He looked at the stone and drew himself together, becoming more remote, more taut. "I know what you're talking about," he admitted.

"Let's go together," she said. She tried to pull him around the stone to the straight and silken path that lay beyond.

But he did not cooperate. "You must go home," he said. "You must not come this way again."

Nicoletta did not listen to him. She did not want warnings. She wanted Jethro. "Where do you live?" she said. "Tell me where you live!" She explored his fingers with hers, slipping between them, pressing down with her thumb, feeling his bones and sinews.

This is what falling in love is, thought Nicoletta. It's looking at a boy and wanting to know every single thing there is to know about him, and wanting to know every inch of him, and every emotion of him, and every word in him.

Jethro's eyelids trembled, closing down over his eyes as if he could shutter himself away, and then they opened wide, and he stared back into her eyes.

He loves me, too, thought Nicoletta. Still holding his hand in one of hers, she lifted her other hand to his face. As if reading mirrors, he did exactly what she did. Fingertips approached cheeks. Nicoletta and Jethro shivered with the heat of first love's first touch.

His hand slid cupped over her chin and around her face. His fingers went into her hair. He drew the gleaming yellow locks through his fingers, and wound them gently over his palm. "You have beautiful hair," he said in a husky voice. His lips pressed together, coming to a decision, while her lips opened, ready.

Kiss me, thought Nicoletta. Please kiss me. If you kiss me, it will seal this. It will be love. I can tell by the way you're standing here that you want to be in love with me. Kiss me, Jethro!

But a car came slowly, noisily, down the road.

They were jolted by the sudden sight and sound of the vehicle.

This had been a place in which the twentieth century did not come, and now it was driving right up.

She knew the car.

It was Christo's.

Jethro's breathing was ragged. "Do not tell him!" whispered Jethro with a ferocity that frightened her. "You must not tell him!" Nicoletta was stunned by the force of Jethro's command. "You have promised to keep a secret! You must keep the promise, Nicoletta!"

Christo swung out of the van, leaving the motor idling.

"*Promise*," breathed Jethro, with a terrible force, as if his lungs were going to explode.

But she did not answer him.

"Hi, Christo," she said. "Do you know Jethro?"

Christo shook his head. She introduced them, using only first names, since she did not know Jethro's last name. The young men stared at each other warily. Christo extended his right hand. They shook hands, also warily, as if they were about to be contestants in some duel.

"I'm glad you came," said Jethro. His voice calm now, even bland. "Would you mind giving Nicoletta a ride home? She shouldn't be down here. We were arguing about it. The woods are dangerous. Nobody should be in these woods without a compass."

Christo was amazed. "You don't seem like the outdoor type," he said to Nicoletta. "Do you hike? Do you camp?"

"No. Never."

"That's why I told her to stay away," said Jethro. "It's dangerous for somebody who's ignorant about it."

"I love the woods," said Christo happily. "I'll teach you,
Nickie. That's what we'll do this weekend! We'll go to the state
forest and hike down to the waterfalls! They're so beautiful in
winter." Christo led Nicoletta to his van as he gave her a long,
lyrical description of frozen waterfalls and gleaming ice.

How easily he used words! Not like Jethro, who could hardly
bear to let a syllable out of his mouth. "Nice to have met you,"
Christo called cheerfully back to Jethro.

How strange romance is, thought Nicoletta. I was following
Jethro and Christopher was following me. To Christo this is the
beginning of a beautiful romance in which we share the great
outdoors. I don't care about the outdoors at all. I don't care about
Christo either. I care about Jethro.

And I wonder about the cave.

And the monster.

And the promise that mattered so much.

To whom was I making that promise? she thought suddenly,
frowning. To the creature? Or Jethro?

Christo, backing his van down the narrow rutted lane, suddenly lifted his right hand from the wheel and stared at it. He
shook his hand slightly.

"What?" said Nicoletta. Her eyes were glued to the place
where Jethro had stood. He stood there no longer. He had circled
the stone, and must even now be tracing the straight path. Even
now Jethro was going toward the cave, on a path that seemed to
go nowhere else, a path he had wanted her to promise she would
never follow again.

But I will, thought Nicoletta. I will follow Jethro forever.

"There's sand on my hand," said Christo. "That guy's hand
was all sandy."

Chapter 8

Never before in her life had Nicoletta intentionally done something stupid and dangerous. Her parents were cautious in all things but money. They had taught Nicoletta and Jamie to steer clear of strangers, to look both ways before crossing streets, to be home before dark. They were full of warnings and guidance, and Nicoletta had spent a lifetime listening carefully and obeying completely.

But not today.

The snow was falling lightly when she left the school building. She had hidden in the library stacks until Christopher had definitely driven away. Hidden among the dusty pages and unread texts until there was not a single soul left in the school whom she knew.

Little homework had been assigned for the night. Nicoletta was able to leave her bookbag in her locker. How strange to be unburdened, to have hands and arms free. She ran all the way, feet flying, hair streaming behind her, heart filled with excitement.

How lovely the woods were, dusted with snow, crisp and clean and pure in the fading afternoon.

The snow was dry and separate. Snowflakes touched her cheeks like kisses.

The road narrowed and she had to slow down, unable to find easy footing on the snow-hidden ruts of the dirt lane. At first she did not even see the boulder; snow had draped it like a cloak. It did not look like a stone, but like an igloo, a place that would be cozy inside. She patted the stone as she rounded it and her glove left a perfect five-fingered print.

On each side of the slim, straight path, the dry weeds stood up like snow bouquets. Ice flowers.

The snow came down more heavily.

There was no sky anymore; just a ceiling of white.

When she came to the place where pools of water lay below each side of the raised pathway, snow had covered the ice, and had Nicoletta not seen the lakes before, she would have thought they were fields; she would have thought it was safe to run over them, and dance upon them.

The cliff wall was hung with frozen water from springs deep in the earth. Snow danced in gusts, spraying against the cliff like surf and falling in drifts at the foot of the rocks.

A piece of the cliff moved toward her.

Nicoletta held out her palm like a crossing guard, as if she could stop an avalanche that way.

It was stone, and yet it walked. It was snow, and yet it bore leaves. It was a person, and yet —

It was the creature.

She could see its eyes now, living pools trapped in that terrible frame.

She could see its feet, formed not so differently from the huge icicles that hung on the cliff: things. Dripping stalagmites from the floor of the cave.

She felt no fear. The snow, falling so gently, so pure and cleanly, seemed protection. Yet snow protected nothing but ugliness. Ugliness it would hide. Filthy city alleys and rusted old cars, abandoned, broken trikes and rotting picnic tables — snow covered anything putrid and turned it to perfect sculpture.

Even the thing, the monstrous thing that had stank and dripped and scraped — it was perfect in its softly rounded snowy wrap.

"Go away," it growled. "What is the matter with you? Don't you understand? *Go away!*"

"I want to find Jethro."

It advanced on her.

She backed up. What if I fall off the path? she thought. What if I fall down on those ponds? How thick is the ice? Will I drown here?

"Go away," it said.

"I know Jethro lives here somewhere," she said. "You must know him. He takes this path. The path stops here! Tell me where he turns off. Tell me where he goes. Tell me where to find him." She could no longer look at the thing. Its face was scaly, like a mineral, and the snow did not cling to its surface, but melted, so that it ran, like an overflowing gutter. She looked past the thing and saw the black hole of the cave. It wanted her. She could feel its eagerness to have her again. She tore her eyes away and wondered how she would get past the cave to wherever Jethro was.

"Why does he matter?" asked the thing.

Why does Jethro matter? thought Nicoletta. I don't know. Why does anybody matter? What makes you care about one person so deeply you cannot sleep?

She said, "He wasn't in school today."

The creature said nothing. It turned around and moved toward its cave.

"Don't go!" said Nicoletta. "I'm worried about him. I like him. I want to talk to him."

It disappeared into the cavern.

Or perhaps, because it was stone and sand itself, it simply blended into, or became part of, the cliff.

She followed it. She ran right after it, inside the flat and glowing walls of the entrance.

"Stop it!" the thing bellowed. Its voice was immense, and the cave echoed with its deep, rolling voice. "Get out!"

"I love him," said Nicoletta.

In the strange silence that followed, she could see the thing's eyes. They had filled with tears.

Only humans cry. Not stones.

"Who are you?" she whispered.

But it did not answer.

The only sound was the sharp unmistakable report of a rifle. Nicoletta whirled.

"Hunters. They think I'm a bear," whispered the thing. "They'll come in here to shoot me. Poachers."

"Have they come in before?" she whispered back.

"They don't usually find the cave opening. Sometimes they see me, though, if I'm careless, and they follow me."

She could hear the loud and laughing voices of men. Cruel laughter, lusting for a kill.

"If they see you move, they'll shoot you," it told her. "They shoot anything that moves."

"I'll go down in the cave with you," said Nicoletta. "We'll be safe together." No snow remained on the humanoid creature. Its stink increased and its stone skin flaked away. Its hair like dead leaves snapped off and littered the floor. As long as she didn't have to touch it, or look too closely, she was not afraid of it.

"No," it said. "You must never, never, never go down in this cave."

"I did before."

"And you only got out because I brought you out. If you go any farther into the cave, the same thing will happen to you that happened to me."

"What happened to you?" she said. She forgot to whisper. She spoke out loud.

From out in the snow came a yell of satisfaction. "I see the cave!" bellowed a voice. "This way! We'll get it this time! Over here!"

The thing grabbed Nicoletta and the horrible rasp of its gruesome skin made her scream. It put its hand over her mouth and she could taste it. A swallow of disease and pollution filled her throat. She struggled against the thing but it lifted her with horrifying absolute strength. She was carried down the tunnel and into a small low-ceilinged pit beside the shaft.

"Don't make any sounds," it breathed into her ear. Its breath was a stench of rot.

She was weeping now, soaking its ghastly skin with her tears. The acid of her very own tears dissolved the thing. Its coating was soaking off onto her.

I've been such a fool, thought Nicoletta. My parents will kill me. I deserve anything I get.

She fought but the thing simply pressed her up against the back of the dark pit. When the slime of the wall came off on her cheek, Nicoletta sagged down and ceased struggling. She tried to crawl right inside herself, and just not be there in mind or in body.

But she was there. And all her senses — smell, sight, sound, touch — all of them brought her close to vomiting with horror.

If I can let the hunters know I am here, thought Nicoletta, they will save me. They'll shoot this horrible animal and take me home.

The hunters came into the cave.

There were two of them.

They had a flashlight.

She saw the light bobble past her little cavern but she knew that if they glanced in her direction, they would see only the stony side of the creature. To their eyes, the thing gripping her would look like cave wall.

She took a breath to scream but the thing's handlike extension clapped so tightly over her mouth she could taste it, toxic and raw.

"This is neat," said one of the hunters. His voice was youthful and awestruck. "I can't imagine why I've never heard of this place. Never even seen the opening before."

"Me either," said the other one. "And I've come around here for years. Why, it's — it's —"

"It's beautiful! I'm calling the TV stations the minute we shoot that bear."

"Let's put the body right outside of the cave opening," agreed the other one. "It'll make a great camera angle."

Their voices faded. The creature's grip on Nicoletta did not.

They walked more deeply into the cave. No! she thought. They mustn't go in farther! The cave will turn! I've been at that end of it! It isn't beautiful, it's the opening to some other terrible place. I've got to warn them. I've got to stop them.

She flung herself at her captor, but its strength was many multiples of her own. Nothing occurred except bruising against its stony surface.

Her heart pounded so hard and so fast that she wondered if she would live through this. Perhaps her own heart would kill her, giving up the struggle.

So distantly that Nicoletta was not confident of her hearing, came two long, thin cries. Human cries. Threads of despair. Cries for help.

The final shrieks before the final fall.

The two hunters, plunging down the black end of the shaft. Hitting bottom, wherever that might be.

She knew what they felt. The textures and the moving air, the shifting sands and the touching walls.

The thing released her. Her mouth and lips were free. Shock kept her silent. The entire cavern was silent.

Silence as total as darkness.

No moans from the fallen pair. No cries of pain. No shouts for help.

They had hit bottom. They were gone. Two eager young men, out for an afternoon of pleasure.

The monster's sand clung to her face and wrists. She could not move. She could not run or fight or think.

After a moment, it picked her up like a pile of coats and carried her out of the cave.

The snow was now falling so heavily that the world was obliterated.

If there was a world. Perhaps this horrible place was the only place on earth, and it was her home.

She wept, and the tears froze on her cheeks.

"I'm sorry," it said. "I had to do that."

"How will they get out?" she said, sobbing.

"They won't."

How matter-of-factly it gave an answer. How will the hunters get out? *They won't.*

She backed away from him. "You *are* a monster," she said, and she did not mean his form, but his soul. "You let them go down in there and fall. You knew they would fall! You knew they would come to a place where there was no bottom." She began to run, slipping and falling. The path was invisible. The snow came down like a curtain between them. When she fell again, she slid perilously close to the ice over the deep, black lake.

He picked her up out of the snow and set her on her feet. "I'll go with you some of the way. In this weather there will be no more of them."

He held her gloved hand and together they walked between the lakes. On the straight and slender path they could not walk abreast, and he walked ahead, clearing the snow for her.

She had given him gender and substance. Her mind had taken him out of the neuter-thing category. The monster was a he, not an it.

They reached the boulder. "Promise you won't come back," he said. His voice was soft and sad.

Her hair prickled. Her skin shivered. Her hands inside the gloves turned to ice.

"You must go home. You must not come this way again."

She looked into the eyes. Deep, brown, human eyes. And a human voice that had said those same words to her once before.

Chapter 9

Her first real dance. Her first real date.

And Nicoletta was as uninterested as if her parents had gone and rented a movie that Nicoletta had seen twice before.

"What is the matter with you?" yelled Jamie.

True love is the matter with me, thought Nicoletta. Jethro is the matter with me. Instead of having Jethro, I'm almost the captive of Christo.

It wasn't that Christo had taken her prisoner. Christo was his usual gentlemanly self. It was more that she was not arguing about it. She was not saying no. She was allowing events with Christo to take place because they did not matter to her at all.

"I don't think you even care about Christo," said Jamie, flicking a wet towel at her half-dressed sister. "Even the middle school knows that Christo asked you out."

"They only know because you told them," said Nicoletta. "How else could they know who Christo is?"

"Nicoletta, you're so annoying. He's a football star, isn't he? Me and my friends went to every game last fall, didn't we? We won the regional championship, didn't we? He has his picture in the paper all the time, doesn't he?" Jamie made several snarling faces at her sister.

Nicoletta never thought of Christo as an athlete. She thought of him exclusively as a baritone in Madrigals. She thought of him, not in a football uniform, but in the glittering turquoise and silver he wore for concerts, a king's courtier, a royal flirt.

Christo was a football player, and she did not even know, had never attended a game, never considered his practice schedule. And Jethro. Did he play sports? What was his schedule? Where did he live?

"You don't even care what you're wearing!" complained Jamie. "You didn't even ask Mom to buy you a new dress for this!"

Her dress lay on the bed, waiting for her to put it on.

She felt as if there were a veil between her mind and her life. The veil was Jethro. She was as consumed by him as if he had set her on fire. It was difficult to see anything else. The rest of the world was out of focus, and she did not care whether she saw anything clearly but Jethro.

Jamie held the dress for her and she stepped carefully into it. It was Jamie who exclaimed over the lovely silken fabric, the way it hung so gracefully from Nicoletta's narrow waist, and dropped intoxicatingly at the neckline, like a crescent moon sweeping from shoulder to shoulder. Nicoletta had borrowed her mother's imitation ruby necklace. The racing pulse at her throat made the dark red stones beat like her own blood.

"You're in love, aren't you?" whispered Jamie suddenly.

Nicoletta turned to see herself in the long mirror.

I'm beautiful, she thought. She blinked, as if expecting the beauty not to be there at the second glance. But it was. She was truly beautiful. She had to look away. It felt like somebody else in that gown.

And it is somebody else! thought Nicoletta. It's somebody in love with Jethro, not somebody in love with Christo.

Jamie was also reflected in the mirror: a scrawny little girl, still with braces and unformed figure — a little girl utterly awestruck by her big sister. For the first time in their lives, Nicoletta was worth something to Jamie. For Nicoletta was in love, and beautiful, and going to a dance with a handsome boy.

"Do you think you'll marry Christo?" said Jamie, getting down to basics. "What's his last name? What will your name be when you get married? I'll be your maid of honor, won't I?"

But Christo's last name did not matter. Only Jethro's.

Who is he? thought Nicoletta. *Where* is he?

Love was like clean ice.

Nicoletta skated through the evening. All things were effortless, all motions were gliding, all conversations spun on her lips.

Christo was proud of her, and proud that he was with her.

And if she glittered, how was he to know she glittered for someone else?

They left the dance shortly after midnight.

Snow had begun again.

There was a full moon, and each snowflake was a falling crystal. The night world was equally black and silver. Even the shadows gleamed.

They drove slowly down the quiet streets, rendered perfect by the first inch of snow.

"Where are we going?" said Nicoletta.

"That road," said Christo. He smiled at her. "I never noticed that road before. It looked quiet."

He wants to kiss, thought Nicoletta. He is going to drive me down Jethro's road, to park at the end of the lane where Jethro's stone will see us. What if the stone tells? I know they talk. I don't want Jethro to find out about Christo.

She was dizzy with the magic of her thoughts. There is no stone, she told herself, and if there is one, nobody talks to it.

Jethro had not been in school. The gloomy skies and early dark of winter had been a perfect reflection of Nicoletta's emptiness when there was no Jethro in Art Appreciation. He was the only art she appreciated.

How she wanted Jethro to see her in this gown!

For she was beautiful. She had been the princess of every girl's dream at that dance. She had been as lovely as if spun from gold, as delicate as lace, as perfect as love.

She saw herself in the snowy night, floating down the path, her long gown flowing behind her, her golden hair glittering with diamonds of snow. She saw herself untouched by cold or by fear, dancing through the dark like a princess in a fairy tale to find her prince.

O Jethro! she thought. Where are you? What are you thinking? Why weren't you in school? Are you ill? Are you afraid of me? What promises do you have to keep? What does the stone know about you that I do not?

Driving with his left hand, Christopher touched her bare shoulder with his right. He was hot and dry, burned by the fever of wanting Nicoletta.

She thought only of Jethro, and of Jethro's hand. The first time he touched Nicoletta, his fingers had not felt human. The first time he touched Christo, he had left behind grains of sand.

A strange and terrible thought had formed in Nicoletta's mind, but she refused to allow it a definite shape.

Christopher kissed her once, and then again. The third time he shuddered slightly, wanting a hundred times more than this — wanting no car, no time limit, no clothing in the way. The calm young man who easily flirted with or touched any girl because it meant nothing, was not the one driving the van tonight.

Touching meant a great deal to Christo tonight.

Think of Christo, Nicoletta told herself, accepting the kisses but not kissing back. But she could not think of him at all. She could hardly see him. He felt evaporated and diffuse. She felt sleazy and duplicitous. What have I done? thought Nicoletta. What have I let happen? How am I going to get out of this? "Good night, Christo," she said courteously. "And thank you. I had a lovely time."

She put her hand on the door handle.

Christo stared at her. "Nickie, we're in the woods, not your driveway."

But she was out of the van, standing in her fragile, silver dancing slippers on the crust of the snow. She knew she would not break through, she would not get snow in these shoes. She touched the ruby necklace. The moon came out from behind the snow-laden clouds, and rested on her face and her throat. The ruby and the red rose of her cheeks were the only heat in the forest.

Like a silver creature of the woods, she found the path, swirling and laughing to herself.

"Nickie?" said Christo. He was out of the van, he was following her. He could not stay on the surface of the crusted snow, as she could. His big feet and strong legs slogged where she had danced. "You don't even have a coat!" he cried.

The boulder carried a shroud of snow. Nicoletta was a candle flickering in the dark. She quickstepped around the immense rock. The boulder shrugged its shoulders as Christo passed and dropped its load of snow upon him. Muffled under layers of white, his cry to Nicoletta did not reach her ears. "Wait up!" he said to her. "Don't do this, Nickie. Nickie, what are you doing?"

She was in a dance choreographed by an unknown, moonlit hand. She had a partner, unseen and unknown, and the only thing was to keep up, to stay with the rhythm, her skirts making scallop shells around her bare stockinged legs, her feet barely touching the white snow, her hands in synchrony, touching, holding, waving.

Christo struggled free from the snow and circled the boulder.

He could see her, her gown luminous as the stars, her hair like golden music. He could not imagine what she was doing, but he did not care. She was too lovely and the evening was too extraordinary for reason. He simply wanted to catch up, to be with her, to see her eyes as she danced this unearthly dance.

When he caught up to her, she was dancing on a balance beam between two black-iced ponds. The path was so narrow his heart stopped. What if she fell? What could she be thinking of? He was too out of breath to shout her name again, he whose breath control and athletic strength were his strong assets. The stillness of the night was so complete it was like crystal, a call from him would shatter the glass in which they danced.

A black, black hole at the end of Nicoletta's narrow danger opened wide, and opened wider.

Christo stared, fascinated, unable to think at all, unable to shout warnings if warnings were needed.

From the side of the ice-dripping rock, walked rock. Moving rock. The rock and Nicoletta danced together for a moment while Christo tried to free himself from ribbons of confusion. What is going on? he thought.

It was possible that the night had ended and he was deep in a dream, one of those electrical-storm dreams, in which vivid pictures leap and toss like lightning in a frightened sky.

"Nicoletta?" he said at last.

She spun, as if seeing him for the first time, and the rock spun with her, and it had a face.

The rock was a person.

Chapter 10

"*You brought him here*," it said to her.

She knew who he was now, but not why or how. She wanted to talk to him. Not just this night, but every night and forever. She wanted him to be the only person she ever talked to.

But he was not a person. He was a thing.

"When do you change?" she said to him. "When are you one of us?"

"I am always one of you," he said desperately. "How could you have brought Christo? How could you betray me?"

"I would never betray you. I love you."

He released her, and the rough granite of him scraped her painfully. There was more red now under the moon: her rubies, her cheeks, and her one drop of blood.

"Go!" he breathed. "Go. Convince him I am not."

Convince him I am not.

Not what? Not who?

She was alone now between the lakes and Christo was trying to join her, his large feet clumsy on the tilting ice and snow. "I'm coming, Christo!" she said, and ran toward him, but she was clumsy now, too. Her partner of the silence and snow was gone; her choreography failed her.

She slipped first, and Christo slipped second.

They were a yard apart, too far to touch, too far to catch.

At first she was not afraid, because she knew that even falling through the ice, the creature would save her, lift her, carry her out.

But the sharp tiny heel of her silver shoe punctured the ice at the same moment that Christo's big black shoe cracked it, and as the frigid water crept up her stockings, she realized that the creature would not save her, any more than it had saved the hunters. What mattered most to it was being unknown, and being untouched, and being safe itself.

Christo and I will drown, she thought. We will fall as far beneath the black water as the hunters fell in the black shaft. We will die in ice and evil cold.

She thrashed desperately, but that only made the hole in the ice larger.

Christo said, in a normal high school boy's voice, "I can't believe I have done anything as stupid as this. Don't tell anybody, that's all I ask." He was crouching at the water's edge, having pulled himself back. He grabbed her hand and waist and yanked her unceremoniously to dry land. "Let's get out of here before we get frostbite." He hustled her along the straight path and back into the woods and back around the boulder.

Nicoletta was afraid the boulder would roll upon them, would crush their wet feet beneath its glacial tons, but it ignored them. Back in the van, Christo turned on the motor and then immediately the heat, with the blower on high.

After a moment he looked at her, reassessing what had happened and who she was.

He knows now, thought Nicoletta. He knows who I love and where I go and what matters most.

But he did not know. People in love seldom do.

"You," said Christo finally, "are not what I expected." He was laughing. He was thrilled. Nicoletta had proved to be full of well-kept secrets, a girl whose hobbies were not the usual, and he was even more proud of being with her than he had been at the dance.

Christo started to list the things they would do together — things he probably thought were unusual and exciting. To

Nicoletta they sounded impossibly dull. They were of this world. They were commonplace.

Nicoletta had a true love now, from another world, a world without explanation or meaning, and she did not care about Christo's calendar.

The light was on in the bedroom Nicoletta shared with Jamie when Christo pulled into the Storms's driveway. Jamie had definitely not gone to bed. Her little face instantly appeared, and she shaded the glass with her two hands so that she could see into the dark.

Christo grinned. "We have to give your little sister a show for her money," he said.

No! thought Nicoletta, shrinking. I can't kiss you now. I'm in love with another — another what?

Man? Boy? Rock? Thing? Beast?

Or was she in love with a murderer?

She thought of the two men falling to the depths of the cave.

Where are we going? they would have said to each other.

Down.

Down forever, down to certain death.

He could have prevented the hunters from dying, she thought.

Then she thought, No, he couldn't. They would have killed him first, shot him, it was self-defense, in a way.

Her thoughts leapt back and forth like a tennis ball over a net.

It came to her, as black and bleak as the lakes in the dark, that she had forgotten those two men. They had fallen out the bottom of her mind just as they fell out the bottom of the cave.

Love is amoral, she thought. Love thinks only of itself, or of The Other.

There is no room in love for passersby.

Those hunters. They had passed by, all right.

Did they have wives? Children? Mothers? Jobs?

Nobody will ever find them, thought Nicoletta. They will never be buried. They will never come home. Nobody will ever know.

Unless I tell.

*   *   *

"Good night," said Christo softly. He walked her up the steps, dizzy with love. Together they stared at the blank wooden face of the door, at the bare nail where last December a Christmas wreath had hung.

Christo's kiss was long and deep and intense. His lips contained enough energy to win football games, to sing entire concerts. When he finally stopped, and tried to find enough breath to speak, he couldn't, and just went back to the car.

Behind Nicoletta the door was jerked open and she fell inside, her heart leaping with memories of caves and black lakes, of dancing in front of rock faces that opened like the jaws of mountain spirits.

"Ooooooh, that was so terrific!" squealed Jamie, flinging her arms around her sister. "He really kissed you! Wow, what a kiss! I was watching through the peephole. Oooooooh, I can't wait to tell my friends."

Nobody could ever accuse a little sister of good timing.

"Get lost, Jamie."

"Forget it. We share a bedroom. I'll never be lost. Tell me everything or I'll never let you sleep. I'll borrow all your clothes. I'll get a parakeet and keep the cage over your bed. I'll spill pancake syrup in your hair."

"Go for it," said Nicoletta. She walked past her pesky sister and into the only room in the teeny house where you were allowed to shut the door and be alone. In the bathroom mirror she stared at herself.

Mirror, mirror, on the wall, who is the fairest of them all?

There were answers behind the silvered glass. If she could only look in deeply enough, she would know.

I didn't look deeply enough into the cave either, she thought.

I have to go back.

Further down.

Deeper in.

Chapter 11

"Daddy and I are going to see the Burgesses today," said Mother. "This is the first free Saturday we've had in so long!"

Mr. Burgess was Daddy's old college roommate. It was a long drive and when Mother and Daddy went to see Sally and Ralph, they stayed all afternoon and sometimes long into the night.

Yes! thought Nicoletta. I'll have the time to scout out the cave. Nicoletta tightened her bathrobe around her and thought of the long, unsupervised day ahead and what yummy food she would eat to sustain herself. Doughnuts, she thought, Gummi bears, ice cream, chocolate chips out of the bag, and barbecue potato chips. She would take some to Jethro. She would wear a backpack filled with junk food, and —

"Nicoletta," said her mother, in her high, firm, order-giving voice, "you'll stay home and baby-sit for Jamie."

"Baby-sit for Jamie?" Nicoletta repeated incredulously. She needed to get out there in the snow and find Jethro! And they were making her stay home and baby-sit her stupid sister who was perfectly capable of taking care of herself?

Nicoletta tipped way backward in her wooden breakfast table chair, rolling her eyes even farther backward, to demonstrate her total disgust.

Luckily Jamie felt the same way. "Baby-sit?" she shrieked.

"Mother! I am eleven years old. I do not need a sitter and I am not a baby. Furthermore, if I did need one, I would want one more capable, more interesting, and more worth your money than Nickie."

It was agreed that the girls could take care of themselves separately, as long as they promised not to fight, not to argue, and not to do anything foolish.

"I promise," said Nicoletta, who had never meant anything less.

"I promise," said Jamie, who lived for fights and arguments and would certainly start both, the minute their parents were out of sight.

Their car backed out of the driveway, leaving deep lacelike treads in the snow. The sky was a thin, helpless blue, as if its own veins had chilled and even the sky could no longer get warm.

But Jamie did not start a fight.

"Make pancake men," she said pleadingly to her sister. This was one of the few episodes out of the *Little House* series that Jamie considered worthy. Nicoletta was excellent at it, too. Nobody could pour pancake batter like Nicoletta.

So Nicoletta made pancake men and then struggled with pancake women, although skirts were harder to pour. They ate by cutting away limbs with the sides of their forks: having first the arms, then the legs.

Jamie drowned some of her men in syrup, pouring it on until their little pancake heads were under water, so to speak.

There was nothing quite so filling as pancakes. When you had had pancakes for breakfast, you were set for a hard day's work. Nicoletta dressed, carefully hiding her excitement from Jamie. Jamie loved Saturday morning cartoons and with luck would not even hear the door close as Nicoletta slipped out. With extremely good luck, she would still be cartooning and junk-fooding when Nicoletta returned in the afternoon.

There had been enough money last year for Nicoletta to

purchase a wonderful winter wardrobe. She wanted to be seen against the snow. A scarlet ski jacket with silver trim zipped tightly against the cold. Charcoal-gray pants tucked into white boots with furry linings. She wore no hat. The last thing she wanted to do was cover her hair.

She loosened it from its elastics and let it flow free, the only gold in a day of silver and white.

"Where are you going?" yelled Jamie, hearing the door open after all.

"Out." Nicoletta liked the single syllable. The strength of it pleased her. The total lack of information that it gave, increased the sense of secrecy and plotting. She stood for a moment in the doorway, planning her strategy. She'd be warm inside her puffy jacket, but the pants were not enough and the boots were more for show than snow. She needed earmuffs in the fierce wind, but would die before wearing them.

"Nicoletta!" screamed her sister, who never called her that. The scream soared upward with rising fear. "Nicoletta!" Loud. Louder than it should be for anything less than blood. "Nicoletta, come here!"

She flew through the house, remembering emergency numbers, fighting for self-control, reminding herself to stay calm. Was Jamie bleeding? Was Jamie —

Jamie was fine. Curled in a ball on the easy chair, with Mother's immense purple velour bathrobe draped around her like Cinderella's gown.

"This better be good," said Nicoletta. "Talk fast before I kill you."

"Kill me for what?" said Jamie.

"Frightening me."

Jamie was gratified to have frightened Nicoletta. Nicoletta could think only of time lost, time she needed to find and talk to Jethro. Time in the winter woods, time behind the swollen boulder. Get to the point! she thought, furious in the wake of her unreasoning fear.

Jamie pointed to the local news channel.

"You called me in here to look at something on TV?" shouted Nicoletta.

"Shut up and listen."

A distraught woman was sobbing. "My husband! My husband Rob!" she said. "We don't know what happened to him! He never came home last night. Or Al either. They must be hurt." The woman's shoulders heaved with weeping. "I don't know," she whispered. "They're lying out there in the snow. I know they are. Too weak to call for help. Or maybe they fell through unsafe ice. I don't know. But Rob didn't come home."

As if she, too, had fallen through unsafe ice, Nicoletta grew colder and colder, sinking to the depths of her soul.

"See," said Jamie, "what happened is, these two hunters went out yesterday morning and they never came home. Isn't that creepy? They took a day off from work to go hunting *and they never came home.*"

I forgot them, she thought. I forgot them right away. I yelled at the monster once and then I forgot again. But those were people. Real people.

"What if she never finds out?" said Jamie in a low, melo-dramatic voice. "You missed it, Nick, but they showed her little kids. The kids are too little to know what's going on. They just held hands and stared at the camera. You know, that goopy, gaping look little kids have."

Children, thought Nicoletta. I went back and danced on the snow while little children waited for a daddy who is not coming home. And I knew, I knew all along.

Something in her congealed. She felt more solid, but not flesh and blood solid. Metallic. As if she were no longer human, but more of a robot, built of wires and connections in a factory.

Because I didn't react like a human, she thought. A human would have gone to the police, called an ambulance, taken rescue teams to the cave to bring the hunters up. And what did I do? I obeyed a voice telling me to keep its secrets.

The reporter's face became long and serious. "In this temperature," she said grimly, "in this weather, considering tonight's forecast, there is little hope that the men will survive, if indeed they are alive at this moment. They must be found today."

Nicoletta's stomach tried to throw up the pancake men.

She forced herself to be calm. She supervised every inside and outside muscle of herself. It seemed even more robotic. And it worked. She knew from Jamie's glance that her body and face revealed nothing.

"Search teams are combing the areas where the men are thought to have been," said the reporter. "We will return with updates." The long, grim face vanished into a perky smile, as if the reporter, too, were a robot programmed for certain expressions. "Now," she said cheerily, "back to your regular programming!"

Jamie, who always preferred regular programming, and never wanted interruptions, sighed happily and tucked herself more deeply into her mother's robe.

Nicoletta backed out of the room. She stared down at the bright, sparkling outfit she had chosen to shine in the snowy woods, so Jethro would see her.

I know where they are . . . but if I tell . . . his secret . . . my promise . . .

Anyway, they're dead. It isn't as if anybody could rescue them now. They have a grave, too — farther underground than an undertaker would put them.

It was not funny. Not funny at all. And yet a snickery laugh came out of her mouth and hung in the air like frost. She had to pull her mouth back into shape with both hands.

What shall I do? Does a promise to a monster count when wives are sobbing and children have lost their father? Of course not.

But in her heart, she knew there had been no promise to a monster. The promise had been to . . .

But even now she could not finish the sentence. It was not possible and she was calm enough to know that much.

But it was true, and she had seen enough to know that as well.

First, I'll find him, she told herself. We'll talk. I'll explain to him that I have to notify authorities. Then —

A small, bright yellow car whipped around the corner, slipping dangerously on the ice, and zooming forward to slip again as it rushed up her driveway. Rachel, who aimed for every ice patch and shrieked with laughter at every skid. Rachel, coming for a Saturday morning gossip.

Nicoletta could not believe this was happening to her. First she had to make breakfast with her sister. Now she had to waste time with her best friend.

Rachel leapt out of the driver's side and Cathy from the passenger side. It wasn't enough that she would be saddled with one friend; now there were two. They slammed their doors hard enough to rock the little car and purposely leapt onto untouched snow, rather than using the path, tagging each other and giggling.

She was framed in the doorway anyhow; there was no escape; so she flung it open and said hi.

"Nickie!" they cried. "You have to tell us everything. We're dying to hear about it."

Her heart tightened. *How could Rachel and Cath know?* She had said nothing! Only Christo had been there, and he'd had no sense of what was going on. He'd been too in love with Nicoletta to see anything.

And yet Rachel and Cathy knew.

Nicoletta struggled to remain composed. She could not talk to anybody until she had talked to Jethro. That was all, that was that.

Rachel flung her arms around Nicoletta. "It's terrible not to see you all the time," she said. "We're so out of touch. Now get inside where it's toasty-oasty warm and tell us all about it." Rachel shoved Nicoletta into her own house.

Cathy tap-danced after them. "You're so lucky, Nickie," she said, admiring her own steps. "Did you dance all night?"

They even knew that she had danced under the moon and across the snow!

"Hi, Jamie," said Rachel. "Are you still worthless or have you improved since we saw you last?"

"I'm flawless," said Jamie. "Get out of my living room. I'm watching television. But if you pay me, I'll describe Christo's good-night kiss. It was very long and —"

Christo.

This was about Christo! The dance at Top o' the Town. Not the dance to find Jethro.

Nicoletta surfaced. It was sticky coming up, as if, like the pancake men, she had drowned under syrup.

How quickly can I get rid of them? she wondered. She would have to give them every detail, assuming she could remember any details; and then what excuse could she use to make them leave her alone? She wondered if there was any way she could get Rachel to drive her to the dead-end road, save her that long hike. She could think of no way to explain being dropped off there.

"And then," said Jamie, accepting a pack of Starburst candy in payment, "Christo staggered back to the car like a drunk. Except he was drunk with Nickie." Jamie laughed insanely. "Men," she said, shaking her head in dismay. Clearly she had expected men to have higher standards in love than her own sister.

"Oh, that's beautiful," sighed Cathy. "Come on, Nickie, into your room for your version. We've already had Christo's and now Jamie's."

"You've already had Christo's?"

"Of course. We had an extra rehearsal this morning. At Anne-Louise's. She has the most wonderful house, Nickie. It's on Fairest Lane, as a matter-of-fact. Her family bought the house three down from your old one, and her living room is huge. The whole chorus can fit in easily. Plus she has a grand piano, not to mention a fabulous electric keyboard. There's nothing that keyboard isn't programmed to do."

"Cathy," muttered Rachel. "I don't think Nickie is thrilled to hear that."

Cathy apologized desperately.

"It doesn't matter," said Nicoletta. It didn't. All that mattered was getting to the boulder, the path, the two lakes, the cave.

And Jethro.

Is he the monster? she thought. How can he be? How can anybody be?

"So," said Rachel, hugging herself with eagerness. She lowered her voice. Excitedly she whispered, "Are you in love with him?"

Nicoletta stared into the faces of her former friends. Still friends, she supposed. Friends because they had not forgotten her . . . and yet, friends she'd forgotten.

Am I in love with him? she thought. Which him do we mean?

She told them many lies. At the time she uttered each sentence, she swore to remember it, so they wouldn't know she was lying, but she tripped continually. She could not remember one lie even through the following lie.

Cathy and Rachel thought it was wonderful. "You're so dizzy with love, you can't even keep your first date straight," accused Rachel. She hugged Nicoletta, cementing something, but Nicoletta did not know what.

"I'm jealous," added Cathy.

The doorbell rang.

"Get it!" yelled Jamie. "I'm busy."

Nicoletta went to the door. In this tiny house, everybody was adjacent to everything and everyone.

It was Christo.

No, she thought. No, not now. I've told enough lies. I can't tell more.

Just seeing her brought a laugh to Christo's lips. "Hi, Nicoletta," he said, trembling over these simple words. It was not a tremble of nervousness, but of sheer pleasure to see her. But of course, it was not only Nicoletta he saw. With a touch of disappointment, he added, "Hi, Cathy. Hi, Rachel."

"We're just leaving," said the girls, nudging each other, pushing the romance along.

Don't leave me alone with Christo! How will I ever get to Jethro if Christo is here? I don't mind lying to you two. If I could explain everything to you, you wouldn't mind. But Christo! He would mind.

For there is no explanation for loving somebody else.

Chapter 12

"Let's all go to the mall!" said Nicoletta. "That would be fun." She clapped her hands like a moron and twirled to make her hair fly out in a golden cloud.

Christo was truly in love. Anything Nicoletta said sounded heavenly to him. "Great idea," he said. He ran his hand up her shoulder and caught at her thick, blonde hair. "You're already in your coat. Were you just leaving with the girls?"

"Yes," said Nicoletta.

Cathy and Rachel looked confused.

"We were talking about Anne-Louise," said Nicoletta. Cathy and Rachel were even more confused.

Christo, however, thought that Nicoletta was a wonderful, generous, and truly forgiving person. He could not get over how easily she had accepted Anne-Louise's presence in the Madrigals, and how well she had dealt with her own loss. He complimented her profusely on her greatness of heart.

Cathy and Rachel looked skeptical.

Christo actually wanted to know if, on the way to the mall, they should swing by Anne-Louise's and pick her up and bring her along. "So the whole gang is together," he said eagerly, as if Nicoletta were part of the gang. Rachel cringed. Cathy held her breath. Boys were so thick.

"Sure," said Nicoletta. "I'd love to get to know her better."

Who is saying these things? she thought. The only thing I'd love to do right now is shake you off, Christo, so I can find Jethro.

They clambered into the van. Christo turned the radio up higher, and then they talked louder, and he turned the radio up even more, and then they shouted and laughed and the interior of the van was a ringing cacophony of music and talk and giggling.

Nicoletta thought of unrequited love. It was dreadful. She could not believe she was a part of it. And yet, it was not unrequited, because Christo did not know. Once he knew, it would qualify. I'm sorry, Christo, she thought.

And then she heard the radio.

The update.

" . . . get a pizza," said Christo, taking Nicoletta's hand. "A new brick-oven pizzeria opened down by the highway exit. Want to go?"

" . . . rather go to the movies later on," said Cathy. "Let's all go, the way we used to. There's a fabulous fantastic cop-chase comedy playing."

Their voices were jackhammers in Nicoletta's skull.

" . . . rescue efforts," said the radio, "are to no avail. The fate of the two missing hunters remains unknown. On the economic front . . ."

"Isn't that scary?" shrieked Rachel. "I mean, those guys just walked off the face of the earth."

Walked off the face of the earth.

It was true. They had. The hunters had fallen down the gullet of the earth, and lay within its bowels.

"I wasn't inviting you for pizza, Cath-Cath," said Christo, friendly and flirty as ever. "Just Nicoletta." He smiled sweetly at Nicoletta and she ducked, as if the smile were a missile.

I was there when they walked off the face of it, she thought. *I know where the face of the earth ends.* And Jethro — what does he do? Cross the boundaries? Go between the face of the earth and whatever lies beyond?

The van whipped on well-plowed roads toward the city and

the mall. Suddenly she saw the little dead-end road, and felt as if her eyes were being ripped out of her head in their effort to see all the way down it, and through the woods, and into the face of the cliff, and down the falling, falling cave.

"Nickie and I had the weirdest adventure the other night," said Christo, laughing and pointing. He turned down the volume of the radio and addressed the other girls. "We were going to park down at the end of that road. It dead-ends, you know, in a forest."

"We know," said Rachel in a sultry voice, implying that she, too, had parked a hundred times. Everybody laughed at her.

"Well," said Christo, in an introductory voice, as if he had much to say. "We go running through the woods. Nick and I. In the middle of the night! Ice and snow and moonshine. And we're running. Past boulders and trees and icicles hanging from the sky."

"Icicles hanging from the sky?" said Cathy, pretending to gag. "Christo you are getting altogether too romantic here. Next thing you know, you'll be writing greeting cards."

"Nickie?" repeated Rachel incredulously. "In the woods after dark? Come on."

"Nicoletta loves the outdoors," Christo told her.

"*Nicoletta?*" said Rachel.

"And," said Christo, "we spotted a thing. A Bigfoot. A monster. A Yeti. Something."

"I'll bet," said Cathy, giggling. "If I were running around in the woods in the middle of the night in the snow, I'd be seeing monsters, too."

"I'm serious," said Christo. He pulled into Fairest Lane without slowing for the curve, and the van spun momentarily out of control. "Oops," said Christo, yanking it back. He missed a tree by inches.

What if we had been killed? thought Nicoletta. Jethro would never know what happened to me.

She sneaked a corner-of-the-eye look at Christo. He had an excited look to him; not a preconcert look, but a prefootball game look. He was an athlete right now.

A hunter.

She had thought he had been confused or too swept away in his emotions to retain the memory of the stone that danced with Nicoletta between the lakes. She had thought he'd forgotten the warts of sand that covered its humanoid features, and its hair like old bones of thin fingers. Instead he had been making plans.

Christo pulled into the driveway of a house so similar to Nicoletta's old one that for a moment she thought she had fallen backward two years, the way the hunters had fallen backward into their particular hole. He honked the horn in a lengthy musical rhythm that must have made the neighbors crazy. Especially the neighbors Nicoletta remembered. It was a Madrigals' call. The hunters, she thought. What were they originally hunting? Ducks? Deer? Did they have a call, too?

I must make Christo hunt *me*, she thought, not Jethro. Christo must not go back. I betrayed Jethro once before. I can't let it happen again.

Anne-Louise came running out, laughing. "Want to go to the mall with us?" shouted Christo. She signaled yes and ran back for her coat and purse. "So what I'm going to do," said Christo to his three passengers, "is go back there and catch it."

"Catch what?" said Rachel.

There, thought Nicoletta. I admitted it. It's Jethro.

"The thing," said Christo. "Bigfoot. The monster. Whatever it is."

Rachel and Cathy exchanged looks. Give-us-a-break looks. This-nonsense-is-annoying-us looks.

Good, thought Nicoletta. If they laugh at him enough, we can get away from it. We'll make him forget it. I have to make him forget it.

"Or shoot it," said Christo, his voice as relaxed as if he were deciding on a flavor of ice cream for a sundae. "Whatever."

Shoot it? Nicoletta's heart felt shot. It isn't an "it," she thought, it's Jethro, you can't shoot him, *I won't let you shoot him!*

"I'd be the only person in North America who ever actually

caught one." Christo beat out a rhythm on the steering wheel with his fists. "What a trophy, huh? Can you imagine the television coverage? I bet there's not a TV show in America I couldn't get on." His grin was different now. Not the sweet tremulous smile of first love, but a hard calculating grin.

A hunter. Ready to hunt.

Anne-Louise came running out of the house.

"After I shoot it, I guess I could have it stuffed," mused Christo.

Nicoletta clung to the seat belt.

"Christo," said Rachel. "Enough. Anne-Louise thinks we are civilized and interesting. Talking about shooting monsters in the woods will not do."

But Cathy was interested. She leaned forward. She tapped Nicoletta's shoulder. "Did you see it, too, Nickie?" she whispered, as if "it" were there, and might overhear, and so she needed to be careful.

Anne-Louise climbed into the van and yanked the sliding door shut after her. The van rocked when it slammed. She sat down breathlessly in the back with Cathy and Rachel and then, recognizing the front seat passenger, cried, "Nicoletta! Oh, what a pleasure! I've heard so much about you!"

"Nice to see you, too," said Nicoletta.

Cathy said louder, "Did you see it, too, Nickie?"

"Yes," said Nicoletta frantically. "I said hi. Nice to have Anne-Louise along."

"The monster," said Cathy irritably.

"No," said Nicoletta. "I didn't see anything. Of course not. There wasn't anything to see. Christo was seeing shadows."

Christo was genuinely angry. "I was not! You actually touched it, Nickie. Remember? Right there by the water and the cliff? Before we fell in?"

"You guys were running around in the dark in the woods where there were cliffs to fall off and water to fall in?" shrieked Rachel. "That sounds like the most horrible night on earth. Christo, remind me never to go on a date with you."

"It was Nicoletta's idea," said Christo defensively. "She knows the people who live around there."

"Who?" demanded Rachel. "Who lives around there?"

Nicoletta tried to shrug. "Nobody. Nothing. There wasn't anybody there."

"There was so a monster!" said Christo. He was really annoyed that she was not backing his story up. "And there was a cave! You were there, Nickie. You know I'm not making it up."

"A cave?" said Anne-Louise. "I wonder if that's what happened to those poor hunters. Where is this cave?"

Nicoletta was colder than she had ever been in the ice and snow.

Anne-Louise put a heavy, demanding hand on Nicoletta's shoulder. "Where is this cave?" she repeated. "We must notify the authorities. Who is this friend of yours who lives near there? He must show the rescue teams where to look."

Nicoletta heard her voice climb an octave and become brittle and screamy. "Christo is just being silly, Anne-Louise. Keep going to the mall, Christo. I need to buy . . . I need to look for . . . I'm out of . . . "

But she could not think of anything she needed or was out of.

Except time.

Chapter 13

At the mall, the teenagers gathered around a large, slablike direct-ory of stores and entertainments. Christo was giving orders. First, he decreed, Anne-Louise was to stop her noise about the author-ities. This had nothing to do with the two missing hunters. He was not going to tell her where the cave was. It would not become her business until she saw him on television. He was going by himself tomorrow morning to capture it. It would be his personal trophy. Second, Cathy and Rachel were to stop nagging and asking questions and not believing him. Third, Nicoletta was to tell him Jethro's last name and phone number, so he could get in touch with this person who undoubtedly knew the woods best.

Cathy and Rachel said they didn't know what anybody else was going to do about Christo's sudden personality change into staff sergeant, but they personally were going to try on shoes. Good-bye. And they would be happy to see Christo again once he turned back into a fun person.

Anne-Louise said that if Nicoletta and Christo wanted to hunt monsters and leave hunters to their hideous deaths, it was on their consciences not hers, and she was looking for shoes, too. So there.

Nicoletta was thinking that although her grasp of local geog-raphy was not great, the rear mall parking lot might back onto the woods. She might be able to walk through from this end and find the path, the two lakes, and Jethro. She waved good-bye to the other three girls.

What do I think will happen if I find the cave? Do I think Jethro will explain this away. Do I believe there could be an explanation? Do I expect to haul the hunters' bodies up so they can be found, and meanwhile hide Jethro? Do I expect to bring Jethro home with me, in whatever form he exists today, and ask my parents to let him sleep on the living room couch for a few years?

The mall was its usual bland self. Nothing ever changed there. The shiny, dark floors, the softly sliding escalators, the windows full of shoes and toys, the people sitting beneath indoor trees eating frozen yogurt. For a moment Nicoletta did not know which world was more strange: the world of the cave or the mall.

Christo, however, was not bland. He was full of the hunt. His muscles, his stride, his speech — they all talked together. He wanted this capture. He wanted this television coverage. This fame. This triumph.

It came to her in an unusual moment of understanding that he was not only hunting the thing he had seen in the forest; he was also hunting Nicoletta herself.

He was going to bring her a trophy she could not refuse.

He was going to show off his physical prowess, not on the football field where she had never even bothered to look, but in the forest, which she had claimed to love.

It was deeply flattering. She could not prevent herself from basking in this. Christo — admired by every girl in town — Christo wanted to impress only Nicoletta.

And she, after all, was not thinking only of Jethro. She wanted to impress Christo right back. But later. Much later. Right now she had to get to Jethro first. Warn him. Save him. Keep him.

As if, she thought in another moment of unwanted clarity, as if Jethro is *my* trophy before he's Christo's trophy.

She could think of nothing to say that was not stupid. Let's get French fries. Let's go with the others and try on sneakers. Let's check out the new videos and T-shirts and perfumes and pizza toppings. This nonsense when Christo was saying: Let's shoot the monster. And stuff it. Let's go out there and get the thing. "You don't want to come," he assured her. "You'd get squeamish." He laughed a strong male laugh, full of plans and promises. "In the morning," said Christo, "I'll take my father's shotgun."

The hunters had had shotguns. And what had happened to them?

She had a third all-too-clear vision.

It was not Jethro she had to worry about. Jethro was safe. The cave was his and he knew it.

It was Christo — innocent, show-off, excited Christo.

What had happened to the hunters would happen to him. He, too, would fall forever down. If she let Christo go on this expedition, she would betray him as well. She knew the length and depth of the fall Christo would take. She knew where he would hit bottom.

She knew he would never come out.

Never again sing or play ball. Never flirt or grow old.

Now as she looked at Christo, he seemed infinitely desirable. Perfect in every way. A person the world must have, a person who must live out his life span.

Christo, looking down at her, saw emotion in her eyes. He saw desire and fear and hope but he read it as love. Not a wish that he would live, but a wish that he would be hers.

Right there in the blandness of the encircling mall, among tired mothers pushing strollers and bored teenagers sipping soda, he kissed her with the sort of passion reserved for movies. The sort of intensity that belonged on late night drama.

He was embracing her with a ferocity she did not expect from a Madrigal singer. Perhaps this was Christo the football player, perhaps she was a goalpost he was trying to reach.

But no. He was kissing with the ferocity of a hunter.

When it ended, people were smiling softly and indulgently, enjoying this glimpse of true love. Christo was dizzy, backlit with the glow of his crush on her. He pulled slightly back from her to admire her from a distance of several inches instead of eyelashes against eyelashes.

But Nicoletta only wondered if Jethro would ever kiss her like that.

The day passed as, unbelievably, all days do.

It was a fact of life that fascinated Nicoletta. Even the worst days draw to a close. Sometimes a day seems to have the potential of lying there forever, trapping its victims as if they were treads on a circling escalator. But it never happens. The shopping ends, the van brings you home. The sun goes down, and the table is set for supper.

She endured her family. She swallowed her meal. She stared at a television screen. She held a book on her lap.

Outside, the snow fell yet again. They had never had such a winter for snow. The wind picked up, singing its own songs, sobbing its own laments. It dug tunnels in the drifts, as if hunting for its own set of hidden bodies.

Nicoletta undressed for the night.

Naked, she examined her body. What body did Jethro possess, he of the sandy hands and the granite face?

If I wait till morning, she thought, Christo will already have left on his hunt.

So I cannot wait till morning.

Chapter 14

The night was young. She had heard that phrase and never understood it. But now at one in the morning, she knew the meaning. She ran easily over the crusted snow, jumping the immense piles the plows had shoved against the curbs. She, too, was young. They had been born together, she and the night.

But the dirt road was far and the roads, with their walls of hard-packed, exhaust-blackened snow, obstructed her.

She was afraid of being seen. If a police car happened by . . . if grown-ups returning from parties noticed her . . . would they not stop? Demand to know why a lone girl was running down deserted streets at such an hour?

But the snow loaned Nicoletta enough hiding places to last a lifetime. Every pair of headlights caused her to bend a knee, and wait patiently behind a snow mountain until the vehicle passed by, and then she rose to her feet and ran on.

The night grew older. After one it became two, and was fast reaching three when finally she came to the end of the paved road, and found herself in the woods she wanted. She was exhausted. When the running ended, the trembling of legs and joints began, as if her body wanted to give up now, before its goal.

The boulder waited for her. It had gained in stature, for the snow had drifted upon it, increasing its height and breadth. As she trudged wearily up to it, snow fell from its stony mouth like words she did not comprehend.

She stopped walking. She had a sense of the boulder taking aim. The moon was only a sliver, and the stars were diamond dust. It was not enough to see by. And yet she saw.

And was seen.

In the pure, pure black of the night, she felt eyes. A thousand eyes, searching her like a thousand fingers. "Jethro," she whispered.

She wet her lips for courage and the damp froze and her mouth was encrusted with ice, the way Jethro's body was encrusted with sand. "Jethro," she cried, louder.

There was not a breath of wind. Just icy air hunched down against the floor of the forest as if it planned not to shift for months. She waded through the cold and it hung onto her pants legs and shot through the lining of her jacket.

When she reached the boulder, she put her mittened hand against it for support. But there was no support. There was not even any rock. She fell forward, her hand arriving nowhere at all. She screamed, remembering her brief fall in the cave.

But this fall, too, was brief.

There was so much snow that her arm went through white right up to the elbow and then she touched rock. But under its blanket, the rock was not warm and friendly. It seemed to lunge forward, as if to hurtle her away from itself.

"Jethro!" she shrieked.

The trees leaned closer and listened harder. She pressed her back against the great rock, even though it did not want to shelter her. "Jethro!"

Her voice was the only sound in the silent black. It lay like an alien in another atmosphere. Nothing answered.

She would have to go to the cave in this terrible dark.

She remembered that first portion of her life when every day she had acted out *Little House on the Prairie*. She preferred being Laura, of course, because Laura had more fun, but every now and then it was her turn to be Mary. Nicoletta had always wanted to change the course of history and give Mary antibiotics so she didn't go blind. That was the only really awful thing in *Little House*. Oh, you could have your best friend read aloud to you for ten minutes and be your eyes for half an hour, but then you lost interest and had better things to do, and you didn't really like to think about Mary being stuck inside herself. Caught there in the dark. It used to make Nicoletta feel guilty and crawly that she could run away from blindness. Run into the sun and see and know the shapes and colors of the world, while Mary had to sit quietly at the table, forever and ever and ever in the dark.

The woods were so very dark.

She even thought she understood the meaning of forever, it was that dark.

If she did not find Jethro, she might lose her balance and slide into the black lakes and she, too, would be forever and ever in the dark.

A hand took hers firmly and guided her down the straight path toward the lakes. She was grateful for help and tightened her grip on the hand and even said thank you.

But there was no one there.

She was holding a stick. She could not even remember picking it up. It was weirdly forked, as if it really had once been a hand. She threw it hard into the trees to get it off her but it clung to her mitten and went nowhere. She began to cry soundlessly, because she was afraid the rest of the twigs and trees would attack if she made an ugly noise.

"Don't be afraid." The voice came from nowhere, from nothing. Now she screamed silently, twice as afraid. "They're trying to help," it said.

She was frozen. She had neither breath nor blood.

"It's me. I don't want you to look. I don't want you to know. You shouldn't have come, Nicoletta. Why do you keep coming when I keep telling you to stay away?"

Jethro. Oh, Jethro! "I had to warn you." She could not see

anything. She knew his voice but he was not there. Nothing was there.

"Warn me of what?"

"Christo is coming back in the morning," she said. She began to cry again, and it was a mistake, for the tears froze separately on her cheeks and lay like rounded crystals upon her skin. "He wants to get you. Shoot you. Stuff you. He wants to take you for a trophy and go on television with you."

"Don't worry." Jethro's voice was consoling and gentle. "He won't find me. He'll find only the bottom of the cave."

The bottom of the cave.

Handsome, flirty, athletic Christo taking one step too many. Tumbling backward, screaming his final scream, hands flailing to stop himself, body twisting as helplessly as a pinecone falling from a tree.

Landing on the sharp spikes of stalagmites, dying slowly perhaps, his bones mingled with the bones of the hunters.

Oh, Christo! You don't deserve that!

He'll find only the bottom of the cave. How could Jethro say a thing of such horror in a voice of such comfort?

Fireworks of shock rocketed behind her blind eyes.

"Anyway," said Jethro, "the hunters will be glad to see him. They need company."

"What do you mean? Weren't they killed?"

"No one is killed by a fall into that cave."

"Jethro! Then I have to call the police! And the fire department! They'll bring ladders and ropes! We'll get the hunters out! We'll —"

"No, Nicoletta. No one gets out of the cave."

"You get out!"

"It took me a hundred years to learn how."

Exaggeration annoyed her. "Don't be ridiculous. Jethro, where are you? I can't really see you."

"I don't want you to really see me," he said quietly. "I don't want you to be as scared of me as you would be."

"I've seen you before! I know you in that shape. Jethro, *I need you.*"

There was no sound in the woods except the sound of her own breathing. Perhaps Jethro did not breathe. Perhaps he was all rock and no lungs. But then, how did he speak? Or did he not? Was she making it up? Was she out here in the woods by herself, talking to trees, losing her mind?

"You need me?" said Jethro. His voice quavered.

Humans have two great requirements of life. To be needed is as important as love. Now she knew that he was human, that he was the boy who sat beside her in art as well as the creature wrapped in stone. "I need you," she repeated. She slid her scarlet mitten off her hand and extended her bare fingers into the night.

The hand that closed around them rasped with the rough edges of stone. But the sob that came from his chest was a child's.

Chapter 15

They sat on the boulder, wrapped in snow as if in quilts. It was a high, round throne and the woods were their kingdom. The night was old now. The silver sliver of moon had come to rest directly above them, and its frail light gleamed on the old snow and shimmered on her gold hair.

She kept his hands in her lap like possessions. They were real hands. They had turned real between her own, as if the oven of her caring had burnt away the bad parts. "You are a real boy," she said to him.

"I was once. It was a long time ago."

She snuggled against him as if expecting a cozy bedtime story of the sort her parents loved to tell.

"Long ago," said Jethro. He told his story in short spurts, letting each phrase lie there in the dark, as if each must mellow and grow old like the night before he could go on to the next. "Long before the Pilgrims," said Jethro, "ancient sailors from an ancient land shipwrecked here."

The town was only a few miles from the sea, but she never thought of it that way. There was no public beach and Nicoletta rarely even caught a glimpse of the ocean. People with beaches were people with privacy.

"They found the cave," said Jethro slowly, "and explored it for gold."

Yes. She could believe that. Those gleaming walls and incredible patterns of royal rock — anybody would expect to find treasure.

"There was none. The men who went first fell to the bottom, and could not be rescued by the others." His voice waited until she had fully imagined the men in the bottom who could not be rescued. "They had to be abandoned," he said, his voice a tissue of sorrow.

"Still alive?" asked Nicoletta.

"Still alive."

Wounded and broken. Screaming from the bottom of a well of blackness. Hearing no words of comfort from above. But instead, words of farewell. *We're sorry, we've got to go now. Die bravely.*

"In their society," said Jethro, "the soul could not depart from the body unless the body was burned at sea with its ship. But they, of course, could never return to the ship. And so the men at the bottom of the cave never died. Their souls could not leave. Their bodies . . . dissolved over the decades." His voice was soft. With revulsion or pity, she did not know. "Until," he said, "they became the cave itself. Things with warts of sand and crusts of mineral."

His hands took her golden hair, and he wove his fingers through it, and then he kissed her hair, kissed that long thick rope, but he did not kiss her face. "The ones who fell," said Jethro, "put a curse on the cave."

A chill of horrified excitement flashed down Nicoletta's spine. She had never heard a human being utter those words. *A curse be upon you.*

"What was the curse?" She whispered because he did. Their voices were hissing and lightweight, like falling snow.

"Whoever entered that cave," said Jethro, "would be forever abandoned by the world. Just as they had been."

Was he one of them? Ancient as earth? But the boy she knew from Art was her age. A breathing, speaking boy with thick, dark hair and hidden eyes.

"And did Indians fall in?" she asked.

"The Indians always had a sense of the earth and its mysteries. They knew better than to go near the cave."

He seemed to stop. He seemed to have nothing more to say. She asked no questions. The moon slid across the black, black sky. "Then," said Jethro, "white men came again to these shores. To farm and hunt and eventually to explore." Now he was speaking with difficulty, and the accents of his voice were lifting and strange. "My father and I," he said, "found the cave. So beautiful! I had never seen anything beautiful. We did not have a beautiful life. We did not have beautiful possessions. So I stayed in the outer chambers, touching the smooth rock. Staring at the light patterns on the brimstone. Dazzled," he said. "I was dazzled. But my father . . . "

How softly, how caressingly, he spoke the word *father*. A shaft of moonlight fell upon the monstrous shape of him and she could see the boy inside the rock. His eyes might have been carved from a vein of gold. He smiled at her, the sculpture of his face shifting as if it lived. It was a smile of ineffable sadness.

"My father went on in."

She turned to look at him.

"My father fell, of course. He fell among the abandoned, and they kept him."

He stopped. The warmth of the great rock dissipated. It was cold. She waited for Jethro to descend through the centuries and return to her.

"I didn't leave the cave. If I had run back out . . . things would have been different. But I loved my father," he said. His voice broke. "I offered myself in exchange. I told the spirits at the bottom of the cave that they could have me if they would give up my father. They were willing. My father was willing. He said he would come back for me. He emerged at the same moment that I fell into the cave on purpose."

Jethro paused for a long time. "I try to remember that," he told Nicoletta. "I try to remember that I stepped off the edge because I wanted to."

"Were you hurt?"

He smiled again, his sadness so great that Nicoletta wept when he did not. "I broke no bones," he said finally. He said it as if something else had broken.

"What did your father do? He must have run back to the house and the town and gotten everybody to bring ropes and ladders."

Jethro's smile was not normal. "There was a curse on the cave," he said. "I told you that." His words seemed trapped by the frost. They hung in front of his lips, crystallized in the air.

She had been listening to the story without listening. It was a problem for her in school, too. She heard but did not keep the teachers' words. She moved her mind backward, to retrieve Jethro's speech. "*Whoever entered,*" she repeated slowly, "*would be forever abandoned by the world. Just as they had been.*"

Jethro nodded.

The moon was hidden by a cloud.

Jethro put a hand gently over her eyes. "Don't move," he said softly. "Don't look again."

His hand was heavy. Stonelike. "Your father?" she said. "Abandoned you?"

"He walked away. He walked out of the cave and into the daylight. He never came back. Nobody ever came back. I called and called. Day after day I called. He was my father! He loved me. I know he did. Even though there was nothing else beautiful in our lives, that was beautiful. He loved me."

She opened her eyes under the weight of his hands and saw only the underside of a rock. She closed her eyes again.

"Even though I gave myself up for him," said Jethro, his voice caught as if it, too, were falling to a terrible fate, "I didn't understand that it was forever. I was sure he would return and rescue me."

Rescue. A lovely word. Certain and sure. I will rescue you, Jethro, thought Nicoletta. I love you. I will rescue you from all curses and dark fallings.

"But he didn't, of course," said Jethro.

Jethro cried out. A strange terrible moan like the earth shifting. A groan so deep and so long she knew that he was still calling for his father to rescue him.

Being a monster was not as terrible as being abandoned by his father. Nothing on earth could be worse. Forgotten by your father? A child goes on loving a father who drinks too much, or beats him, or does drugs . . . but a father who leaves the son to endure horror forever . . . and even forgets that he did that . . . it was the ultimate divorce.

Abandoned. The word took on a terrible force. She could see his feet — that father's feet — as they walked away. Never to turn around. She could hear the cries, echoing over the years: that son, calling his father's name. Never to hear an answer.

"I try not to hate him," said Jethro. "I try to remember that there were no choices for him. The curse carried him away from me and kept him away. But he was my father!" The voice rose like the howl of a dying animal into the winter air. "He was my father! I thought he would come! I waited and waited and waited."

The voice sagged, and fell, and splintered on the forest floor.

"Oh, Jethro!" she said, and hugged him. He was sharp and craggy but the tighter she held her arms the more he softened. She felt him becoming the boy again, felt the power of her caring for him fight the power of the curse upon him. He removed his heavy hand from her eyes but she kept them closed for a while anyhow.

"You can emerge from the cave and be a real person some of the time," she said.

"It's a gift of the light. Sunlight, usually. I am surprised that the moonlight is giving me this now. Sunshine is a friend. It doesn't end the curse, but sometimes it gives me a doorway to the world. Haven't you noticed that I am only in school on sunny days? I cannot touch the world except on bright days."

"I will make all your days bright," said Nicoletta.

"You have," he said, his voice husky with emotion. "I think of you when I cannot leave."

For a long time they sat in each other's arms. Moonlight

glittered on the fallen snow and danced on the icy fingers of trees. Very carefully she turned to look at him. He was Jethro. She sighed with relief. He had been in there all along, and she — she, Nicoletta Storms — had freed him with her presence. "At least I'll see you in school," she said.

"No. I can't go again."

"Why not? *Why not?* You have to! Oh, Jethro, you have to come back to school! I have to see you!" She gripped his arms and held him hard.

"You must forget about me."

"I can't. I won't. You don't want me to. I don't want to. We're not going to forget about each other."

He said nothing.

"Why do you come to school?" she asked him.

"To dream of how it might have been. You are my age. The age, anyway, that I was once. The age when I fell. I hear human voices, I recognize laughter. I see human play and friendship."

Oh, the loneliness of the dark!

She pictured her family. How loving they were. How warm the small house was. She thought of Jethro, returning every time to the dark and the rage of the trapped undead. She kissed him, hungrily, to kiss away his loss. Around them the trees leaned closer and looked deeper. "Jethro, it feels as if the woods are alive," she whispered.

"They are," said Jethro. "We were all something else once. Every tree and stone. Every lake and ledge."

Horror surrounded her. She breathed it into her lungs and felt it crawl into her hair, like bats. She could not look into the woods.

"You must go home. You must never come again."

"But I love you."

He flinched. He pushed her away, and then could not bear that, because nobody had loved him in so very long. He held her more tightly than ever, cherishing the thought. *Somebody loved him.*

Love works only when it circles, and it *had* circled. It had enclosed them both. She loved him and he loved her back. He had to love her enough to make her stay away.

"Never come near the cave again. They know about you. They will look for you now, and guide your steps so that you fall. They will take you, Nicoletta. What else do they have to do for all eternity? Nothing. They will never be buried by fire at sea. You must go and never come back."

She was unmoved. Nobody would tell her never to do anything. Nobody would tell her that she could find true love and then have to walk away from it! No. She would always come back.

"Nicoletta," he said. His voice was hollow now, like a reed . . . or a cave.

"If you get too close, not only will you fall, I — cursed by the cave — I would do to you what my own father did to me."

She was looking into his eyes, eyes like precious gemstones. I love you, she thought.

He said, "*I would abandon you.*"

Abandon her? She could not believe it. He loved her. Love did not abandon.

"Abandon you forever, Nicoletta. In the dark. Turning to stone. Forgotten. I would not come back. Nobody would ever come back for you."

The moon hid behind wispy clouds. The night was too old to be called night. Jethro left. He had been there, and then he was not. She was alone on the stone in the dark.

For he did love her.

And to prove it, he had to leave. And so did she.

Chapter 16

It had taken great courage to walk into the woods.

It took none to walk out.

If Jethro was not afraid of what the trees and ledges had once been, how could she be afraid? She said good-bye to the boulder, but it said and did nothing, which surprised her. She had expected a response after the conversation and the agony it had heard; the loving it had seen.

When she reached the paved road, she would have to put away these things. Enter into her other life.

How distant it seemed — her other world.

Nicoletta touched the pavement.

Dawn was coming. Quickly the sun threw scarlet threads into the sky, and quickly the snow turned pink in greeting. As if they were flirting and blushing. Like me, she thought. She smiled to herself, and then smiled at the sun.

She walked swiftly. She was happy.

What is there to be happy about? she thought. That the sun rises? That I love Jethro but he doesn't want me to come again?

And yet she was happy in a liquid way, as if she were still all one, a water glass of pure happiness, a crystal cylinder of delight.

Love, she thought. I know what it is now. It's every molecule of you. It connects you to yourself, even if you cannot be connected to the person who caused it.

Jethro. Oh, it was a beautiful name!

A car turned down the DEAD END road.

She had not wanted the other world to appear so soon.

A second vehicle followed it.

She considered hiding. Stepping off the road into the trees. She knew that the trees would take her in. Circle her, and blind the cars to her presence for Jethro's sake. Snow, its sides packed like a ski jump by a plow, and a little, green holly tree without berries were on either side of her. She could hunch down behind the sharp, leather leaves and not be seen.

The first vehicle was Christo's van. The second vehicle was a television network van.

Nicoletta had omitted the part that counted. She had entertained herself. She had run to Jethro for talk and love and comfort and daydreams. But the important part of what she had needed to do before morning, she had skipped.

Christo, who was equally liquid and crystal with love. Christo, who was hot and surging with the need to show off, to hunt, to capture or to destroy.

Not only had Christo come. He had brought teams. Witnesses. Camera film. And, no doubt, weapons.

She thought of the cave. The long fall that Christo and his TV crew would take. The horrible slime and sand and narrowing walls of shining stone. The knowledge that they were doomed. Of course, they would not have that knowledge as they fell. They would think there was a way out. Or that rescue would come.

How many days, or weeks . . . *or years* . . . would they struggle against their fate? How long before they became, as Jethro had become, part of the cave? Just another outcropping of sand and rock and dripping water? Would she, Nicoletta, in that other world have grown up and had children and grandchildren and been buried herself by the time Christo understood and surrendered to his fate?

The van rushed down the narrow road.

Christo drove too fast, gripping the wheel of his car, leaning forward as if trying to see beyond the windshield and through the woods, behind the rock and into the cave. He looked neither left nor right, only ahead. He didn't see the packed snow and the holly, let alone Nicoletta. She had a glimpse of his profile as he sped past. How handsome he was. How young and perfect.

And how excited. He thought this would be an adventure. And oh! it would be. But not one in which he conquered.

She could not let him fall! Nor could she let those poor strangers in the van meet that fate.

The television van came much more slowly. Its driver was middle-aged and frowning, studying the road, the snow, the sky, as if he were worrying about a change in the weather, the studio deadline, his taxes, his wife, and his aching feet all at the same time.

He could have been her father.

He was surely somebody's father. Would he, like the hunters, end up forever fallen?

I have to do something, she thought. But what? I can't talk them out of it. The more information I give them, the more eager they'll be. The more I explain, the quicker they'll rush to see for themselves. And even if they stay away from the cave, even if I can convince them to stay in the meadow, or between the lakes, or among the trees . . . they'll try to shoot Jethro.

I have no control. I have no moves. I have no way to turn.

This is not the world of the ancient Indians who understood that there were mysteries, and that mysteries should not be touched. This is the world of the television networks, who think that everything on earth belongs to them and ought to be captured on their cameras.

Perhaps she owed Christo nothing; after all, she did not love him; it was he who loved her. Perhaps she should let them go, and let Jethro control what happened.

But love was too precious. Even if it was not hers, and would never be hers, how could she be part of its ending? She did not love Christo, but it counted that he loved her.

The television van was almost upon her.

She flung herself out from behind the piled snow and the little holly tree . . . directly under the wheels of the van.

"She jumped!" said the van driver constantly. "I swear it. The girl jumped right in front of me."

"I slipped," Nicoletta explained. It was not easy to talk because of the pain. The broken leg was so very broken. Pieces of bone stuck out of her flesh like long white splinters. "Snow," she explained. "Ice. No sand on the road yet. It's my fault. I should have been more careful."

Whatever spell Christo had cast to coax a network to send a crew, had dried up. The people who had been eager to film whatever this kid thought he'd seen, especially since it was near the disappearing point of the two hunters, were now interested in nothing but getting through a terrible day. The van driver was desperate to be sure everybody understood it was not his fault. He said this to Nicoletta's parents and to the doctors and the admitting secretary in the emergency room and to Christo.

Christo had questions of his own to ask Nicoletta, but being severely hurt provided its own camouflage. She need only close her eyes, rest her long lashes on her pale cheeks, and whisper. "I'm tired, Christo, visit me tomorrow." And he had to leave. No options.

The cast was big and white and old-fashioned. No vinyl and metal athletic brace for a break this bad; solid heavy-duty plaster and bandage was like a rock attached to her leg. She had always rather hoped to be wearing a cast one day, and attract lots of sympathetic attention, and have to use crutches.

But now she faced a new nightmare.

How will I go back to Jethro? thought Nicoletta. I can't get through the woods with this. I can't use crutches in the snow.

Not only had she stopped Christo and the TV crew from looking for Jethro, she had stopped herself.

People asked what she had been doing, anyway, on some

remote road at the crack of dawn? There was only one acceptable excuse and she used it. "I've taken up jogging, you know. I've been running every morning."

Her parents had not known this, but then, they didn't get up before dawn and could not say she hadn't been.

Jamie was too jealous of the attention Nicoletta was getting to ask difficult questions. Jamie kept looking around for cute interns instead.

When Nicoletta woke up in the afternoon, she was alone in a quiet hospital room with pastel walls. The other bed was empty. There was something eerie about the flat white sheets and the untouched, neatly folded, cotton blanket on the other bed. It was waiting for its next victim.

The door was closed. She had no sense of noise or action or even human beings around her. She might have been alone at the bottom of the cave, she was so alone in the bare, pale room.

Her leg hurt.

Her head ached.

I'll never even be able to tell Jethro what I did for him, she thought, in a burst of self-pity. I'll hobble around by myself and nobody will care.

The door was flung open, banging heavily into the pastel plaster wall.

The Madrigals burst into the room, singing as they came. It was so corny. They were singing an old European hiking song: "And as we go, we love to sing, our knapsacks on our backs. Foll-der-oolllll, foll-der-eeeeee, our knapsacks on our backs."

She was so glad to see them that it made her cry. It was hokey, but it was beautiful. It was friendship.

"Now, now," said Ms. Quincy, "we won't stay long, it's too exhausting for somebody as badly hurt as you are. We just wanted you to be sure you know that you're among friends."

Nicoletta looked up, thinking, Ms. Quincy had a lot of nerve, when she'd kicked Nicoletta away from those friends. But out loud she said, "Hi, everybody. I'm glad to see you."

They all kissed her, and Christo's kiss was no different from anybody else's. She wanted to catch his hand, and see if he was all right. Ask what he was thinking. But she didn't really want to know.

Rachel had brought colored pens so everybody could sign the cast. Rachel herself wrote, "*I love you, Nickie! Get well soon!*"

This meant everybody could write, *I love you, Nickie*, and they did. David and Jeff, whom she hardly knew, wrote, "*I love you, Nickie, get well soon.*" Cathy did, Lindsay did, even Anne-Louise. "*Love you, Nickie!*"

Christo was last. She had to do something. She was out of action, but he might return to the cave anyway. She had to exert some sort of pull on him.

"Why were you there?" he breathed. "What were you doing? It was awfully far from home to be jogging."

"I knew you were coming, Christo," she murmured. "I wanted to watch you in action. I wanted to be part of it." She squeezed his hand. "Promise me you won't do anything unless I'm along to watch you, Christo?"

Everything about him softened. The love he had for her surfaced so visibly that the girl Madrigals were touched and the boy Madrigals were embarrassed. Nicoletta blushed, but not from love. Because he believed her. Because love, among all the other things it was, was gullible. Everybody had written, "Love you, Nickie," but he wrote on her cast, "*I love you more. Christo.*"

The Madrigals left, singing again, this time a burbling Renaissance song that imitated brooks and flutes. It was a lullabye, and Nicoletta slept, deep and long.

She dreamed that she was falling.

Falling in dreadfully icy cold, wind whipping through her hair and freezing her lungs. She dreamed that her hand was reaching for something to catch. Anything! A branch, a rock, a ladder, a rope —

— but found only sand.

The flat of her palm slid across the grit, finding nothing to hold, nothing at all, and the black forever hole below her opened its mouth.

In her sleep she screamed silently, because everything in that terrible world was dark and silent, and in one last desperate try she tightened her grip.

She found a hand. It held her. It saved her. She woke. It was Jethro's hand. He had come. He was safe. He had not been hurt, and nobody had hurt him. He was here in a pastel hospital room.

He leaned over her bed and found her lips. He kissed her as lightly as air and whispered, "Nicoletta. *Oh, Nicoletta.* I love you."

Even when used by strangers like David and Jeff, or people at whom she was angry like Ms. Quincy, those three words remained beautiful. But from the lips of the boy she loved, those three words were the most beautiful on earth.

"I love you, too," she whispered.

A rare smile illuminated his face, momentarily safe from its terrible burdens. They held hands, and his was graveled and rasping, and hers was soft and silken.

Chapter 17

Jethro yelled at Nicoletta, albeit softly. "You could have been killed!"

"I know that now, but there wasn't time to think of that then."

"What were you thinking of?" he demanded.

"You."

The quiet of the hospital room deepened, and the pale colors of the walls intensified. Her hand in his felt warmer and his hand in hers felt gentler. "I can't stay long," he said.

"Why not? Stay forever."

He smiled sadly. He understood what forever meant. She had no grasp.

"Then I'll talk fast. Jethro, I have ideas." Her eyes burned with excitement. "The thing is," she said, "to bury them. Right?"

"To bury them?" repeated Jethro.

"The ancient souls! They didn't get buried. That's the problem, right? So we have to bury them. We'll blast the cave! We'll dynamite them up! Or else we'll flood the cave! Or else we'll bring torches. We'll get toy wooden boats to count as their ships and set fire to those!"

He did not respond.

"Jethro! Don't you think those ideas are terrific?"

He said instead, "Who do you think you will have if you have me?"

Now she was the one to repeat words that meant nothing to her. "Who will I have if I have you?"

"Nicoletta," he said. "What if you have me . . . as a thing?"

She did not want to think about that.

"You screamed the first time I touched you. Because I am part of the cave. It's in me now. I don't even know why I came here, I could get caught in my other shape. There's no way out of my other being, Nicoletta." His sentences, normally so hard to come by, tumbled and fell on top of each other, like hunters in caves. "You told me yourself what your friend Christo wanted to do to me. Shoot me. Or exhibit me."

"Well, I won't let him."

"How many times do you plan to step in front of trucks?"

After the fact, Nicoletta was aware of what she had done. She certainly did not want death. That was what this was all about! She wanted life, and she wanted it for both of them. Life and love, hope and joy. No. She did not plan to step in front of any more trucks. "Jethro, there has to be a way out for us."

His eyes looked into a deep distance she could not follow. Did not want to follow. Did not want to think about. "Think of rescue," she said urgently. "We have to work on this, Jethro." She gripped him with both her hands. "What's the point of love if we can't be together?"

His chest rose and fell. She wanted his shirt off, so she could touch his skin and rest her cheek against that beating heart.

His lips moved silently, but she could not read the words. Was he repeating that lovely word *rescue*? Was he imagining that it really could be done? That there really was a way out?

He said, "Love always has a point. Even if it stays within. Or is hidden. Or is helpless."

Nicoletta was angry with him. That was stupid. Who would want a helpless love? Who would want a hidden love?

"Okay," she said, "if you don't want to try anything drastic, what we'll do is tell my parents. We'll explain. They're wonderful people. We'll —"

"And think of what could go wrong," he interrupted. "What if your father fell into the cave? Or your mother? Or your little sister? To be lost forever instead?"

She wanted to joke. My little sister wouldn't be such a loss. But he knew nothing of jokes. "You don't even want to try dynamite?" she said.

"How would you get it?"

"My father bought some to blow up stumps in the backyard. But he never got around to it. It's just there in the garage."

He shook his head. The silence she had first found fascinating annoyed Nicoletta now. "We have to work out a strategy!" she said sharply. "We need to make plans."

But he said nothing, keeping his thoughts. Her hospital room darkened, more infected by his bleak hopelessness than her eager love.

A nurse bustled into the room. She was the sort of woman who called her patients "we." "How are we feeling, dear?" she said, thrusting a thermometer into Nicoletta's mouth so that answers were not possible. "Let's take our blood pressure," she said. She pumped the cuff up so tightly on Nicoletta's arm that Nicoletta had to hold her breath to keep from crying. She did not want to be a sissy in front of Jethro. She stayed in control by trying to read her blood pressure upside down, watching the mercury bounce on the tiny dial. She failed. "What is it?" she asked the nurse.

"Fine," said the nurse. "Keep the thermometer in your mouth."

"But what were the numbers?" mumbled Nicoletta. She hated medical people who kept your own bodily facts to themselves.

Reluctantly, as if answering might start a riot, the nurse said, "One-ten over seventy."

Nicoletta, who had studied blood pressure in biology last year, was delighted. "I'm in great health then," she said happily. The thermometer fell out of her mouth and onto the sheets. The nurse picked it up grumpily. Then she placed two cool fingers on Nicoletta's wrist.

Nicoletta looked at Jethro to share amusement at an old-fashioned nurse. Jethro was not there. A thing, a dark and dripping thing, like a statue leaking its own stone, was propped against the wall. Crusted as if with old pus, it could have been a corpse left to dry.

A scream rose in Nicoletta's throat. Horror as deep as the cave possessed her. He had changed right there, right in this room. In public, in front of people, he had become a monster. She could not look at him, she could not bear it that beautiful Jethro had turned into this.

"My goodness!" exclaimed the nurse. "Your pulse just sky-rocketed. Whatever are you thinking about?"

I cannot scream, she thought. People will come. The nurse just has to leave quietly with her little chart and her little cart. I cannot scream.

She screamed.

The nurse followed Nicoletta's eyes and saw a monster.

In the split second before the nurse, too, screamed in horror, Nicoletta saw Jethro's eyes hidden beneath the oozing grit of his curse. Shame and hurt filled his eyes like tears. Fear followed, swallowing any other emotions.

Jethro was terrified.

Oh, Jethro! she thought. Your life isn't a life, it's a nightmare. Your body isn't a body, it's a trap.

Jethro vanished from the room before the nurse could finish reacting. Nicoletta heard his steps, lugging himself out of the room, down the hall, trying to escape.

There was nothing left of him there but a gritty handprint on a pastel wall.

The nurse was made of stronger stuff than Nicoletta had thought. She caught her scream and ran out of the room after Jethro, shouting for security.

No, thought Nicoletta, let him get away! Please let him get away!

She needed to run interference, needed to make excuses, think up lies, anything! Her leg lay on the mattress, heavy and white and unmoving. She literally could not get off the bed.

"Okay, okay," said a grumpy voice in the hallway outside Nicoletta's door. "We've phoned for security. Somebody will be up in a few minutes. Now what was the intruder doing?"

There was a pause. Nicoletta recognized it. The nurse had no idea what to say without sounding ridiculous or hysterical. "He was — he was just standing there," said the nurse lamely.

"What did he look like?" said the grumpy voice. "Race? Age?"

The nurse said nothing for a moment. Then she said, "I'm not sure. Ask the patient."

She's sure, thought Nicoletta. She knows what she saw. She saw a monster. But she can't say that. The words won't come out of her mouth.

Security never came in to ask Nicoletta anything. An aide, not the nurse, arrived later to finish charting Nicoletta's vital signs. Nicoletta said nothing about an intruder. The aide said nothing.

She thought of Jethro's journey home. How would he get there?

How could she ever refer to that cave as home?

Home. She knew now that a house was only a house; the building on Fairest Lane was a place to buy and sell, to decorate, and to leave. But a home is a place in which to be cherished. A home is love and parents, shelter and protection, laughter and chores, shared meals and jokes.

Home.

He had none.

And how with that curse upon him, could she bring him home? Find safety for him? Find release?

Her parents and Jamie burst into the room, loaded down with Nicoletta's schoolbooks and homework, a potted flower, a silly T-shirt from the hospital gift shop, and a balloon bouquet. The balloons rushed to the ceiling, dotting it purple and silver and scarlet and gold.

She wondered if Jethro had even seen a balloon bouquet. Or ever would.

"I'm so glad to see you!" cried Nicoletta. "Oh, Mommy! Daddy! Jamie!"

"You're even glad to see me?" said Jamie. "You *are* sick!"

"Darling," said her mother, hugging. "You look like you've had a good long nap. Feeling better?"

"Lots."

"You come home tomorrow," said her father. He looked worn and worried. He touched her cheek, as if to reassure himself that this was Nicoletta, his baby girl, his darling daughter.

"Tomorrow? I just got here." She thought of a father, years and years go, who left a son inside the earth and never looked back.

"Isn't it wonderful?" agreed her father. "Then just another day of rest at home and you're on crutches and back in school. Orthopedic decisions are very different from when I broke a leg. When I broke my leg skiing, back in the dark ages, why, I was in the hospital for ten days."

They talked about the dark ages: her parents' childhoods, in which there had been no fast food, no video games, no answering machines, and no instant replays.

Nicoletta thought of Jethro, for whom all ages were dark.

I know what I could do, she thought. I could do what Jethro did for his father. *I could offer myself to the spirits of the cave.* I could exchange myself for him.

How romantic that would be!

Greatness of heart would be required. She would step down and he would step up. She would take the dark and he could have the light.

Jethro would have his fair share of laughter and love; he would smile in the sun, with no fear of turning to horror and stone. He would have his chances, at last, for life, liberty, and the pursuit of happiness. The dark ages would end for him.

And she, Nicoletta . . . she . . . would inherit the dark ages.

Dark. Forever and ever, world without end.

Dark and all that *dark* meant. Unknown. Unseen. Things that crawled and bit and flew and slithered. Things that crept up legs and settled in hair. Things that screamed and moaned and wept in the entrapment of their souls.

Could she really do that? Was she, Nicoletta, strong enough to accept darkness and terror, fear and slime — forever?

But it would not be forever, of course. He would come back for her. He would —

He would not.

He would not even remember. He would abandon her. Everybody would abandon her.

She thought of the Madrigals. How quickly they had abandoned her for Anne-Louise. She thought of Ms. Quincy, who had praised her voice for so long, only to abandon her the instant she heard a better one. It would all be like that, she thought. My entire life. Except my life would not have a span. It would not end. There would be no way out. It would be eternal.

Oh, Jethro! Jethro!

I don't want you caught in your dark ages. I want you here on earth with me.

"Sweetie, don't cry," said her mother. "It isn't that bad of a break. All will be well. I promise."

She rested on her mother's promise.

She thought of Jethro going back, and down, and in. To become part of the walls and the fall and the blackness, to live among the spirits he would not describe because they were too awful for her to hear about.

"Don't cry," said her mother, rocking. "All will be well."

Chapter 18

"A snow picnic?" repeated Nicoletta.

"Yes!" said Anne-Louise. "It was my idea. And you'll be our mascot!"

Your mascot? thought Nicoletta. I get it. You're the soprano, Anne-Louise. I'm the puppy. The rag doll. The mascot. Drop dead, Anne-Louise, just drop dead.

Christo said, "I'm driving!"

Rachel said, "I packed the sandwiches."

Cathy said, "But I made them, so don't be afraid of food poisoning, Nickie."

Nicoletta had to laugh. She got her crutches. Christo's van was not large enough for so many Madrigals, but if they really squished and squashed, they could fit in a very uncomfortable but delightful way. The three leftovers followed in a leftover car. Nicoletta felt sorry for them, trailing behind.

Her white packed leg with its scrawls of Madrigal names stuck out in front of her, between the two bucket seats.

Christo said, "We're going to that meadow you showed me, Nick. I thought I might climb the cliff."

Anne-Louise gave a little shriek of fright. "Christo! You might fall!"

Christo smiled arrogantly. Falling happened to other climbers. Not to Christo.

"It'll be icy," warned Anne-Louise. She patted Christo's knee excitedly.

Nicoletta definitely knew who had a crush on whom. Well, it was useful in a way. Christo would be deflected. It would free Nicoletta up for Jethro.

"Okay, Nickie," said Rachel. "The time has come. What is this crazy story Christo keeps telling us about rock people?" The packed singers burst into laughter and the whole van shook.

Christo just grinned. "You'll stop laughing when I catch it," he said.

"Actually," Anne-Louise said, turning to speak clearly, and be sure everybody knew that she knew first, "Christo brought his gun. He's not going to climb. He's going to hunt."

"I'm against hunting," said Rachel.

"I usually am, too," said Cathy, "but this is a rock he's after. The worst that can happen, I figure, is there'll be two rocks after he shoots at it."

Nicoletta's brain felt as solid as the cast on her leg. She had plaster in her skull. What was happening? The cave and Jethro were becoming public territory. There were no taboos, there was no fear, there was no stopping them now. Even Cathy was laughing about hunting. It occurred to Nicoletta that she could not pretend Jethro was against hunting.

In fact, he and his companions in the cave were the most vicious hunters of all. For they hunted the hunters.

"I want a souvenir," said Anne-Louise, in a little girl singsong voice.

Nicoletta hated her. She hated the flirting, the silliness, the fakery. She hated every single thing about Anne-Louise. Drop dead, she thought. Out loud she said, "It won't be any fun picnicking there, Christo. Let's go to the state park or the town lake."

"Forget it," said Cathy. "He's told us and told us about this place, how romantic and weird it is, what strange things we'll see. We're on. This is it, Nickie."

They turned into the lane that said DEAD END.

They drove past the few houses and the high, winter-tired hedges.

They drove right up the dirt road and came to stop where the ruts were too deep for a suburban van. "How will we ever get through all this snow?" cried Anne-Louise, pretending fear. "How will we ever find our way in those woods?"

"Not to worry," said Christo, comforting her. He was completely sucked in by her acting.

Nobody except Nicoletta seemed bothered by Anne-Louise. The altos, tenors, and basses piled out, the leftover car with its leftover people caught up, the boys hoisted the coolers and then they were faced with the problem of Nicoletta's cast and crutches.

"See?" said Nicoletta. "I really think the town lake would be a good idea. That way you can prop me up on a bench right near where we park, and we'll still have a good view, and yet we —"

"Nickie," said Rachel, "hush. The boys are going to carry you. This is the most romantic moment of your life, so enjoy it."

Christo and Jeff made a carrying seat of their linked arms and David helped her sit. With David holding her cast at the ankle as if she were a ladder he was lugging, Christo and Jeff carried her.

They went past the boulder.

Straight as folded paper, the path led them through the snow-crusted meadow. Weeds from last summer poked out of last week's snow, brown and dried and somehow evil. The weeds tilted, watching the trespassers.

The two lakes were free of ice. They lay waiting. Tiny waves lapped the two shores like hungry tongues.

"Ooooh, it's so pretty!" squealed Anne-Louise.

The sound of their crunching feet was like an army. Jethro was surely hidden safely away; he would have heard them coming.

I couldn't stop them! Nicoletta thought at Jethro. It isn't my fault! I wouldn't have come, but I have to keep an eye on them.

The air was silent and the cave was invisible. They stopped

walking. Only Anne-Louise found the place pretty. Rachel swallowed and wet her lips. "The water looks dangerous," she whispered. "It looks — as if it wants one of us."

Nobody argued.

Nobody said she was being silly.

Nobody tried to walk between the two lakes, either.

The boys set Nicoletta down. They set the big cooler down, too, and Nicoletta used it for a chair.

Ice had melted on the side of the cliff, and then frozen again. It hung in thin, vicious spikes from its crags and outcroppings. There was no color. The stone was dark and threatening. The day was grim and silent.

Christo's voice came out slightly higher than it should have. "I'm walking between the two lakes," he said, as if somebody had accused him of not doing it. "The cave is over there. When the thing came out and attacked Nicoletta, it came out of there."

"Nothing attacked me," said Nicoletta.

"It touched you," said Christo.

"There was nothing here," said Nicoletta.

"I believe you, Christo!" sang Anne-Louise. "I know there was something here. I'll go with you, Christo!"

Anne-Louise and Christo walked carefully as if they were on a balance beam. The water reached up to catch their ankles. A moment passed before Rachel and Cathy and David and Jeff walked after them. Did they not see the cliff snarl? Did they not see the hunger of the cave, how it licked its lips with wanting them?

"There *is* a cave!" cried Rachel. "Oh, Christo, you were right! Oh my heavens! Look inside. It's beautiful!"

No, thought Nicoletta. No, Rachel, it's not beautiful. Don't go in, don't go in.

But now her tongue was also plaster and did not move, but filled her mouth and prevented her speech.

No one went in.

A cave gives pause. Even with walls shining like jewels, the dark depths are frightening and the unknown beyond the light should remain unknown.

The Madrigals posed at the entrance, as if waiting for their cue to sing, needing costumes, or a director to bring them in.

"Anne-Louise," said a voice, "you go first."

Chapter 19

The screams of Anne-Louise were etched in the air, like diamond initials on glass. Indeed, glass seemed to separate the safe from the fallen.

The Madrigals were collected as if about to concertize. But it was horror that held them, not an audience. They, in fact, were the audience. They had aisle seats to the end of Anne-Louise.

Anne-Louise, whose voice was not so beautiful when screaming in terror, was on the far side of the glass.

The screams went on and on and then stopped. They stopped completely. The silence that followed was even more complete.

Nobody attempted to go in after her.

Nobody tried to rescue her.

Were they too afraid? Or too smart to risk the same ending?

Nicoletta had the excuse of an immovable leg, a helpless body. None of the others had an excuse.

But Nicoletta had known what would happen. None of the others could have known. And so Nicoletta Storms was the one with no excuse at all, no excuse ever.

Whose voice sent Anne-Louise tumbling forever into the dark?

Was it me? thought Nicoletta. Did I shout *Anne-Louise, you go first*! I who knew what would happen to the one who went first?

Did I want revenge that much? How sick and twisted I am, to destroy a classmate over a singing group.

I'm sorry! thought Nicoletta. As if being sorry would change anything.

Time stopped.

The sun did not move in the sky and the teenagers did not move beneath it.

Sound ceased.

Nothing cried out within the cave and nobody spoke without.

The glass wall broke.

Anne-Louise, babbling and twitching, fingers curling and uncurling, eyes too wide to blink, staggered out of the cave.

Still nobody spoke. Still nobody moved.

They were like a group photograph of themselves. A still shot of Madrigals from another era.

"It's in there," whispered Anne-Louise. "You were right, Christo. It's in there! It picked me up. It caught me."

Anne-Louise addressed Christo but did not seem to see him. Instead she staggered away from the cliff, hands out as if holding a rope nobody else could see. On an invisible lifeline she hauled herself in Nicoletta's direction. There was sand in her hair, as if she were a bride at some dreadful wedding. Her guests had not thrown confetti.

"It's there?" breathed Christo. Excitement possessed him. "It really exists? You saw it? You touched it?"

"Don't go in!" screamed Anne-Louise. Her voice was huge and roiling, nothing like a soprano's. It was ugly and swollen. "Don't go in!" she shouted. She did not let go of her lifeline, but kept hauling herself between the lakes, past Nicoletta. She fell to her knees, and Nicoletta saw that the kneecaps were torn and bruised from an earlier fall. Still Anne-Louise did not stop, but crawled, sobbing, trying to find the straight path and the way out.

"She's right, Christo," said Rachel. She sounded quite normal. "Don't go in there. What we'll do is come back with a truck and ropes. Obviously it's slippery and the cave falls off. There are people who go into caves for hobbies. I've read about them. They're called spelunkers. We'll get in touch with a club and bring a group that knows what they're doing. We'll —"

"No!" said Christo. "It's my find! I'm getting it!"

Jethro saved Anne-Louise, thought Nicoletta. She wanted to call *thank you!* to him. She wanted to shout *I love you!* in his direction. She wanted to put her arms around him and tell him that he was good and kind.

How many people had he saved in the past? Nicoletta had been horrified because Jethro let the hunters fall. But he hadn't let Nicoletta fall. He hadn't let Anne-Louise fall.

He would let Christo fall. He would have to.

"Fine," said Christo in the furious voice of one who means the opposite. "Fine! I'll take everybody back to the van. Fine! We'll picnic at the lake. And then I'm coming back and I'm getting it."

Anne-Louise was walking upright now, a stagger to her gait as if something in her had permanently snapped. Rachel and Cathy were running to catch up and help her. The rest of the Madrigals, saying little, crept between the lakes, safely away from the stretching black elastic of the water, picked up the pace, and headed for the van.

For a moment, Nicoletta thought they would abandon her; that half the curse would come true. She prayed they would, because if she sat long enough, Jethro would come to her. Her Jethro. Jethro with the smooth quiet features, the heavy falling hair, the dark, motionless eyes.

But the boys remembered they had two burdens: a girl and a cooler. They hoisted her up, silently and with great tension, wanting to run, not wanting to admit it.

"You'll see, Nicoletta," said Christo eagerly. "I'll get it."

He wants "it" for me, she thought. "It" will be his trophy to lay at my feet, a golden retriever laying the gunshot duck before his master.

She knew now that Christo could never get "it." "It" would

always win, because "it" had greater, deeper, more ancient and more horrible weapons.

She did not want Christo to fall, and not be saved.

She did not want Jethro to have to face that moment. To know that he could rescue . . . and would not.

She did not want coming here to be a hobby. She did not want to think of the collection that would lie at the bottom of the cave. Or, if Jethro were caught on the outside, the collection he would be in, the display he would make.

The boys staggered in the snow, losing their footing.

Nicoletta looked back. The cliff face was nothing but rock and dripping ice. The lakes were nothing but dark surfaces. The hole in the wall was not visible.

And then part of the rock moved. Changed. Was light, and then dark. A dark wand rose upward. An arm. After a time in the air, like a flag without wind, the hand moved.

It was Jethro.

Terrible grief engulfed her. Was that his good-bye? Would she never see Jethro again? "Put me down!" she cried. "I have to go back!" Her heart was swept out of her, rushing like wind and desperation toward the last wave.

But the boys trudged on.

Chapter 20

Nobody would return anywhere that night.

The snow came down like a monster itself. It came in bulk, in dump-truck loads, smothering every car and bush and front step.

At least school would be canceled. At least Christo would be unable to get his van out of his driveway.

Long after Jamie had fallen asleep, Nicoletta raised the shades and sat up in bed, watching the beauty and the rage of the weather. The wind was not a single whooshing entity but a thousand tiny spinners. The night was dark with desperate clouds letting go, but yellow pools of streetlights illuminated the falling snow.

Jethro came.

She had not expected him. She had thought him gone forever. She had been in mourning, believing in his good-bye, sure that he had backed off for good.

"Jethro!" she cried, and then twisted quickly to see if she had awakened Jamie. Jamie slept on. She put a hand over her mouth to keep herself from speaking again.

When he moved, Nicoletta could see him. When he stopped, she could not. He was part of the landscape. He could have been a dark wind himself, or a heavy clot of snow on rock.

She looked at her sleeping sister. Jamie's mouth was slightly opened and in sleep she seemed glued to the sheets, fastened down by the blankets. She wouldn't wake unless Nicoletta fell right on top of her.

Nicoletta found her crutches, and slowly — far too slowly; what if Jethro left before she could get outside? — she made it down the stairs and reached the coat closet, wrapped herself tightly and hobbled to the back door to let herself out in the storm.

The wind aimed at her face. It threw pellets of ice in her eyes and tried to damage her bare cheeks. The three back steps could have been cliffs themselves. The distance between herself and the garage seemed like miles. "Jethro!" she shouted, but the wind reached into her throat first and seized the words.

"Jethro!"

Nobody could have heard her; she could not even hear herself.

She tried to wade through the snow but it was impossible. It would have been like swimming and the broken leg could not swim.

Why was he not at the door, waiting for her?

She gulped in snow, and put a hand blue with cold over her mouth. She should have worn mittens but she had expected to be out here only a moment before Jethro found her.

She launched the tip of her crutches into the snow ahead of her and attempted to get through the drifts.

There he was! By the garage door! She shouted his name twice, and he did not respond, and she shouted a third time, and he turned — or rather, it turned — and she waved the whole crutch in order to be seen.

He seemed to turn and to stoop. As if he were on an errand. Carrying something. When at last she knew Jethro had seen her, he looked away. What is this? thought Nicoletta. What is going on?

But she had been seeing things. Of course he came to her, white with snow. Snow purified and cleansed. Again he lifted her, and carried her this time into the garage, sitting her on the edge of her father's workbench, her good knee dangling down while the white plaster tip of her cast rested on the top of her mother's car. "You came," she said. "I knew you would come."

He said nothing.

For a frigid, suffocating moment she thought it was somebody else. Not Jethro. Some — creature — who —

She looked and at least knew his eyes: those dark pools of grief.

"Jethro, I don't want you to live like this."

"No," he agreed.

She could feel no pulse in him, no heartbeat, no lifting of a chest with lungs. He was stone beside her.

"You stay here and live. I will go down for you."

He did not smile, for there was no face to him that could do that. And yet he lightened and seemed glad. "No," he said again. The thing that was his hand tightened on hers.

"I don't want you to suffer anymore."

He said nothing.

"I've thought about it. It's your turn for life, Jethro. I will go down."

The words came as from a fissure in a rock. "No one should suffer what I have. Certainly not you."

"Aren't you even tempted? Aren't you even daydreaming about what it would be like to be alive and well and normal and loved?"

"Always."

"Well?"

"Nicoletta, I will never be well and normal and loved."

"*I* love you!"

He was silent for a long time. The storm shrieked as it tried to fling the roof off the house. The snow whuffling into deepening drifts. "Thank you," he said finally.

"There won't be school tomorrow," she said.

He did not seem to know why.

"Canceled," she explained. "Snow is too deep."

He nodded.

Oh, tonight of all nights she did not want his silence! She

wanted to talk! To know. To understand. To share. "When school begins again, will you be in Art?"

"No."

"Jethro, you have to come. Where else will I see you?"

His silence was longer than ever. She was determined to wait him out, to make him talk. She won. He said, "This is only pain and grief."

"What is?"

"Loving."

"You're wrong! It can end well! I want you to stay."

"Like this?" Bitterness conquered him. "Why would I want to be seen like this? What do you think will happen? Christo will exhibit me in a cage." He did not point out that if she had never come back to his cave, if she had never been followed by Christo, he would not be at risk. But they both knew it.

His voice rose like the wind, screaming with the pain of his nightmare. "I don't want anybody to see me. I didn't want you to see me!"

What would it be like, she wondered, to be so ghastly you did not even want the people who loved you to see you? What would it be like to look down at your own body and be nauseated? To be trapped — a fine soul; a good human — in such ugliness that another human would want to put you in a cage and exhibit you?

Nicoletta was freezing to death. It was not just Jethro's body in which she could feel no pulse, no heartbeat, no lungs. "I have to get inside," she said. "I'm so cold. I don't think I can move. Jethro, carry me inside?"

He said nothing, but lifted her. Her skin scraped against him and she hoped that it was deep, and would bleed, and leave a scar, so she would have something to remember him by.

He took her up the back steps and opened the door for her. He saw how she lived; the warmth and clutter, the letters and the photographs, the dishes and the chairs. The goodness of family and the rightness of life.

"I love you, too," he said, his voice cracking like old ice. "But try to see. I can't risk anything more, Nicoletta. You can't risk anything more. I can't be caught. I can't let Christo fall. He loves you. I care about anybody who loves you."

"You saved Anne-Louise," she said softly. "You're a good person. It isn't fair when somebody good suffers! Let me rescue you. I know there must be a way out of this."

His voice was oddly generous, as if he were giving her something. "When your leg is better," he said, "come to the cave. But don't come before that. Promise me. I need your promise."

"No."

"Nicoletta! Why won't you promise?"

"I love you. I want to see you."

"*Don't come.*" He set her down. The one side of her was flooded with the warmth of her home and its furnace. The other side was crusted with snow turning to sleet.

She began arguing with him. Reasons why she must come, why they must get together, why they needed each other, and could think of some way somehow to save each other, because that was what true love did; it conquered, it triumphed.

She thought it was a wonderful speech.

She knew that she had changed his mind, that he understood because she had said it so clearly.

But when she put her hand out, there was nothing there.

A snowdrift pressed against the door and a snow-clumped branch from a heavy-laden fir tree tipped over the railing and tried to reach inside the kitchen. But no boy, no monster, no rock.

No Jethro.

He had left her, and she had not even sensed it.

He had gone, and she had not even heard.

"No!" she shouted out into the snow. "Who do you think you are anyway? Don't you vanish like that!"

Only the snow answered.

Only the wind heard.

"I don't promise, Jethro!" she shrieked.

The side door to the garage banged.

Jethro had not come to see her. She had been right when she thought he stooped and carried. He had come for the dynamite.

Tears froze on her cheeks but hope was resurrected. He had thought of a way out. He was going to use one of her suggestions. He would blow up the cave, and bury the curse, and when she came back to find him, they would be together!

Chapter 21

"Nicoletta, darling," said Ms. Quincy.

Nicoletta turned away, saw who was speaking, and very nearly continued on. How she yearned to be rude to the teacher she had once adored. She looked now at Ms. Quincy and saw not a friend, but a conductor who set friendship aside if she could improve the concert by doing so.

Nicoletta did not even know what was fair, let alone what was right.

In fairness, should the best soprano win? Or in fairness, should the hard-working, long-term soprano stay?

What was right? What was good teaching? What was good music?

Were the concert, the blend, the voices always first, and rightly so?

Or did loyalty, friendship, and committee time count?

She wondered if Ms. Quincy had wondered about these things, or if Ms. Quincy, like so many adults, was sure of her way? When she became an adult, would Nicoletta know the way?

She thought of Jethro, who knew the way but could not take it.

Of Jethro's father, who knew the way once but lost the memory of it.

Of Art Appreciation and Jethro's empty chair.

She said, "Hello, Ms. Quincy, how are you?" Manners were

important. You always had them to go by. When you stood to lose all else, there were still manners.

"Fine, thank you, darling," said Ms. Quincy, relieved that Nicoletta was going to be polite.

Politeness is a safety zone, thought Nicoletta. She thought of Jethro coming out of her garage. The dynamite that no longer lay in the box on the shelf. Had he done what he had set out to do? She must go! She must see what had happened. She must find him and know.

Practically speaking, this meant she would have to get a ride from somebody. Who?

"Anne-Louise," said Ms. Quincy, "has let me down."

Down, thought Nicoletta. You have no idea, Ms. Quincy, what the word *down* means to Anne-Louise now. You have no idea how far down Anne-Louise actually went. "I'm sorry to hear that," said Nicoletta politely. "But I'm sure it will work out in the end."

"No, darling. She has quit Madrigals! Can you believe such a thing?" Clearly Ms. Quincy could not. "And here we are in the middle of the winter season with several upcoming events!" Ms. Quincy was actually wringing her hands, an interesting gesture Nicoletta had never seen anybody do. "Nicoletta, please forgive me. Please come back. We need you."

Back to Madrigals.

Back in the group she loved, in the center of things, the whirl of activity and companionship and singing. Back, if she chose, as Christo's girlfriend, twice the center of things with that status.

But never . . . if she rejoined Madrigals . . . never again to sit in Art Appreciation. Waiting. Gazing on the boy she loved.

She knew Jethro was not coming back to school. He had said so quite clearly. And yet she knew she would see him again. She had to. A person you loved could not simply never be seen again. It was not fair.

In the end, things — especially things of true love — should be fair.

Three days of school since the roads were finally cleared, and each afternoon as she went to Art, her heart quickened, and a smile lay behind her lips. Let him come! Let me see that profile. The boy who was in darkness when they watched slides and remained dark when the lights came on.

He did not come.

If she did not continue in Art Appreciation, she would never know if he came back. If she did not rejoin Madrigals, she could not gather back those friendships and pleasures either. "I'll think about it, Ms. Quincy."

It had never occurred to the woman that Nicoletta might say no. There was a certain revenge in seeing Ms. Quincy's shock. "Nicoletta," said Ms. Quincy severely, "you are cutting off your nose to spite your face."

Nicoletta had never heard that saying before and had to consider it.

"You will hurt yourself more than you will hurt the group," said Ms. Quincy, putting it another way.

Nicoletta wondered if that was true. "I'll let you know on Monday, Ms. Quincy," said Nicoletta. "First I'll talk to Anne-Louise."

Anne-Louise was fully recovered. In fact, she was laughing about it. "I can't believe how I behaved," she said. "Isn't it funny?"

If it's so funny, thought Nicoletta, why did you quit Madrigals?

"You know what we should do?" said Anne-Louise.

"What?"

"Let's go back to the cave," said Anne-Louise. "I mean, when I got home the other day, my mother said my eyes were glazed over. She thought I had cataracts or something. My mother said, 'Anne-Louise, what happened out there anyway?' And do you know what, Nicoletta?"

"What?"

"I can't remember exactly what happened. Let's go back and see. I'm curious. I don't understand what scared us all so much. It was only a cave."

"It's more than a cave. It needs victims," said Nicoletta. "You must not go back. You must never go back, Anne-Louise."

Anne-Louise shrugged. "I'm going back to the cave now, Nicoletta. I *have* to see it," said Anne-Louise. "Do you want to come?"

What way out, thought Nicoletta, would preserve us all? What way out saves Jethro, but gives him to me? Keeps us from exploring or falling? Gives Jethro life as a boy and not a monster?

But did it matter anymore? She thought she knew what way Jethro had decided would work.

No way.

The snow was so high it covered the DEAD END sign. The trees were like branch children with snow blankets pulled up to their shoulders.

Anne-Louise's car reached the end of the road. Here the immense amount of snow had been piled by the plows into sheer-sided mountains. The path was not visible. There was no way in to the boulder.

The road, indeed, was a dead end.

The girls got out of the car. Nicoletta had learned how to use her cast; it was just a heavier, more annoying leg than she had had before. She did not need the crutches for pain or balance.

They surveyed the problem. The snow was taller than they were. Shovels, possibly pick axes, would be necessary to break through. And beyond the snow-plowed mountains, it would still be nearly up to Nicoletta's waist. There was more snow here than elsewhere, as if the snow had conspired to conceal the path until spring.

Anne-Louise looked confused. She rattled her car keys. She was losing touch with what she wanted to do, and thinking of leaving.

Yes, leave! thought Nicoletta. Leave me here. I'll get to him somehow; I know I will, because he needs me and I need him. He can't have left me forever. Jethro! she called through her heart and her mind. I'm coming!

Christo pulled in behind them. Oh, Christo, why do you always show up, as if I cared about you? she thought.

But he kissed her, because he knew nothing. "We'll just go around," he said.

She had never thought of that; never thought of just walking back to where the plows had not packed the snow so high. Christo went first, kicking a path. Anne-Louise went second, widening the path.

Nicoletta went third, dragging her cast.

The boulder had never seemed so huge. Snow had fallen from the surrounding trees, pitting the soft layers on the boulder. It looked volcanic, as if seething hot lava was bubbling just beneath the snow, waiting for them to put out a wrong foot.

But only to Nicoletta's eyes. To Christo they seemed the right places to step, where the snow was dented. He slogged forward, a football player with a goal in mind. A camera swung from his shoulder.

Nicoletta thought of the order in which they were going. Victims at the head of the line. "Stop," she said. "Stop, Christo!" It's dangerous for them, she thought. But not for me. Love will save me. Love always triumphs. I know it does! Jethro will save me, and we will be together.

"Nickie, I'm never stopping," said Christo. "I'm going to figure out what's happening here if it kills me."

The boulder moved.

It rolled right in front of them. The ground began to shake. Nicoletta had never known how terrible, how awe-full an earthquake is. Nothing in life was so dependable as the ground under her feet. Now it tossed her off, as if she were going to have to fly; she could no longer stand, the old order of human beings was ended.

Anne-Louise's scream pierced the sky, but the sky cared

nothing for humans without sense and her scream flattened to nothing under the gray ceiling.

The stone rolled onto Christo's ankle and pinned him.

A huge and terrible noise came from beyond; greater noise than Nicoletta had ever heard; a shattering of rock and earth deeper than man had ever mined. Jethro had dynamited the entrance to the cave.

And then, and only then, Nicoletta knew what way out Jethro had thought of. Not one of hers. But his own.

For there was no way out that preserved them all.

Nicoletta was right that love triumphs. Jethro loved her. And he had put that first. He loved her enough to prevent her from coming back, from bringing her friends, from risking their lives.

He had closed his door forever. Himself inside.

They will all be buried this time, she thought. Every sorrowful spirit will find its rest. Buried at last. *Including Jethro.*

The shaking dashed Nicoletta against a tree.

Jethro gave me life, she thought. For the second time in his terrible life, he sacrificed himself for the person he loved. He wanted me to have my life: sharing a bedroom with a little sister, singing in Madrigals, and eating in the cafeteria.

He wanted no more hunters falling, no more Christos, no more Anne-Louises. He did not want me to risk myself again. He did not want another person on this earth to abandon, or to be abandoned.

Jethro. I love you.

The earth ceased its leaping. The stone rolled off Christo. He was only bruised. He got up easily.

The path through the meadow had received no snow. It was clear as a summer day, straight as the edge of a page. Christo and Anne-Louise led the way, Nicoletta following, her good leg walking and the other leg dragging.

There was no rock face left. There were no ponds. A jumble of fallen stone and rock lay where once a tall cliff and two circles of water had been.

"Wow," said Christo reverently, and lifted his camera. He got into camera athletics, squatting and whirling and arching for the best angle.

Nothing else moved.

Not a rock. Not a stone. Not a crystal.

"I didn't abandon you, Jethro," whispered Nicoletta. "I want you to know that. I came this afternoon to find you. So we could be together after all. I didn't know this was your plan. I swear I didn't. I thought you were only going to bury *them*."

There was only silence. The rocks that had made such a tremendous crash had made the only sound they ever would. They were done with motion and noise. And Jethro? Was he, too, done with motion and noise?

Jethro. I love you.

"Wow!" Christo kept saying. He bounded from rock to rock. "What do you think set it off? Was it an earthquake? I never heard of earthquakes in this part of the country. Wow!"

It was my father's dynamite, thought Nicoletta. But it was Jethro's courage.

Are you well and truly buried now, Jethro? Is the curse over? Are you safe in heaven?

Or deep within this cruel earth, are you still there? Your upward path closed? Still in the dark, forever and ever caught with the raging undead? Never again to hear laughter? Never again to hold a hand?

Oh, Jethro, I hope what you did for me worked for you, too!

I love you. Jethro! Be safe!

Christo finished the roll of film. "Let's go home," he said. "I want to call the television studio. The newspapers. I think my science teachers would love to see this, too."

Love, love, love. How Christo had misspelled that precious word. Only Nicoletta knew what love was. And only Jethro had shown it.

"Jethro!" she screamed then. It was too much to keep inside herself. "*Jethro!*" she shrieked, trying to explode his spirit as the dynamite had exploded the rocks. She tried to run toward him, or where he had been, tried to find the place from which he had waved, his stone arm lifted to say farewell.

But of course she could not move, for the cast kept her in place, and the broken, destroyed surface of the earth presented a thousand rocky obstacles. "Jethro!" she screamed. "Jethro!"

She hated silence. How dare Jethro be silent? She wanted him to answer! She wanted him to speak!

Her tears spilled down her face and fell on her pleading hands.

It seemed to her as she wept, that the tears were full of sand, not salt, and that when they dried on her hands, she had some of Jethro in her palm.

"Be safe!" she cried. "Be at rest! Oh, Jethro, be safe!"

Christo said, "What are you talking about?" He shepherded the two girls toward the van.

Talking? thought Nicoletta. I am trying to be heard through hundreds of years of abandonment, and through thousands of tons of rock. I am screaming! I am screaming for the soul of a boy who loved me.

Anne-Louise rattled her car keys.

Christo rewound his film.

They reached the boulder. Nicoletta rested her hand on the snowcap it wore. There was nothing. Snow. Rock. Solidity. She put the same hand on her heart. It was as cracked as crystal thrown from the cliff. And no one knew, or heard.

"Jethro," she whispered.

It seemed to her that for a tender moment, the frozen trees of the woods, the lakes and ledges and stones of the earth, bent toward her and understood her sorrow.

Christo opened the van door for Nicoletta, and boosted her in. "Where does that Jethro kid live anyway?"

She looked into the silent woods and thought of Jethro, silent forever. "He moved," said Nicoletta. Let it be true, she prayed. Let him be safe wherever he moved to, wherever he lies.

Jethro, it was too much. To die for me was too much. I wanted you alive! I wanted us together! You can't do that with death. With death you can't be together.

Christo started the engine.

She looked down at her hand. Caught in the tiny cup of her curved palm was a grain of sand glittering like a diamond. She closed her fingers to keep her diamond safe. The way, with his death, Jethro had kept her safe.

They left in the little lane with its dwindling ruts, and the trees closed around the road as if it had never been.

Her breath was hot in the icy van. It clouded the window. With the hand that held no diamond, she traced a heart in the mist on the glass. She wrote no initials within the heart, for she did not know Jethro's, and Christo would expect his initials to go beside hers.

They drove on, and the van heated up, and the warm air erased the heart.

But Jethro would not be erased. Jethro had lived and loved. He had loved *her*. Nicoletta Storms opened her hand. The diamond lay still and silent in her palm.

And always would.

TWINS

Chapter 1

They were sending Mary Lee to boarding school. She could not believe it. Identical twins — *separated?*

Mary Lee's lovely olive skin was stretched with fear. Her beautiful hazel eyes, with their fringe of long black lashes, were wide with panic.

Each swing of hair, each lift of brow, was mirrored in her identical twin. If it had been a fairy tale, and one twin had said, "Mirror, Mirror on the Wall, Who Is the Fairest of Them All?" the mirror could have made no answer. For *two* qualified.

"Listen," said Mary Lee, striving to stay calm. Her parents admired calm. "Madrigal and I have never been separated! You don't understand because you're ordinary people. But we're identical twins. We're not regular sisters. If you send one of us away, we won't be whole!"

"Nevertheless," said her mother, looking sad but sure of herself, "you are going."

Mother, who adored having identical twins, who loved dressing them just the same, and fixing their hair just the same, and admiring them in their perfect synchrony, now wanted them split up?

Mary Lee was shaking. There was no need to look at her twin, because whatever one did, the other did. Madrigal would also be shaking. One of the oddities of identical twins was that the girls themselves could never tell who started anything. Madrigal might well have started trembling first, and Mary Lee second. One of them was always the echo of the other.

There was no possibility of remaining calm. Frantic, Mary Lee cried, "Mother, you can't do this to us!"

Her parents were strangely still, perhaps braced against her screaming, perhaps rehearsed for it, dreading the moment when Madrigal, too, began screaming.

"We have given it a great deal of thought, sweetheart," said her father quietly, "and this is the right thing to do."

"You've spent seventeen years making us match!" shrieked Mary Lee. "And you pulled it off! Nobody can tell us apart. We are one. Now what has brought this on? What set you off? How can you possibly think separation is the right thing to do to us?"

Both girls were there, of course, because where one twin was, the other always was, too. And, yet, Mother and Father seemed to be talking only to Mary Lee. As if Mary Lee had come undone. As if Mary Lee needed to be repaired. As if boarding school were the solution to Mary Lee.

Sadly, her mother stroked Mary Lee's heavy black hair. Loosely caught behind her head in a cluster of bright yellow ribbons, the hair slid free and weighted down her shoulders. Mother's eyes were bright with unshed tears, and her heart was racing with sorrow.

Mary Lee could not imagine what was going on. Separation could only break the hearts of all four of them.

"Try to understand," said her mother brokenly.

But Mary Lee had no use for that instruction. "What is there to understand? You are ripping us away from our own selves!"

"Listen to your phrasing, Mary Lee. Madrigal is not *your* self," said Mother. "She is *her* self. We have allowed ourselves and the world to treat you as a unit. We were wrong. You are not one. You are two."

She and Madrigal were not run-of-the-mill sisters. Mary Lee could not imagine being shipped away like a package, wrapped in brown paper, tied with string. Waking up in the morning without her twin. Dressing without her twin. Going to class without —

It was unthinkable. She would not do it. "You brought identical twins into the world. You must accept what we are! We are one."

Mother was suddenly harsh and angry. "Mary Lee, listen to yourself. You say 'we' instead of 'I.' You say 'us' instead of 'me.' It isn't healthy. You need to be a girl named Mary Lee, not half a twinset. You must fly alone. Sing solo."

Mary Lee had never heard such a horrible idea. *Fly alone? Sing solo?* "Identical twins can't do that. You're fighting a biological fact."

"The fact," said Father, "is that we have decided to separate you and your sister. You will simply have to trust us that this is a necessary action. For your mental health and Madrigal's. Madrigal will stay home under our supervision. You will go to boarding school."

The house seemed to float around Mary Lee as if its rooms had fallen apart like badly stacked toy blocks. She turned to her sister, knowing that the force of her own turn would turn Madrigal as well. They did not imitate each other so much as simultaneously broadcast. They never knew which of them was first and which the follower. It was too quick for that. "We won't let them, will we, Madrigal?"

Her twin sister smiled. A smile Mary Lee did not share at all. Her twin sister said, "I think it's a good idea."

One thousand nine hundred and twelve miles to the school.

On the big featureless airplane, in a gray sky, with a gray heart, Mary Lee felt each of those miles pulse through her. One thousand nine hundred and twelve spaces between Mary Lee and her twin.

How can I do this? she thought, sick with fear. In my whole life I've never entered a room or a building without Madrigal.

This was not quite true. But she could count the exceptions.

There was the first week of fifth grade, when the elementary school faculty decreed that Mary Lee and Madrigal must have different teachers. The second week they gave up.

There was the time Mary Lee went shopping at the mall with Scarlett Maxsom, the way other girls did — with a friend. How strange it had been to have no twin along. To laugh with somebody whose laugh was not partly her own. She had had the fleeting thought that it would be fun to have a friend.

There was the sweet and funny afternoon that she and Van, Scarlett's brother, had had strawberry sundaes together. Not a date, really, just a lovely coincidence for Mary Lee to cherish.

In fact, the twins had never dated. They never did anything without each other. Their presence overwhelmed boys. Girls as beautiful and as incredibly alike as these two were not girls so much as an Event.

It was odd how that brief hour with Van had also acquired the status of an Event. She remembered it like a beloved movie, and replayed it in her heart, and even Madrigal did not know how often Mary Lee thought of that afternoon.

But the largest Event of her life was Separation. Already it had a capital letter: It was as huge as the sky and as impenetrable as marble.

"You are not to telephone," Mother and Father had said sternly. "You must write letters instead."

Not telephone? Not hear my sister's voice?

"I *have* to phone," pleaded Mary Lee. "I have to have something left." She turned to Madrigal. "Don't listen to them. Phone me anyway, when they're not home."

"I think they're right," said her twin.

The betrayal was so huge and painful that Mary Lee could not even think about it. She knew if Madrigal had fought back, Separation would not have occurred. But Madrigal had not fought back. Madrigal hadn't argued once. Not once. It was a slap that left a bruise on her heart. Once Mary Lee had the sick thought that her twin was not going to miss her. She killed that thought in a hurry!

Madrigal, left at home, would be as devastated as Mary Lee, shipped away.

She could not understand anything that was happening. Mother and Father actually seemed to hover over her that final week before she left home. As if she were in danger. As if people near her were unsafe. At night she wept into her pillow. In the morning, Mother's eyes were red, and Father's eyes were circled, but Madrigal's eyes were clear and bright.

How could it be? Mother and Father who had always seemed to love her so much had shuffled her off like an old deck of cards.

The mountains were high and crisp. Gray stone buildings sat on a wide grass campus. Thick dark woods enclosed the school like a fortress of old.

She was alone. It had never happened to her before. Ordinary people were often alone, but identical twins, never. What a hideous sensation it was — to be alone! How did people stand it? She was so glad not to be ordinary.

Identical twins, thank heaven, could communicate by invisible waves. Not ultraviolet, not X, not micro, not radio, but twin waves. Through the air and her soul, Mary Lee reached for her twin.

Nothing happened.

The waves were silent.

In her worst nightmares, Mary Lee had never expected this. Even if death were to come, she had expected to share it with Madrigal.

She was alone. And Madrigal had agreed to it.

Her father had actually had the nerve to cuddle her at the airport, to say good-bye privately, as if he were doing a good thing, a fatherly warm thing. "Be my brave soldier," he said to her.

Mary Lee hated that comparison.

"Put your best foot forward and try hard. Make friends. Stay alive."

My best feet walk in step with my twin's, she thought, fighting tears.

She crossed that school campus, and in the heavy grass left but one set of footprints. Neither of them looked like a best foot to Mary Lee. And what a queer trio of orders: try, make friends, stay alive. Of course she was going to stay alive. You didn't die of loneliness. Although no doubt she would feel dead, without Madrigal. As for "make friends," she didn't want any friend except Madrigal! As for "try" — well, yes, he was right about that. She did have to try. He was leaving her with no choice except trying.

It's too hard, she thought, already exhausted, and she hadn't even introduced herself to a single person.

The dormitory was large. So many strange girls to identify and names to learn. They seemed to know each other already, and have the passwords and jokes of intimate groups. The third floor, to which Mary Lee was assigned, seemed more a gathering of teams than a crowd of potential friends.

"Hi," she said to the girls, "I'm Mary Lee?" Her voice stumbled, the end of the sentence questioningly up in the air, for that was how it felt, not introducing Madrigal, too. Floaty and undecided. Half an introduction for half a set.

But all the girls had been new once, and they moved forward as if they expected to be best friends.

"I'm Bianca," said her first roommate, smiling.

"I'm Mindy," said her second roommate, and she actually swept Mary Lee into a hug.

"We're glad to have you," they both said. "We'll show you the ropes, because this is our third year here. They put you with us because we can help."

Okay, she said to herself. This won't be the end of the world. People are nice. Somehow I can survive.

The calendar of the school year stretched out hideously long.

September until June? She couldn't go home until Christmas! Oh, that was evil, making her stay here four entire months by herself.

No matter how nice Mindy and Bianca were, Mary Lee could only half-respond. And it didn't help that, on the third floor, there was already a Marilyn, a Merrill, and a Mary. Mary Lee was yet another similar name to overload people's memories. Nobody could get her name right. Mindy and Bianca decided to call her ML. It made her feel like a corporate logo, a piece of stock.

Madrigal I need you, she begged over the miles. But the twin waves remained silent.

It was worse than being alone: She felt unoccupied. A partly emptied mind and soul.

In the beginning, Mindy and Bianca escorted her everywhere, introducing her with smiles and hugs. But Mary Lee, homesick and heartsick, just stood there: the kind of boarder no school wants, because her only contribution is to lower morale.

The school year continued like a night without sleep.

Mary Lee had never had to make friends before. She had been equipped with an escort since birth. And even though she was so lonely her heart hurt, and she would have taken any pharmaceutical in production to ease the pain, she did not reach out.

Through the blinding loneliness, she saw that Mother and Father had been right: She was crippled by her twinness.

When Madrigal and Mary Lee sashayed into a room, action and speech ceased. People were fascinated. Twins are unusual. Identical twins are striking. Beautiful identical twins are an Event.

Mary Lee was just another pretty black-haired girl on a campus stocked with pretty girls. No longer an Event, she let herself become the reverse. A Non-Event.

At dinner, for which seats were assigned, companionship was enforced at a full table. But for breakfast and lunch, girls came when they were hungry, or awake. Some tables were empty while others were jammed. Mary Lee ached to join a packed table, yet sat at an empty one, yearning for the twin back home, for the life back home, the friends and school and parents and good things.

Whatever good there was at boarding school, Mary Lee ignored.

Within days she was branded: the sort of loser who sat alone; who had no friends and never would. Mindy and Bianca dutifully continued to be nice, and quietly asked the dorm mother if Mary Lee could be transferred to another room.

Mary Lee observed the dorm friendships. How lovely they were! How much Mary Lee wanted one for herself. If she had not had a twin, perhaps she would have possessed such a thing with Scarlett. Or Van. But the chance had gone by, she had been too absorbed by Madrigal to consider it, or to act upon it, and now Scarlett and Van and all that was home and good and safe were lost to her.

Among their other terrible orders when they enforced Separation, Mother and Father had ordered Mary Lee to tell nobody that she was an identical twin. "Am I supposed to hide it like some scandalous past?" she wept.

"No," said Father, "you're supposed to forget it, like some crippling past."

Forget that you were an identical twin? How could she?

In boarding school there was little history. It was as if they had all dumped something behind. They had all abandoned a twin or a parent or a past. They lived in the present, and Mary Lee's present did not include a twin. People didn't ask for background, and they quit asking Mary Lee anything.

When she thought of home — which was constantly — she thought mostly of questions she should have asked Mother and Father. There had to be more to this than they had explained. Why, if there had been too much togetherness, didn't they just make Mary Lee take different courses at school? Sign up for different sports? Get involved with different activities? Why couldn't she have gone to one of the private day schools in town — why pick a school nearly two thousand miles away?

Now and then Bianca and Mindy yelled at her, and told her to make an effort, and said if she was lonely it was her own fault.

My own fault, she thought. It must be all my fault, and none of Madrigal's fault, or Mother and Father wouldn't have done it this way. But what did I do?

She struggled to communicate with Madrigal by letter. The twins had certainly never written to each other before. In fact, they often skipped speaking. There was no need. They knew each other's thoughts and plans without speech.

One thousand nine hundred and twelve miles proved something terrible. Something Mary Lee would have been happier not knowing.

Dear Madrigal . . . wrote Mary Lee twice a week. What to say next? *It's terrible here; I miss you so; I want to come home!*

She couldn't write that. The whole point was that Mary Lee and Madrigal had passed the point of normalcy and must be separated to be whole. And what was this whining, but proof?

So Mary Lee wrote lies. *I am on the field hockey team,* she wrote, although she was not.

My roommates Mindy and Bianca are wonderful, she wrote. That much was true. It was Mary Lee who was not proving to be a wonderful roommate.

My English teacher, Mrs. Spinney, thinks my writing is brilliant, she wrote, although Mrs. Spinney had given her C-minus on her last two papers.

Madrigal's letters were also full of lies.

She did not write nearly as often as Mary Lee. *I am having a great year. What a good idea this was! What wonderful times I'm having.*

No doubt Mother and Father supervised the writing of such paragraphs. She pictured them, ripping up the letter in which Madrigal wept and sobbed and confessed how awful it was without her twin, and dictating those hateful sentences: *I am having a great year. What a good idea this was! What wonderful times I'm having.*

Sometimes she remembered another sentence. Madrigal, Mother had said, will stay home under our supervision.

The twins had always behaved perfectly. When had they ever needed supervision?

Certainly boarding school was supervised. Mary Lee got used to it, as people get used to any form of torture. With cruel slowness, Christmas holidays inched closer.

Twenty days at home. Twenty days with Madrigal. Twenty days in which Mary Lee would not stand before a mirror, because she would be, and would have, a mirror. Her living twin. Her other self.

No one ever returned home from boarding school as joyfully as Mary Lee.

But it did not happen.

There stood the identical twin. Madrigal, her mirror, her lost fraction, remained lost. Mary Lee could no longer read Madrigal. She was no longer joined in heart and mind with this sister.

Mother and Father had accomplished their wish.

The twins were Separate.

When they were eleven, they had been forced to have separate bedrooms. It had taken them years to learn how to sleep with walls between them. Now the wall between them was invisible, but higher. The twins might as well have been divorced.

. . . and Madrigal was glad.

"But Madrigal," whispered Mary Lee. She was beyond heartsick. She was seasick, as if they stood on a tossing boat. "You must want me back!"

Her sister sighed. "Of course I do, Mree Lee." Mree Lee was Madrigal's baby nickname for Mary Lee. Madrigal kissed her, but it was a kiss of duty. A kiss because she had to.

"Why?" cried Mary Lee. "What's happened? I miss you so much! It's so hard, Madrigal. At school most of the day and night I try to hear you, but I don't get through! It's like being *anybody*."

Madrigal would comfort her now. Because that had been their special pride, their special secret. *We are not like anybody. We are us.*

"Life has changed," said her sister briefly.

Fear rose up like floodwater to drown Mary Lee. "But *we* haven't changed!"

Her sister's eyes moved in an expression Mary Lee could not duplicate. Mouth curved with an emotion Mary Lee did not know. Two words came out of her sister's mouth like spinning tops. "Jon Pear," said Madrigal. "My boyfriend. *Jon Pear*."

Mary Lee was stunned.

Boyfriend? What boyfriend?

Had her identical twin mentioned Jon Pear in letters?

No.

Had Mother and Father mentioned that Madrigal had a boyfriend?

No.

Had Mary Lee felt that her sister had a man in her life?

No.

"I'd love to meet him," she said shyly. How extraordinary, to be shy with her own twin!

Madrigal shook her head firmly. "He knows I have a twin," she said, "and I imagine people in school have told him we are identical. But I don't want him to see you. I want him to think only of me. Not a set of me."

"You don't want your boyfriend to meet me? I'm half of you!"

Madrigal made a face. "Don't be so melodramatic, Mree Lee."

"But you're keeping me offstage! Hidden away, like a family scandal!" Mary Lee found herself fussing with her hair, poking at her buttons, tugging on her earrings. Not once did her twin move with her. The simultaneous broadcast had ceased.

"Mree Lee," said her sister, being patient, putting up with her. "Come on now. Your girls' school has a companion boys' school. Boys are stacked ten deep just across the street from you. A thousand of them! Pick one."

"Of course I want a boyfriend," said Mary Lee, "but that has nothing to do with us. I want us."

Madrigal fixed her with a stare for which Mary Lee had no

return. "I have a different *us* now, Mree Lee," she said. "You are not to interfere."

Mary Lee could not think about this Jon Pear, this different *us*. It was too huge and terrible. In only a few days she would be back at boarding school. She had to make Madrigal understand her desperation. "Madrigal, please visit me. Spend a long weekend with me. It would help if you came just for a little while."

"I'm busy," said Madrigal. "I have Jon Pear now, Mree Lee. You've got to adapt. You even share the same ski slope with the boys' school. You ought to be able to meet someone cute. Trust me on this one. What you need is a boyfriend. Just pick one."

If she could pick, it would be Van. But she could not pick, for she did not go to the old high school, and would soon be shoved back on a plane and shipped away to boarding school. She could not pick there, either, where her uselessness hung around like negative ions.

Madrigal lost interest in Mary Lee's problems and left the house, and where she went, Mary Lee did not know, and could not feel; and when she came home, Madrigal did not tell.

"I hope you're happy," sobbed Mary Lee to her parents. "We're no longer identical. We're no longer a mixture. We're two instead of one."

"We aren't happy," said Father, "but we are right, Mary Lee."

A strange foggy sorrow seemed to envelope her parents. They hugged her, but distantly. It went way beyond giving her away, they acted as if they had sold her into another world. Made a pact, a deal, and she would never know the terms. "What is happening?" she said brokenly. "Why are you doing this to me?"

"We are doing this *for* you, sweetheart," said her mother. "You must trust us."

Trust them? She actually laughed.

Christmas vacation ended.

Mary Lee was once again flying through gray skies with a gray heart.

Jon Pear, she thought. What is he like? And if he loves Madrigal, would he not love me exactly the same? For are we not exactly the same?

I wish, she said to the invisible stars behind the featureless clouds, *I wish for Madrigal's life.*

Chapter 2

"I'm coming," cried Madrigal on the telephone. "We'll go skiing! We'll have a lovely lovely time. I'll meet all your friends and gossip and we'll show off and be *us*."

"Mother and Father said you could come? Mother and Father said you could telephone?" whispered Mary Lee.

"No. They did not. But I love you, twin of mine, and you need me, and so I have arranged it in spite of them."

Oh, Madrigal! Mary Lee had given up hoping for a visit. Her heart had grown as cold as the February outdoors, and she had thought that only the arrival of summer vacation could end her loneliness.

She began laughing, planning, hoping. She pirouetted around her dorm. "Mindy, guess what! My identical twin is coming!"

Mindy had long since ceased to try with this annoying personality-free roomie. "Give me a break. You don't have a twin."

"I do, I do! You'll love her." Mary Lee could not stop laughing. She felt thinner and lighter and giddier.

"You remembered this twin in *February*, ML?" Mindy exchanged skeptical looks with the ceiling. "Right."

"Right!" laughed Mary Lee.

The next day at meals, she assaulted tables and gatherings that she had ignored long enough that they now ignored her. "I'm an identical twin!" she cried. "And my twin is coming to visit for the three-day weekend!"

The popular girls exchanged long looks.

"It happens at this time of year," said Marilyn with a shrug. "Too much winter. The useless ones get crazy. They start believing in identical twins."

Mary Lee flushed.

The popular girls laughed, their mouths gaping. "So, Mary Lee," said one of Bianca's buddies, "if your supposed identical twin is *really* identical to you. . . " — A cruel smile flickered on the pretty round face — "like — who cares?"

"Stop," said Bianca, obeying the roommate rule. You stick up for your roommate even when she's a dork. "Leave Mary Lee alone." (A skill, of course, that everyone was now pretty good at.)

Madrigal arrived.

She stalked onto that campus, and it was hers. She was the Event Mary Lee had longed to be. She overwhelmed the girls in Mary Lee's dorm and made them her own possessions. By the end of the very first evening, the twins were sitting at the very best table, among the most desirable girls. But it was Madrigal and Madrigal alone to whom they spoke.

Maddy, they said affectionately, come to our room and listen to tapes. Maddy, sit with us. Ski with us tomorrow, Maddy. Have hot chocolate with us, Maddy.

In spite of the identical look that had confused people for seventeen years at home, the girls on Third were able to tell Mary Lee and Madrigal apart. Mary Lee was shocked. Back home, she was always answering to Madrigal and Madrigal answering to Mary Lee. How could Bianca and Mindy and Merrill and Marilyn so easily know which dark skinned dark haired dark eyed beauty was Madrigal?

Madrigal had personality.

Mary Lee, whose school this was, remained wallpaper.

This visit for which Mary Lee had had such high hopes was the most horrible weekend of her life. She was taught a terrible and unwanted truth: It is *not* the surface that matters. For the surfaces of the twins were identical. In five months of living with them, she had displayed nothing to these girls. Twenty-four hours with Madrigal, and they had a best friend.

I am not identical. She is better. And everybody but me knew all along. It's why I was the one sent to boarding school — Mother and Father knew — Madrigal is the worthy one. I am nothing but an echo.

She tried to twin-wave this dreadful thought to Madrigal, so Madrigal would sweep her up in hugs and love, understand completely and deeply. She needed Madrigal to deny it and prove the silly theory wrong.

Madrigal, however, did not notice. The twin who should have instantly comprehended the situation was simply enjoying herself. Laughing away, having a good old time.

And at night, in the dorm, Madrigal on a lumpy guest cot — she refused offers of bunks — Madrigal entertained them with stories of high school. Of handsome wonderful Jon Pear, and their exciting wild dates. Of Jon Pear's romantic escapades and his crazy insane ideas.

It didn't even sound like home to Mary Lee. Mother and Father, who all but fingerprinted the kids their little girls played with, letting Madrigal go out at any hour of the day or night with this wild-acting Jon Pear? There seemed to be no curfews, no rules, no supervision.

Supervision. She remembered that word. Mother had claimed to keep Madrigal at home for "supervision."

"Wow, you get to do *anything*, don't you?" said Bianca enviously. She brushed Madrigal's gorgeous fall of black hair, playing with it and fixing it, as if this were an incredible treat, as if Mary Lee, with the same hair, had not been around all year.

Sunday was the final day of a too long and too lonely visit. Mary Lee said to her sister, "I'm not going to ski today. You go on with Bianca and Mindy. I'm going to work on my report."

They were fixing each other's hair as they often had, a perfect reflection of the other without mirrors. Mary Lee stared at her lovely self; and at the self who was actually somebody else. Those hazel green eyes, so clear and true — so deep and unreadable. That rich olive skin, like a curtain between them. The long black lashes, finer than any mascara, dropping like a fringe to separate their lives. Each girl had caught her heavy black hair back twice, high on top of the head, and again low at the neck.

Who are you? thought Mary Lee. *I don't even know you!*

"Of course you're going to ski," said Madrigal. "That's what's across the street. A ski slope. So you ski. Don't be such a baby, Mree Lee."

"I'm not as coordinated as you are," said Mary Lee.

Her sister poked her. "We are identical in leg muscles, too," said Madrigal. "Now we're going to ski. There are people out there I intend to impress. Two of us are more impressive than one of us."

Who is out there for you to impress? thought Mary Lee. You own them all already.

It would happen, though. They would go out there, the two of them, and only one of them — Madrigal — would impress somebody.

Madrigal's ski outfit was stunning.

Jacket and pants looked as if they had begun life as a taffeta Christmas ball gown: darkly striking crimson and green plaid with black velvet trim and black boots. Madrigal was no oddity, but a trendsetter. Every other girl on the slopes was now out of date.

Including Madrigal's twin.

For Mary Lee wore the same neon solids everyone else had that winter: Hers was turquoise. The color, which had seemed so splendid, which would hold its own against the lemon-yellow and hot-orange and lime-green of other skiiers, was now pathetically out of style.

She was ashamed of her turquoise. She felt obvious. She felt loud and lacking in taste.

In fact, Mary Lee felt like an imposter. As if she and her sister had not started life as equally divided halves; as if Madrigal had drawn nine tenths of the personality, and Mary Lee the slight remaining fraction.

They could both wear their hair in the same black cloud of excitement, paint their lips the same dark rose, throw back their heads to laugh the same laugh . . . but even identical, Madrigal was more.

Despair overtook Mary Lee. She prayed that Madrigal was not reading her mind right now. What if Madrigal knew Mary Lee was eaten with jealousy over her own twin?

She thought to herself: Okay, this is my fault, this loneliness at school. It was a decision I stupidly made, not to try my hardest, not to be my best. But how can I start over? How do I make friends where I shrugged them off before?

Madrigal did not waver in her affection. Even now, during the mild argument that was the closest they had ever come to fighting, Madrigal tilted forward to touch her twin's cheek with her lips.

"Okay, okay," said Mary Lee reluctantly, breaking down, "we'll ski. But you'd better break your leg in the same place I break mine, Madrigal."

Madrigal laughed. "I have too much at stake to allow for hospital time."

She meant Jon Pear.

Mary Lee's cheeks grew hot. Unwanted jealousy whipped like an approaching blizzard through the snow of her heart.

Perhaps that was the great difference that people saw or suspected. Perhaps having a boy in your life lifted your spirits so high that everyone else wanted to hang onto the edge of your soaring heart. Take a free ride to love.

Mary Lee no longer knew what love was. Her twin had discarded her, her parents had shipped her away. If you could not trust the love of your family, could you trust the love of some unknown boy, or of anyone?

The mountain on which they skied rose beyond the playing fields. Girls supposedly came to the school for the famous academics, but as far as Mary Lee could tell, they came for the nearby boys and the winter sports. The two schools shared an indoor skating rink, so figure skating and ice hockey could be practiced year round. Each ski team could be at the top of the mountain within minutes of the end of classes.

So while there were several hundred girls that Mary Lee had failed to impress, there were also several hundred boys. Could Madrigal have her eyes on one of them? Why would somebody as deeply in love with a boy as Madrigal said she was with Jon Pear look at anyone else?

What was Jon Pear like? What if she met a boy as wonderful as Jon Pear? For he must be wonderful, or Madrigal would not adore him so.

"Do you and Jon Pear talk about me?" she said, wanting to be a necessary part of her sister's conversation with Jon Pear.

Madrigal turned away from the twin who looked exactly like her to look in the mirror instead. When she spoke, her generous lips played with the single word and lingered upon it. "No."

Madrigal smiled into the mirror and the mirror, of course, smiled back, equally satisfied. Madrigal's lips moved, and Mary Lee read them: *Mirror, Mirror, On the Wall, Who Is the Fairest of Them All?*

Mary Lee was chilled. The mirror cannot answer that question, she thought. We are equally fair.

Another word from Mother's lecture flickered in Mary Lee's memory like a reminder on the calendar: *unhealthy.*

"But Jon Pear must wonder what it's like," said Mary Lee quickly. "Everybody wants to know what it's like to be identical twins."

"I'm sure he does," said Madrigal, giving her twin a hard look, "but he has the good manners not to refer to it."

Mary Lee was cut to the bone.

"I don't think he actually believes that I could have an identical twin," said Madrigal, laughing now. She seemed to flirt with her reflection. "He's in love with me. He says, '*Two of Madrigal? Impossible.*' " Madrigal went on ahead, dancing out the dormitory door in her dashing glittering ski suit. She was greeted with cries of ecstasy and friendship from girls who had never bothered with Mary Lee.

"Oh, Madrigal! This is such fun!"

"How neat to be an identical twin!"

"Tell us all about it. What's it really like?"

They did not ask Mary Lee what it was like.

Mary Lee became part of the masses, blending in with ordinary skiers, while Madrigal was fascinating and special and An Identical Twin.

The boarding school's bus carried the skiers and their equipment the single mile to the lifts. Everybody got out, carefully manouvering long skis and poles and making put-your-eye-out jokes.

Madrigal scampered ahead of Mary Lee. Way ahead. Deep in a throng of new, but close, friends. Laughing and teasing and thoroughly enjoying herself.

Mary Lee pulled out an old ugly knit cap and stuffed her heavy hair beneath it. The cap was not a good match for the turquoise ski suit; it was royal blue: together the colors snarled. Mary Lee became plain. An inconvenient blue splat.

She struggled even to trudge in her sister's wake, her abandoned heart no longer pumping as it should.

Halfway to the lifts, Madrigal paused. Around her, the crowd had expanded as if it were being multiplied by some geometric factor; as if some magic algebra class were using the creatures on this slope for their problematic equations, moving and multiplying what had once been human beings.

Fear clogged Mary Lee's arteries and thoughts.

Mary Lee, came a pulsing wordless communication. *Come.*

Madrigal was calling. The lovely unspoken words had returned.

Madrigal just figured out how lonely and lost I am without her. So we're back. Twins again, touching without speech again!

Madrigal entered the immense lodge, and Mary Lee flew in the building, too, broken heart mending as she ran.

"*I knew you'd come.*" They said it together, inflections on the same syllables, lips equally lingering on the *m*.

Madrigal huffed out a breath of relief. "I was afraid we'd lost it, Mree Lee."

"Me, too," said Mary Lee, her eyes filling.

The twins embraced. The joy was almost too much to bear.

Madrigal pushed Mary Lee into a girls' room. "I feel so bad because you have on that old rag of a ski suit and I've got such a beauty. Listen, Mree Lee."

Mary Lee's heart turned over with love for this twin who outshone her.

"We'll switch," said Madrigal. "You be the star here. This is your school. I don't know what's the matter with me, trying to leap into your life as well as my own."

How she loved this sister, who would come through for her in the end. We're still twins, Mary Lee thought, passionately relieved. "It's okay," she said. "You look perfect in it."

Madrigal giggled. "Then so would you, Miss Identical Twin."

They undressed with lightning speed, the way they had since they were toddlers. "You be Madrigal, Mree Lee," said her twin, zipping Mary Lee into the gleaming taffeta plaid.

"What do you mean?"

"We'll switch." Madrigal's wild smile demanded a return, and Mary Lee gave it, smiling wildly back, though comprehending nothing.

"You join them as Madrigal. You answer when they say Maddy. You be the one they want. You laugh and ski and be silly with them. You have hot chocolate and listen to tapes and dance in the dark as their brand-new extra-special-Event friend." Madrigal yanked the ugly blue cap down over *her* hair this time. "Then tonight, when they've completely confused which of us is which, we'll tell who's who. It'll be hysterical. Everybody will have a good laugh. It'll help. I promise. It'll get you started up again, like a stalled motor."

Madrigal lifted her hands to hold her sister's, and, of course, her sister's hands had lifted at the same second to hold hers. In the unfathomable way of identical minds, they had each chosen to wear a silver ring on the third finger of the right hand, to wear clear polish, no watch, and two slim silver bracelets.

Madrigal pushed Mary Lee gently in the small of her back, sending her sister out into the group, shining like a Christmas decoration.

Mary Lee was enveloped in Third Floor girls. Mindy and Bianca and Marilyn cried, "Madrigal! What happened to you? Where'd you go?"

"Come on!"

"Time's wasting!"

"Snow's melting!"

So many exclamation points. So much excitement. All because they thought she was somebody else.

Chapter 3

With so many friends clustered around her, the new Madrigal was slow to reach the ski lift. Girls bumped companionably against her, and giggled, and offered sticks of gum or candy. Where once they had seemed sharks swarming, chewing at her with cruel appetites, they were now pleasant smiling girls having a good time together.

Is there a lovelier word in the English language, thought Mary Lee, than *friends*?

A shock of disloyalty hit her. Of course there was a lovelier word than *friends*. *Twins* was lovelier; lovelier by far.

She looked to see where the new Mary Lee was, but her twin, since she was alone, and therefore able to wriggle through the crowds, had actually arrived first at the chair lift. In spite of such a crush of people waiting in line, no one stepped up to share the seat with the new Mary Lee.

Alone, swinging on the chair lift, went the turquoise suit and the ugly blue cap. The lift careened forward several feet, jerked to a partial stop, and then jerked on. The head of the girl jerked with it, as if on a stem, not a neck.

Not one other person at the mountain was all by herself.

She felt terribly, desperately, sorry for that girl.

You're Madrigal right now, Mary Lee reminded herself. Stop worrying about that loser. Tonight she'll evaporate. You'll dispose of pitiful Mary Lee. You'll be popular, identical-twinned Mary Lee.

Mindy pushed the group to the head of the lift line, talking and laughing. Mindy, the roommate who still wanted to eat with her, still trudged to the library with her, still cheerfully yelled her name across the campus. "Madrigal, we have another long week-end in March," said Mindy. "Won't you visit then? Or — I know! Would you like to visit me over spring vacation? We'll be going to the islands, of course. You don't need a tan, you were born with the perfect tan, but I'm hideous and have to spruce up my skin. You'll come, won't you."

Mindy spoke with the complete assurance of one who knows her invitation is irresistable.

"Honestly, Madrigal," said Bianca, "you really floored us when we found out there was an identical twin."

"You're not like your sister at all," said Mindy.

"You," pointed out Bianca, "are interesting."

Mary Lee killed time by yanking the ribbons out of her hair and letting her black tresses spread in the wind. Far ahead and up the mountain, her twin reversed the hair motion, tucking hers even more completely up under the blue cap. Pretty gleaming ski costumes by the dozen shone around, and the girl they thought was Mary Lee stood out like a mistake.

"It's amazing that you and your twin could be so different," said Mindy.

They don't bother to use the name Mary Lee, thought Mary Lee. I'm not even a name to them. I'm a person not worth naming.

She willed them to say "Mary Lee" out loud, but they did not.

"I wish you were the one at school here, Madrigal," said Bianca. "We'd have so much fun."

The snow seemed to laugh. The entire mountain shook its head and snickered. The terrible cliff below the ski lifts was not rimmed with crags and rocks, but the razor teeth of sharks.

It's too late, thought Mary Lee. I can't get another chance. I've ruined it for Mary Lee. She isn't interesting and she isn't worth inviting anywhere.

Once these girls knew the truth, they would moan and groan and scatter. There would be no lasting friendships. Oh, Madrigal would get away with it; they would think she was funny; clever, even, to have pulled off such good mimicry. But the moment Madrigal left, Mary Lee's life would be empty once more.

I don't want Mindy and Bianca to like me because I'm somebody else. I really do want to be a separate person, the way Mother and Father said we need to be; and I want to be a *likeable* separate person. With friends of my own.

She truly saw the light, as if the snow and the sun had been laid out today to clear her eyes.

Mother and Father had been right; acting in kindness, not cruelty. Twinship had gotten unhealthy — two living and breathing and moving as one.

Next three-day weekend, she decided, I'll go home. Argue with Mother and Father. Reverse their decision. Agree to anything. I'll play horrible sports like field hockey and take hideous subjects like History of the Cold War. I'll take over cleaning the toilets and learn how to change the oil in the cars. Anything. I just want to go home.

The sun hit the snow so hard, even sunglasses were no help. The glittering rays were as hard as metal.

The lifts continued to deposit skiers at the top of the mountain, and groups continued to spill out, ski down, whirl and flourish on the snow. A group in scarlet and black; a family whose children did not bother with poles; a row of brawny men, whose weight would surely crush the skis instead of cross the snow.

And then a pause.

A pause in which Mary Lee's yearning to go home was so immense, so filling, it seemed to her it was written on the sky, as well as in her heart.

A pause in which the Mary Lee who was actually Madrigal

seemed for a moment stuck on the lift. Stuck alone and friendless. Perhaps equally stuck in life.

The gondola in which the twin sat by herself leaped forward again, and the thin metal rod that curved over the top of the seat and held the gondola to the cables, snapped. Over the roar of the snowmakers and the shouts of the skiers, no sound was audible.

The gondola flipped, as if unearthly hands were shaking the contents out. The contents that were Mary Lee's twin. Skis tangled, turquoise legs twisted, a knit cap caught on the protective bar, but the girl herself fell like a silent stone.

Madrigal! My twin! No!

"No!" screamed Mary Lee. She could not run. She wore skis. She who spoke to her twin without words shrieked every word she knew to stop the falling. "No! Hang on! Don't fall!" She kicked one foot free of the thick shining ski boot, planning to burst away from Bianca and Mindy, run faster than anyone could, get beneath her tumbling sister, catch her, save her —

But she did not even get the second boot off.

Her twin's body spiralled only once, and then, headfirst, fell prisoner to gravity. Not on soft snow, not neatly feet first, not easily into cushioning hands, but viciously, cruelly, horribly onto the rock scree which divided the bunny slope from the advanced.

The end of identical twins took only a moment.

The mountain had had no respect for their twinship. The rocks had not cared. Gravity had not given it a second thought.

Slick steep snow. So easy to ski down. So hard to run up. The gondola itself did not fall all the way, but hung, like a loose tooth, swinging lightly in the wind. Occupied by a ghost skiier.

"Don't look!" cried Mindy, holding her back. "You mustn't go over there," said Bianca forcefully, pushing her away.

Mary Lee fought them. "It's my sister," she panted, "it's my twin."

The ski instructors turned swiftly into an emergency crew.

She has to be alive, thought Mary Lee. If Madrigal died, I would die, too. I feel it. My heart would stop, my brain would darken. So she's alive, because I am.

The place filled with grown-ups of the most obnoxious kind. People trying to make her go into the lodge and sit down. People trying to block her view. People saying she couldn't help. "Stop this!" she shrieked at them, pummeling with her fists, kicking with her fat, useless boots. "Let me through!"

They were too padded to feel her blows, and the boots were too heavy for her to bruise any shins. She might have been a rag doll for all she accomplished.

Mrs. Spinney, who coached the girls' ski team as well as teaching English, skiied right down into the group. "Who was hurt?" she shouted, clutching at everybody.

"Mary Lee," said Bianca. "Oh, Mrs. Spinney, it was Mary Lee, and she was never happy here." Bianca began crying horribly.

The rescue crew had an orange sled, long and scooped out, like an Indian canoe, and into this they strapped the victim. When the rescuers dragged the sled the rest of the way down the slope, people drew back, as if in the presence of something special. And they were. For whoever had lived and breathed, whoever had suffered and rejoiced, no longer occupied that body. The girl on the stretcher was only a series of rises beneath a dark brown blanket.

"Is she — ?" began Mrs. Spinney. "Is she — ?"

"Dead," whispered Bianca.

Dead.

Mary Lee tried to think about that word, but it could not have a connection to her and her family. Certainly not to her twin. The high scream of the siren seemed very important. They were rushing to save Madrigal, of course. Because they had to save Madrigal, of course. Because this was her identical twin, of course, and life could not go on for Mary Lee unless Madrigal were there.

The headmaster of the boys' school was the most senior available adult. "Madrigal?" he said to her gently.

She shook her head. "Mary Lee."

"Yes," he said. "Mary Lee had a terrible accident. Mary Lee" — even the headmaster, who had been in Vietnam, and whose gory stories thrilled his boys, had trouble ending the sentence. But he did — "is dead."

"No," she said numbly. "No, she's not. You see . . . "

But he did not see. He decided it would be best for her grieving process (he actually said this) for her to look upon and touch the body of her sister, to see the terrible wounds and know that her sister really was dead.

This turned out not to be the right step in the grieving process, for the remaining twin began shrieking and sobbing when she saw the ruin that had been her darling sister. "No, no, no!" screamed Mary Lee.

When the ambulance arrived, the crew assessed the situation and took the living sister, not the dead one, to the hospital.

"Now, Maddy," said the nurse soothingly. "Your friends are all here, waiting to sit with you. We've phoned your parents, and they're arranging a flight to get here. This little shot will just relax you enough to get you through the rest of the night, that's all."

"Mary Lee," she said for the thousandth time.

"Yes," agreed the nurse. "It's very very sad. I'm not a twin, myself, although I always wanted to be, you know, and when I was pregnant each time, I said to myself, I said, maybe it'll be twins. I would have loved twins."

The shot took effect very fast, and Mary Lee, swirling down into the darkness, thought perhaps death had felt like this. A swirling down. Perhaps at the bottom she would find Madrigal, or perhaps she was asleep during this, dreaming a terrible cruel nightmare, and the swirling would waken her, and Madrigal would be there, laughing and lovely.

I'll have to tell Jon Pear, thought Mary Lee, just before she lost awareness. He loves her, and I'll have to tell him she no longer exists.

The tranquilizer was worthy of the name. She slipped into the comfort of knowing nothing.

When Mary Lee awoke in the morning, she was in a vanilla-plain room, under crispy sheets, with white waffled blankets. Next to her bed was its identical twin. White and waffled. Waiting.

I want Madrigal in that bed, thought Mary Lee. I want Madrigal to be alive. I want the ski slope to be a nightmare. Is this the psych ward? If I've done something terrible or shameful, it's okay, as long as my twin is alive.

A nurse walked in, smiling. A doll-like smile, pursed and red. "Good morning, Maddy."

"Mary Lee," she said hopelessly.

The nurse was followed by a doctor, and the two women looked weirdly alike, the same steady lipsticky smile coating the doctor's face.

"Yes," said the doctor, taking Mary Lee's hand as if to console her, but turning her wrist and taking her pulse instead. "Mary Lee is dead, Maddy. It's a terrible tragedy. Mom and Dad are on their way. I spoke to them last night."

How blurry and strange this was. The twins had never called Mother "Mom" and never called Father "Dad." The family never called Madrigal Maddy, either.

"Did you tell my parents that Mary Lee died?" said Mary Lee, even more heartsick. This was terrible. She could at least have called Mother and Father herself. What a weakling she was. Poor Mother and Father were sitting on some plane even now, picturing the wrong daughter dead on a slab.

Madrigal, or what was left of her, probably lay somewhere in this very hospital. They would have taken off the ugly turquoise ski suit and put her into — no. She would be wearing nothing. It would not matter at all that her bare flesh was against cold steel. Madrigal would never know anything again.

This was so horrible, Mary Lee could not stand being in the building. "I need to go back to the school," she said, weeping without brushing her cheeks.

"Good for you," said the doctor. "That's what we want, Maddy. Courage to face this. Identical twins! My, my. It's a double whammy for you. Now, your sister's roommates are coming to pick you up. Bianca and Mindy will be here in a minute and they'll stay with you all day. You don't need to worry about being alone, Maddy, until Mom and Dad get here."

"I'm Mary Lee," she said tiredly. "You see — "

The doctor hushed her. "Mom and Dad already talked to me about the problem," she said. "You two were over-identifying. It happens. Parents make mistakes, and Mom and Dad made their share. Identical twins aren't easy to bring up, and separating you two was very wise. It's just a terrible shame the equipment snapped. Let's not blame Mom and Dad."

Mary Lee thought that, next time it snapped, maybe the equipment should be holding this doctor.

Bianca and Mindy crept into the room like great big fashionable mice. "Maddy?" they whispered.

It was too much to fight off. Why argue with Mindy and Bianca? Why argue with anybody? In a few hours Mother and Father would arrive, and they would know the instant they were in the room with her that she was —

— *the daughter they had not wanted to keep at home.*

The daughter who had died was the one they had cherished more.

Could she bear to see the shock in Mother's eyes — that it was Madrigal who had died? Could she bear to see the jolt in Father's face — that they were left with Mary Lee?

A dread even more cold and horrid than her twin's death enveloped her. What if Mother and Father wished that she, Mary Lee, *had* been the one on the gondola? What if, when they realized Mary Lee was alive and well . . . what if they were sorry?

She walked numbly between Bianca and Mindy. They had not

thought to bring her a change of clothing, and she had to wear the ski suit that was Madrigal's. When they finally reached the dorm — interrupted by a hundred people crying, "We're so sorry; Oh, this is awful; Oh, what a tragedy; Oh, poor Maddy, you lost your sister, we're so sorry about Mary Lee, Maddy" — she wanted only to shut the door and be alone.

But boarding schools are not arranged for alone-ness.

She stripped off Madrigal's ski suit and thought that when she got home she would burn it, for it did not deserve to live, when Madrigal could not. She opened her closet to find something plain and dark to wear. Perhaps her black T-shirt with the pleated pocket and her black jeans.

"Maddy!" said Bianca. "That's sick. You can't start by dressing in your sister's clothes." Bianca flipped open the suitcase that Madrigal had brought. "Here. Wear this cute little skirt."

"I'll wear the jeans," said Mary Lee wearily. "Bianca, I appreciate your concern, but I'd rather be alone."

"We can't let you be alone," said Mindy. "We promised the doctor."

"Promised her why?"

"Because she doesn't want you to think of following your sister. She says identical twins can get a little screwy."

Following my sister, thought Mary Lee. *If only you could do that! I would follow her and bring her back. I would —*

They meant suicide. They had been told to stay with her to prevent her from killing herself.

"I'm not the type," said Mary Lee, "and neither was my sister. She loved life."

"Actually, she wasn't very happy," said Bianca.

"And she sure didn't love life here," added Mindy.

Mree Lee, you be Madrigal.

And she was. Clothing was all it took.

Mindy and Bianca talked on and on, sure that it was Madrigal to whom they offered comfort.

Mary Lee wanted her parents desperately. She stood by the

window, waiting and watching. They would come in an airport taxi. It would be orange. She would see it against the snow. She would run to her mother and be hugged; turn to her father and be held.

Nothing could bring Madrigal back home.

But surely, surely, there would be enough love left to bring Mary Lee back home!

Chapter 4

From the dorm window, she watched the orange taxi pull up in front of the administration building. Her mother and father got out. The Dean of Students walked swiftly down his wide stone steps, hand extended to shake theirs, as if congratulating them on the death of a twin. Everybody nodded heads up and down and then shook heads back and forth: a strange head-dance upon the mysteries of death.

Her parents were frail black outlines against the harsh glitter of snowbanks. Clinging to each other, they followed the Dean into his office. From the Dean, they would learn the details of the accident, be told exactly how their daughter died, exactly what arrangements had been made.

"Now, Madrigal," said Bianca, "be brave for your parents. They're going to need you."

"At least they have you," said Mindy. "It's a terrible thing to lose a daughter, but then again, Mary Lee must have been the daughter they didn't much — "

"*Mindy!*" said Bianca. "Ssssshhh."

"I just meant that when you send one twin to boarding school and keep the other one at home with you, it could mean that — "

"Mindy!" said Bianca. "Shut up."

But it's true, thought Mary Lee. It was Mary Lee they disposed of. Now they just have to dispose of her again.

She began shivering, waves of cold passing through her and over her, as if she were sea water, going through a tide. Bianca yanked a blanket off her bed and wrapped her in it. "Poor Maddy," whispered Bianca. "Be brave."

I could have been friends with this nice girl, thought Mary Lee, and I didn't try. I wanted to be an Event without trying.

Mree Lee, you be Madrigal.

What did that mean?

She knew, because her sister had been sane, that Madrigal had not meant to die; had not meant that her twin should actually step into her life. But the opportunity was here. Perhaps the need was here. What if her parents really did need Madrigal . . . and did not need, and did not want, Mary Lee?

For one terrible sick moment, Mary Lee actually considered going on with the pretense that she was Madrigal.

For one terrible sick moment, Mary Lee saw herself in Madrigal's life: at home, popular, dating Jon Pear, the only daughter, the light of her parents' world.

How much better *that* life would be than the one she had now! How much more fun and exciting! How much more —

Mary Lee buried her face in the blanket. She had learned a great deal during this hard year. She knew more about who she was, and who she wanted to be. Throw that away? Be somebody else?

But of course, it was only halfway somebody else. Mary Lee was, even with death between them, an overlapping fraction with her identical twin.

She dropped the blanket and looked into the large three-way mirror that stood on top of Mindy's desk. Mindy never studied at her desk. She studied lying on her bed. The desk was for makeup.

The girl who looked back at Mary Lee, eyes swollen from weeping, looked — of course — exactly like Madrigal. Nobody would ever know if . . .

Nonsense. Mother gave birth to me. She will know! I'm her

baby, her daughter, her firstborn, in fact, because I came twenty-four minutes before Madrigal.

Across the campus, the door to the administration building opened, and Mother, Father, and the Dean emerged. Slowly, tiredly, whipped by grief and shock, her parents made their way after the Dean toward the dormitory and their remaining daughter.

But what do I do, if she doesn't know? What if my own mother comes to hug me and cannot tell which twin I am? What if I have to introduce myself? Hi, Mother, I'm Mary Lee.

Mree Lee, you be Madrigal.

She tried to think of the essential morality of it. Was it amoral to shift into another person's life and clothes, name and world? Was it what Madrigal would have wanted? Was it what Mother and Father would want?

She tried to imagine taking on Madrigal's life.

Another loophole came to mind. The boyfriend!

Of course, Jon Pear would know. Whereas she wouldn't even recognize Jon Pear! In a heartbeat, he'd be able to tell that she had no memories of their dates; that those lips might look the same as the ones he had kissed, but these lips had never kissed a boy ever, let alone him.

She tried to visualize Jon Pear, but could think only of Scarlett's brother, Van. Immediately, she missed Van. He was the boy next door; he was the birthday cake and the soft icing; he was the summer wind and the new leaf.

Scarlett and Van were not twins, and yet both were seniors. Van had been kept back in first grade because he was hyperactive and the second-grade teachers didn't want him yet. Nobody would know it now. He had become the preppy type, with friends named Geordie and Kip. He played water polo and wore blue blazers with khaki pants, and his thin blond hair was smooth silk across his high forehead.

How can I be daydreaming about Van, she thought, when my sister is dead?

She wondered if Jon Pear knew. If the news had broken

publicly. Was he even now screaming in the agony of loss, asking himself, "Why couldn't it have been the other one — that twin — that sister we never bothered to talk about?"

But, of course, Jon Pear thought it *was* the sister. Everybody thought it was the sister.

Her parents had reached the dorm, and the Dean had gotten to the door first and was holding it for them.

Mary Lee faced the door like a captured prisoner facing the judge. She would leave it to fate. To chance. To Mother and Father.

If they opened the door and knew — knew that she was Mary Lee — knew who had lived and who had died — well, then, she would be Mary Lee.

But if they did not . . .

If Mary Lee was so inconsequential to them that they did not feel, did not see, did not instantly know . . .

Mree Lee, you be Madrigal.

. . . then she would be Madrigal.

Bianca rushed out to meet them. Perhaps she thought a good roomie had a duty to introduce herself to the bereaved parents. "Maddy is so upset," cried Bianca. "Thank goodness you're here. She needs you so."

Who could this person be, that Bianca called Maddy? Mother and Father wouldn't even know the nickname!

Madrigal, don't be mad at me! Whatever happens now, please forgive me. Forgive me for being the one who gets life.

The door opened.

Mother came in first. There was a strange light in her eyes. With a desperate sort of hope, she faced her living child. What do you hope for, Mother? thought Mary Lee. I want to give you what you want! I love you so. You choose here. I will be the daughter you want to have alive.

But Mother did not speak. She held out her arms, instead; her wonderful arms, the arms of comfort and love and assurance.

Mary Lee rushed forward, sinking into her mother's embrace. Inside those arms, the world was safe and good; nobody died, and nobody got hurt. "Oh, Mother," she whispered. "Oh, Mother."

Father put his ten fingers into her hair, as he always had, gripping her fiercely like a caveman parent.

"You saw it happen, sweetie?" he said. "Was it terrible? Was it quick? Did she cry out?"

She could not speak. Her throat filled with the horror and she could only weep. Who am I? she thought. Tell me who I am.

Locked between her parents, she waited to hear a name. It was like waiting to be christened; waiting to be graduated.

"We've been staying with Madrigal," said Mindy.

"We didn't want Madrigal to be alone," added Bianca.

"We'd be glad to pack up her belongings for you to take back," said Mindy. "I'm a very good packer. It comes from living abroad so much. And Madrigal shouldn't have to do it."

"Or if there's too much pain involved," said Bianca, "we could arrange to take them to the Salvation Army."

Mother said, "We're thankful for all you did for both our girls. If you'd pack Mary Lee's things, that would help. Just ship everything home."

Mary Lee stepped away from Mother and Father. They were in agreement with Mindy and Bianca. It was Mary Lee who had died, and whose things must be packed, must be shipped as easily as once they had shipped the girl herself.

Her mother gave a funny little sigh and her father a strange little shiver. They did not hug her again. When she was able to see past the blur of fear, her parents were looking into the open closet of the daughter they thought dead: the clothes of Mary Lee. The stacked books, the open assignments, the tumbled sweaters, the precious jewelry.

The Dean said, "Madrigal?"

She felt herself within her skin, behind her eyes, under her hair. She felt her soul and her past. Shall I be Mary Lee? she asked herself in the silence of her fright.

The Dean repeated, "Madrigal?"

With eyes so afraid they went blind, she faced a future and a past. I am dead, thought Mary Lee. Madrigal lives. She said to the walls and the witnesses, "Yes."

Chapter 5

On the long and largely silent flight home, she stayed inside her mind and thought of Madrigal. There would be a funeral . . . but Madrigal's name would not be mentioned. Were you well and truly on your way to the next world if they buried you under another name? Would Madrigal forgive Mary Lee for this? Would Madrigal want this strange immortality; this life of hers that went on without her?

The steward gave her a tiny, white foam pillow, about the right size for a newborn baby, and into this pillow Mary Lee spilled her tears and behind this pillow Mary Lee hid her eyes.

Madrigal, how can I go on without you?

Is this how?

By becoming you?

She could not seem to talk to her parents. She recognized them; they were indeed Mother and Father. And yet strangers. How could parents not know their child?

She wanted fiercely to hear her mother call her Mary Lee. . . but what if her mother didn't mind that Mary Lee was gone. . . . What if Mother could not bear it that she had lost Madrigal?

Over and over, terrible conflicting thoughts tumbled through her mind, and over and over were swept away by torrents of tears for the twin she no longer had.

When the long day was over, and they had reached home, she

remembered to enter not her own half-empty room, but Madrigal's full and busy one. She brushed her hair not with her own brush, but with the one lying carelessly on Madrigal's chest of drawers.

"Good night, Madrigal," said her father.

"Good night, Father."

"Will you be all right, Madrigal?" asked her mother.

"Yes, Mother. Will you be all right?"

They stared at each other, the remaining pieces of their family of four, the way you would stare at a person who had lost a limb. Where is his arm? you would think, wrenching your eyes away. Where is his leg?

Where is my twin? thought Mary Lee.

The sharing of mind and skin continued to the final instant of her sister's physical existence on earth. Her parents chose cremation. "I don't want you to do that!" Mary Lee had cried hysterically.

"Some things," said Father, "must be . . . " He paused, and his pause was heavy, and in the thick creamy silence she knew as if Father had been her twin what word he meant to use — *destroyed* — but he substituted; he said " . . . finished."

Cremation.

One-and-a-half hours of burning in a furnace. The waves of heat and terror were unspeakable.

She felt them both.

Mother and Father said it was not possible, but they knew nothing; they never had; they were ordinary people; they were not *us*.

I am not dead, Mary Lee thought, and yet she felt dead; she felt burned and ashy and scattered in the wind.

The names Madrigal and Mary Lee collided with each other, and hurt, like cutting knives. She did not know what to call herself in her heart.

Her heart hurt, her wrists and ankles and knees hurt, her head hurt, her throat hurt.

She was so very alone.

If she had thought herself separated from Madrigal by one thousand nine hundred and twelve miles, it was nothing compared to the separation of death.

She could not cry enough to rid herself of all the tears, and still the aching came on, traveling from one joint to another.

The memorial service was packed. So many students were there. She was a teenager herself, and knew teenagers. Many had come because it was a school day, and they wanted to get out of class. Many had come because death fascinated them. They wanted to see how it was done. Many had come because identical twins fascinated them, and they wanted to see what was left. Many had come because they wanted to see Madrigal in her new life, and wanted to console her. And perhaps a few . . . but what few? For her only friend had been her twin . . . had come to say good-bye to Mary Lee.

She sobbed for the girl who was not having a funeral . . . for no one knew she was dead. Could Madrigal rest? No words had been said over Madrigal; they were expended on Mary Lee, who lived.

She sat listening to her heart beat, wearing Madrigal's pretty black swirly skirt and Madrigal's gauzy white blouse and Madrigal's shining black heels. At the last moment she had added Madrigal's sunglasses, pretending she had to hide her red-rimmed weeping eyes. She was hiding Mary Lee's red-rimmed weeping eyes.

From behind the dark glasses, when they stood in the receiving line, she stared at every person her age. But the teenagers did not go through the line. Perhaps they lacked experience at funerals, or had bad manners, or were afraid to talk of death. For not one fellow student came up to shake hands, to hug, or to speak.

If she had not had the glasses to hide behind, she would have sobbed all over again. Mary Lee is dead! she thought. Can't you tell me you're sorry? You think it's me! Don't I matter even one sentence worth? Can't you put yourself out long enough to say you're sorry about Mary Lee?

But people hardly mentioned Mary Lee. Even dead, she was the other twin. The sent-away twin. Her parents' friends and the parents of the kids her age patted her shoulder. "Poor Madrigal," they said, "you must be brave." And then they said to Mother and Father, "This is so awful. We're so sorry. What can we do to help?"

But nobody could think of anything anybody could do to help. Death has that quality of being beyond help. And so her mother just smiled sweetly and her father wrinkled his forehead tightly to keep his eyes from filling up, and the line of mourners — or at least, attenders — moved on.

No one introduced himself as Jon Pear. It was frightening, because surely he would come! His girlfriend's identical twin's funeral? Surely he would come! But perhaps he knew her secret, perhaps he alone could see behind the shaded lenses, and knew she was masquerading. Perhaps he had actually gone through the line already and she had missed it, felt nothing, known nothing.

She saw Scarlett and Van among the mourners, and her heart leaped, wanting to be friends with them, wanting the ordinary delight of their company . . . but they did not come to speak to her. They filed out of the building and back onto the bus without a syllable of condolence.

Is this what memorial services are like? she thought. It can't be! This is so unloving. They seem to be at a spectator sport, not a funeral.

A terrible benediciton seemed to lie over the fate of Mary Lee. *Rest in peace. Nobody will miss you.*

Is it a crime, she thought, to use some one else's funeral as your own? A crime to take over another's room and closet and life and cassettes and telephone number?

There she was at night, in Madrigal's bed, between Madrigal's sheets, and by day, wearing Madrigal's clothing and using Madrigal's lipstick. She chose from Madrigal's earrings, and stared across the bedroom at Madrigal's choice of posters, and sat on Madrigal's side of the dinner table, and answered questions Mother and Father put to Madrigal.

It was the ultimate trespass, and yet, at the same time, the ultimate identical twin-ness.

She hoped for a message, that a twin could talk from beyond death.

But if it was true for any twin, it was not true for them.

The days passed.

The nights ended.

The days returned.

Mother and Father hardly mentioned the dead twin. Mary Lee might never have existed. All sorrow was given to the living, breathing Madrigal. "Are you all right, dear?"

"Are you feeling more like yourself, dear?"

"Shall we go shopping tomorrow, dear, and find some new clothes?"

"Do you feel up to returning to school, dear?"

So she made up the message that her twin would send if she could send, and the message she decided on was this: *Mree Lee, you be Madrigal. You be the popular one, who lives at home, and have Mother and Father . . . and Jon Pear.*

To have it all.

Everybody said they wanted it all.

But Mary Lee had it all now, and she did not want it. She wanted to share it with Madrigal, halve it, give it back.

Am I some sort of mental murderer, pushing my sister out of the ski lift with the hands of my hopes? Do I have it all because I asked Madrigal to give me her life?

"We think you need to go back to school in the morning, Madrigal," said her mother.

School. Madrigal's school. Madrigal's boyfriend, of whom she had never even seen a photograph. Yet if Mother and Father had not known, how could Jon Pear?

I can do it, thought Mary Lee. *I can have it all.* "Yes, all right," she said calmly. "I'll go to school tomorrow."

Chapter 6

The drive to the high school was not easy. She was not sure who held the wheel, who shifted the gears, whose eyes checked the rearview mirror and whose foot pressed the accelerator.

I am not dead, Mary Lee reminded herself. Even though I went to my funeral service, and even though the house is a forest of sad little cards about my loss, I am not dead.

She checked to be sure. She had chosen a white shirt, whose lacy front rose and fell as she breathed, and a nearly ankle-length black skirt. Romantic mourning. But over the shirt, a hot pink jacket, because she had gotten a great surprise going through Madrigal's closet. Madrigal twinless — Madrigal on her own — was brilliant and loud. Madrigal had replaced her entire wardrobe. She had discarded the colors and styles of their togetherness.

She felt faintly sick studying this new closet, this gathering of clothes she must now wear. How quickly, how completely, how vividly, Madrigal had tossed off what they had shared for so long! Whereas Mary Lee had clung obstinately to everything, blocking herself from friendship and pleasure.

A tiny betrayed part of Mary Lee remembered how Madrigal had shrugged when Mary Lee was sent away. She put the memory away, on a mental shelf where she would never have to look at it again.

The Separation had made it all too clear which twin spoke and which one echoed, who strode and who imitated. I must not echo, she thought, for there is no one else to speak first. I must not imitate, for there is no example to follow. I am Madrigal now.

The radio blared. Mary Lee sang along for a few measures to be sure that she still had a voice, was still a person. She drove into the student parking lot only to realize that she did not know where Madrigal's assigned slot was. Fear of being caught turned her hands and spine to cold jelly. She circled the lot and finally chose the Visitors Only slot. Appropriate. Rarely had a student so completely been a visitor.

It was a human fantasy to remain on earth after death. To see what it was like when you no longer existed. See how people had felt about you. Measure the space you left behind.

A thrill of guilt and fear made her breathe faster, less steadily.

She was also, she reminded herself, in love. With Jon Pear. How did a girl in love act? What if she acted wrong? Why on earth had Jon Pear not come to the service? How could he have chosen to stay away from the funeral of the identical twin of the girl he loved?

Were he to discover she was a trick, a substitute, a mere stand-in for the real thing, what would he do? Hate her? Hit her? Expose her? Stomp away from her?

The high school was immense. Its original brick building had graceful white columns and a center dome that glistened in the winter sun. It was now engulfed by several additions.

Engulfed, she thought, and then she was. Drowning in running feet and panicked hearts and screaming silent voices. She shook them away from her, like a Labrador shaking away water.

She looked out the car's windshield and calmed herself by studying the architecture of the school. Each addition was in the style of its time. *I, too, must be in style*, she thought.

Madrigal's style had changed. Mary Lee must do it perfectly, and do it constantly, or her new life would dwindle away.

She tilted the visor down to check herself in the mirror glued to it. The sympathetic hazel eyes looked gently back, and the thick, questioning brows were black velvet against the dark skin.

She was stunning in an outfit meant to catch the eye and keep it.

That was the thing. To keep the eye.

If only she knew whose eye!

He would expect her to know everything, and she knew nothing.

These things she knew: Her stride must be longer; she must possess the halls and floors. Her chin must be higher, and her eyes not linger. Above all, she must never hesitate. Hesitation is weakness.

The moment she entered the first class, her nervousness would be visible to Madrigal's classmates. If she hesitated, if she floundered, they would turn on her like feral dogs at bare ankles.

Even worse — what if nobody suspected, but she failed anyhow? What if she was such a faded copy of Madrigal that people lost interest?

I am Madrigal, she said to herself. And then out loud. "I am Madrigal. I own this school. And I own Jon Pear, whoever he may be. Once I walk the halls, it will be made clear to me."

She was arriving at ten in the morning. School, of course, began at eight-thirty. But Madrigal would make an entrance, because Madrigal had remained an Event.

If I make mistakes, thought Mary Lee, I'll dip my head, hide the tears behind my tumbling forward hair, explain that death has confused me.

It would not be a lie. Death, especially this death, was quite confusing.

She (whoever she was; at this instant she herself had no idea) held the car handle as she held her two selves. Carefully. Cautiously.

Jon Pear might be watching. It must begin now. Every motion and thought must be Madrigal. She slammed the car door shut at the same moment she took the first step toward the school. Madrigal had connected her Events, whipping from one to the next. Mary Lee stalked up wide marble stairs that led to the front hall, and entered the high school under the frosted glass of the central dome.

"Madrigal," said the principal immediately, scurrying out of his office to take her hands. "Poor poor Madrigal." He was in late middle age, and had lost most of his hair. That hair he had left was combed desperately around his baldness. "We had a Remembrance Service here at the school, of course," said the principal, hanging onto her like a suitor.

A Remembrance Service, thought Mary Lee, almost pleased. I wonder what they said about me. I wonder who spoke. I wonder what poems and prayers they used.

"And the next day," added the principal, "we had a Moment of Silence."

A moment? Mary Lee had died and they gave her a moment? She pulled her hand out of his greasy clasp and wanted to wash with strong soap.

"You're upset, Madrigal," the principal said, putting the same hand on her shoulder, resting it on the hair that lay on her shoulder. Her hair could feel his sweaty palm; she had always had hair like that; hair with a sense of touch. "It is an unusual situation," said the principal, "and none of us can possibly understand the depth of your emotions. I just want you to know that we understand."

"You can hardly do both," she pointed out. It was Madrigal's voice speaking, for Mary Lee would never have ridiculed an adult. "Either you understand or you do not, and in this case, you do not."

He flinched. "Of course," he said quickly. "Of course, Madrigal."

He was afraid of her. His smile stretched in a queer oval, like a rubber band around spread fingers.

"Walk me to my class," she commanded.

He moved like a good little boy and walked nervously ahead, turning twice to be sure she was still there. The creases in his charcoal suit wrinkled with each kneebend.

The first hurdle was over. Because she did not know, of course, what nor where Madrigal's class was.

She kept her stride long, but measured; setting the pace, allowing the principal to dictate nothing, and yet following him, because she had to. It was an art, and she was good at it. It came from twinship, she supposed, the constant struggle both to lead and to follow.

Struggle. A word she had never used. Had she and Madrigal been involved in a struggle, and only Madrigal had known?

Down the hall, so far away he seemed framed by openings, like a portrait with many mats, was Van. One hour, one dish of ice cream — did that a crush make?

She wanted to run to him, crying, Van, it's me, Mary Lee! The one you flirted with that afternoon, before they told me I had to leave. Van, I don't have Madrigal now, and I need somebody, because nobody can be alone! Please, Van, be mine.

But Van, who must have recognized her, simply stood there, his posture oddly hostile, feet spread, hands out, like a deputy in an old western, ready for the duel.

She caught herself. She was not Mary Lee. Van thought that he had buried Mary Lee. Besides, she was expecting Jon Pear. She must stay within her new life, lest her story dissolve.

The principal halted at an open classroom door, and Mary Lee stopped just before treading on his heels. She forgot Van in the face of so many new problems. For no teacher's name was printed on the door. No subject title was given, no clues passed out.

They walked in. The room was unadorned with equipment. Therefore the subject was not science.

She glanced at a sea of faces, could focus on none of them, and desperately surveyed the front of the room instead. The blackboard was covered with French verbs.

New problems leaped up and assaulted her plans. How good had Madrigal been at French? Where had Madrigal sat? Had she acquired the correct accent? Did she do her homework? Did she get along with the French teacher? Did she come for extra help?

"Madrigal is back," said the principal in a low voice.

"Ah, Madrigal," said the French teacher, clasping her hands prayerfully in front of her flat bosom, "*Je suis tellement désolé.*"

How could you be desolate? thought Mary Lee. You didn't even know me.

She remembered, as if she had had an entire hour to relive it, her hour with Van Maxsom.

Is Van *désolé*? Did he think sad thoughts of me during the Moment of Silence? Is he sorry that I am gone? That he cannot even visit my grave, because there is none?

Then why didn't he come up at the service and tell me how sorry he is that my wonderful sister died? Why didn't anybody speak to me? I mean, to Madrigal?

She could have responded to the teacher in French, but did not. "Thank you," she said. There were empty desks. But with whom would Madrigal have sat? Who were her friends?

Not that she and Madrigal had had friends. They had needed no friends. They were each other.

The loss of it was suddenly so immense, so terrible, that she could not maintain control after all, neither of time nor space nor soul. She held everything in her body absolutely still, but it was not protection; the tears still came, soaking her cheeks.

Madrigal! Come back! Please be alive! I love you so!

My twin is cut away. I am severed. The stem without the blossom.

"Poor Maddy!" cried one of the girls. "We're so sorry. What a blow it must have been! And you saw it happen. Poor, poor Maddy."

The class chimed in, sounding rehearsed, each student flinging out a short consolation. "Madrigal, we're so glad you're back," they chorused. "We're so glad you're all right." They did not mention being sorry the dead girl was not all right.

I left no space, thought Mary Lee. Rest in Peace, Mary Lee. Nobody will miss you.

She walked to the back of the room where she sat alone. She

wanted to break down on this old marred desk, rip her hair, wear it loose and messy, and scream at these people who could not be bothered to mention her name. She wanted to beat her fists on her chest, rend her clothing, and crash her car.

"*Continuez, Madame*," she instructed the French teacher.

The French teacher did not call upon her.

Madrigal would have volunteered answers to establish that she was not rocked by catastrophe. But Madrigal's replacement could not find the voice with which she had practiced in the car. And she did not even know for whom she felt the most grief: the dead girl or the living. *Doesn't anybody miss me, too?*

Her heart said to itself: I will be friends with anybody who utters my name. Anybody who says "Poor Mary Lee," I will love that person.

French class drew to a close.

One minute before the bell, she allowed her eyes to drift.

He was there.

Watching her.

It had to be him.

It could be no one else.

Yellow flecks, like gold beneath the waters, glittered in his eyes.

Jon Pear.

His red cheeks grew redder, a rising fever for her. His breathing was too fast, and his wide chest rose and fell like a signal, forcing her own pulse faster. Next to him the other boys, even though they were seniors, were mere reeds, without muscle or brawn. He was a man.

He was so handsome! And yet not handsome at all, but roughly crude, a mix that gave her the same sinking dizziness she'd felt when she entered the school.

Jon Pear, she thought, and the two words of his name seemed precious and perfect. Jon Pear. And now he's mine. I have it all!

But she said nothing to him. She could think of nothing to say. She knew not one single thing with which to start a conversation.

His smile broke, like thin ice over black water. Like danger.

Mary Lee would have fallen in love with somebody quiet and loving, somebody sweet and endearing. With Van, in fact. But Jon Pear's look was not romantic. Not affectionate, but fierce. Their eyes locked as if in combat.

She was afraid of him. Slowly she made a partial turn away from Jon Pear, pretending to hear the French assignment.

He slowly winked, slowly shifted his own gaze, slowly bestowed upon her the corner of a smile. It was only a wink but it was sickeningly violent. And completely sexy.

Her blood pounded in her ears.

The bell rang.

It startled her heart.

People leaped up. Mary Lee would have leaped up, too, but she was Madrigal. Madrigal, of course, showed no such childish eagerness, but rose gracefully, and stacked her books by size.

He was next to her.

She shivered with extraordinary heat, and felt herself glow.

He touched her cheek in an unusual way, dotting it vertically with the very tip of his fingers. She thought the touch would penetrate right into her brain, and give her away. Through the pads of his fingers he would discover somebody else's brain living in that identical flesh.

But it did not happen. "Did you miss our little gifts to each other, Madrigal?" he whispered.

No time to feel safe. For this was a test. She could not know what little gifts he had given her.

Earrings? Madrigal had an enormous collection.

A book of love poems? There had been one by the bed.

A museum scarf? One lay carelessly draped over the chairback.

What to answer?

Between people in love, there could be only one answer.

"I missed everything," she whispered back.

How he laughed! His laugh hurtled over her, a stream in spring, full of melted snow, flooding her. "I knew you would," said Jon Pear. He moved her heavy black hair away from her forehead and kissed the skin beneath.

She trembled violently, for it was her first kiss. But he had no knowledge of her inexperience. Nothing told him the skin that brushed his lips belonged to Mary Lee.

Courage grew in her. "Come," she said. "Walk me to my next class, Jon Pear."

His eyes were like a tiger's, the pupils vertical. "You want to do it again, don't you," he said to her.

"Of course," she said, heart beating wildly, wondering what *it* was.

"I am Jon Pear," he said softly, as if beginning an incantation. As if he were an emperor reminding his subject who he was. She found it difficult to believe that Madrigal had ever been anybody's subject.

He cupped her two cheeks in his two hands, and she felt eerily possessed. As if she were not a person, but a china souvenir to grace a mantel. An object that could be dusted and cherished. Or thrown against the wall.

Was he toying with her? Had he introduced himself because he knew that she was Mary Lee?

"Jon Pear," she repeated, perfectly matching his emphasis. She was, after all, a twin; she could match with the best.

His shadowy eyes seemed old and distant, having nothing to do with his clear childlike skin. He was a combination of sweet and rough that had neither age nor gender.

Take risks, she said to herself, fly alone in this empty sky. She withdrew from Jon Pear's touch and exited alone from the room.

His emotions were as readable as a twin's — they rushed and flushed with strength. She was amazed at the force of his feelings. He did not like her leaving without his instruction, not one bit.

What if she had ruined it? Should she whirl around and rush back to him, and let him —

She had been correct.

He followed. He begged. He said he needed her. He said he was sorry he had asked for so much so soon.

She could not recall that he had asked for anything.

They had had a secret language, those two. She burned with jealousy, and with grief.

She and Jon Pear were strangely alone in the crowded hall, and yet strangely under observation. She saw in her peripheral vision a hundred students lining the walls, slipping past in single file, or standing at a distance, staring. What a great impression Madrigal and Jon Pear must have made! Why, she and Jon Pear were ringed as by autograph-seeking fans. By people thirsty to see and touch and have inside information.

They're envious, thought Mary Lee, because I have him and they don't.

"Jon Pear," she repeated, tucking his name into her own heart, knowing already that nobody ever called him by just one of his names, or by a nickname.

He took her hand, and it seemed that their hands merged and became one. He looked into her hazel eyes, and his yellow eyes focussed for her as if, from now on, she would see only what Jon Pear saw.

She felt herself rising to meet him, rushing to fall in love with him. It really was a falling sensation, and yet also rising, a tornado of excitement, spinning up and spinning down at the same moment, until she was nothing but a whirl of emotion.

The ring of listening students leaned forward, wanting to overhear. She recognized friends of friends: Geordie, Kip, Kelly, Stephen, Katie, Courtney.

"Shall we choose again?" he said, his voice cracking like ice. Black ice, perhaps, that drivers never saw until it was too late, the car out of control before the driver knew there was trouble.

Her hair, which had always had feelings, prickled beneath his palm, each strand fighting to be free. Whatever choice Jon Pear meant, it was not love, and not nice. Evil soaked his speech.

She wanted to be away from him, to merge and blend with the

students along the wall. Instead she was an exhibit at some sort of side show. And what was the show? The choice? What had Jon Pear and Madrigal done on the side, that frightened and drew people?

Fear riddled her, like a shotgun burst in the chest.

Jon Pear laughed again, and this time his laugh was low and musty. It crept beneath things and saw behind things. His gold-stained eyes and white teeth smiled in unison.

Madrigal loved this person? But he is frightening. I am afraid of him.

She would never have used the word boyfriend to describe Jon Pear. He seemed neither boy nor friend.

"I am your twin now," whispered Jon Pear. "At last, you have somebody who truly understands you. A twin of the heart and soul instead of the flesh and blood."

The chorus of classmates on the outskirts of their lives seemed to sigh and hiss.

She looked into the gathering and could no longer recognize faces, could not even recognize features, nor tell noses from mouths from eyes.

Jon Pear came very close. He took her hands away from her face, as if they were his hands; as if he owned them; as if she had them only on loan.

What was he doing?

Again his fingertips dotted her cheeks, but —

What did he —

Jon Pear held a small glass vial beneath her eye. He caught her tears within it, and capped them with a tiny black rubber stopper. The vial, on a heavy gold chain around his neck, fell back against his chest and swung there.

She stepped back from him, staring from the glitter of his yellow eyes to the captured tears. One tear remained caught in her long lashes, and this he touched with a bare finger, transferring the tear to himself. He looked down onto her tear like somebody telling fortunes, and a wild and boyish smile crossed his face.

He ate the tear.

Chapter 7

How safe boarding school seemed now. How attractive the many miles!

How pleasant the laughing girls who had ignored her.

Madrigal loved this person? thought Mary Lee. On her cheek she could feel dots where Jon Pear's fingertips had touched her skin. Perhaps he had branded her.

He is evil. My sister, my wonderful sister, would never love somebody like this! There is some terrible misunderstanding here.

Just as Mary Lee had always been able to feel her hair, so she could feel her stolen tear. She and the tear were on the inside of the glass vial, slipping on smooth vertical sides, back and forth on the slippery silk vest Jon Pear wore. Why was he dressed like that? Why didn't he wear jeans and a shirt like everybody else? What kind of statement was Jon Pear making?

I am your twin now. Now there was a sick and frightening statement. "I lost my twin, Jon Pear. You cannot replace her. Nobody — nothing — could replace her."

His face shifted. His expressions were a deck of cards being shuffled. He dealt himself to the bottom. Blank and hidden and oddly threatening.

She looked into the crowd where she saw Scarlett, pretty sweet Scarlett. Who needs a boyfriend? Especially this one. I want a girlfriend. A girl to talk to, and weep with, and gossip with, and know me to the bone.

She gave the boy whom Madrigal had loved one more chance. She waited for Jon Pear to express his sorrow. This was the moment for him to say he understood the magnitude of her loss; he knew she must be bleeding as if cut by a guillotine. She would forgive Jon Pear anything if he, too, ached and wept for the lost twin.

But Jon Pear's laughter hung in the air, threatening the standing students. "You don't miss her, Madrigal."

He closed in on her, and she thought he would strangle her, but he kissed her instead, and even though she wanted to run from Jon Pear, she found him so attractive that she also wanted to hurl herself upon him. To kiss until they both died of exhaustion, like a fairy tale in which lovers dance themselves to a frenzied end.

"You don't miss her," he breathed, and his breath was fever hot against her throat. "You got rid of her. Clever you. Everything according to plan. I like that in a woman, Madrigal."

Where his kisses touched, her skin felt stained. She blistered, as if he had the power to cremate her! To turn her, like her sister, into ashes.

"We are the 'us' now, Madrigal. We are the twins. You and I, Madrigal. You didn't need her. You need me."

It seemed to take so much breath to speak. More breath than she could possibly drag into her lungs. She was not going to think about what he had said about planning. He could stain this place with his speech, and he could stain her throat with his kisses, but he was not going to stain her memories of Madrigal. She was going to put him in his place, and that place was far from her. "Twins have to be born," she said. "Twins cannot be made."

But now his big firm hands covered her cheeks, and his fine strong nose tilted down against hers, and his golden eyes stared hypnotically through her own. "I love you," he whispered.

I love you.

There was a no more appealing thought in the world. Jon Pear loved her; she could see that. Even though it was a different beautiful girl he loved. His golden eyes were swimming with emotion, and that emotion was adoration.

As she had been half a person at boarding school, so she half-yearned to have Jon Pear and half-yearned to run away, to put even those two thousand boarding-school miles between herself and his eyes and his vial of tears.

Half is crippled; half cannot quite make decisions. In the moment before she said, *Yes, anything, Jon Pear, yes, you and I will be the twins now*, Scarlett came between them.

Pretty in a soft and doe-eyed way, Scarlett walked forward as if she were actually retreating. She was a deer at the edge of the meadow. Timid, shrinking beauty. "I didn't speak to you at the funeral," said Scarlett. Even her voice shrank, as if she were afraid to get close to Madrigal.

Immediately Mary Lee knew she had hit on it. *They were afraid of her.* Whoever Madrigal had become, her classmates feared her. But how could that be? Madrigal was, after all, just another seventeen-year-old girl! You couldn't be afraid of —

"I miss Mary Lee," said Scarlett. Her sweet face crumpled in pain. "I think about her all the time. It was a tragedy, Madrigal. You know what I think of you, but still I'm sorry. You must feel pain beyond anything I would, for you were twins."

Scarlett thought so little of Madrigal? Mary Lee tried to catch the meaning, but Jon Pear spoke. "Mary Lee didn't matter," he said carelessly. "Who needed that second reflection in the mirror?" Jon Pear's smile seemed like a passageway to some dark place. He took the ribbon and pins out of her black hair and held the heavy weightlike ropes in his large hands. Then, evilly, he twined the ropes beneath her chin as if he intended to make a knot and hang her on a hook.

She tried to take her hair back, but he kept it, as he had kept the tear.

"I want to put flowers on Mary Lee's grave," said Scarlett, "but I don't know where it is."

She loved Scarlett for being the one to miss Mary Lee. "There is no grave," she admitted, and the loss assaulted her again. Surely it was a terrible omission, to have no place on earth marking the loss of a life. "She is on the wind now. She is part of the air and the sky."

"But that's beautiful!" cried Scarlett. "That sounds just like Mary Lee. Wind and sky."

Van broke through the crowd, ferociously, as if the student body formed a locked door and he had to clobber people to get through. He approached as if he'd be willing to break wrists to break in.

Jon Pear and Madrigal are an Event, the way Madrigal and I were an Event. I want to be an Event. I do not want to be half, or forgotten, or lost, like boarding school. Jon Pear will make me an Event.

Van left the circle like a warrior with the courage to leave his troops. Alone, he walked toward Jon Pear and Madrigal, as if getting this close was also an Event.

When he looked at Mary Lee, Van sucked in his breath and held it for so long, she had to smile. She forgot Jon Pear, though he still held her hair and her arm. How lovely Scarlett and Van were; how beautiful the friendship of sister and brother. It would be good to have real friends. Mary Lee had drawn a new life, but that didn't mean she had to use every molecule of Madrigal's. She could choose some of her own.

She remembered with a start of surprise that Madrigal had despised Scarlett.

But I'll be friends with her, thought Mary Lee joyfully. Real girlfriends, like other girls. "Scarlett," she said eagerly, "this afternoon would you like to go to the mall with me?"

"No," said Van sharply. "She would not. She has other plans, Madrigal. She always will."

From the gathered, tightening circle of students came another hiss, another murmur, *She always will.*

"How brotherly," said Jon Pear. "Of course, after that

unfortunate little episode, Scarlett, I can see how you would need a brother around rather often."

Scarlet paled, pressed her lips together, and lowered her head.

Van stepped between his sister and Jon Pear, and moved her back, as if he were herding her, as if he were her guard dog, and she were a vulnerable lamb. They withdrew into the circle of students, and there they vanished, and Mary Lee could no longer tell one face from another, but instead the students boiled, like water, bubbling and increasing and raising steam.

What little incident? Why did they hold Madrigal responsible?

"There's no need to discuss Mary Lee again," said Jon Pear. He seemed to be addressing the entire school, for his voice soared as if he carried a microphone. "She may not be buried beneath the soil, but Madrigal and I have buried her. Refrain from mentioning Mary Lee again."

People faded and blurred.

Walls left and returned.

Mary Lee found that she was walking beside Jon Pear again, deeply exhausted, as if they had hiked miles together over rugged terrain in difficult weather. "Why did you fall in love with me?" she whispered.

"For your name. Madrigal. Song of the murmuring waters."

She tried to remember what Van looked like but found that she could not. Van, she thought, first syllable of vanish. Perhaps that's all he is, a thing that goes away.

She did not know why she was putting so much value on a mere hour anyway, a mere hour months ago where nothing really had been shared except a snack.

I could be Jon Pear's song of the murmuring waters, she thought.

"And," said Jon Pear, "because you are the twin I have always needed."

She could not snuff out her twinship like a candle. "I'm not your twin, Jon Pear."

Jon Pear's laughter went in and out like tides slapping underground caverns. It passed from good to evil and back.

"Ah, but you are, Madrigal. You and I are twins of the soul."

She was drawn to him like a child to sticky candy, and could not tear herself away.

Jon Pear walked her to her car.

The school day had been so short! Where had it gone, that collection of classes, acquaintances, and curiosity?

She was filled with thoughts of Jon Pear. They seemed to have multiplied in her, so that there was room for nothing else: his strangeness, his beauty, his familiarity, his ugliness . . . his evil.

She could take neither her mind nor her thoughts off Jon Pear.

Who are you? she thought, for she knew he was nobody ordinary. She wanted knowledge about him. She wanted detail and background. All girls who have crushes on boys want more: they want to see his house, and see his clothes; they want to talk to his friends and see him in sports; they want to read his papers and touch his books and know his life.

She wanted to know which car was his, what he drove, where he was going, but he simply stood waiting for her to drive away.

"Tell me everything," she said to him.

He laughed. It was an ordinary laugh. "You know everything, Madrigal. I didn't leave anything out."

"I want to hear it all again. I love it. I want you to tell me everything over and over, like bedtime stories."

He smiled, and the smile was like Van's: warm and easy.

He slid the key in the ignition for her, and turned it, and the radio came on with the engine. A fifties rock station. Mary Lee loved that stuff. So soft and easy. But when she danced her shoulders to it, she remembered her dead sister, who would never dance again.

She needed to be alone after all. Scream into the wind and sky, cry out for the sister she had lost. She waited for the tears to come; the tears she wanted, for they would make her feel both better and worse. The only way I will ever feel about Madrigal now, she thought.

No tears came.

Her eyes were dry. Her thoughts were still mainly of Jon Pear, and the dead twin had hardly a sliver, hardly a splinter, of her emotions. And not a single tear. "I can't even cry for her," she said desperately.

"I have your tear," Jon Pear reminded her. His smile increased, blocking roads and mirrors and thought.

She stared at the tiny glass tube on the thick gold chain. "What will you do with it?" she whispered.

His smile grew even larger, like a mushroom cloud. An explosion. "I like this game, Madrigal," he said. "I'm glad you thought of a new one. We've played the old ones enough."

When she got home, the house seemed more isolated than Mary Lee remembered, the neighborhood more remote, the road less used. Even the house itself looked smaller, its windows blank and dead.

How silent, how sinister, her own driveway felt.

The sky had grown dark early. Shadows were vapor, wafting up from the frozen earth, caressing her legs.

The key trembled in her hand.

She missed boarding school — the chaos and shrieking of hundreds of girls. The lights always on, the radios always playing, the laughter and the arguments always from one room or another.

She tried to picture Madrigal and Jon Pear laughing and arguing, kissing and exchanging gifts.

It was Madrigal's key, of course, because Mary Lee had had to give up everything of her own, and adopt Madrigal's possessions. The key did not go into the lock easily, and when it did go in, would not open the lock.

She stood on the front step, pushing and turning and clicking and still the door did not open. The shadows behind her crawled up and touched the backs of her legs.

And were they shadows? Or the ghost of Madrigal, trying to come back?

Who was that twin? And who was Jon Pear? What would happen if Jon Pear could read her soul, and imitate her movements, and know her choices the way an identical twin did? Did she want to know Jon Pear the way she once knew Madrigal?

Eventually the key moved and the lock opened. But it was only the key to a piece of architecture, and not the key to any question in her heart.

She could think of nothing and no one but Jon Pear. When she did her nails, when she emptied the dishwasher, when she listened to her parents' chatter, when she watched television . . . hardly a fraction of her participated. The rest was with Jon Pear.

And it was, as he had decreed, like twinship again.

The ordinary world had relatives: parents, brothers, sisters, aunts, uncles, grandparents, cousins. But only twins shared molecules and thoughts. Only twins knew each other's interior.

Now she felt not quite separate from Jon Pear, either.

And completely, hideously, separated from Madrigal.

The evening was heart-quiet.

Mary Lee went silently away from her parents, who had been silently with her. To the bare wood stairs she went — stairs she and an identical person had spent a lifetime running up and down. She went into Madrigal's room.

My room, she thought. I'm Madrigal.

But she was not Madrigal, and she walked in a trespasser. She stood carefully in front of the mirror. Once they had not needed mirrors. She pretended the reflection was her twin. Oh Madrigal, tell me Jon Pear lied! Tell me you had enough love to go around! Tell me you could love this Jon Pear and your love for me was not diminished by it.

But it was difficult to think of Madrigal, for she was entwined with thoughts of Jon Pear.

She took the room apart, inch by inch, studying everything,

looking perhaps for an inscription in a book — *love and kisses, Jon Pear*. But there was none.

A treasured greeting card. Scribbled-on, ripped-off notebook paper.

There was none.

Mary Lee was not surprised to find the same three paperback novels she, too, had purchased, two thousand miles and silence away.

The extraordinary linkage of Madrigal and Mary Lee had often extended to shopping.

Vividly, Mary Lee remembered a morning of rage. Not hers. Madrigal's. In her separate bedroom a year ago, before her own mirror, Mary Lee had stared at herself that morning, bored with the way she did her hair. I'll part it on the side instead, she had decided. The left side. I'll hold it back with my new green barrette.

During her one and only mall expedition with Scarlett, they'd stumbled on a basket piled with gaudy barrettes, marked down from outrageous boutique pricing to affordable leftovers. Mary Lee and Scarlett sorted through every one. Scarlett chose a silver-and-gold braid, while Mary Lee settled on an emerald-green tortoiseshell.

Mary Lee ran downstairs that day to catch up to Madrigal, who was already having breakfast, only to find that Madrigal, too, had suddenly decided to part her hair on the left, and Madrigal, too, at a different store in a different mall with a different shopping partner, had nevertheless found the exact same emerald-green barrette to hold back her hair.

Mary Lee was entranced. Out of an entire nation of goods! That two sisters in different malls would choose the identical tiny object!

But Madrigal had flung back her head, and *screamed*, a scream of pure wrath, and flung her barrette into the trash. She'd stomped up and down, taking a decade off her age, acting like a toddler in a tantrum. "Why did you have twins?" she screamed at Mother and Father. "I hate sharing my decisions with her! I want to be *one* person! Make her go away!"

How quickly Mary Lee had torn the barrette out of her hair. How swiftly she, too, stomped down, going even further than her twin, crushing the offending barrette beneath the hard sole of the brown loafers — shoes she rarely wore, preferring sneakers. Shoes that Madrigal also rarely wore and, dressing separately that morning, had also chosen.

But later Mary Lee fished Madrigal's barrette out of the trash, washed it off, and kept it. Very soon after that morning, Mother and Father had decided on the boarding school. But even at boarding school, Mary Lee could not bring herself to wear the green barrette. Madrigal would feel it. Two thousand miles away, would get a headache right on the spot where Mary Lee held her hair down with it.

She had meant, over Christmas, and later over the long weekend of Madrigal's visit, to talk about the barrette incident, to see if Madrigal felt better about that stuff now that it had come to an end. But the time had never come to discuss barrettes. *I could wear it now*, she thought, and knew that she never would, for even the ash and wind of Madrigal would hate her for it.

She left Madrigal's room, with its secrets, and went into her own former bedroom. The bed had a comforter, but no sheets and blankets beneath it. The floor had only a carpet. The closet only musty air. The dresser drawers were empty. For her own possessions had not, after all, been shipped back.

Too painful, Mother had said.

We can't bear it, Father had said.

The school agreed to dispose of Mary Lee's things.

Dispose.

It was a garbage word. A trash word.

The possessions of Mary Lee had been disposed of.

She wanted to run down the stairs and fling herself on her parents, let out her pain and anguish. *I made a mistake! Everybody made a mistake! We switched clothes, that's all! And it's me, it's Mary Lee, I'm still here, please be glad, please be glad that I'm the one who lived.*

Yes, she thought, I will do that. I cannot just adopt my sister's life.

Bravely, she left the empty room and headed for her mother and father to tell the truth.

At the top of the stairs she paused, hearing soft conversation between Mother and Father. "I don't miss her," said Father.

"I don't either. But it still hurts so much."

"Of course it hurts," said Father. "But if we must lose a daughter, better it should be that one."

"What kind of parents are we?" said Mother. "And what are we doing now? I'm sure it's another terrible mistake."

"Having twins was the mistake," said Father.

Mary Lee was stabbed through the heart.

She crept back into the room that was not hers, and stood in front of the mirror, trying to grasp the reality that it was only a reflection and never never never again a twin.

Oh, Madrigal! They don't miss me! They think it was a mistake ever to have had me. They wanted only you!

The mirror spoke to her.

Mary Lee shuddered convulsively. Ridiculous. The mirror —

The mirror spoke again.

For a moment she thought it was her sister, living between the silver and the glass. She even heard her sister's voice, whispering out of the long ago as if, in another life, the twins had lived in a fairy tale. Madrigal had once stood before this very different mirror, murmuring, "Mirror, Mirror on the Wall, Who Is the Fairest of Them All?"

And to Madrigal, the mirror had replied, *There are two of you, exactly the same.*

No! I will not be somebody's double. I will not be interchangeable parts, like something out of a factory! I will not have a twin.

Mary Lee stared at her reflection: the closest she would ever come to seeing her twin again.

When the twins had been Separated, it had been like divorce. Mary Lee got the clean slate and the plane ticket. Madrigal got the new wardrobe and the boyfriend. They had not split the beauty, for their beauty could not be divided.

Madrigal, if we hadn't changed ski jackets, you'd be listening to this mirror. And when you said, "Mirror, Mirror on the Wall, Who Is the Fairest of Them All?" the mirror would say, "You, Madrigal. Only you. Is that what you dreamed of, Madrigal? Being the fairest of them all? Which is something only one can do, and never two?"

The mirror held onto her. "You," spoke the mirror, its voice silvered and shining.

This was not happening. No. She was reading a children's fairy tale. Remembering a children's story.

"Say it," ordered the mirror.

"Mirror, mirror, on the wall," she whispered. But she didn't care who was the fairest of them all. She didn't even care about being fair. She wanted only to be loved.

"Who is the fairest of them all?" finished the mirror.

The silence was liquid.

"*You are*," said the mirror. And it laughed, as Jon Pear had laughed, its laugh oozing out like slime from under the silver layer.

Chapter 8

Madrigal is back.

The news whirled like winter winds through the long and heavy corridors of the school. On the second day she was in class, hostility hung in the halls.

The school was overlaid with apprehension. It lay like another textbook on top of everybody's burdens.

Madrigal is back.

Madrigal herself — Mary Lee, that is — was thinking only of Jon Pear.

A good night's sleep had been impossible. But even a bad night's sleep showed her how ridiculous yesterday had been. Of course she had been afraid, but to call her twin's boyfriend evil? Nonsense. Jon Pear, said her mind and heart, Jon Pear Jon Pear Jon Pear.

She was as nervous as a cat on a string, jerking and looking and tying herself in knots.

But Jon Pear was not around.

She found her way to European history without him. This was not a subject Mary Lee had taken at boarding school. It was going to be a challenge, suddenly starting in midwinter. The text was dauntingly thick.

Again Mary Lee sat in the back row, but today she had company — Van. What a pleasure! "It was so nice of Scarlett," she said to Van, "to tell me she was sorry about Madrigal."

Van stared at her.

She'd used the wrong name. She colored deeply. "I mean Mary Lee, of course. I've lost half of myself. I keep forgetting who I am. Because half of me — isn't."

"That's sick," said Van.

"No, that's twins." She tried to imprint the name Madrigal on her tongue. But the name didn't feel like hers. It felt like a summons, as if she were calling Madrigal back. If only she could!

Mary Lee forgot European history.

Grief filled every cell of her body. It was time to weep, to bawl, throw back her head and wail and keen. But it didn't happen. She wept without tears and without sound, a huge and terrible despair for the beloved life that was gone forever.

I have no tears, she thought. Jon Pear took them.

As if he were sitting next to her, she saw the swinging vial of her captured tears. For a moment, she was so fearful she might have been dropped herself into the tube. Her soul encased in glass, fixed by a rubber stopper.

Why can't I cry? she thought. Does Jon Pear have some power over me now that he possesses my tears? Does he own me?

Stop this, she thought. Stop this pitiful absurd train of thought! Some people become deadheads. Some people become glue freaks. Jon Pear is a tear collector. It's a little weird, but Madrigal loved him, so he's lovable.

Van lifted his hand. Mary Lee misunderstood, reached over and clung to it. He took his hand back as she had jerked hers away from the principal. Wishing for harsh soap to scrub off the touch.

Get a grip! thought Mary Lee. Do something, girl, do anything; collect tears, just don't keep having these creepy ideas about people! "That time Scarlett and I went shopping together," she said to Van, and caught herself again, "I mean — she and Mary Lee went shopping — and I caught up to them — that was so much fun. Your sister's a lovely person."

Van was kind, serious, and brotherly, with all those wonderful traits like medieval knights: gallant and true. She pretended her hour with him was a hundred hours, a week, a hundred weeks. True love.

Van looked at her as searchingly as an explorer hunting for the Northwest passage. "I don't know what you're up to, Madrigal, but don't think for one minute I'll let you near my sister again."

She was getting a pounding headache. She didn't want Van to give her headaches. She was in the mood for love and companionship and laughter.

"And so," said the teacher, "we will split into pairs to discuss the oral presentations you will be giving next month. Madrigal, do you feel up to this? If so, you and Van will work together."

Van gave a strange laugh. His eyes were bright as fever.

Could Van have had a crush on Madrigal? Was he jealous of Jon Pear? So jealous he couldn't even let his sister be friends with her?

If that was true, even Van didn't miss Mary Lee, but had moved right on to Madrigal.

But I could still make it work, she thought. The thing is to bury Mary Lee and really be Madrigal. Take advantage of Van's crush on her. I mean, me. Jon Pear's a little scary. Not my type. I'll drop him. I want to be friends with easy people, like Scarlett and Van.

She said softly, "I'd love to work with Van."

The class turned as one to gape at her. Van's laugh was out loud, and out of bounds. A wild twisting laugh.

Mary Lee wrapped her fingers around the edge of her desk, because she needed something, in this strange world, to hang onto.

Van shoved his desk hard and quick right against hers. He meant to slam her fingers between the desks! Just in time, she yanked her fingers back. The two desks hit hard enough to break bones. She stared at her undamaged hand and then into his eyes.

"Sorry," lied Van, smirking, and she knew — and he knew that she knew — he was only sorry he had not caught her fingers.

Not all the knights of old were gallant. Some were black and evil.

She focused her green eyes on Van, knitting her thick eyebrows above them, trying to find out what was going on.

"You hate me for that day with Mary Lee, don't you, Madrigal?" said Van. "You hate us all. You came into the world a split. A division. The rest of us were born whole, and you'll never forgive us, will you? Well, you have what you want now, Madrigal. You got rid of your sweet sister forever. Leave us alone. Stay with your new twin, Jon Pear. He's your type."

Van's gotten into drugs since I saw him last, she thought.

"Madrigal and I can't come to an agreement on the topic," Van told the teacher. "Would you reassign us?"

Maybe I just need lunch, she thought. Lack of nutrients is making me light-headed and absurd.

"Of course," said the teacher smoothly. "Who will volunteer to work with Madrigal?"

Nobody volunteered.

Nobody moved.

Nobody turned.

No pages flipped. No pencils wrote. No voices spoke.

She was a prisoner in this classroom, with its wall of windows and the straight indifferent backs of people who were not her friends.

Madrigal, whose life she had wanted so much, *had no friends*.

Madrigal had only enemies. People who wanted to crush her fingers between desks.

What have I done? thought Mary Lee.

Van followed her.

If he had been her ghost, he couldn't have stuck closer.

He was staring at her from down the hall, he was staring at her from the library, he was staring at her in the cafeteria, he was staring at her across the computer carrels.

She wanted him to be the Van of the strawberry sundae, not

the Van of the smashed fingers. She looked at her hand. It was unbruised. It had not, after all, been damaged. Only her own nerves were damaging her right now.

Van was studying her. He was so cute. He had that wholesome look, that After-School-TV-Special look, the dear brother who takes care of the dear sister. Perhaps, had he known how, he would have said he was sorry for his behavior in European history.

She smiled at him. Mary Lee's smile. Then of course it was necessary to pull it back, find Madrigal's smile and paste that on instead.

Van stared on, trying to figure her out.

Me, too, Van, thought Mary Lee. I cannot figure out Madrigal's life. If I fail to accomplish even that, what's the point in having it?

At lunch, she joined in the cafeteria line and filled her tray. Food was so satisfying. Boyfriends were not a simple pleasure. But food did not hide itself behind strange actions and strange code words. Food was your friend. Mary Lee loved meals, she loved between meals, thinking about future meals, and remembering past meals.

Pizza day, so she chose extra cheese. She loved pizza, especially the way you dragged the strings of mozzarella through the air, and whipped them around your finger and ate them off your finger, laughing. She took two milks, because pizza induced thirst. She took a green Jell-O, because it had a castle turret of real whipped cream. She emerged from the kitchen tray-filling line and into the cafeteria.

Red tables seating six filled an immense noisy screaming room. Some tables were pushed up against each other. Mary Lee looked into the packed room and knew most of them: people from when she was a twin, and had a person to sit with every moment of her life. People for whom she had been half a set, and who required a name tag to get the right twin.

But no friends.

It was like boarding school. Packed tables for the winners. Spare, empty, distant tables for the losers.

Twins

She wanted to fling her pizza tray against the wall and run out of the school. Run out of this life. Where could she sit? Everybody else had a friend!

She saw Scarlett.

Oh, yes, thank you for Scarlett.

She walked swiftly to Scarlett and sat down.

Scarlett was utterly and completely astonished. She exchanged a glance with the other girl seated next to her and both stared at Mary Lee.

I mean Madrigal, she corrected herself quickly.

"Emily," said Scarlett in a strange voice, "I'd like you to meet Madrigal."

"Emily Sherwood," said Emily, without smiling. "Do you have a last name, Madrigal? I have heard you spoken of all day long, but nobody uses your last name."

"She doesn't need one," said Scarlett. "How many Madrigals do you know?"

"Actually, dozens. I've sung in Madrigal choirs for years. You know what your name is, of course. Renaissance song."

Nobody ate. Nobody touched a fork or a cup. They sat very still, watching her, as if they expected her to do something. As if they were braced and ready for the worst.

Mary Lee was crazy for explanations. "Does it seem to you that everybody is hesitating?" she said. "Does it seem to you that everybody is on edge?"

Scarlett and Emily merely looked at her.

A snake sentence slithered through the silent cafeteria. *Madrigal is back.*

And then, unexpectedly, Van was also back. His handsome thin features were hideously distorted. Van jerked Mary Lee's chair violently backward, dumping her out. Mary Lee nearly hit the floor, but caught herself. "Get away from my sister!" he said angrily.

"I — I thought we were friends," whispered Mary Lee.

The whole cafeteria was watching. Several hundred people

were watching. She felt their eyes. *Everybody here knows things I don't.*

"Friends!" said Van contemptuously. "*You?*"

Mary Lee was glad she had not touched the pizza. Glad she had not sipped the milk. Empty, she felt stronger. "What do you want, Van?" Her throat closed. Only a husky remnant of a voice rasped out the sentence.

"I want," said Van, "a ski accident to happen to the right person, Madrigal."

Mary Lee no longer knew what universe she occupied. What language she spoke. Talk to my parents, she thought. They think the ski accident happened to the right person.

"Hush, Van," said Scarlett quickly. "Sit down! Madrigal's just lost her sister."

"The sister they shipped away in the faint hope of keeping her sane," said Van. "The sister they thought they could rescue! The sister they were trying to protect! They figured they'd get poor Mary Lee away from Madrigal before *her* character was ruined, too. But no! Some stupid ski accident has to take the sister who was —"

"Don't make a scene," said Scarlett. "Please, Van."

The words raced through Mary Lee's mind.

Was Van saying that Mother and Father had been attempting to save Mary Lee from her own twin? That there was something so wrong with Madrigal it required hiding Mary Lee on the opposite side of the nation?

Mary Lee was so cold, so frozen, she might actually have been on a mountain, surrounded with snow.

Why had Madrigal come to visit? After saying over and over that she had better things to do, why had Madrigal changed her mind and decided to come to the boarding school? She had not had Mother and Father's permission. She'd arranged it herself. Used the credit cards and gone. Mary Lee thought that was so neat when Madrigal told her: you wonderful brave good dear sister, Mary Lee had thought. Yes! Coming to see your twin no matter what blockades are thrown in your way. True love!

But had it been . . . true hate?

Jon Pear had actually said — and she had not listened; he was so scary that not listening was what you did around him — that Madrigal had pulled it off, had destroyed the sister as planned.

I refuse to let these people poison me, thought Mary Lee. My twin sister was perfect. I'm not listening to their terrible words. People who say terrible things are terrible themselves, and I'm writing off Van. That's it, I'm done pretending that hour meant anything. It didn't mean anything to Van, so it doesn't mean anything to me, either.

Then Jon Pear was there.

How had he done it? How had he appeared like this? Why was his schedule not filled with classes like other people?

He and Van were looking at each other like pit bulls eager to rip off each other's flesh. Except that Jon Pear was smiling. "Scenes," said Jon Pear, "seem to be Scarlett's specialty."

Mary Lee didn't want anybody to start anything. How was she supposed to have an ordinary life? "Please! Let's just sit together and have pizza and be friends."

Van stared at her incredulously. "You? Friends? Get real, Madrigal."

"I have lots of friends," she said quickly. "Everybody in French told me how sorry they are for me."

"Everybody in French is afraid of you," said Van.

She knew that. She couldn't keep up the pretense any more. The smiles had been quivers of fear. The sympathy cards that piled up at the house were letters of protection.

I have no friends, she thought.

She wanted to die, the way at boarding school she had wanted to die. Friends were everything, *everything*!

Jon Pear spoke so softly it was not speech, but thought etched with a sharp metal tool upon the opposite brain. "You have me, Madrigal," said Jon Pear. "I am your twin now. Come. We will work on your next gift."

"No!" shouted Van. "We won't let you! Everybody knows

what kinds of things you do! There aren't any victims left around here. You can't get away with it again."

"I'm not Madrigal," Mary Lee said, desperate now. There had to be a way out. "I'm Mary Lee."

"You think we'd fall for that?" Van was shaking with rage. "You think we'd believe for one minute that you're sweet Mary Lee? Get out of town, Madrigal. Take your sick boyfriend and go. Nobody would care. Nobody would miss you."

She went.

She could not stand alone, not against an entire school, and besides, Jon Pear cared. He was a friend and, in the end, aren't friends everything?

Chapter 9

I have a boyfriend, thought Mary Lee.

A pillar in a falling world. Somebody to walk with. Somebody who wants to walk with me. Somebody who wants to walk with me only.

Jon Pear seemed to have no classes, no teachers, no school, nothing but the task of moving Madrigal from place to place. He seemed able to stay with her for good.

But is it for good? said the corners of her heart and the depths of her gut. *Or is it for evil?*

His arm lay around her. It was strangely light, as if he were made of aluminum instead of flesh and bone. If she hugged Jon Pear, would she feel ribs and spine? Was he even human?

Mary Lee needed answers.

She began carefully. "Being a twin," she said to Jon Pear, "is like being an occupied country, with an occupying army watching every move. Since I'm not used to being single, I'm trying to understand who Madrigal was just before the accident."

"Who Madrigal *is*," said Jon Pear easily. "It would have been a cute game if Van and Scarlett had believed you were Mary Lee, but they didn't." He smiled at her, a wide shining smile. "And who *you* are, Madrigal, is evil." The smile was happy as sunbeams, yellow dust on warm summer days.

"Not pure evil, of course," he said. His eyes were gold. "I'm pure. You're mixed. But you always surrender to me, because being bad is so much more fun. You're good at bad, Madrigal."

Mary Lee refused to think that. We were identical. I would have known if I had a sister who was good at bad.

Jon Pear drew his finger around Mary Lee's face, as if he were drawing her portrait. As if he could style her personality, and her actions, and even her smile. She knew it was the truth, then, that Madrigal had been good at bad. Would she, Mary Lee, surrender to Jon Pear? Did Mother and Father know? Had they read in Madrigal's heart what Mary Lee hadn't? A turning to evil for the fun of it?

But what was it they did together, Madrigal and Jon Pear? Whatever it was, it involved victims: Scarlett and others.

"Scarlett," she whispered through thickened tongue and brain, "and the others . . . what . . . ?"

"Who cares about them? They're history, we worked them over." His gold-stained eyes were as impossible to understand as medieval stained glass windows. "Choose another one, Madrigal. It's your turn. I saved your turn when you were offing Mary Lee."

The flecks of gold left his eyes and hung in the air between their faces, like a veil. His eyes, without gold, were black stones at the bottom of some endless shaft.

Mary Lee held her hair behind her head, using her hand for a barrette and thought of Madrigal, flinging away the elegant green ornament as if she were . . . *flinging away her twin.*

Mary Lee wanted to hide. To hide she had to get home, and to get home she had to get away from Jon Pear and from school.

Time to tell Mother and Father who I am, she thought.

How bizarre if they did not believe her, either. What if she had to resort to a laboratory! Genetic blood typing, or something, to prove which twin lived. Prove she was Mary Lee.

"I can't choose now," she said, forcing herself to sound irritable instead of afraid. "It's only my second day back and my heart hurts. I need to be away from all this pressure."

"You love pressure," he snapped.

A shiver raced all the way up her spine into her hair, down between her eyes, and back to her ribs, an all-encompassing shudder.

How do I get out of this? I'll be a victim myself if I'm not careful of Jon Pear. He will hate me for tricking him. He's dangerous. But I can't go on being Madrigal, either. She's dangerous, too.

Jon Pear's eyes tracked the shudder. His shining smile hid behind twitching lips.

"My darling Madrigal," he whispered. "Song of the murmuring waters. We go on, you and I, regardless of your feelings after the fact."

After the fact of what? The — she hated the word; it was a sick ugly horrid word — the *offing* of Mary Lee?

His eyes were boiling. His patience burned off, leaving the real Jon Pear snarling at her. "Pick, Madrigal!" He spit the consonants. "Choose!" He lingered on the vowels. "Who shall it be?"

She had to close her eyes. "Jon Pear, why did you take my tear?"

"What do you mean, why? I love to scare people. People are always scared when you do something they don't understand. Look at you. You were terrified even though you knew perfectly well what I was doing."

"What were you doing?" she said.

Jon Pear was getting really annoyed. He took the gold chain off and dropped it over her head. Her own tear hung beneath her own throat. She jerked off the rubber cap and poured the tear out on the floor. She was being superstitious and stupid, but she hated him wearing her tear. "My sister — " she began.

"Stop using her for an excuse! Once you began loving me, you didn't have room to love anybody else, and you know it. You have a very limited capacity for love, Madrigal."

He kissed her. The kiss was both demanding and giving. She actually enjoyed it, actually wanted more, at the same time she wanted to run.

"You're whiplash," she whispered.

He loved that. He lifted her like a china doll and swung her around. "My darling whiplash," he said, "please choose." He seemed younger than he had, and sweeter.

If I knew the rules to the game, thought Mary Lee, I could play. And if I knew the rules to the game, I could also end it.

He kissed her throat.

She would stop this game as it happened, as she saw the mystery unravel. Perhaps she could be the heroine of this high school! The savior! She'd win those hostile people back as her friends. She'd be the most popular girl in school after all, if she could stop Jon Pear in his tracks. Therefore, she would start in with him. She'd gather facts. Then, cleverly, she'd end whatever charade Jon Pear was playing. "You choose, Jon Pear. I'm too tired."

He doubled over laughing. "All right. We'll cruise the town and pick somebody up. Van has warned everybody here. But there are two private schools and another high school and the Arts and Music High School. We'll go to Arts. Any kid that decides to do nothing but play the oboe all day long is flaky, and they'll go along with flaky suggestions. Once they've gotten started, of course, there's no way out."

Mary Lee felt tough and competent. I will provide the way out, she said to herself. Didn't I survive all by myself at boarding school? I can handle anything.

Jon Pear led her out of the school. Even though she was going to trick him, she felt like a follower, not a leader planning to go in some other direction. Her opposition was melting. She was being steered by him as if she were a wheel. His wheel.

Jon Pear crossed town and found the Arts and Music High School. There, the driveways were so lined by the vertical points of cedar trees, the school was invisible. Only the hedges were real.

The interior of Jon Pear's car was sleek and electronic, stupendously expensive, technologically years ahead of anything Mary Lee had ever driven. He must have a very rich family, thought Mary Lee. She wondered if Madrigal had visited Jon Pear at home. He didn't seem like the kind of person who had a home, or parents, or closets, or breakfast.

Jon Pear frowned. His big lips drew into an odd pout, his golden eyes hooded by his own brows.

The marching band was practicing formations on a field beyond the student parking lots. A single student watched from the pavement. Jeans, jacket, and short hair made it difficult to tell whether it was a boy or a girl.

Jon Pear smiled. "There," he said softly, a hunter spotting a deer. "We've got one."

Mary Lee saw that surrendering to Bad did not require her to do Bad. It only required that she go along with it. "What will you do?" she asked, sick and fascinated at the same time.

Jon Pear laughed. "What will *we* do?" he corrected her.

Chapter 10

Jon Pear parked, leaving the car without a word. She sat in the passenger seat, knowing that neither she nor that student in jeans should be a passenger of Jon Pear's.

It was a girl, lots of makeup on a gamin face, hazel eyes, and tipped nose. Her legs and tiny feet treated the band's marches like ballet music, and she danced in slow motion as Jon Pear spoke to her.

Again and again, she giggled, tilting her head flirtily, dancing.

Jon Pear was at his handsomest. His golden-certain self gleamed like a trophy before her. When she paused to hug herself against the cold, he whipped off his jacket like her male dance partner and roped her close to him with its empty sleeves. They both laughed, and he leaned down, and she leaned up, and they touched — not lips, but foreheads.

Jon Pear escorted her to the car.

She, too, had surrendered. Whatever he had offered her, she was eager to have.

Mary Lee trembled, but the girl was laughing.

"Hi," she said to Mary Lee, ducking into the backseat. "Jon Pear says you're getting up a party to go into the city. I never go in unless I'm with friends because you know it's so dangerous. But when you're in a group, of course, you're not afraid, so this is really great. I've been noticing Jon Pear around the high school. I don't go to Arts yet, but I keep applying, maybe some semester I'll qualify, but of course right now I'm only a sophomore at the regular high school with you. This is pretty neat, what a great car! I usually don't hang out with seniors. In fact I hardly even know any seniors. My name is Katy, and you're Madrigal, aren't you? I love your name. Jon Pear says it means song of the murmuring waters. Are we just going to party? See a movie? What will we be doing? Who else is going?"

Katy did not seem nervous, but as if babbling was normal for her.

Jon Pear eased his car off the Arts campus. His eyes were icier than the wind, and his smile more cruel.

The car, utterly silent, without the slightest bump or jostle, moved on like soft butter being spread. At a stoplight, where the car ceased traveling forward so gently, so imperceptibly, that Mary Lee could not even compare it to normal vehicles, she thought: I'm just getting out. There's a McDonald's over there, I'll just use the phone, call Mother and Father, leave Katy and Jon Pear to whatever —

The door handle did not move.

The temperature in Mary Lee's body dropped several degrees. Without attracting any attention she slipped her fingers to the door lock on the window ledge. She could not pull it up.

Jon Pear was smiling broadly. He did not look at Mary Lee. He did not look at Katy in his rearview mirror. He smiled down the road and into the night he had planned.

Van had supposedly "warned" everybody in the high school — but two thousand students attended that high school. Nobody knew "everybody." When people said "everybody," they meant the hundred or so kids they actually knew.

So this is what a victim looks like, thought Mary Lee. *Katy.* "Don't you have to call your parents, Katy?" said Mary Lee.

Now she had Jon Pear's attention? "What are you up to?" he hissed incredulously.

Katy was bouncing eagerly, a ballet dance from the waist up.

"Heck no. My parents never care what I'm doing. I mean, they don't even care what they're doing, you know what I mean?"

"I know what you mean," said Jon Pear sympathetically.

Mary Lee didn't. What kind of parents were those?

Jon Pear passed the fast food places: Burger King, Roy Rogers, Arby's, Subway, and Dunkin' Donuts vanished. He passed motels and garages, discount stores, and factories.

He accelerated, and drove upward onto the raised super-highway that led into the depths of the city.

"Jon Pear, this is a limited access road," said Katy. "I mean, like, from this road we sure aren't going to stop at any houses. I thought, you know, lots of people were going to the party. How are you going to pick anybody up? Did you actually mean to get on at the next entrance? Because I know a shortcut if what you want is — "

"We'll meet everybody else there," said Jon Pear.

Who will they be? thought Mary Lee. Who are the other players in this game? If I don't go along with Jon Pear, I won't get answers and be able to stop him . . . but what if I can't stop him? What if Katy and I end up in serious trouble? And neither of our parents will know where we are?

It seemed more and more possible that her identical twin had gone on dates not to dance, not to see movies, not to park the car and kiss . . . but to hurt people.

"I don't want to go after all," said Mary Lee. "Take me back to the school. I have to get my car. Katy, I'll take you home."

"Oh, I don't want to go home," said Katy quickly. "I mean, this is pretty exciting. I don't get to do stuff very often."

Jon Pear's laughter filled the glossy car. He clicked on a CD and turned the volume up high enough to move tectonic plates. Rap. Words of rage and hate blended with screaming instruments.

Seventy-five miles an hour. Impossible to open a door and escape, even if the doors opened. The driver, however, controlled the locks.

The suburbs ended.

The city began.

It was a city whose symphony and museum, fabulous depart-ment stores, and famous shops lay in the very center. Ring upon ring of abandoned wrecks of buildings circled the safe part. The safe part — joke; this was not a city with safe parts — was contained in a very small area. People drove into the city only on the raised highway, keeping themselves a story higher than the human debris below.

It was a place where garbage was permanent and graffiti was vicious. The homeless died in pain, and the drug dealers prowled like packs of animals looking for victims.

Mary Lee did not like to look out the window whenever she went into the city, because the alien world down there was so horrid she could not believe they were citizens of the same country. Guilt and fear cancelled each other out, and she just wanted not to see it, and not to let it see her.

Jon Pear got off the highway.

"Not here," said Mary Lee in alarm.

The road onto which he exited was pockmarked like a disease. Shadows moved of their own accord, and fallen trash crawled with rats.

"Jon Pear, you got off too soon," said Katy nervously. "People never get off the highway here. Get back on! The only safe exit is another mile up. This is a terrible neighborhood, even I know that. Jon Pear, we can't drive here!"

Jon Pear smiled and drove here. He drove very slowly, the way only a big, heavy car with automatic transmission can move: creeping like a flood over flat land. So slowly they could see into the broken windows and falling metal fire escapes, down the trash-barricaded alleys and past the sagging doors of empty buildings.

A gang in leather and chains moved out of the shadows to see what was entering their territory.

"Jon Pear," said Mary Lee, too afraid to look and much too afraid not to look, "what are you doing?"

It was impossible to imagine that human beings lived here. It was another planet . . . as the mind of Jon Pear was another planet.

The gang could have enveloped the car, but perhaps they were too surprised, for they simply watched, and Jon Pear turned the corner.

Here, not even streetlights worked; they were long destroyed. Not even cats prowled. A stripped car lay rusting on the sidewalk. Distant sirens as distant as foreign lands whined.

Jon Pear stopped the car.

What if the car breaks down here? thought Mary Lee.

She tried to picture her sister doing this and could not. Madrigal, to whom beauty and order and perfection mattered?

"You better sit up front with us, Katy," said Jon Pear. "Madrigal, move over closer to me. Katy, get out of the car and get in front with Madrigal."

"I don't want to get out," said Katy, terrified.

Jon Pear swivelled in the driver's seat. He extended his right arm in a leisurely manner, so it lay over the back of the seat. His golden smile filled his entire face, and he swivelled his head and widened the smile even more.

Katy had no smile whatsoever.

"What do you think we're going to do?" said Jon Pear. "Leave you here?"

There was a soft friendly click, and the locks on the four doors rose, like tiny antennas.

"Come, Katy," said Jon Pear, "come sit in front with us. Just open your door and walk around."

I can't let her do that, thought Mary Lee. He might — he might actually — no. Nobody would do that. But what if he — no. I refuse to believe that —

Katy got out.

Jon Pear, his smile completely intact, as if he had become a wax figure of himself and would gloat for eternity, reached back, shut her door himself, and locked up.

"No," whispered Mary Lee, and she was not saying *no* to Jon Pear, or *no* to the neighborhood, but *no* to Madrigal, who had done this before.

Jon Pear put the car in drive but did not set his foot on the accelerator, so that the car moved of its own accord, only a few miles an hour, and Katy could keep up with them if she ran fast enough.

Katy pounded on the metal of the car. "Stop the car! Let me in! What are you doing? Do you want me to get killed?" She was screaming. Her own screams would bring the gang.

Mary Lee was immobilized. This, then, was the entertainment of her own twin. Evil without vampires, evil without rituals, evil without curses or violence.

The simple and entertaining evil of just driving away.

Katy's face was distorted with terror. Her fingers scrabbled helplessly against the safety glass.

"I love panic," said Jon Pear. "Look what it does to her face."

I should kick him, thought Mary Lee, disable the car, call the police, hit him with the tire iron. "Jon Pear," she said. The words hardly formed in her mouth. Or perhaps her mouth hardly formed words. Everything was wrong with everything. "Stop the car. We have to let Katy back in."

"We never let them back in, Madrigal. Don't be ridiculous."

We *never*. So her twin had done this more than once and, presumably, once to Scarlett. No wonder Van hated her.

But why hadn't police been called? Why hadn't authorities stopped Jon Pear and Madrigal? If the whole school knew, why weren't people doing anything?

She would have to tell her parents. But what parents would believe that their sweet beautiful darling daughter had a hobby like this?

No trigger pulled. No match lit. No poisons given.

Just driving away. That was all you had to do. Drive away.

"What did you do to Scarlett?" said Mary Lee.

"Me?" He lowered his eyes. "I beg your pardon. *You* chose Scarlett."

Katy screamed and scrabbled and crawled on the sides of the car.

"And what happened?" said Mary Lee.

"You well know. You orchestrated it."

"Tell me again."

Jon Pear relaxed. "Oh, you just want a bedtime story. You just want to wallow in the details again. Well, she was much more scared than Katy. I like talking about it."

"Talk" was a nice, friendly, folksy word. This was not "talk." This was obscenity.

"Scarlett didn't even run after us. She just folded up on the sidewalk. Then rats came out to investigate. She didn't get bitten or anything, but they walked on her. She went insane for a while, I guess. It was so neat. We followed her block after block, just watching. She was seeing rats everywhere. She ran deeper into the tenements instead of out. She kept screaming 'Help!' As if anybody here would help anybody. They were probably all laughing, too, if they heard over their radios and televisions."

Katy stumbled and fell, leaping up with the strength of terror, trying to climb right up the car. Jon Pear, amused, accelerated. "Don't you love it when they panic so much they aren't human anymore," he said.

Katy was not human anymore. Panic had scraped off everything but the desire to survive.

"That was beautiful. I love fear," whispered Jon Pear. "I love panic."

Jon Pear turned a corner.

A dozen blocks away were the glittering prosperous lights of safe downtown. If Katy kept running, she'd make it. But Mary Lee could not even roll down the window to yell instructions. Jon Pear had sealed the car.

And even if Katy arrived in the safe part, what then? Did she have the money to phone? Would she go to the police? Would she call those parents that didn't care where she was?

"Why didn't the Maxsoms do something to — " she could not say *us*. "I mean, why didn't Scarlett and Van — "

"They never tell," said Jon Pear. "I don't know why. People are ashamed. Victims always think it's their fault. That's one of the neat things about this, don't you think? They blame themselves. They tell half of it, or none of it, or lie about it, or wait months."

He paused, not worrying about traffic, because no one sane would drive here, and looked back to see if Katy was emerging from the pools of dark. She wasn't. Perhaps she was already trapped.

"Old Scarlett was so blown away," said Jon Pear, "that even though a fire truck happened by and found her, she got her story so wrong it was comic. She got the times wrong and the description of the car wrong and the rats wrong. You and I really couldn't have done it! Hysterical. Scarlett set us free. Van's a little irritated, of course. Scarlett spent two weeks in a mental ward, getting rid of rat visions. I found a rat and put it in her locker, and she ended up back in the hospital. The only thing wrong was I wasn't there to see her face when she opened the locker. There's no point in doing this stuff if you don't get to see them panic."

Mary Lee would have preferred to find that Jon Pear had fangs and supernatural skills. But he was just a teenager without a soul or a heart, without a conscience or a care.

And so was my identical twin.

Jon Pear explained himself with the open heart of a lover. "Jon Pear has always been alone," he said, as if Jon Pear were some third party. "Who would have guessed that he'd find a partner?" He held her hand as he drove, and squeezed it affectionately.

Jon Pear swam under the water of evil. It lapped up against Mary Lee, as if she were a pebble on the lake of evil, soon to be covered by a wave of it.

"It's wrong," she said to him.

"Of course it's wrong. That's the fun part." This time he held her in his arms as if about to declare wedding vows. "Oh Madrigal!" he breathed. He drank in her beauty, and Mary Lee saw that he truly was in love.

She would have thought evil people were incapable of love, but she was wrong: Evil could love just as deeply.

For Jon Pear loved Madrigal.

"Oh, Madrigal, I'm so glad Mary Lee is gone out of our lives," said Jon Pear. "Those foolish, friendly, forgiving thoughts she was always cluttering up your mind with are gone forever."

Mary Lee spun out into space, as if she were a black hole, an eternal sorrow. He kissed her and in spite of the horror it was a wonderful kiss, because it was truly full of love. Who would have thought that love could flourish in an evil soul?

"You're just like me," Jon Pear told her. "For you, people are no different from sheep or ants or hamsters. Just breathers, to provide entertainment."

The gold curtain dropped over his eyes.

"And now," said Jon Pear lovingly, opening her door, "I want to see you scared, too."

Chapter 11

I just won't move, she said to herself.

I'll just stand very still, right here in the street.

Nothing can happen to me in the middle of the pavement.

Jon Pear sat within the locked car, the tiny little lights on his dashboard flickering upward under his chin. He was laughing, his mouth open, his white teeth tinted by the lights.

His glittering golden eyes waited for her to panic.

His chest lifted and fell too fast, a panting dog ready to bite.

She could not look at him. He was not human.

Mary Lee looked away, down the street into the total black and up the street where Jon Pear's headlights made queerly yellow shadows. She needed an ally. Somebody to stand with.

This is no different from boarding school, she thought, no different from the cafeteria. All anybody wants in life is somebody to stand with!

Mary Lee called out to Katy, but terror had robbed her of the air to support her voice. Only a mumble came from her mouth. Nobody came to her aid.

A rat, however, came to her feet.

She had not known a rat would be that large, that sure of itself. She had not known its little eyes would fix on hers, making its little rat plans. She had not known its long, hairless tail would be so plump.

The rat grabbed her dangling shoelace in its teeth, its teeth yellowy green. Now the scream Mary Lee had not been able to produce invented itself.

She felt her face change shape and her jaw stretch, she felt her eyes scream along with her mouth, widening and gaping. She heard the terrible sound of her own horror scraping its way out of her lungs.

She kicked. She didn't want even her shoe to touch the rat. She had to get it off her! Get away!

Mary Lee, too, tried to mount the car body, tried to tip the windows down, tried to tear the doors off the hinges — anything — just to get inside, be safe, be civilized.

Jon Pear was delighted.

Bright-eyed, he watched her.

The rat followed.

She choked on her own scream.

How silent was the city. How soundless the rat.

There was no urban din. No radio. No engine. No horn. No bark.

Just the heaving of her own chest, the sucking of her own lungs.

She ran. She had to run. She didn't know if she was running from Jon Pear — sitting all normal and cozy like an ordinary high-school boy waiting for the light to change — or from the rat.

Only the rat followed her.

The street belonged to the rat. She had to leave the street. She had to run faster than the rat. She would go into this building — she would — but no human beings went into this building. She made it up the first step, and up the second, and while her foot was still in midair, reaching for the third, she saw how the doors and windows were solid: blank, with splintered plywood nailed on to make empty boxes of night out of ordinary buildings.

The third step collapsed. Sneaker and sock were slashed as her foot went down. Down into air, down into nothing, down where probably not just rats but also snakes hid! Down with spiders and things that bit and things that chewed.

Mary Lee had not known she possessed as many screams. They came rolling out of her like links on a chain, one after another, huge shining polished screams.

Jon Pear was backing up his car. He was not a good backer. The car veered first to the left and then to the right. She hoped he would crash into some unyielding brick building and total his car, but he wasn't going fast enough for that.

Rolling down his window with the little push button, Jon Pear grinned at her. Loose and easy, like a cheerleader at a game. "Hey, Maddy, what's happening?" He giggled.

Mary Lee thought: My sister Madrigal enjoyed hurting people. Madrigal did this. More than once. She sat in that car with Jon Pear, with the windows up and the doors locked, and she laughed while her face turned green in the light and her victim screamed among the rats.

My twin.

Katy staggered around the corner. Her eyes were unnaturally wide. Her hands were filthy and also her kneecaps; she'd fallen in a gutter and the trash had stuck to her.

Jon Pear vaulted out of the car. He escorted Katy to the car like a boyfriend privileged to have such a pretty date for the prom.

"Jon Pear," whispered Mary Lee. "Jon Pear, I can't get my foot out. I'm stuck."

"Dear, dear," said Jon Pear, tucking Katy into the front passenger seat, and gently fastening her seatbelt, and gently closing her door. Jon Pear waved at Mary Lee. "Bye, bye, Madrigal," he said softly, blowing her a kiss.

He strolled around the car to get in and drive away.

Lock him out, Katy! thought Mary Lee. Lock Jon Pear out in the street and drive away! I don't care what happens to me as long as Jon Pear gets his! Lock the doors, Katy.

Katy scrunched against the door, clinging to herself and the armrest.

Mary Lee's screams were all used up now, tired and pointless, and the tears began.

Jon Pear scared Madrigal so much that my sister had to participate, thought Mary Lee. My sister didn't really want to do this. Jon Pear forced her . . .

No. The sister who visited her at boarding school hadn't been afraid of her boyfriend. The thought of Jon Pear had brought only smiles to Madrigal's face.

No wonder Van hates me, thought Mary Lee. No wonder Scarlett is afraid of me.

Jon Pear rested on the back of the car, like a horse trainer lounging against the fence.

She knew what he wanted. He wanted her to beg. Say please, say the magic word.

He wanted power.

He wanted proof that he could give fear and take away fear.

He could start panic and take away panic.

I will stop him, she thought, I will end him. I will never never never let Jon Pear hurt anybody else again!

"Please, Jon Pear," she begged. "Please don't leave me here."

He stomped down on the broken step, breaking it more, and giving her room to pull her foot out. He helped her into the backseat. Very gentlemanly. When she sagged down onto the leather, the soft-as-butter leather, the warm once-alive leather, she felt safe and civilized again.

Jon Pear actually said thank you to Mary Lee when he started the car. "That was great, Madrigal," he said. "You were great. You were as scared as any of them. Because you knew I'd really drive away. You really knew what to be scared of."

Jon Pear laughed happily and changed radio stations.

"Wasn't that a high, Katy?" said Jon Pear. He flashed his marvelous smile at her. The smile had a life and character of its own. He was the sponsor of the smile, but it wasn't his. He'd just bought it somewhere. "Weren't you thrilled, Katy? There's nothing like having your life in danger."

Katy burst into tears.

They reached a red light in the center of downtown, ten blocks and a million emotional miles from where he had dumped Katy. Theater patrons bustled in their finery, and the late-night restaurant crowd rustled in and out bright-lit doors. The music of pianos and small bands spilled out onto the friendly sidewalks.

Jon Pear took Katy's hands away from her face as if those were his own, as if Katy had them on loan. Her face was stricken and tearstained. He chose a tear, lifting it carefully with a bare finger. He looked down onto the tear like somebody telling fortunes, and a wild and boyish smile crossed his face.

He ate the tear.

Mary Lee made herself think of good things. Of parents and warmth, of sunshine and autumn leaves, of laughter and sharing. Once she would also have thought of twins, but there was no beauty in that thought now.

"Tears are the soul," said Jon Pear. "Tears are pain."

No, thought Mary Lee, tears are just proof. Just a weird creepy way of showing that you made somebody cry.

She saw there was just something animal about Jon Pear; he was closer to the rat. He was a boy, a high school boy, but a wilding. He was so handsome, so well-packaged! It was hard to tell, beneath the good clothing and the great hair, the shining smile and the fine speech, that he was less, not more.

Subhuman, she thought. That's what it is.

How much, she thought, as Jon Pear's car moved through the city and got back on the highway, how much did Mother and Father know? They knew I was in danger. Did they know exactly what Madrigal was up to? Did somebody's parents call them? Did Madrigal brag? Did they follow her?

Now the two thousand miles her mother and father had chosen seemed like a fine gift. If only it had worked! Mary Lee would have been happier to be lonely and confused all her life, than to know what kind of person Madrigal had really been.

I have to be sure Mother and Father know that I'm really Mary Lee. We have to bury Madrigal, and we have to bury her deep and forever.

And Jon Pear . . . how do we bury Jon Pear?

Mary Lee made plan after plan. But nothing would really work. Jon Pear would slide out of whatever came and wait a while and then — here or elsewhere — start up again.

Katy and I will go to the police, she thought. The simple solution is always best. We'll tell the authorities and have Jon Pear imprisoned.

But Jon Pear had been here before. How clever he was! In moments, he had Katy giggling to please him. He had Katy admitting that the night had been a real high. He had Katy pressing her lips together in a one-person kiss, listening to a hint that Jon Pear might ask her out again one day.

It chilled Mary Lee more than the rat.

Katy was cooperating.

Katy wouldn't tell a soul.

So there would be no police to stop Jon Pear. No principal, no parent, no passerby.

Only Mary Lee.

They took Katy home. She actually said thank-you after she said good-bye. Jon Pear laughed all the way to the high school.

How Mary Lee yearned to be in her own car! Doors locked, wheels pointed toward the safety of home.

There had evidently been some event at the school, for late as it was, people were pouring out of the building, laughing, cheering, and thrusting fists of victory into the air. Boys were whapping each other on the back, and girls were hopping up and down with delight.

How nice to enjoy a sport like basketball, where the worst that can happen is you lose. Whereas Madrigal's sport . . .

"Jon Pear," said Mary Lee, "we're not going to hurt anybody again. This hobby is over."

It startled him. "What are you trying to pull?" said Jon Pear suspiciously.

"This is truly bad! You have to stop being so rotten."

Jon Pear laughed. "Too much fun. You should have seen your face, Madrigal. You were so scared. You were jelly. You were panic. You were gone, girl. And everybody is jealous of me. I do what I want. They want to, too, but they're timid, see. My plan is to get them all. We'll have a whole school of people who will do anything to anybody."

"You will not! They won't cooperate with you. This school is full of good people! Kind, generous, decent people."

He was skeptical. "Name one."

It was easy to name one. Easy to name two. Scarlett and Van were kind, generous, decent people.

"Van," she told Jon Pear. Just uttering Van's name made her feel better. "Van is a good person."

She had made a mistake.

A huge and serious mistake.

Everything about Jon Pear darkened and deepened. He moved back from her, and she saw, for a splintered second, the creature that was beneath his skin. A creature with no compassion, no humanity. A soul as empty as the glass vial in which he had dropped her tear.

"You like him," said Jon Pear. He was truly shocked. "*You like Van!*"

She had forgotten that Jon Pear loved Madrigal. Trusted Madrigal. Confided in her.

She had betrayed Jon Pear. And in so doing, had betrayed Van. For Jon Pear, who had simply wanted entertainment, now had a greater motive.

The desire to hurt Van flared on Jon Pear like sunspots. It blinded Mary Lee, as if looking Jon Pear's way required special lenses.

Jon Pear got out of his car and searched the crowds.

Coming through the high school door were Van and Scarlett.

"Why, Van," said Jon Pear, his smile growing.

"Why, Van," said Jon Pear, gliding forward like a creature of the water, without legs, without steps.

Chapter 12

Van stepped in front of Scarlett.

As if standing first in line ever saved the second person.

But Mary Lee loved him for it. Once I was that close to my sister, she thought. Once Madrigal and I trusted each other and looked out for each other.

When the twins were little, Mother used to say, they'd fall asleep at the exact same moment, the rhythm of their breathing identical. They would eat their cereal in synchrony, each little right hand moving a spoon as the other did. They would run to the schoolbus stop, each skip timed like a choreographed dance number.

Where did you go, Madrigal? asked Mary Lee.

But she could not spend time on a ruined sister. She had to move on. "Leave Van and Scarlett alone," said Mary Lee. Her voice felt old, as if she had dug it out of some dusty history text.

Jon Pear, of course, never even looked at her, but continued to advance upon Van.

She stepped between them.

"Madrigal, this is my game," said Jon Pear, never lowering his eyes to hers.

"These are people. They aren't a game." She stepped in front of him again.

He was incredulous. Nobody blocked the path of Jon Pear.

"What is going on here?" demanded Jon Pear. "Who do you think you are?" His voice was no longer water rippling over the rocks. It was the rock itself, sharp. "I do anything I want."

"No."

"Madrigal," said Jon Pear. "You're making me angry, Madrigal."

She shrugged. The pretense of being Madrigal felt as if it had lasted for weeks. Drained her like a wasting disease.

Jon Pear wanted to shove her away. She could feel his yearning to push her trembling on the other side of his own extended hand. He controlled himself, but just barely. The violence in Jon Pear was growing. She felt as if she were standing over a geographic fault line.

Who is Jon Pear? she thought, staring at his fury.

She knew nothing of his history and nothing of his present. Did not know his address. Did not have his phone number. Jon Pear had never mentioned parents — never quoted them, referred to them, groaned about their rules, hoped for their approval. He had mentioned no sisters or brothers. No dogs, no bedroom, no possession had been worth describing. He seemed to play no sport and, although he attended classes, he seemed not to be enrolled in them.

He was just there.

"If your plan, Madrigal," said Van quietly, "is to pretend you're on our side, so you can get us to go along with you, or divide us, you need to know we can see through you. You're as sick as Jon Pear is."

She wanted desperately to have Van know who she really was.

"It won't work, Madrigal," said Van. "We've played too many of your games. We're not playing this time. We're going to our car. You are not getting near us. Neither of you. You are not to touch us, nor speak to us. Ever again."

Mary Lee's heart was breaking. She flushed in shame, her olive skin turning hot and beautiful.

Jon Pear said, "Madrigal?" She could not tell whether he shook from rage or adoration.

Van and Scarlett took a single stride toward their car, but Jon Pear leaped between them and safety. He spoke to Madrigal, but he stared into the eyes of Van and Scarlett.

"Remember the day we saw somebody drowning, Madrigal?" said Jon Pear. "Remember how you and I stood on the shore and watched? Remember how bright and gaudy the autumn leaves were, drifting down on the water where he went under? Remember how he came to the surface again and signalled us? He knew we were there, Madrigal."

The miasma of his evil spread like a fishnet. Mary Lee tried to step away, but his voice caught her. She was prisoner of his voice the way she had been prisoner of the broken step.

"The last time he came up, and didn't have enough strength to call out to us, we waved at him." Jon Pear's eyes glittered like diamonds. "You and I, Madrigal. Remember what fun that was, when he went down? He knew we could have done something. And he knew we wouldn't. That's the most fun," Jon Pear confided. "When you *could* do something, but you don't. And they realize it, the victims. They know you chose to let them drown."

Scarlett was weeping.

Van continued to appear preppy and perfect, athletic and interesting. But his complexion drained of color, and beneath his tan he was gray. As gray as the skies and the heart that had accompanied Mary Lee on her plane trips.

Mary Lee, too, struggled for air she would never find and reached out with frozen fingers to haul herself to safety, and found only a maple leaf. In a voice that had no sound, only horror, she said, *My sister did that?*

Her knees buckled. Half-fainting, Mary Lee ended not unconscious but kneeling in front of Jon Pear, as if begging for mercy.

"I don't do mercy," said Jon Pear. "I don't do anything I could go to jail for, either. I just stand there. Watching. What happens, happens. I love watching it."

She felt herself folding, growing smaller and smaller. She had nothing inside now but agony. What he was was bad. Not a mirage, not a ghost, not a vampire, but a completely bad person. And either Madrigal had been born the same, or he had taught her to be the same.

"And you do, too, Madrigal. Don't pretend now that you didn't enjoy it as much as I did. Don't try to get Van Maxsom back by pretending you're really a nice person. You're Madrigal, who stands laughing while people die." He smiled a real smile, the smile of a person who found life satisfying.

"I will do nothing with you, Jon Pear!" she shouted. "I will stop you."

How he laughed. His eyes bright. "Nothing stops me. Least of all you, Madrigal! I'll have whatever victim I want. Including you, if I want you."

In the parking lot that Mary Lee had thought empty, students appeared. They formed a distant circle, silent and watching.

"Ah, this is what I like," said Jon Pear. "A larger audience."

She knew them. Geordie, Kip, Stephen, Rog, Kelly, Courtney, Nate . . . and Katy.

Jon Pear's voice like a satin wedding gown, tempting her down a terrible aisle. "Join me, Madrigal. You and I are twins now, remember. The perfect match."

"No, Jon Pear. Never."

"I own you, Madrigal. I know everything you ever did. I even know you murdered your own sister. Mary Lee was far away but she was still there. You couldn't stand it! You couldn't stand those soft little thoughts of hers wafting home, you couldn't stand that whimpering — *come visit me*. You decided miles weren't enough. You wanted her completely and forever gone."

She spread her legs for balance, and gripped her waist with her two hands for courage. "I am not Madrigal. I do not know what Madrigal had in mind for Mary Lee, but nothing happened to Mary Lee. It happened to Madrigal herself. The body was identified by a ski suit and I, Mary Lee, took advantage. I thought she had the better life, and I thought I wanted her life. Now I see that Madrigal's life was ugly and barren and cruel.

And you, too, Jon Pear. You are ugly and barren and cruel. And I will stop you."

The night air was less cold. The wind was more quiet.

"*You* are Mary Lee?" whispered Scarlett.

"She is not!" shouted Jon Pear. He jumped up and down, as if trying to crush the opposition under his feet. "I know everything, and I would have known."

Mary Lee folded her arms across her heart. Either the memory of her twin or the violence of Jon Pear was going to destroy her if she didn't keep a very tight hold. "You know very little, Jon Pear. You know nothing of love. You corrupted Madrigal, but you will not have me."

"You are *Madrigal*!"

"I am Mary Lee."

"Impossible! Nothing fools me. *I would have known.*" He clung to the little vial of tears, and Mary Lee saw suddenly that it was for his sake he had the gold chain and the talisman: It made him feel bigger and better.

She grabbed the chain and jerked it hard, snapping it against the back of Jon Pear's own neck, and she threw it into the weeds where it belonged.

There was silence.

There was darkness.

There was astonishment.

Scarlett whispered, "You *are* Mary Lee!" She pivoted slowly, creeping around behind the safety of her brother, hardly daring to believe.

"I'm sorry." Mary Lee was weeping. "Oh, Scarlett, for all the things my sister did, I'm sorry. I didn't know! I knew some other Madrigal. I don't know who this one was, that Madrigal who hurt everybody and liked it."

Scarlett placed a gentle kiss on Mary Lee's cheek. It was unbearably similar to the kiss of twins. "We forgive you for what Madrigal was, and what she did."

Mary Lee left Jon Pear standing alone. She left him humiliated and tricked. She left after calling him ugly. She stood with Van and Scarlett, with Kip and Geordie, Courtney and Nate.

No one can bear to be left standing alone and friendless.

No one can bear to see a circle of people closing in on him.

The worse kind of person you are, the more you need other people. You have to brag. You have to show off. You have to swagger.

Jon Pear would show them.

He would have something to swagger about.

Chapter 13

As if they had been in a VCR clicked to PAUSE, they now clicked to PLAY.

People moved back to their cars. Chatter and laughter returned. Tonight's athletic event was over; now they must remind each other of the next one, and promise to be there, and to win.

"Winter Sleigh Day is Saturday," they called to each other.

"I'm in the relay race," Stephen said. "What are you doing?"

"I'm selling T-shirts," said Kelly.

"I'm selling hot chocolate," said Courtney.

"I'm renting ice skates," said Rog.

Van and Scarlett walked Mary Lee to her car. Van opened the door for her, and checked to see that the other doors were locked, and waited until she had her key out. "I'm stunned," he said. "I have to admit — I only half-believe you, Mary Lee. Madrigal, you see, was so crafty. She could fool anybody."

"She fooled me," said Mary Lee.

Scarlett said, giving a great gift to Mary Lee, "I don't believe for one minute that Madrigal was going to hurt you when she went to visit. That's typical Jon Pear. He turns a perfectly nice visit to a sister into something evil and violent. I'm sure Madrigal really missed you."

Van looked at his sister. His eyes were flat and his mouth was tight. He believed Madrigal had planned to hurt her sister. He had no trouble believing it at all.

What he had trouble believing was that Madrigal didn't pull it off — that it was Mary Lee who had survived.

Like photographic negatives, in the half-illumination of half-working parking-lot lights, students in cars were ghosts on black. Muffled, their engines began. Slowly, nosing forward like migrating herds, they found the exits and drove away.

Van and Scarlett went to their car.

Mary Lee turned the key in her engine.

Van and Scarlett slammed their own doors and locked them.

Mary Lee's key turned, but her engine didn't.

Van and Scarlett started up and drove away.

Mary Lee tried the key again, and the engine was silent, and again, and the engine was silent, and —

Jon Pear slid into the passenger seat.

"I locked the door!" she said.

He laughed. "I have a key, of course. And I took the precaution of disabling your car, of course. Wave good-bye to your little friends, Mary Lee."

But her little friends were gone, nothing but red rear lights vanishing down the road. The last parting student waved good-bye. Did that person know? Did that driver see who had gotten into the car with her? Was that person doing for a hobby exactly what Madrigal and Jon Pear had done — committing the sin of just driving away?

"Winter Sleigh Day," said Jon Pear meditatively. "Let's spell that differently, Mary Lee. Winter Slay Day." His smile was back. "Whom shall we slay, my new little twin?" His fingers closed over Mary Lee's wrist.

"So you are really Mary Lee." He shook his head. "Fascinating. Madrigal tried to talk back to me once, too."

"She did?" Mary Lee felt a thread of hope for her sister.

"You are braver than she is. You're trying a second time."

I am braver than Madrigal?

"But it won't work. I will make you my twin just the way I made Madrigal my twin. You and I will be twins in evil."

"Never! Anyway, Jon Pear, you're not evil. You're ordinary. You're just mean and low. You're just ugly and pointless. The world has lots of people like you."

Jon Pear was furious. What could be a greater insult than being called ordinary? "I am evil," he told her. He tilted her chin up as if to kiss her lips, but kept tilting as if to snap her neck. "And you tried it, Mary Lee. You were a passenger in the car that put old Katy out in the street."

"I didn't know what was going to happen," she said.

Jon Pear laughed. His laughter rose like smoky pollution from some ancient factory. "You knew something bad was going to happen, and you wanted to see what it was. Don't lie, Mary Lee. But even if you didn't lie, you're still caught. See, once you go bad, you stay bad. You get only one chance. You don't get to say, 'Oh, let's not count this, I'm sorry now, I want to be nice again.' "

"Yes, you can. You can say you're sorry." She wondered what he was going to do to her. He was stronger. He could run faster.

"People love to say they're sorry," he agreed, "and maybe somebody somewhere gives you points for it. But you stay bad, whether you're sorry or not."

There was a sort of purity to Jon Pear. Weren't most people a mixture? Didn't most people, no matter how ugly, have some redeeming quality? Jon Pear was scum, acid.

"How did you disable my car?" she said sharply.

"Oh, right, I'm going to tell you so you can do it to mine." He snorted.

How strange, she thought. It never occurred to me to do it to his, I just wanted to change the subject and maybe even figure out how to get it going again.

"I may have been fooled by a change of clothing, Mary Lee," whispered Jon Pear, and the whisper whistled through the silent frightened night. "But you! You were fooled by Madrigal's entire life."

"Not her entire life," said Mary Lee. "Some of our lives — most of our lives — Madrigal was good."

He snorted. "Madrigal was born bad and got worse. Madrigal hated being a twin. She hated you for flirting with Van that day and she hated you for going to the mall with Scarlett. She hated you for looking the same and sounding the same and acting the same as her. She thought boarding school would be enough, but it wasn't. You were still an aura in the house. Your mother and father still missed you. Your room was still there. She could feel your messages. How you were lonely and scared. Of course, she was glad about that, but she hated it that you still had a thought wave to her."

It was just as well that Mary Lee did not still have a thought wave to her twin. Don't tell me her plans for that visit, thought Mary Lee. Don't give me any details about what Madrigal said she'd do to me.

"Winter Sleigh Day," said Jon Pear. "What is it, anyway?"

Beyond the tennis courts and the big oval track, beyond the stand of pine trees that bordered the school campus, a charming lake emptied into a wild white-water river. Winter Sleigh Day used it all: courts, track, trees, lake, and river. It was a day of merrymaking, the highlight of the season, the most fun and the most friendly.

An idea came to Mary Lee.

"Madrigal and I," said Mary Lee, "always loved Winter Sleigh Day. We wore matching purple-velvet snowsuits when we were little, and Mother curled our hair out around the white trim of our hoods, and we would make maple sugar candy on the snow, and fly down the hill on the toboggan."

"Spare me the infant memories," said Jon Pear. "The past does not interest me unless I am in it."

Mary Lee said, "You must have been in it somewhere. How did you get here? Where did you come from?"

Jon Pear laughed without sound. "My parents are boring. Stupid. Dull. My whole life would be boring stupid and dull, but

I decided to have fun. And I'm going to have fun, Mary Lee, and I'm going to have fun with you."

She wet her lips in spite of the fact that Jon Pear would see her anxiety, and use it against her. "Winter Sleigh Day is such a pretty holiday." She closed her eyes and spoke from the darkness. "They have ice carving and snowman contests. They bring in sled dogs. Ice skating and cross-country skiing are competitive events, and there are also silly events, like snowball wars and icicle eating. So no disrupting Winter Sleigh Day, Jon Pear. It's an important day. You need to confine your silly little pranks to school days. No fooling around on Winter Sleigh Day."

"I don't fool around!" said Jon Pear. He muttered to himself. "Pranks!"

"Childish," said Mary Lee. "You're just frustrated. Now, I want you to make a real effort to act more adult. You're not very mature, and if you just try hard, Jon Pear, you can — "

"I can see why Madrigal hated you," said Jon Pear. "You're a lecturing frumpy little middle-aged — "

"I'm just trying to help, Jon Pear. Have you thought of counseling? Well, we'll save that for another day, when you're not so moody. Saturday is Winter Sleigh Day, and you absolutely must not do anything naughty."

"Naughty!" exploded Jon Pear.

"Furthermore, if you were really a man, and had any abilities of your own — "

He wanted to hit her. Every muscle in him gathered for striking. Mary Lee flinched, expecting pain.

But he did nothing. "I don't do violence," said Jon Pear very softly. "I just watch it. I let it happen. So I won't hurt you with my fists, Mary Lee. But I will use Winter Sleigh Day, since it has such a perfect name. Winter Slay Day." Jon Pear was night fog, a wet clinging blanket of evil.

"Do anything you want next week in school," said Mary Lee, all prissy, "but promise me you won't touch Winter Sleigh Day."

"I don't make promises," said Jon Pear, "and if I did, do you really think I would keep them?" Jon Pear laughed. He got out of the car and unhooked the hood. From his pocket he produced something small and round, which she couldn't see very well through the crack, and screwed it back on. He let go of the hood, and it slammed itself down.

The engine started.

He stepped back so she couldn't just run him over, leaving him in the student parking lot.

"We'll have a contest, you and me, Mary Lee. Welcome to my playground. There are no rules. There is no such thing as fair play. I don't give warnings. I will win."

When she got home, Mother and Father were waiting up for her. They were frightened. They were dressed in jackets and gloves to go out after her, search for her — but they hadn't. Perhaps they knew better. Perhaps they had tried to find Madrigal before — and regretted it.

She went straight to the truth.

"There's something I have to tell you. I'm Mary Lee, not Madrigal. When she was killed, everybody thought it was me. Just the ski suit. That was all anybody based it on. And I let them. I wanted Madrigal's life. Madrigal had you! She had home, and everything I missed so much. So I stepped into her clothing and her bedroom and her life, even her boyfriend and her classes. But I'm sorry now. Madrigal didn't have a life that I want."

She had not surprised them. She saw that they knew; had known from the first. "Mother?" she said shakily. "Father?"

They hugged her swiftly and encompassed her with their love.

"*You knew?*" she cried.

"Of course we knew," said Mother softly. "Right away. What we did not know was what to do next. We were afraid. Parents should not be afraid."

"Sweetie," said her father, "I don't know what you found out about Madrigal. I don't know what you ever knew. There was something very wrong with your sister. There always had been.

She was a scary little girl. She didn't take it out on you, and we thought you were her lifeline to being good. We thought she would outgrow the things she did, and be more like you; be nice. Really nice, not just nice to get something she wanted."

"But it got worse," said Mother. "Each year, she was scarier and scarier. Angry. Mostly she was very very angry. And after a long time, we realized she was angry at you, her twin! Angry that you existed. Angry that she shared her beautiful looks with you."

"Madrigal would stand in front of the mirror," said Mother, "and like a demented queen in a fairy tale, cry, 'Mirror Mirror on the Wall, Who Is the Fairest of Them All?' Then she would be enraged because she wasn't. There was a pair of fairest."

"When your back was turned, Mary Lee," Father said, "she would look at you with such hatred, we trembled. We tried to talk to her about it, and she had her own solution: separate the two of you. So we did."

Did Madrigal always feel that way, wondered Mary Lee, or did it happen over the years? Did Jon Pear come first or during or after?

Oh, Madrigal! I didn't want to be the fairest of them all. I wanted us both to be the fairest of them all! We could have done it. You didn't need to throw us away.

"We failed you," said her father.

"Yes, you did!" cried Mary Lee. "Why did you ship me away? Why didn't you send Madrigal away?"

"Where would we have sent her? Who would have taken her? Besides, we thought we could turn her around. We thought when we had just one daughter at home, and we could concentrate on her, that we could make her good."

"It just gave her more space to be bad in," said Mother. "It was a terrible mistake. I go back over her life all the time, trying to see where the first mistake was, and the second, and the third. But I don't find them. All I find are two little girls I loved so much."

"Why did you let me be Madrigal?" she said. She was angry

herself. She wanted parents who didn't make such big mistakes. Parents who could tell what was going to happen instead of going all the wrong ways.

"We knew you wouldn't behave like Madrigal. We knew you'd be good. You wanted her life so much. We should have said, 'Mary Lee, forget it. This is Madrigal who died.' But — we were so shaken up, we were so flustered, it was all so horrible — and we let it happen. We just stood there and let it happen."

Mary Lee knew the real horror then. The worst, absolutely worst thing, is to see something wrong, and then just stand there and let it happen.

I've seen something wrong, thought Mary Lee, and its name is Jon Pear, and I'm not going to let him happen again.

The reunion with her parents lasted long into the night, but at last she was in her room; Madrigal's room. The day had lasted a generation.

The mirror was dusty.

"I'm mad at you, Madrigal," she said, as if her reflection were the twin who had been her reflection. "You knew better. I don't care how powerful or how exciting Jon Pear was. You could have chosen not to be a part of it. *How could you do that?* When you and I were part and share of each other, how could you choose evil over good?"

There was no message, for there was no Madrigal.

"Madrigal," she whispered. She touched the mirror, as a thousand times a thousand she had touched her real living twin. "I forgive you. You are still my twin. My beloved twin. Still my beloved sister. You are still half of me, and I am still half of you."

The glass turned warm at her touch, alive and full of hope. "*I still love you, Madrigal.*"

Mary Lee straightened her shoulders. "Rest in peace, Madrigal. I am Mary Lee and I will beat Jon Pear."

Chapter 14

The marching band gathered between the track oval and the lake. Brass players warmed their mouthpieces, huffing constantly. Third-graders in crayon-colored ski suits got ready for their ice-skating relay races.

Fourth-graders drank hot chocolate, while fifth-graders prepared maple-sugar-on-snow candy. The big boys got ready for snow wrestling. Forts for the snowball war were being built. The log cabin with the huge stone fireplace was the only warm spot at Sleigh Day, and children raced in to dry their mittens and raced out to get them wet again.

Where Mary Lee stood, the ice on the lake was not solidly frozen. A little brook kept it mushy. Little orange signs on thin metal rods said over and over THIN ICE, THIN ICE, THIN ICE.

Jon Pear held her from behind, his arms encircling her.

The day grew colder, the sky thinner, its blue watered down with winter chill. People stood closer and shivered, and made fists of their fingers inside their mittens. People curled their toes inside their boots and tucked their hands beneath their arms.

"Where does the relay team skate?" asked Jon Pear.

"Way over there," said Mary Lee. "The ice is three full inches thick over there."

"But over here," said Jon Pear, as if he had discovered treasure, "it isn't."

Her mother and father were laughing with the other parents. Judges and PTA officers, teachers, and older brothers and sisters home from college, were everywhere. She took a step toward the crowd she yearned for: Van and Scarlett, Kip, Geordie and Courtney.

Jon Pear did not move. His weight kept her tethered. "This is a good vantage point," remarked Jon Pear. "If anything goes wrong, we'll have a good view." Jon Pear was enjoying himself. If she fought against his grip, he'd enjoy it more. If she didn't fight, he'd win.

Sweet, innocent, brightly clad children, thinking only of snow and ribbons, ice and prizes, swarmed and danced, skated and raced.

The crowd of her classmates suddenly surged toward Mary Lee and Jon Pear. How grim their expressions were. How determined they looked.

They were coming for revenge.

Would they include Mary Lee in it? Would they make her pay for Madrigal's deeds? Did they even believe that she was Mary Lee?

Mary Lee tried a third time to step free of Jon Pear and, as she leaned and struggled, he released her so suddenly she fell onto the hard ground and cried out in pain.

Jon Pear smiled.

Van lifted her up.

Scarlett moved between her and Jon Pear.

And the students surrounded Jon Pear.

Home-grown justice, thought Mary Lee. They have come to do away with Jon Pear.

The boys were armed. Not with knives, not with guns, not with stones. They carried icicles. Long vicious sharp icicles. Nothing would melt in this weather. And icicles would penetrate a heart as well as steel.

"No," whispered Mary Lee.

"Yes," said the crowd. They surrounded Jon Pear. He merely continued to smile, his expression filled with superior loathing.

The crowd hated that smile. They would wipe it off.

"It's time, Jon Pear," said Van. "You're going to get yours."

Jon Pear raised his eyebrows skeptically.

"You pride yourself on standing by and watching people suffer," said Katy. "We're going to see how that feels. Because we're going to stand by and watch *you* suffer."

Jon Pear laughed.

"We won't actually do anything to you," added Courtney. "We'll be passive."

"I think," said Geordie, "that he should drown the way he and Madrigal watched that man drown." Armed with ice, Geordie hardly looked passive. He looked truly and willingly violent.

A flicker crossed Jon Pear's face. He was not so sure of this situation after all.

"I vote to have Jon Pear drown," said Katy.

Jon Pear was taller and broader than most, and he gazed around, casually, as if bored. But he saw no way out, and he was not bored.

"Second," said Van.

"All in favor?" said Katy.

"Aye," chorused the students.

"All opposed?" said Katy, and they laughed because nobody would be opposed to the end of Jon Pear.

"I'm opposed," said Mary Lee. Her voice hung like spun sugar in the freezing air.

They stepped away from Mary Lee, and Mary Lee stepped away from them, and even further from Jon Pear. "It isn't right," she said. "You have to give people what you would like them to give you." She swallowed. "We have to be decent, whether Jon Pear is or not."

Jon Pear's laugh flipped in wild peals like a Frisbee.

"Listen to him!" shouted Van. "He knows you're nothing but a patsy, saying he should go free! Does he have you in his spell the way he had Madrigal? There has to be an end to people like Jon Pear! Let him drown."

The group agreed, chorus-like, singing and swaying along.

They pressed forward, and Jon Pear was forced back a step, and then two steps, and then the heel of his boot was in the mush and sliding down.

"No!" said Mary Lee. "We can't."

"Watch us," said Courtney.

They were a mob, and they were going on without her.

She had not stopped her twin, she had not stopped Jon Pear, she could not stop this mob. She had no silver tongue and had convinced nobody of anything.

On Jon Pear's face, a tear of panic formed. He swung wildly, looking for a way out, and the tear was flung out over the ice and replaced by another tear.

"He's scared!" said Katy. "Oh, good! He's scared!"

Across the lake, a little skater left the course.

Head down, feet pumping, the small bright-blue-clad racer was thinking only of speed. The shouts from the crowd, shouts of his name — *Bryan! Bryan!* — meant nothing; Bryan thought they were his fans.

His legs were short and, even on skates, his strides were short.

The judge abandoned his position at the end of the race course and ran — not on skates, but on slippery rubber boots — to stop Bryan.

Parents left the shore, and shouting, skidding, falling, tried to stop Bryan.

The little boy flew across the last of the solid ice, and vanished as quick as a stone through the possessive mush of the bad ice.

Jon Pear was closest.

"Save him!" shrieked Mary Lee. "Jon Pear! Go out after him!"

But Jon Pear had only himself on his mind, and the mob had only Jon Pear. Mary Lee ran out on the ice, passing them, screaming, "Jon Pear! Do something good for a change!"

She too wore no skates, and her rubber soles slipped. But she knew this lake. It was shallow at this end. If she fell through, she was tall enough to stand. She just had to get to Bryan, yank him up, pull him out of the water that would stop his heart.

She fell through the ice yards from where Bryan had gone down. She righted herself, smashing the ice between them with her fists. The cold was so bad, it was like being burned. She felt as if her legs would be amputated by the water itself.

On the shore, the teenagers abandoned Jon Pear and flung themselves through the ice, to help from their side.

But they were too far and too late.

Mary Lee waded forward somehow, making herself an icebreaker, using muscles she had not possessed when she was fighting Jon Pear.

The bright bright blue of Bryan's jacket showed through the cold cold water.

Mary Lee pulled him up, dragging him out of the water, holding him high. Geordie and Van reached her, and the teenagers passed the little boy from arm to arm, a bucket brigade, handing him at last to the parents on dry land.

When the ambulance had arrived, and Bryan was breathing and yelling that he didn't want to go to the hospital, he still wanted to be in his race, they relaxed.

Relaxed enough to remember who and where they were.

And Katy said, "Where's Jon Pear?"

Nobody still held an icicle. Nobody still formed a mob. They were just kids, thrilled to have saved a life, proud of themselves, and very very wet and cold.

Jon Pear was nowhere. They stared across the churned and broken ice at the long expanse of frozen lake where the skating had begun again.

"Maybe he was supernatural," whispered Katy. "Maybe he dematerialized."

Mary Lee knew better. But she didn't know where Jon Pear was. Where could he have gone? How did he get there without anybody noticing?

"Come on, Mary Lee," said Scarlet, "I brought a change of clothing. You'll have to put it on — quick — before you die of exposure."

Mary Lee still looked for Jon Pear. He wasn't the kind of person you wanted to lose track of. You didn't want him at your back.

"Mary Lee, your ski suit's turning to ice right on your body," said Scarlett. "Move it."

But when she moved it, she saw the colors in the water. Bright bleeding colors. Beneath the churned ice. Floating in the frigid water.

She stepped forward, to see more clearly, and Geordie and Kip, Kenneth and Stephen, stepped between her and the ice.

"It'll freeze over again," said Geordie.

"Temperature's dropping as we speak," said Kip.

"Time to go in," said Van.

This mob. Her new friends. Had they held him under? Had they trampled him when she thought they were rushing to rescue Bryan? Or had Jon Pear slipped of his own accord, and just as *he* never rescued anybody, nobody rescued him?

Which of these boys and girls had shrugged and let him drown? Or had he let himself drown? Had he known, for a few seconds at least, how evil he was?

I will never know what Madrigal really planned to do on that visit, she thought. I will never know why she switched ski suits with me, or what would have happened if the ski lift hadn't broken.

And unless I ask, I will never know how Jon Pear found his way beneath the ice, to stay there until spring.

"Carry her," advised Katy. "I think she's going into shock herself. Lift her up on your shoulders and carry her to the warming cabin."

They were ready to let the ice freeze over, and the past stay past.

They lifted her up and ran, a bunch of boys holding a pretty girl in the air. She jounced in the aching cold, held up by the flat palms of nice young men, who had taken justice into those same hands. People shouted and cheered, thinking she was the princess of Winter Sleigh Day. Thinking there must have been a vote they didn't know about.

There was a vote, thought Mary Lee. And I voted no. I have to remember that. I wasn't able to stop evil, but I didn't stand and watch it, either. Jon Pear didn't win. I won.

I'm Mary Lee. And I'm glad.

Catriana

Boneville